THE
TrAVeLeR

SEAL BOOKS

JOHN TWELVE HAWKS

THE

TrAVeLeR

A Novel

Seal Books and colophon are trademarks of
Random House of Canada Limited.

THE TRAVELER
Seal Books/published by arrangement with Doubleday Canada
Doubleday Canada edition published 2005
Seal Books edition published June 2006

ISBN-13: 978-0-7704-2972-0
ISBN-10: 0-7704-2972-6

Cover images: (woman) Tom Maday/Luckypix.com;
   (man) Andrea Pistolesi/Getty Images
Cover design: Michael J. Windsor

Seal Books are published by Random House of Canada Limited.
"Seal Books" and the portrayal of a seal are the property of Random House
of Canada Limited.

Visit Random House of Canada Limited's website: www.randomhouse.ca

PRINTED AND BOUND IN THE USA

OPM 10   9   8   7   6   5   4   3   2   1

FOR MY PATHFINDERS

THE

TrAVeleR

KNIGHT, DEATH, AND THE DEVIL

Maya reached out and took her father's hand as they walked from the Underground to the light. Thorn didn't push her away or tell Maya to concentrate on the position of her body. Smiling, he guided her up a narrow staircase to a long, sloping tunnel with white tile walls. The Underground authority had installed steel bars on one side of the tunnel and this barrier made the ordinary passageway look like part of an enormous prison. If she had been traveling alone, Maya might have felt trapped and uncomfortable, but there was nothing to worry about because Father was with her.

It's the perfect day, she thought. Well, maybe it was the second most perfect day. She still remembered two years ago when Father had missed her birthday and Christmas only to show up on Boxing Day with a taxi full of presents for Maya and her mother. That morning was bright and full of surprises, but this Saturday seemed to promise a more durable happiness. Instead of the usual trip to the empty warehouse near Canary Wharf, where her father taught her how to kick and punch and use weapons, they had spent the day at the London Zoo, where he had told her different stories about each of the animals. Father had traveled all over the world and could describe Paraguay or Egypt as if he were a tour guide.

People had glanced at them as they strolled past the cages. Most Harlequins tried to blend into the crowd, but her father stood out in a group of ordinary citizens. He was German, with a strong nose, shoulder-length hair, and dark blue eyes. Thorn dressed in somber colors and wore a steel *kara* bracelet that looked like a broken shackle.

Maya had found a battered art history book in the closet of their rented flat in East London. Near the front of the book was a picture by Albrecht Dürer called *Knight, Death, and the Devil*. She liked to stare at the picture even though it made her feel strange. The armored knight was like her father, calm and brave, riding through the mountains as Death held up an hourglass and the Devil followed, pretending to be a squire. Thorn also carried a sword, but his was concealed inside a metal tube with a leather shoulder strap.

Although she was proud of Thorn, he also made her feel embarrassed and self-conscious. Sometimes she just wanted to be an ordinary girl with a pudgy father who worked in an office—a happy man who bought ice-cream cones and told jokes about kangaroos. The world around her, with its bright fashions and pop music and television shows, was a constant temptation. She wanted to fall into that warm water and let the current pull her away. It was exhausting to be Thorn's daughter, always avoiding the surveillance of the Vast Machine, always watching for enemies, always aware of the angle of attack.

Maya was twelve years old, but still wasn't strong enough to use a Harlequin sword. As a substitute, Father had taken a walking stick from the closet and given it to her before they left the flat that morning. Maya had Thorn's white skin and strong features and her Sikh mother's thick black hair. Her eyes were such a pale blue that from a certain angle they looked translucent. She hated it when well-meaning women approached her mother and complimented Maya's appearance. In a few years, she'd be old enough to disguise herself and look as ordinary as possible.

They left the zoo and strolled through Regent's Park. It was late April and young men were kicking footballs across the muddy lawn while parents pushed bundled-up babies in perambulators. The whole city seemed to be out enjoying the sunshine after three days of rain. Maya and her father took the Piccadilly line to the Arsenal station; it was getting dark when they reached the street-level exit. There was an Indian restaurant in Finsbury Park and Thorn had made reservations for an early supper. Maya heard noises—blaring air horns and shouting in the distance—and wondered if there was some kind of political demonstration. Then Father led her through the turnstile and out into a war.

Standing on the sidewalk, she saw a mob of people marching up Highbury Hill Road. There weren't any protest signs and banners, and Maya realized that she was watching the end of a football match. The Arsenal Stadium was straight down the road and a team with blue and white colors—that was Chelsea—had just played there. The Chelsea supporters were coming out of the visitors' gate on the west end of the stadium and heading down a narrow street lined with row houses. Normally it was a quick walk to the station entrance, but now the North London street had turned into a gauntlet. The police were protecting Chelsea from Arsenal football thugs who were trying to attack them and start fights.

Policemen on the edges. Blue and white in the center. Red throwing bottles and trying to break through the line. Citizens caught in front of the crowd scrambled between parked cars and knocked over rubbish bins. Flowering hawthorns grew at the edge of the curb and their pink blossoms trembled whenever someone was shoved against a tree. Petals fluttered through the air and fell upon the surging mass.

The main crowd was approaching the Tube station, about one hundred meters away. Thorn could have gone to the left and headed up Gillespie Road, but he remained on the sidewalk and studied the people surrounding them. He smiled slightly, confident of his own power and amused by the pointless violence of the drones. Along with the sword, he was carrying at least one knife and a handgun obtained from contacts in America. If he wished, he could kill a great many of these people, but this was a public confrontation and the police were in the area. Maya glanced up at her father. We should run away, she thought. These people are completely mad. But Thorn glared at his daughter as if he had just sensed her fear and Maya stayed silent.

Everyone was shouting. The voices merged into one angry roar. Maya heard a high-pitched whistle. The wail of a police siren. A beer bottle sailed through the air and exploded into fragments a few feet away from where they were standing. Suddenly, a flying wedge of red shirts and scarves plowed through the police lines, and she saw men kicking and throwing punches. Blood streamed down a policeman's face, but he raised his truncheon and fought back.

She squeezed Father's hand. "They're coming toward us," she said. "We need to get out of the way."

Thorn turned around and pulled his daughter back into the entrance of the Tube station as if to find refuge there. But now the police were driving the Chelsea supporters forward like a herd of cattle and she was surrounded by men wearing blue. Caught in the crowd, Maya and her father were pushed past the ticket booth where the elderly clerk cowered behind the thick glass.

Father vaulted over the turnstile and Maya followed. Now they were back in the long tunnel, heading down to the trains. It's all right, she thought. We're safe now. Then she realized that men wearing red had forced their way into the tunnel and were running beside them. One of the men was carrying a wool sock filled with something heavy—rocks, ball bearings—and he swung it like a club at the old man just in front of her, knocking off the man's glasses and breaking his nose. A gang of Arsenal thugs slammed a Chelsea supporter against the steel bars on the left side of the tunnel. The man tried to get away as they kicked and beat him. More blood. And no police anywhere.

Thorn grabbed the back of Maya's jacket and dragged her through the fighting. A man tried to attack them and Father stopped him instantly with a quick, snapping punch to the throat. Maya hurried down the tunnel, trying to reach the stairway. Before she could react, something like a rope came over her right shoulder and across her chest. Maya looked down and saw that Thorn had just tied a blue and white Chelsea scarf around her body.

In an instant she realized that the day at the zoo, the amusing stories, and the trip to the restaurant were all part of a plan. Father had known about the football game, had probably been here before and timed their arrival. She glanced over her shoulder and saw Thorn smile and nod as if he had just told her an amusing story. Then he turned and walked away.

Maya spun around as three Arsenal supporters ran forward, yelling at her. Don't think. React. She jabbed the walking stick like a javelin and the steel tip hit the tallest man's forehead with a crack. Blood spurted from his head and he began to fall, but she was already spinning around to trip the second man with the stick. As he stumbled backward, she jumped high and kicked his face. He spun around and hit the floor. Down. He's down. She ran forward and kicked him again.

As she regained her balance, the third man caught her from behind and lifted her off the ground. He squeezed tightly, trying to break her ribs, but Maya dropped the stick, reached back with both hands, and grabbed his ears. The man screamed as she flipped him over her shoulder and onto the floor.

Maya reached the stairway, took the stairs two at a time, and saw Father standing on the platform next to the open doors of a train. He grabbed her with his right hand and used his left to force their way into the car. The doors moved back and forth and finally closed. Arsenal supporters ran up to the train, pounding on the glass with their fists, but the train lurched forward and headed down the tunnel.

People were packed together. She heard a woman weeping as the boy in front of her pressed a handkerchief against his mouth and nose. The car went around a curve and she fell against her father, burying her face in his wool overcoat. She hated him and loved him, wanted to attack him and embrace him—all at the same time. Don't cry, she thought. He's watching you. Harlequins don't cry. And she bit her lower lip so hard that she broke the skin and tasted her own blood.

1

Maya flew into Ruzyne Airport late in the afternoon and took the shuttle bus into Prague. Her choice of transportation was a minor act of rebellion. A Harlequin would have rented a car or found a taxicab. In a taxi, you could always cut the driver's throat and take control. Airplanes and buses were dangerous choices, little traps with only a few ways to get out.

No one is going to kill me, she thought. No one cares. Travelers inherited their powers and so the Tabula tried to exterminate everyone in the same family. The Harlequins defended the Travelers and their Pathfinder teachers, but this was a voluntary decision. A Harlequin child could renounce the way of the sword, accept a citizen name, and find a place in the Vast Machine. If he stayed out of trouble, the Tabula would leave him alone.

A few years ago, Maya had visited John Mitchell Kramer, the only son of Greenman, a British Harlequin who was killed by a Tabula car bomb in Athens. Kramer had become a pig farmer in Yorkshire, and Maya watched him trudge through the muck with buckets of feed for his squealing animals. "As far as they know, you haven't stepped over the line," he told her. "It's your choice, Maya. You can still walk away and have a normal life."

Maya decided to become Judith Strand, a young woman who had taken a few courses in product design at the University of Salford in Manchester. She moved to London, started working as an assistant at a design firm, and was eventually offered a full-time job. Her three years in the city had been a series of private challenges and small victories. Maya still remembered the first time she left her flat without carrying weapons. There was no protection from the Tabula and she felt weak and exposed. Every person on the street was watching her; everyone who approached was a possible assassin. She waited for the bullet or the knife, but nothing happened.

Gradually, she stayed out for longer periods of time and tested her new attitude toward the world. Maya didn't glance at windows to see if she was being followed. When she ate in a restaurant with her new friends, she didn't hide a gun in the alleyway and sit with her back to the wall.

In April, she violated a major Harlequin rule and started to see a psychiatrist. For five expensive sessions she sat in a book-lined room in Bloomsbury. She wanted to talk about her childhood and that first betrayal at the Arsenal Tube station, but it just wasn't possible. Dr. Bennett was a tidy little man who knew a great deal about wine and antique porcelain. Maya still remembered his confusion when she called him a citizen.

"Well, of course I'm a citizen," he said. "I was born and raised in Britain."

"It's just a label that my father uses. Ninety-nine percent of the population are either citizens or drones."

Dr. Bennett took off his gold-rimmed spectacles and polished the lenses with a green flannel cloth. "Would you mind explaining this?"

"Citizens are people who think they understand what's going on in the world."

"I don't understand *everything*, Judith. I never said that. But I'm well informed about current events. I watch the news every morning while I'm on my treadmill."

Maya hesitated, and then decided to tell him the truth. "The facts you know are mostly an illusion. The real struggle of history is going on beneath the surface."

Dr. Bennett gave her a condescending smile. "Tell me about the drones."

"Drones are people who are so overwhelmed by the challenge of surviving that they're unaware of anything outside of their day-to-day lives."

"You mean poor people?"

"They can be poor or trapped in the Third World, but they're still capable of transforming themselves. Father used to say, 'Citizens ignore the truth. Drones are just too tired.'"

Dr. Bennett slipped his glasses back on and picked up his notepad. "Perhaps we should talk about your parents."

Therapy ended with that question. What could she say about Thorn? Her father was a Harlequin who had survived five Tabula assassination attempts. He was proud and cruel and very brave. Maya's mother was from a Sikh family that had been allies with the Harlequins for several generations. In honor of her mother, she wore a steel *kara* bracelet on her right wrist.

Late that summer she celebrated her twenty-sixth birthday and one of the women at the design firm took her on a tour of the boutiques in West London. Maya bought some stylish, brightly colored clothes. She began to watch television and tried to believe the news. At times she felt happy—almost happy—and welcomed the endless distractions of the Vast Machine. There was always some new fear to worry about or a new product that everyone wanted to buy.

Although Maya was no longer carrying weapons, she occasionally dropped by a kickboxing school in South London and sparred with the instructor. On Tuesdays and Thursdays, she attended an advanced class at a kendo academy and fought with a bamboo *shinai* sword. Maya tried to pretend that she was just staying in shape, like the other people in her office who jogged or played tennis, but she knew that it was more than that. When you were fighting you were completely in the moment, focused on defending yourself and destroying your opponent. Nothing she did in civilian life could match that intensity.

Now she was in Prague to see her father, and all the familiar Harlequin paranoia came back with its full power. After buying the ticket at the airport kiosk, she got on the shuttle bus and sat near the back. This was a bad defensive position, but it wasn't going to bother her. Maya watched an elderly couple and a group of German tourists climb onto the bus and arrange their luggage. She tried to distract herself by thinking about Thorn, but her body took control and forced her to choose another seat near the emergency exit. Defeated by her training and filled with rage, she clenched her hands and stared out the window.

It had started drizzling when they left the terminal and was raining heavily by the time they reached the downtown area. Prague was built on both sides of a river, but the narrow streets and gray stone buildings made her feel as if she were trapped in a hedge maze. Cathedrals and castles dotted the city, and their pointed towers jabbed at the sky.

At the bus stop, Maya was presented with more choices. She could walk to her hotel or wave down a cruising taxi. The legendary Japanese Harlequin, Sparrow, once wrote that true warriors should "cultivate randomness." In a few words, he had suggested an entire philosophy. A Harlequin rejected mindless routines and comfortable habits. You lived a life of discipline, but you weren't afraid of disorder.

It was raining. She was getting wet. The most predictable choice was to take the taxi waiting by the curb. Maya hesitated for a few seconds and then decided to act like a normal citizen. Clutching her bags with one hand, she yanked open the door and got into the backseat. The driver was a squat little man with a beard who looked like a troll. She gave him the name of her hotel, but he didn't react.

"It's the Hotel Kampa," she said in English. "Is there a problem?"

"No problem," the driver answered and pulled out into the street.

The Hotel Kampa was a large four-story building, solid and respectable, with green window awnings. It was placed on a cobblestone side street near the Charles Bridge. Maya paid the driver, but when she tried to open the car door it was locked.

"Open the bloody door."

"I'm sorry, madam." The troll pushed a button and the lock clicked open. Smiling, he watched Maya get out of his cab.

She let the doorman carry her luggage into the hotel. Going to see her father, she had felt the need to carry the usual weapons; they were concealed in a camera tripod. Her appearance didn't suggest a particular nationality and the doorman spoke to her in French and English. For the trip to Prague she had discarded her colorful London clothes and wore half boots, a black pullover, and loose gray pants. There was a Harlequin style of clothing that emphasized dark, expensive fabrics and custom tailoring. Nothing tight or flashy. Nothing that would slow you down in combat.

Club chairs and little tables were in the lobby. A faded tapestry hung on the wall. In a side dining area, a group of elderly women were drinking tea and cooing over a tray of pastries. At the front desk, the hotel clerk glanced at the tripod and the video camera case and appeared satisfied. It was a Harlequin rule that you must always have an explanation for who you are and why you're at a particular location. The video equipment was a typical prop. The doorman and the clerk probably thought she was some kind of filmmaker.

Her hotel room was a suite on the third floor, dark and filled with fake Victorian lamps and overstuffed furniture.

One window faced the street and another overlooked the hotel's outdoor garden restaurant. It was still raining; the restaurant was closed. The striped table umbrellas were sodden with water and the restaurant chairs leaned like tired soldiers against the round tables. Maya glanced under the bed and found a little welcoming present from her father—a grappling hook and fifty meters of climbing rope. If the wrong sort of person knocked on the door, she could be out the window and away from the hotel in about ten seconds.

She took off her coat, splashed some water on her face, then placed the tripod on the bed. When she passed through the airport security checks, people always wasted a great deal of time inspecting the video camera and its various lenses. The real weapons were hidden in the tripod. There were two knives in one leg—a weighted throwing knife and a stiletto for stabbing. She placed them in their sheaths and slipped them beneath elastic bandages on her forearms. Carefully, she rolled down the sleeves of the sweater and checked herself in the mirror. The sweater was loose enough that both weapons were completely concealed. Maya crossed her wrists, moved her arms quickly, and a knife appeared in her right hand.

The sword blade was in the second leg of the tripod. The third leg concealed the sword's hilt and guard piece. Maya attached them to the blade. The guard piece was on a pivot that could be pushed sideways. When she carried the sword on the street, the guard piece was parallel to the blade so that the entire weapon became one straight line. When it was necessary to fight, the guard snapped into its proper position.

Along with the tripod and the camera, she had brought a four-foot-long metal tube with a shoulder strap. The tube looked vaguely technical, like something that an artist would bring to her studio. It was used as a sword carrier when walking around the city. Maya could get the sword out of the tube in two seconds, and it took one more second to attack. Her father had taught her how to use the weapon when she was a teenager and she had developed her technique in a kendo class with a Japanese instructor.

Harlequins were also trained to use handguns and assault rifles. Maya's favorite weapon was a combat shotgun, preferably a twelve gauge with a pistol grip and folding stock. The use of an old-fashioned sword along with modern weapons was accepted—and valued—as part of the Harlequin style. Guns were a necessary evil, but swords existed outside of the modern age, free of the control and compromise of the Vast Machine. Training with a sword taught balance, strategy, and ruthlessness. Like a Sikh's kirpan, a Harlequin's sword connected each fighter with both a spiritual obligation and a warrior tradition.

Thorn also believed there were practical reasons for swords. Concealed within equipment like the tripod, they could pass through airport security systems. A sword was silent and so unexpected that there was a shock value when using it on an unsuspecting enemy. Maya visualized an attack. Fake to the head of your opponent, then down low to the side of the knee. A little resistance. The crack of bone and cartilage. And you've cut off someone's leg.

A brown envelope lay within the coils of the escape rope. Maya ripped it open and read the address and time for her meeting. Seven o'clock. The Betlémské náměsti quarter in the Old Town. She placed the sword on her lap, turned off all the lights, and tried to meditate.

Images floated through her brain, memories of the only time she had fought alone as a Harlequin. She was seventeen then and her father had brought her over to Brussels to protect a Zen monk who was visiting Europe. The monk was a Pathfinder, one of the spiritual teachers who could show a potential Traveler how to cross over to another realm. Although the Harlequins weren't sworn to protect Pathfinders, they helped them whenever possible. The monk was a great teacher—and he was on the Tabula death list.

That night in Brussels, Maya's father and his French friend Linden were upstairs near the monk's hotel suite. Maya was told to guard the entrance to the service elevator in the basement. When two Tabula mercenaries arrived, there was no one there to help her. She shot one man in the throat with an automatic and hacked the other merc to death with her sword. Blood splattered over her gray maid's uniform, covering her arms and hands. Maya was crying hysterically when Linden found her.

Two years later, the monk died in a car accident. All that blood and pain were useless. Calm down, she told herself. Find some private mantra. Our Travelers who art in Heaven. Damn them all.

* * *

IT STOPPED RAINING around six and she decided to walk to Thorn's apartment. Leaving the hotel, she found Mostecká Street and followed it to the Charles Bridge. The stone Gothic bridge was wide and lit with colored lights that illuminated a long line of statues. A backpacker played his guitar in front of a hat while a street artist used charcoal to draw a sketch of an elderly female tourist. A statue of a Czech martyr saint was placed halfway across the bridge, and she remembered hearing that it was a good luck charm. There was no such thing as luck, but she touched the bronze plaque below the statue and whispered to herself: "May someone love me and may I love him in return."

Ashamed of this display of weakness, she walked a little faster and continued across the bridge to Old Town. Stores and churches and cellar nightclubs were squeezed together like passengers on a crowded train. The young Czechs and foreign backpackers stood outside the pubs, looking bored and smoking marijuana.

Thorn lived on Konviktská Street one block north of the secret prison on Bartolomějská. During the Cold War, the security police had taken over a convent and used it for their holding cells and torture chambers. Now the Sisters of Mercy were back in charge and the police had moved into other buildings nearby. As Maya walked around the quarter, she realized why Thorn had settled here. Prague still had a medieval appearance, and most Harlequins hated anything that appeared new. The city had decent medical care, good transportation, and Internet communications. A third factor was even more important: the Czech police had learned their ethics in the communist era. If Thorn bribed the right people he could get access to police files and passports.

*　*　*

MAYA ONCE MET a Gypsy in Barcelona who explained to her why he had the right to pick pockets and rob tourist hotels. When the Romans crucified Jesus, they prepared a golden nail to hammer into the Savior's heart. A Gypsy—apparently there were Gypsies in ancient Jerusalem—had taken the nail, and therefore God gave them permission to steal until the end of time. Harlequins weren't Gypsies, but Maya decided that the mindset was pretty much the same. Her father and his friends had a highly developed sense of honor and their own private morality. They were disciplined and loyal to each other, but they were contemptuous of any citizen-made law. Harlequins believed they had the right to kill and destroy because of their vow to protect the Travelers.

*　*　*

SHE STROLLED PAST the Church of the Holy Rood, then glanced across the street to number 18 Konviktská. It was a red doorway wedged between a plumbing-parts store and a lingerie shop where the window mannequin wore a garter belt and a pair of sequined stockings. There were two other floors above the street and all the upper windows were either shuttered or tinted a hazy gray. Harlequins had at least three exits in their houses, and one of them was always secret. This building had the red door and a second door in the back alley. There was probably a secret passageway that led downstairs to the lingerie shop.

She flicked open the top of the sword carrier and tilted it slightly forward so that the sword handle slid out a few inches. Back in London, the summons had come the usual way: an unmarked manila envelope shoved under her door. She had no idea whether or not Thorn was still alive and waiting in this building. If the Tabula had found out that she was involved in the hotel killings nine years ago, it was easier to lure her out of England and execute her in a foreign city.

Crossing the street, Maya stopped in front of the lingerie shop and looked at the display window. She searched for a traditional Harlequin sign such as a mask or a piece of clothing with a diamond pattern, anything to calm her growing tension. It was seven o'clock. Slowly she moved down the sidewalk and saw a chalk mark on the concrete. It was an oval shape and three straight lines: an abstract suggestion of a Harlequin's lute. If the Tabula had done this, they would have taken more care and made the drawing resemble the instrument. Instead, the mark was casual and scuffed—as if a bored child had placed it there.

She pressed the doorbell, heard a whirring sound, and saw that a surveillance camera was hidden inside the metal canopy above the door frame. The door lock clicked open and she stepped inside. Maya was standing in a small foyer leading to a steep metal staircase. The door behind her glided shut and a three-inch bolt slid into a lock. Trapped. She drew her sword, snapped the hilt into position, and started upstairs. At the top of the stairs was another steel door and a second doorbell. She pushed the button and an electronic voice came out of the little speaker.

"Voice print please."

"Go to hell."

A computer analyzed her voice and three seconds later the second door clicked open. Maya entered a large white room with a polished wood floor. Her father's apartment was spare and clean. There was nothing plastic, nothing false or shrill. A half wall defined the entryway and living room. The area contained a leather chair and a glass coffee table with a single yellow orchid in a vase.

Two framed posters hung on the wall. One advertised an exhibit of Japanese samurai swords at the Nezu Institute of Fine Arts in Tokyo. Way of the sword. Life of the warrior. The second poster showed a 1914 assemblage called *Three Standard Stoppages* by Marcel Duchamp. The Frenchman had dropped three meter-long strings on a Prussian blue canvas and then had traced their outlines. Like any Harlequin, Duchamp didn't fight against randomness and uncertainty: he had used it to create his art.

She heard bare feet moving across the floor, then a young man with a shaved head came around the corner holding a German-made submachine gun. The man was smiling and his gun was tilted downward at a forty-five-degree angle. If he were foolish enough to raise the weapon, she decided to step to the left and slash open his face with her sword.

"Welcome to Prague," he said in English with a Russian accent. "Your father will be with you in a minute."

The young man wore drawstring pants and a sleeveless T-shirt with Japanese characters stenciled on the fabric. Maya could see that his arms and neck were decorated with numerous tattoos. Snakes. Demons. A vision of Hell. She didn't have to see him naked to know that he was a walking epic of some kind. Harlequins always seemed to collect misfits and freaks to serve them.

Maya replaced the sword in the carrying case. "What's your name?"

"Alexi."

"How long have you worked for Thorn?"

"It isn't work." The young man looked very pleased with himself. "I help your father and he helps me. I'm training to be a master of the martial arts."

"And he's doing very well," her father said. She heard the voice first and then Thorn came rolling around the corner in an electric wheelchair. His Harlequin sword was in a scabbard attached to an armrest. Thorn had grown a beard in the last two years. His arms and upper chest were still powerful and it almost made you forget his shriveled, useless legs.

Thorn stopped moving and smiled at his daughter. "Good evening, Maya."

The last time she had seen her father was in Peshawar the night that Linden had brought him down from the mountains of the North-West Frontier. Thorn was unconscious and Linden's clothes were covered with blood.

Using faked newspaper articles, the Tabula had lured Thorn, Linden, a Chinese Harlequin named Willow, and an Australian Harlequin named Libra to a tribal area in Pakistan. Thorn was convinced that two children—a twelve-year-old boy and his ten-year-old sister—were Travelers who were in danger from a fanatical religious leader. The four Harlequins and their allies were ambushed at a mountain pass by Tabula mercenaries. Willow and Libra were killed. Thorn's spinal cord was hit by a chunk of shrapnel and he was paralyzed from the waist down.

Two years later her father was living in a Prague apartment with a tattooed freak for a servant and everything was wonderful—let's forget about the past and move on. At that moment, Maya was almost glad that her father was a paraplegic. If he hadn't been injured, he would have denied that the ambush had occurred.

"So how are you, Maya?" Thorn turned to the Russian. "I haven't seen my daughter for some time."

The fact that he used the word "daughter" made her furious. It meant that he had brought her to Prague to ask for a favor. "More than two years," she said.

"Two years?" Alexi smiled. "I think you have much to talk about."

Thorn gestured with his hand and the Russian picked up a scanner from a side table. The scanner looked like a small airport security wand, but it was designed to detect the tracer beads used by the Tabula. The beads were the size of pearls and gave off a signal that could be tracked by GPS satellites. There were radio tracer beads and special ones that gave off infrared signals.

"Don't waste your time looking for a bead. The Tabula aren't interested in me."

"Just being careful."

"I'm not a Harlequin and they know it."

The scanner didn't beep. Alexi retreated from the room and Thorn motioned to the chair. Maya knew that her father had mentally rehearsed the conversation. He had probably spent a few hours thinking about his clothing and where to put the furniture. To hell with it. She was going to catch him by surprise.

"Nice servant you got there." She sat down on the chair as Thorn rolled over to her. "Very colorful."

Normally, in private conversations, they would speak to each other in German. Thorn was making a concession to his daughter. Maya had passports for several different nationalities, but these days she considered herself British. "Yes, the ink work." Her father smiled. "Alexi has a tattoo artist creating a picture of the First Realm on his body. Not very pleasant, but that's his choice."

"Yes. We all have free choice. Even Harlequins."

"You don't seem happy to see me, Maya."

She had planned to be controlled and disciplined, but the words began spilling out. "I got you out of Pakistan—basically bribed or threatened half the officials in the country to get you on that plane. And then we're in Dublin and Mother Blessing takes charge and that's okay—it's her territory. I call her satellite phone number the next day and she tells me, 'Your father is paralyzed from the waist down. He'll never walk again.' And then she hangs up on me and immediately cancels her phone line. That's it. Bang. All over. I don't hear from you for two years."

"We were protecting you, Maya. It's very dangerous these days."

"Tell that to tattoo boy. I've watched you use danger and security as excuses for everything, but that doesn't work anymore. There are no more battles. No more Harlequins, really—just a handful like you and Linden and Mother Blessing."

"Shepherd is living in California."

"Three or four people can't change anything. The war is over. Don't you realize that? The Tabula won. We lost. *Wir haben verloren.*"

The German words seemed to touch him a little deeper than her English. Thorn pushed the hand control on his wheelchair and turned away slightly so that she couldn't see his eyes.

"You're also a Harlequin, Maya. That's your true self. Your past and your future."

"I'm not a Harlequin and I'm not like you. You should know that by now."

"We need your help. It's important."

"It's always important."

"I need you to go to America. We'll pay for everything. Make all the arrangements."

"America is Shepherd's territory. Let him handle it."

Her father used the full power of his voice. "Shepherd has encountered an unusual situation. He doesn't know what to do."

"I have a real life now. I'm not part of this anymore."

Moving the control stick, Thorn made a graceful figure

eight around the room. "Ahhh, yes. A citizen life in the Vast Machine. So pleasant and distracting. Tell me all about it."

"You've never asked before."

"Don't you work in some kind of office?"

"I'm an industrial designer. I work with a team developing product containers for different companies. Last week I created a new perfume bottle."

"Sounds challenging. I'm sure you're very successful. And what about the rest of your world? Any boyfriends I should know about?"

"No."

"There was that barrister—what's his name?" Thorn knew, of course. But he pretended to search through his memory. "Connor Ramsey. Wealthy. Good-looking. Well-connected family. And then he left you for that other woman. Apparently, he'd been seeing her the whole time he was with you."

Maya felt like Thorn had just slapped her. She should have guessed that he would use his London contacts to get information. He always seemed to know everything.

"That's not your concern."

"Don't waste your time worrying about Ramsey. Some mercs working for Mother Blessing blew up his car a few months ago. Now he believes that terrorists are after him. He's hired bodyguards. Lives in fear. And that's good. Isn't it? Mr. Ramsey needed to be punished for deceiving my little girl."

Thorn spun the wheelchair around and smiled at her. Maya knew that she should act outraged, but she couldn't. She thought about Connor embracing her on the pier in Brighton, then Connor sitting in a restaurant three weeks later announcing that she wasn't suitable for marriage. Maya had read about the car explosion in the papers, but hadn't connected her father to the attack.

"You didn't have to do that."

"But I did." Thorn moved back to the coffee table.

"Blowing up a car doesn't change anything. I'm still not going to America."

"Who mentioned America? We're just having a conversation."

Her Harlequin training told her that she should go on the attack. Like Thorn, she had prepared for the meeting. "Tell me something, Father. Just one fact. Do you love me?"

"You're my daughter, Maya."

"Answer the question."

"Since your mother died, you're the only precious thing in my life."

"All right. Let's accept that statement for the moment." She leaned forward in the chair. "The Tabula and the Harlequins used to be fairly equal adversaries, but the Vast Machine changed the balance of power. As far as I know, there are no more Travelers and only a few Harlequins."

"The Tabula can use face scanners, electronic surveillance, cooperation from government officials, and—"

"I don't want a reason. We're not talking about that. Just facts and conclusions. In Pakistan you were injured and two people were killed. I always liked Libra. He used to take me to the theater when he visited London. And Willow was a strong, graceful woman."

"Both fighters accepted the risk," Thorn said. "They both had a Proud Death."

"Yes, they're dead. Set up and destroyed for nothing. And now you want me to die the same way."

Thorn gripped the arms of the wheelchair and, for a moment, she thought he was going to force himself to stand up, an act of pure will. "Something extraordinary has happened," he said. "For the first time, we have a spy on the other side. Linden is in contact with him."

"It's just another trap."

"Perhaps. But all the information we've received has been accurate. A few weeks ago, we learned about two possible Travelers in the United States. They're brothers. I protected their father, Matthew Corrigan, many years ago. Before he went underground, I gave him a talisman."

"Do the Tabula know about these brothers?"

"Yes. They're watching them twenty-four hours a day."

"Why don't the Tabula just kill them? That's what they usually do."

"All I know is that the Corrigans are in danger and we have to help them as soon as possible. Shepherd comes from a Harlequin family. His grandfather saved hundreds of lives. But an unborn Traveler wouldn't trust him. Shepherd isn't very organized or intelligent. He's a—"

"A fool."

"Exactly. You could handle everything, Maya. All you have to do is find the Corrigans and take them to a safe place."

"Maybe they're just ordinary citizens."

"We don't know that until we question them. You're right about one thing, there aren't any more Travelers. This might be our last chance."

"You don't need me. Just hire some mercs."

"The Tabula have more money and power. Mercenaries always betray us."

"Then do it yourself."

"I'm crippled, Maya. Stuck here, in this apartment, in this wheelchair. You're the only one who can lead."

For a few seconds she actually wanted to draw the sword and charge into battle, and then she remembered the fight in the London Underground station. A father should protect his daughter. Instead, Thorn had destroyed her childhood.

She stood up and walked to the door. "I'm going back to London."

"Don't you remember what I taught you? *Verdammt durch das Fleisch. Gerettet durch das Blut . . .*"

Damned by the flesh. Saved by the blood. Maya had heard the Harlequin phrase—and hated it—since she was a little girl.

"Tell your slogans to your new Russian friend. They don't work with me."

"If there are no more Travelers, then the Tabula have finally conquered history. In one or two generations, the Fourth Realm will become a cold, sterile place where everyone is watched and controlled."

"It's that way already."

"This is our obligation, Maya. It's who we are." Thorn's voice was full of pain and regret. "I've often wished for a different life, wished that I was born ignorant and blind. But I could never turn away and deny the past, deny all those Harlequins who sacrificed themselves for such an important cause."

"You gave me weapons and taught me how to kill. Now you're sending me out to be destroyed."

Thorn looked small and frail in the wheelchair. His voice was a harsh whisper. "I would die for you."

"But I'm not dying for a cause that doesn't exist anymore."

Maya reached for Thorn's shoulder. It was a farewell gesture, a chance to connect with him one last time—but his angry expression made her pull her hand away.

"Goodbye, Father." She turned to the door and opened the latch. "I have one small chance to be happy. I can't let you take it away from me."

2

Nathan Boone sat in a second-floor room of the warehouse across the street from the lingerie shop. Peering through a nightscope, he watched Maya leave Thorn's building and head down the sidewalk. Boone had already photographed Thorn's daughter arriving at the airport terminal, but he enjoyed seeing her again. So much of his work these days involved staring at a computer monitor, checking phone calls and credit card bills, reading medical reports and police bulletins from a dozen different countries. To see an actual Harlequin helped him reconnect with the reality of what he was doing. The enemy still existed—at least a few of them did—and it was his responsibility to eliminate them.

Two years ago, after the shoot-out in Pakistan, he found Maya living in London. Her public behavior indicated that she had rejected the violence of the Harlequins and had decided to have a normal life. The Brethren had considered executing Maya, but Boone sent them a lengthy e-mail recommending against it. He knew that she might lead him to Thorn, Linden, or Mother Blessing. All three Harlequins were still dangerous. They needed to be tracked down and destroyed.

Maya would have noticed anyone following her around London, so Boone sent a squad of technicians to her apartment and had them insert tracer beads in every piece of her luggage. After she obtained a job and started to live a public life, the Brethren's computers constantly monitored her phone calls, e-mails, and credit card transactions. The first alert came after Maya sent an e-mail to her supervisor asking for time off to visit "a sick relative." When she purchased a Friday plane ticket to Prague, Boone decided that the city was a logical place for Thorn to hide. He had three days to fly to Europe and come up with a plan.

That morning one of Boone's employees had read the note left in Maya's hotel room by the young Russian who worked for Thorn. Now Boone knew the location of Thorn's apartment, and it would be just a matter of minutes until he would be face-to-face with the Harlequin.

Boone heard Loutka's voice come from his radio headset. "Now what?" Loutka asked. "Do we follow her?"

"That's Halver's job. He can handle it. Thorn is the primary target. We'll deal with Maya later tonight."

Loutka and the three technicians sat in the back of a delivery van parked near the corner. Loutka was a Czech police lieutenant and was supposed to handle the local authorities. The technicians were there to do their special jobs and go home.

With Loutka's help, Boone had also hired two professional killers in Prague. The mercenaries sat on the floor behind him, waiting for orders. The Magyar was a big man who couldn't speak English. His Serb friend, an ex-soldier, knew four languages and seemed intelligent, but Boone didn't trust him. He was the kind of person who might run away if there was resistance.

It was cold in the room and Boone was wearing an all-weather parka and a knit cap. His military haircut and steel eyeglasses made him look disciplined and fit, like a chemical engineer who ran marathons on the weekend.

"Let's go," Loutka said.

"No."

"Maya is walking back to her hotel. I don't think that Thorn will get any more visitors tonight."

"You don't understand these people. I do. They deliberately do things that are unpredictable. Thorn may decide to leave the house. Maya may decide to return. Let's give it five minutes and see what happens."

Boone lowered the nightscope and continued to watch the street. For the last six years he had worked for the Brethren, a small group of men from different countries united by a particular vision of the future. The Brethren—who were called "the Tabula" by their enemies—were committed to the destruction of both the Harlequins and the Travelers.

Boone was a liaison between the Brethren and their mercenaries. He found it easy to deal with people like the Serb and Lieutenant Loutka. A mercenary always wanted money or some kind of favor. First you negotiated a price, then you decided if you were going to pay it.

Although Boone received a generous salary from the Brethren, he never felt that he was a mercenary. Two years ago, he was allowed to read a collection of books called The Knowledge that gave him a larger vision of the Brethren's goals and philosophy. The Knowledge showed Boone that he was part of a historical battle against the forces of disorder. The Brethren and their allies were on the verge of establishing a perfectly controlled society, but this new system would not survive if Travelers were allowed to leave the system, then return to challenge the accepted view. Peace and prosperity were possible only if people stopped asking new questions and accepted the available answers.

The Travelers brought chaos into the world, but Boone didn't hate them. A Traveler was born with the power to cross over; there was nothing they could do about their strange inheritance. The Harlequins were different.

Although there were Harlequin families, each man or woman made a choice to protect the Travelers. Their deliberate randomness contradicted the rules that governed Boone's life.

A few years earlier, Boone had traveled to Hong Kong to kill a Harlequin named Crow. Searching the man's body, he found the usual weapons and false passports along with an electronic device called a random number generator. The RNG was a miniature computer that produced a mathematically random number whenever you pushed the button. Sometimes Harlequins used RNGs to make decisions. An odd number might mean yes, an even number no. Push a button and the RNG would tell you which door to enter.

Boone remembered sitting in a hotel room and studying the device. How could a person live this way? As far as he was concerned, anyone who used random numbers to guide his life should be hunted down and exterminated. Order and discipline were the values that kept Western civilization from falling apart. You only had to look at the edges of the society to see what would happen if people allowed their life decisions to be determined by random choices.

Two minutes had gone by. He pressed a button on his watch and the device flashed his pulse rate and then his body temperature. This was a stressful situation, and it pleased Boone to see that his pulse rate was only six points higher than average. He knew his pulse rate at rest and during exercise as well as his body fat percentage, cholesterol number, and daily calorie consumption.

A match snapped and a few seconds later he smelled tobacco smoke. Turning around, he saw that the Serb was puffing on a cigarette.

"Put that out."

"Why?"

"I don't like to breathe toxic air."

The Serb grinned. "You're not breathing anything, my friend. It's my cigarette."

Boone stood up and moved away from the window. His face was impassive as he evaluated the opposition. Was this man dangerous? Did he need to be intimidated for the success of the operation? How quickly could he respond?

Boone slid his right hand into one of the upper side pockets of his parka, felt the taped razor, and held it tightly between his thumb and index finger. "Put the cigarette out immediately."

"When I'm finished."

Boone swung downward and chopped off the tip of the cigarette. Before the Serb could react, Boone grabbed the mercenary's collar and held the edge of the razor a quarter inch away from the man's right eye.

"If I slashed your eyes open, my face would be the last thing you would ever see. You'd think about me for the rest of your life, Josef. The image would be burned in your brain."

"Please," the Serb mumbled. "Please, don't . . ."

Boone stepped back and returned the razor to his pocket. He glanced at the Magyar. The big man looked impressed.

As he returned to the window, Lieutenant Loutka's voice came out of his radio headset. "What's going on? Why are we waiting?"

"We're not waiting anymore," Boone said. "Tell Skip and Jamie it's time for them to earn their salary."

Skip and Jamie Todd were two brothers from Chicago who specialized in electronic surveillance. They were both short and plump, and were wearing identical brown coveralls. As Boone watched through his nightscope, the two men pulled an aluminum ladder out of the van and carried it down the sidewalk to the lingerie shop. They looked like electricians who had been called in to fix a wiring problem.

Skip snapped open the ladder and Jamie climbed up to the sign hanging over the window of the lingerie shop. A radio-controlled miniature camera had been placed on the edge of the sign earlier that day. It had taken a video of Maya when she stood on the sidewalk.

Thorn had installed a surveillance camera inside the canopy that protected his front door. Jamie climbed the ladder a second time, removed the camera, and replaced it with a miniature DVD player. When the brothers were finished, they folded up their ladder and carried it back to the van. For three minutes of work, they had earned $10,000 and a free visit to a brothel on Korunni Street.

"Get ready," Boone told Lieutenant Loutka. "We're coming down."

"What about Harkness?"

"Tell him to stay in the van. We'll bring him upstairs when it's safe."

Boone slipped the nightscope into his pocket and motioned to the local hires. "It's time to go."

The Serb spoke to the Magyar and the two men got to their feet.

"Be careful when we enter the apartment," Boone said. "Harlequins are very dangerous. If attacked, they respond immediately."

The Serb had regained some of his confidence. "Maybe they're dangerous for you. But my friend and I can handle any problem."

"Harlequins aren't normal. They spend their entire childhood learning how to kill their enemies."

The three men went down into the street and met Loutka. The police lieutenant looked pale beneath the streetlight. "What if it doesn't work?" he asked.

"If you're scared, you can stay in the van with Harkness, but you're not going to get paid. Don't worry. When I organize an operation, everything works."

Boone led the men across the street to Thorn's door and drew his laser-guided automatic pistol. A radio control was in his left hand. He clicked the yellow button and the DVD started to play an image of Maya standing on the sidewalk half an hour earlier. Look left. Look right. Everyone was ready. He pushed the door buzzer and waited. Upstairs, the young Russian—it probably wouldn't be Thorn—went over to a closed-circuit television monitor, glanced at the screen, and saw Maya. The lock clicked open. They were inside.

The four men climbed upstairs. When they reached the first-floor landing, Loutka took out a voice recorder.

"Voice print please," said an electronic voice.

Loutka switched on the recorder and played the audio captured earlier that day in the taxicab. "Open the bloody door," Maya said. "Open the—"

The electric door lock clicked and Boone was the first person inside. The tattooed Russian stood there holding a dish towel and looking very surprised. Boone raised the automatic and fired at close range. The 9-mm bullet hit the Russian's chest like a giant fist and he was hurled backward.

Trying to get a bonus for the next kill, the Magyar ran around the half wall that divided the room. Boone heard the big man scream. He ran forward, followed by Loutka and the Serb. They entered a kitchen area and saw that the Magyar was lying facedown on Thorn's lap, his legs on the floor, his shoulders wedged between the arms of the wheelchair. Thorn was trying to push the body away and grab his sword.

"Get his arms," said Boone. "Come on! Do it!"

The Serb and Loutka grabbed Thorn's arms, controlling him. Blood spurted over the wheelchair. When Boone pulled the Magyar away he saw the handle of a throwing knife protruding from the base of the dead man's throat. Thorn had killed him with the knife, but the Magyar had fallen forward and hit the chair.

"Step back. Move him over there," Boone told them. "Careful. Don't get blood on your shoes." He pulled out some plastic restraining straps and fastened Thorn's wrists and legs together. When he was done, he stepped back and studied the crippled Harlequin. Thorn was defeated, but he looked as proud and arrogant as ever.

"A pleasure to meet you, Thorn. I'm Nathan Boone. I just missed you two years ago in Pakistan. It got dark very quickly, didn't it?"

"I don't talk to Tabula mercenaries," Thorn said quietly. Boone had heard the Harlequin's voice on recordings from phone taps. The real thing was deeper, more intimidating.

Boone looked around the room. "I like your apartment, Thorn. I really do. It's clean and simple. Tasteful colors. Instead of cluttering up the place with junk, you've gone for the minimalist look."

"If you wish to kill me, do your job. Don't waste my time with useless conversation."

Boone motioned to Loutka and the Serb. The two men dragged the Magyar's body out to the living room.

"The long war is over. The Travelers have vanished and the Harlequins have been defeated. I could kill you right now, but I need your help to finish my job."

"I won't betray anyone."

"Cooperate and we'll let Maya live a normal life. If not, then she'll have a very unpleasant death. My mercenaries spent two days raping that Chinese Harlequin when we captured her in Pakistan. They liked the fact that she struggled and fought back. I guess the local women just give up in a similar situation."

Thorn stayed silent, and Boone wondered if he was considering the offer. Did he love his daughter? Were Harlequins capable of such an emotion? Thorn's arm muscles tensed as he tried to rip apart the restraining straps. He gave up and slumped back into the wheelchair.

Boone switched on his headset and spoke into the microphone. "Mr. Harkness, please come upstairs with your materials. The area is secure."

The Serb and Loutka pulled Thorn out of the wheelchair, carried him into the bedroom, and dumped him on the floor. Harkness appeared a few minutes later, struggling with the unwieldy carrying case. He was an older

Englishman who rarely spoke, but Boone found it difficult to sit beside him in a restaurant. There was something about the man's yellow teeth and pale complexion that suggested death and decay.

"I know what you Harlequins dream about. A Proud Death. Isn't that the expression? I could arrange that for you—a death that was noble and that gave some dignity to the end of your life. But you'd have to give me something in return. Tell me how to find your two friends, Linden and Mother Blessing. If you refuse, there's a more humiliating alternative . . ."

Harkness placed the carrying case in front of the bedroom doorway. There were airholes on top, covered with a thick wire mesh. Claws scratched the metal floor of the case and Boone heard a raspy breathing sound.

He took the razor out of his pocket. "While you Harlequins were trapped in your medieval dreams, the Brethren have gained a new source of knowledge. They've overcome the challenges of genetic engineering."

Boone cut into the skin beneath the Harlequin's eyes. The creature inside the case could smell Thorn's blood. It made an odd laughing sound, then banged against the side panel and tore at the wire mesh with its claws.

"This animal has been genetically designed to be aggressive and fearless. It's compelled to attack without thought for its own survival. This won't be a Proud Death. You'll be eaten like a piece of meat."

Lieutenant Loutka left the hallway and went back to the living room. The Serb looked curious and frightened. He stood a few feet behind Harkness in the doorway.

"Last chance. Give me one fact. Acknowledge our victory."

Thorn rolled into a new position and stared at the carrying case. Boone realized that the Harlequin would fight when the creature attacked, trying to crush it with his body.

"Think anything you wish," he said slowly, "but this is a Proud Death."

Boone went back to the doorway and drew his gun. He would have to kill the animal after it finished with Thorn. The laughing sound stopped and the creature assumed the silence of a hunter, waiting. Boone nodded to Harkness. The old man straddled the case and slowly pulled the panel upward.

3

By the time she reached the Charles Bridge, Maya realized that she was being followed. Thorn once said that eyes projected energy. If you were sensitive enough, you could feel the waves coming toward you. When Maya was growing up in London, her father occasionally hired street thieves to follow her home after school. She had to spot them and hit them with the steel ball bearings she carried in her book bag.

It got darker after she crossed the bridge and turned left onto Saská Street. She decided to go to the Church of Our Lady Beneath the Chain; there was an unlit courtyard there with different ways to escape. Just keep walking, she told herself. Don't look over your shoulder. Saská Street was narrow and crooked. The occasional streetlamp glowed with a dark yellow light. Maya passed an alleyway, doubled back, and stepped into its shadows. She crouched behind a trash dumpster and waited.

Ten seconds passed. Twenty seconds. Then the little troll taxi driver who had taken her to the hotel came down the sidewalk. Never hesitate. Always react. As he passed the mouth of the alleyway, she pulled out the stiletto and came up behind him, holding his shoulder with her left hand and pressing the knife point against the nape of his neck.

"Don't move. Don't run away." Her voice was soft, almost seductive. "We're going to step to the right now and I don't want any trouble."

She pulled him around, dragged him into the shadows, and pushed him up against the dumpster. Now the blade was pointed at his Adam's apple.

"Tell me everything. No lies. And perhaps I won't kill you. Do you understand?"

Terrified, the troll nodded his head slightly.

"Who hired you?"

"An American."

"What's his name?"

"I don't know. He was a friend of Police Lieutenant Loutka."

"And what were your instructions?"

"To follow you. That's all. Pick you up with the taxi and follow you tonight."

"Is someone waiting for me at the hotel?"

"I don't know. I swear that's true." He started to whimper. "Please don't hurt me."

Thorn would have stabbed him right away, but Maya decided that she wasn't going to give in to that madness. If she murdered this foolish little man, then her own life would be destroyed.

"I'm going to walk up the street and you're going to go the other way, back to the bridge. Do you understand?"

The troll nodded quickly. "Yes," he whispered.

"If I see you again, you're dead."

Maya stepped back out onto the sidewalk and headed toward the church, then she remembered her father. Had the troll followed her all the way to Thorn's apartment? How much did they know?

She hurried back to the alleyway and heard the troll's voice. Clutching a cell phone, he babbled to his master. As she stepped out of the shadows, he gasped and dropped the phone onto the cobblestones. Maya grabbed his hair, pulled him up straight, and inserted the point of the stiletto into his left ear.

This was the instant when the blade could pause. Maya was aware of the choice she was making and the dark passageway that opened before her. Don't do this, she thought. You still have a chance. But pride and anger pulled her forward.

"Listen to me," she said. "This is the last thing you will ever know. A Harlequin killed you."

He struggled with her, trying to break away, but she drove the knife down the ear canal and into his brain.

* * *

MAYA LET GO of the taxi driver and he collapsed in front of her. Blood filled his mouth and trickled from his nose. His eyes were open and he looked surprised, as if someone had just told him unpleasant news.

She wiped off the stiletto and concealed the weapon beneath her sweater. Staying in the shadows, she dragged the dead man to the end of the alleyway and covered him with garbage bags taken from a dumpster. In the morning, someone would find the body and call the police.

Don't run, Maya told herself. Don't show that you're scared. She tried to look calm as she walked back across the river. When she reached Konviktská Street, she climbed a fire escape to the roof of the lingerie shop and jumped over the five-foot gap to Thorn's building. No skylight or fire door. She'd have to find another way in.

Maya jumped back to the next roof and went down the block of buildings until she discovered a rooftop clothesline stretched between two metal poles. She cut the clothesline with her knife, returned to her father's building, and lashed the cord around a vent pipe. It was dark except for the glow of a single streetlight and a new moon that looked like a thin yellow line slashed in the sky.

She tested the cord and made sure that it would hold. Carefully, she went over the low wall on the edge of the roof and lowered herself hand over hand to the second-floor window. Peering through the glass, she saw that the apartment was filled with grayish-white smoke. Maya pushed back from the building and kicked in the glass. Smoke poured out of the hole and was absorbed by the night. She kicked again and again, knocking out the sharp edges of glass still held by the window frame.

Too much smoke, she thought. Careful or you'll be trapped. She pushed back as far as possible, then swung through the hole. Smoke drifted up to the ceiling and flowed out of the shattered window; there were a few feet of clear space above the floor. Maya got down on her hands and knees. She crawled across the living room and found the Russian lying dead beside the glass coffee table. Gunshot. Chest wound. A pool of blood surrounded his upper body.

"Father!" She stood up, staggered around the half wall, and found a pile of books and cushions burning in the middle of the dining-room table. Near the kitchen, she stumbled over another body: a big man with a knife in his throat.

Had they captured her father? Was he a prisoner? She stepped over the big man and walked down a hallway to the next room. A bed and two lampshades were burning. Bloody handprints were smeared on the white walls.

A man lay on his side near the bed. His face was turned away from her, but she recognized her father's clothes and long hair. Smoke swirled around her body as she went down on her hands and knees and crawled toward him like a child. She was coughing. Crying. "Father!" she kept shouting. "Father!"

And then she saw his face.

Gabriel Corrigan and his older brother, Michael, had grown up on the road, and they considered themselves to be expert concerning truck stops, tourist cabins, and roadside museums displaying dinosaur bones. During their long hours traveling, their mother sat between them in the backseat, reading books or telling stories. One of their favorite tales was about Edward V and his brother, the Duke of York, the two young princes locked in the Tower of London by Richard III. According to their mother, the princes were about to be smothered by one of Richard's henchmen, but they found a secret passageway and swam across a moat to freedom. Disguised in rags and assisted by Merlin and Robin Hood, the brothers had adventures in fifteenth-century England.

When they were boys, the Corrigan brothers pretended to be the lost princes at public parks and highway rest stops. But now that they were adults, Michael had a different view of the game. "I looked it up in a history book," he said. "Richard III got away with it. Both princes were killed."

"What difference does that make?" Gabriel asked.

"She lied, Gabe. It was just another fabrication. Mom told us all these stories when we were growing up, but she never told us the truth."

* * *

GABRIEL ACCEPTED MICHAEL'S opinion: it was better to know all the facts. But sometimes he entertained himself with one of his mother's stories. On Sunday, he left Los Angeles before dawn and rode his motorcycle through the darkness to the town of Hemet. He felt like a lost prince, alone and unrecognized, as he bought fuel at a discount gas station and ate breakfast at a small coffee shop. As he turned off the freeway, the sun emerged from the ground like a bright orange bubble. It broke free of gravity and floated up into the sky.

* * *

THE HEMET AIRPORT consisted of one asphalt runway with weeds pushing out of the cracks, a tie-down area for the planes, and a shabby collection of trailers and temporary buildings. The HALO office was in a double-wide trailer near the south end of the runway. Gabriel parked his bike near the entrance and unfastened the shock cords that held his gear.

High-altitude jumps were expensive, and Gabriel had told Nick Clark, the HALO instructor, that he was rationing himself to one jump a month. Only twelve days had passed and now he was back again. When he entered the trailer, Nick grinned at him like a bookie greeting one of his steady customers.

"Couldn't stay away?"

"I made some more money," Gabriel said, "and I didn't know where to spend it." He handed Nick a wad of cash and went into the men's room to put on thermal underwear and a jumpsuit.

When Gabriel came out, a group of five Korean men had arrived. They wore matching green-and-white uniforms, and carried expensive gear along with laminated cards with useful English phrases. Nick announced that Gabriel was jumping with them, and the Koreans came over to shake the American's hand and take his picture.

"How many HALO jumps you make?" one of the men asked.

"I don't keep a logbook," Gabriel said.

This answer was translated and everyone looked surprised. "Keep logbook," the oldest man told him. "Then you know the number."

Nick told the Koreans to get ready, and the group began to run through a detailed checklist. "These guys are going for a high-altitude jump in each of the seven continents," Nick whispered. "Bet it costs a lot of money. They're wearing special spacesuits when they do it over Antarctica."

Gabriel liked the Koreans—they took the jump seriously—but he preferred to be alone when he ran through his gear check. The preparation itself was a pleasure, almost a form of meditation. He pulled on a flight suit over his clothes; inspected his thermal gloves, helmet, and flex goggles; then inspected the main and reserve chutes, the straps, and the cutaway handle. All these objects appeared quite ordinary on the ground, but they would be transformed when he stepped into the sky.

The Koreans snapped a few more photographs and everyone squeezed into the plane. The men sat beside each other, two to a row, and attached their oxygen hoses to the aircraft console. Nick spoke to the pilot and the plane took off, beginning its slow ascent to thirty thousand feet. The oxygen masks made it difficult to speak and Gabriel was grateful for the end of conversation. Closing his eyes, he concentrated on breathing as the oxygen hissed softly in his mask.

He hated gravity and the demands of his body. The movement of his lungs and the thump of his heart felt like the mechanical responses of a dull machine. Once he had tried to explain this to Michael, but it felt as if they were speaking different languages. "Nobody asked to be born, but we're here anyway," Michael said. "There's only one question we need to answer: Are we standing at the bottom of the hill or up at the top?"

"Maybe the hill isn't important."

Michael looked amused. "We're both going to be at the top," he said. "That's where I'm going and I'm taking you with me."

Past twenty thousand feet, frost crystals appeared on the inside of the plane. Gabriel opened his eyes as Nick pushed his way down the narrow aisle to the back of the plane and opened the door a few inches. As cold wind forced its way into the cabin, Gabriel began to get excited. This was it. The moment of release.

Nick looked down, searching for the drop zone, as he talked to the pilot on the intercom. Finally he motioned for everyone to get ready, and the men pulled on their goggles and tightened their straps. Two or three minutes passed. Nick waved again and tapped his mask. A small bailout bottle of oxygen was attached to each man's left leg. Gabriel pulled his bottle's regulator handle and his own mask popped slightly. After he detached himself from the oxygen console, he was ready to go.

They were as high as Mount Everest and it was very cold. Perhaps the Koreans had considered pausing at the doorway and making a flashy jump, but Nick wanted them back in the safety zone before the oxygen was gone from their bottles. One by one, the Koreans stood up, shuffled over to the doorway, and fell out into the sky. Gabriel had taken the seat closest to the pilot so that he would be the last jumper. He moved slowly and pretended to be adjusting a parachute strap so that he would be completely alone during his descent. When he reached the door, he wasted a few more seconds giving Nick a thumbs-up, and then he was out of the plane and falling.

Gabriel shifted his weight and flipped over onto his back so that he saw nothing but the space above him. The sky was dark blue, darker than anything you could see when standing on the ground. A midnight blue with a distant point of light. Venus. Goddess of Love. An exposed area on his cheek began to sting, but he ignored the pain and concentrated on the sky itself, the absolute purity of the world that surrounded him.

On earth, two minutes was a commercial break on a television show, a half-mile crawl on a crowded freeway, a fragment of a popular love song. But falling through the air, each second expanded like a tiny sponge tossed into water. Gabriel passed through a layer of warm air, and then returned to the coldness. He was filled with thoughts, but not thinking. All the doubts and compromises of his life on earth had melted away.

His wrist altimeter began to beep loudly. Once again, he shifted his weight and flipped over. He stared down at the dull brown Southern California landscape and a line of distant hills. As he came closer to the earth, he could see cars and tract houses and the yellowish haze of air pollution hanging over the freeway. Gabriel wanted to fall forever, but a quiet voice inside his brain commanded him to pull the handle.

He glanced up at the sky—trying to remember exactly how it looked—and then the parachute canopy blossomed above him.

* * *

GABRIEL LIVED IN a house in the western part of Los Angeles that was fifteen feet away from the San Diego Freeway. At night a white river of headlights flowed north through the Sepulveda Pass while a parallel river of brake lights led south to the beach cities and Mexico. After Gabriel's landlord, Mr. Varosian, found seventeen adults and five children living in his house, he had them all deported back to El Salvador, then placed an ad for "one tenant only, no exceptions." He assumed that Gabriel was involved in something illegal—an after-hours club or the sale of stolen car parts. Mr. Varosian didn't care about car parts, but he did have a few rules. "No guns. No drug cookers. No cats."

Gabriel could hear a constant rushing sound as cars and trucks and buses headed south. Every morning he would walk over to the chain-link fence that surrounded the back of his property to see what the freeway had left along its shore. People were constantly throwing things out of their car windows: fast-food wrappers and newspapers, a plastic Barbie doll with teased hair, several cell phones, a wedge of goat cheese with a bite taken out of it, used condoms, gardening tools, and a plastic cremation urn filled with blackened teeth and ashes.

Gang graffiti was sprayed on the detached garage and the front lawn was dotted with weeds, but Gabriel never touched the exterior of the house. It was a disguise, like the rags worn by the lost princes. The previous summer, he had bought a bumper sticker from a religious group at a swap meet that announced "We Are Damned for Eternity Except for the Blood of Our Savior." Gabriel cut off everything but "Damned for Eternity" and slapped the sticker on the front door. When real estate agents and door-to-door salesmen avoided the house, he felt like he had won a small victory.

The inside of the house was clean and pleasant. Every morning, when the sun was at a certain angle, the rooms were filled with light. His mother said that plants cleansed the air and gave you positive thoughts, so he had more than thirty plants in the house, hanging from the ceiling or growing in pots on the floor. Gabriel slept on a futon in one of the bedrooms and kept all of his belongings in a few canvas duffel bags. His kempo helmet and armor were placed on a special frame next to the rack that held a bamboo *shinai* sword and the old Japanese sword left by his father. If he woke up during the night and opened his eyes, it looked like a samurai warrior was guarding him while he slept.

The second bedroom was empty except for several hundred books piled in stacks against the wall. Instead of getting a library card and searching for a particular book, Gabriel read any book that happened to find him. Several of his customers gave him books when they had finished them, and he would pick up discarded books in waiting rooms or on the shoulder of the freeway. There were mass-market paperbacks with lurid covers, technical reports about metal alloys, and three water-stained Dickens novels.

Gabriel didn't belong to a club or a political party. His strongest belief was that he should continue to live off the Grid. In the dictionary, a grid was defined as a network of evenly spaced horizontal and vertical lines that could be used for locating a particular object or point. If you looked at modern civilization in a certain way, it seemed like every commercial enterprise or government program was part of an enormous grid. The different lines and squares could track you down and fix your location; they could find out almost everything about you.

The grid was comprised of straight lines on a flat plain, but it was still possible to live a secret life. You could take a job in the underground economy or keep moving so fast that the lines would never fix your exact location. Gabriel didn't have a bank account or a credit card. He used his real first name but had a false last name on his driver's license. Although he carried two cell phones, one for personal business and one for work, they were both billed to his brother's real estate company.

Gabriel's only connection to the Grid was on a desk in the living room. A year ago, Michael had given him a home computer and arranged for a hookup to a DSL line. Going on the Internet enabled Gabriel to download trance musik from Germany, hypnotic loops of sound produced by DJs affiliated with a mysterious group called Die Neunen

Primitiven. The music helped him go to sleep when he returned to the house for the night. As he closed his eyes, he heard a woman singing: *Lotus eaters lost in New Babylon. Lonely pilgrim find your way home.*

* * *

CAPTIVE IN HIS dream, he fell through darkness, fell through clouds and snow and rain. He hit the roof of a house and passed through the cedar shingles, the tar paper, and the wooden frame. Now he was a child again, standing in the hallway on the second floor of the farmhouse in South Dakota. And the house was burning, his parents' bed, the dresser, and the rocking chair in their room smoking and smoldering and bursting into flame. Get out, he told himself. Find Michael. Hide. But his child self, the small figure walking down the hallway, didn't seem to hear his adult warning.

Something exploded behind a wall, and there was a dull thumping sound. Then the fire roared up the stairway, flowing around the banisters and railing. Terrified, Gabriel stood in the hallway as fire rushed toward him in a wave of heat and pain.

* * *

THE CELL PHONE lying near the futon mattress started ringing. Gabriel pulled his head away from the pillow. It was six o'clock in the morning and sunlight pushed through a crack in the curtains. No fire, he told himself. Another day.

He answered the phone and heard his brother's voice. Michael sounded worried, but that was normal. Since childhood, Michael had played the role of the responsible older brother. Whenever he heard about a motorcycle accident on the radio, Michael called Gabriel on the cell phone just to make sure he was all right.

"Where are you?" Michael asked.

"Home. In bed."

"I called you five times yesterday. Why didn't you call me back?"

"It was Sunday. I didn't feel like talking to anyone. I left the cell phones here and rode down to Hemet for a jump."

"Do whatever you want, Gabe, but tell me where you're going. I start to worry when I don't know where you are."

"Okay. I'll try to remember." Gabriel rolled onto his side and saw his steel-toed boots and riding leathers scattered across the floor. "How was your weekend?"

"The usual. I paid some bills and played golf with two real estate developers. Did you see Mom?"

"Yeah. I dropped by the hospice on Saturday."

"Is everything okay at this new place?"

"She's comfortable."

"It's got to be more than comfortable."

Two years ago, their mother had gone into the hospital for routine bladder surgery and the doctors had discovered a malignant tumor on her abdominal wall. Although she had gone through chemotherapy, the cancer had metastasized and spread throughout her body. Now she was living at a hospice in Tarzana, a suburb in the southwest San Fernando Valley.

The Corrigan brothers had divided up the responsibilities for their mother's care. Gabriel saw her every other day and talked to the hospice workers. His older brother dropped by once a week and paid for everything. Michael was always suspicious of doctors and nurses. Whenever he perceived a lack of diligence, he had their mother transferred to a new facility.

"She doesn't want to leave this place, Michael."

"No one is talking about leaving. I just want the doctors to do their job."

"The doctors aren't important now that she's stopped chemotherapy. It's the nurses and the aides who take care of her."

"If there's the slightest problem, you let me know immediately. And take care of yourself. Are you working today?"

"Yeah. I guess so."

"That fire in Malibu is getting worse and now there's a new fire in the east, near Lake Arrowhead. All the arsonists are out with their matches. Must be the weather."

"I dreamed about fire," Gabriel said. "We were back at our old house in South Dakota. It was burning down and I couldn't get out."

"You've got to stop thinking about that, Gabe. It's a waste of time."

"Don't you want to know who attacked us?"

"Mom has given us a dozen explanations. Pick one of them and get on with your life." A second phone rang in Michael's apartment. "Leave your cell on," he said. "We'll talk this afternoon."

* * *

GABRIEL TOOK A shower, pulled on running shorts and a T-shirt, and went into the kitchen. He mixed some milk, yogurt, and two bananas in a blender. Sipping the drink, he watered all the hanging plants, then returned to the bedroom and began to get dressed. When Gabriel was naked, you could see the scars from his last motorcycle accident: pale white lines on his left leg and arm. His curly brown hair and smooth skin gave him a boyish appearance, but that changed as he pulled on jeans, a long-sleeved T-shirt, and heavy motorcycle boots. The boots were scuffed and scratched from the aggressive way he leaned into turns. His leather jacket was also scratched and machine oil darkened the cuffs and sleeves. Gabriel's two cell phones were attached to a headset with a built-in microphone. Work calls went into his left ear. Personal calls went to the right. While riding he could activate either phone by pressing his hand against an outside pocket.

Carrying one of his motorcycle helmets, Gabriel walked outside to the backyard. It was October in Southern California and a hot Santa Ana wind flowed out of the northern canyons. The sky above him was clear, but when Gabriel looked west he saw a cloud of dark gray smoke from the Malibu fire. There was a closed, edgy feeling in the air, as if the entire city had become a windowless room.

Gabriel opened the garage door and inspected his three motorcycles. If he had to park in a strange neighborhood, he usually rode the Yamaha RD400. It was his smallest bike, dented and temperamental. Only the most deluded thief would think of stealing such a piece of garbage. He also owned a Moto Guzzi V11, a powerful Italian bike that had a shaft drive and a powerful engine. It was his weekend motorcycle that he used for long trips across the desert. This morning, he decided to ride his Honda 600, a midsize sport bike that could easily go over a hundred miles an hour. Gabriel jacked up the back wheel, sprayed the chain with an aerosol lube, and let the solvents seep into the pins and rollers. The Honda had problems with the drive chain, so he found a screwdriver and an adjustable wrench on the workbench and dropped them into his messenger bag.

He relaxed the moment he straddled the bike and started the engine. The motorcycle always made him feel like he could leave the house and the city forever, just ride and ride until he disappeared into the dark haze on the horizon.

*　*　*

WITH NO PARTICULAR destination, Gabriel turned onto Santa Monica Boulevard and headed west. The morning rush hour had started. Women drinking from stainless steel travel mugs drove to work in their Land Rovers while school crossing guards wearing safety vests waited at the intersections. At a red light, Gabriel reached into his outside pocket and switched on his business cell phone.

He worked for two delivery services: Sir Speedy and its competitor, Blue Sky Messengers. Sir Speedy was owned by Artie Dressler, a 380-pound former attorney who rarely left his home in the Silver Lake District. Artie subscribed to several X-rated Web sites and took phone calls while he watched nude college girls paint their toenails. He loathed his competition, Blue Sky Messengers, and its owner, Laura Thompson. Laura had once worked as a film editor and now lived in a dome house up in Topanga Canyon. She believed in a clean colon and orange-colored food.

The phone rang as the light turned green and he heard Artie's raspy New Jersey accent coming out of his headset. "Gabe! It's me! Why'd you turn off your phone?"

"Sorry. I forgot."

"I'm watching a live-cam shot on my computer. Two girls are taking a shower together. It started out okay, but now the steam is messing up the lens."

"Sounds interesting."

"I've got a pickup for you in Santa Monica Canyon."

"Is that near the fire?"

"Nah. It's miles away. No problem. But there's a new fire in Simi Valley. That one's totally out of control."

The motorcycle's handlebars were short and the foot clips and seat were angled so that Gabriel was always leaning forward. He could feel the vibration of the motor and hear the gears changing. When he was going fast, the machine became part of him, an extension of his body. Sometimes the tips of his handlebars were only inches away from speeding cars as he followed the broken white line that separated the lanes. He looked down the street and saw stoplights, pedestrians, trucks making slow turns, and immediately knew if he should stop or speed up or swerve around the obstacles.

Santa Monica Canyon was an enclave of expensive houses built near a two-lane road that led down to the beach. Gabriel picked up a manila envelope lying on someone's doorstep and carried it to a mortgage broker in West Hollywood. When he reached the address, he removed his helmet and entered the office. He hated this part of the job. On the motorcycle, he was free to go anywhere. Standing in front of the receptionist, his body felt slow, weighed down by his heavy boots and jacket.

Back on the bike. Kick-start the engine. Keep moving. "Dear Gabriel, can you hear me?" It was Laura's soothing voice coming into his headset. "I hope you ate a good breakfast this morning. Complex carbohydrates can help stabilize blood sugar."

"Don't worry. I ate something."

"Good. I've got a pickup for you in Century City."

Gabriel knew this address fairly well. He had dated a few of the receptionists and secretaries he had met delivering packages, but he had made only one real friend, a criminal-defense attorney named Maggie Resnick. About a year ago, he had showed up at her office for a delivery, only to wait around while her secretaries looked for a misplaced legal document. Maggie had asked him about his job and they ended up talking for an hour—long after the document had been found. He volunteered to take her riding on his motorcycle and was surprised when she accepted his offer.

Maggie was in her sixties, a small energetic woman who liked to wear red dresses and expensive shoes. Artie said that she defended movie stars and other celebrities who got into trouble, but she rarely talked about her cases. She treated Gabriel like a favorite nephew who wasn't very responsible. "You should go to college," she told him. "Open a bank account. Buy some real estate." Gabriel never followed any of her advice, but he liked the fact that she worried about him.

When he got up to the twenty-second floor, the receptionist sent him down the hallway to Maggie's private office. He walked in and found her smoking a cigarette and talking on the phone.

"Sure you can meet with the district attorney, but there's no deal. And there's no deal because he doesn't have a case. Feel him out, and then call me back. I'll be at lunch but they'll patch it through to the cell." Maggie hung up and flicked some ash off her cigarette. "Bastards. They're all lying bastards."

"You got a package for me?"

"No package. I just wanted to see you. I'll pay Laura for a delivery."

Gabriel sat on the couch and unzipped his jacket. Bottled water was on the coffee table and he poured some into a glass.

Maggie leaned forward, looking very fierce. "If you're dealing drugs, Gabriel, I will personally kill you."

"I'm not dealing drugs."

"You've told me about your brother. You shouldn't get involved in his scams to make money."

"He's buying property, Maggie. That's all. Office buildings."

"I hope so, darling. I'll cut out his tongue if he drags you into something illegal."

"What's going on?"

"I work with an ex-cop turned security consultant. He helps me out if some crazy person is stalking one of my clients. Yesterday we were talking on the phone and, all of sudden, this man says: 'Don't you know a motorcycle messenger named Gabriel? I met him at your birthday party.' And, of course, I say, 'Yes.' And then, he says, 'Some friends of mine asked me about him. Where he works. Where he lives.'"

"Who are these people?"

"He wouldn't tell me," Maggie said. "But you should watch out, darling. Someone powerful is interested in you. Were you involved in a car accident?"

"No."

"Any kind of lawsuit?"

"Of course not."

"What about girlfriends?" She stared at him intently. "Anyone wealthy? Some woman with a husband?"

"I took out that girl I met at your party. Andrea—"

"Andrea Scofield? Her father owns four wineries up in Napa Valley." Maggie laughed. "That's it. Dan Scofield is making sure you're all right."

"We went riding a few times."

"Don't worry, Gabriel. I'll talk to Dan and tell him not to be so protective. Now get out of here. I've got to prepare for an arraignment."

* * *

AS HE WALKED through the basement garage, Gabriel felt afraid and suspicious. Was someone watching him right now? The two men in the SUV? The woman with the briefcase walking to the elevators? He reached into his messenger bag and touched the heavy adjustable wrench. If necessary, he could use it as a weapon.

His parents would have run away the moment they heard someone was asking about them. But he had lived in Los Angeles for five years and no one had kicked in his door. Perhaps he should follow Maggie's advice: go to school and get a real job. If you were connected with the Grid, your life would become more substantial.

As he kick-started the motorcycle, his mother's story returned to him with all its comforting power. He and Michael were the lost princes, disguised in rags, but resourceful and brave. Gabriel roared up the exit ramp, merged into traffic, and cut around a pickup truck. Second gear. Third gear. Faster. And he was moving again, always moving, a small spark of consciousness surrounded by machines.

5

Michael Corrigan believed that the world was a battlefield in a continual state of war. This war included the high-tech military campaigns organized by America and its allies, but there were also smaller conflicts between Third World countries and genocidal attacks against various tribes, races, and religions. There were terrorist bombings and assassinations, crazy snipers shooting people for crazy reasons, street gangs, cults, and disgruntled scientists mailing out anthrax to strangers. Immigrants from the southern countries flooded across the borders to northern countries bringing horrible new viruses and bacteria that ate your flesh. Nature was so annoyed by overpopulation and pollution that it was fighting back with droughts and hurricanes. The ice cap was melting and the sea was rising while the ozone layer was being shredded by jet planes. Sometimes Michael lost track of a particular threat but stayed aware of the general danger. The war would never end. It was only growing larger and more pervasive, claiming new victims in subtle ways.

* * *

MICHAEL LIVED ON the eighth floor of a high-rise con-
dominium in West Los Angeles. It had taken him four hours
to decorate the place. The day he signed the lease, he drove
over to a huge furniture store on Venice Boulevard and
picked out the suggested arrangements for a living room, a
bedroom, and a home office. Michael had offered to rent an
identical apartment for his brother in the same building and
fill it with similar furniture, but Gabriel rejected the proposal. For some perverse reason, his younger brother wanted
to live in what was probably the ugliest home in Los Angeles
and breathe the exhaust from the freeway.

If Michael stepped out onto the little balcony he could
see the Pacific Ocean in the distance, but he had no use for
views and usually kept the curtain closed. After his phone
call to Gabriel, he made some coffee, ate a protein bar, and
started calling real estate investment firms in New York.
Because of the three-hour time difference, they were working in their offices while he was wandering around the living room in his underwear. "Tommy! It's Michael! Did you
get that proposal I sent you? What did you think? What did
the loan committee say?"

Usually the loan committees were cowardly or foolish,
but you couldn't let that stop you. In the last five years,
Michael had found enough investors to buy two office
buildings and he was about to close a deal for a third building on Wilshire Boulevard. Michael expected people to say
no and he already had his counterarguments ready.

Around eight o'clock he opened his closet and picked
out a pair of gray pants and a navy blue blazer. Adjusting a
red silk necktie, he moved through the apartment, passing
from one television set to another. Fires and the powerful
Santa Ana winds were the big story that morning. A fire in
Malibu was threatening the home of a basketball star.
Another fire was out of control east of the mountains, and
the television screen showed images of people tossing photo
albums and armfuls of clothes into their cars.

He took the elevator down to the parking garage and got into his Mercedes. The moment he left his apartment, he felt like a soldier entering a battle to make money. The only person he could count on was Gabriel, but it was obvious that his younger brother was never going to get a real job. Their mother was sick and Michael was still paying for her care. Don't complain, he told himself. Just keep fighting.

After he had saved enough money, he would buy an island somewhere in the Pacific. Neither he nor Gabriel had a girlfriend, and Michael couldn't decide what kind of wives would be suitable for a tropical paradise. In his dream, he and Gabriel were riding horses through the surf and the two wives were slightly out of focus, standing on a bluff wearing long white dresses. The world was warm and sunny and they would be safe, truly safe. Forever.

6

A brush fire was still burning in the western hills and the sky was a mustard-yellow color when Gabriel reached the hospice. He left his motorcycle in the parking lot and went inside. The hospice was a converted two-story motel with beds for sixteen patients with terminal illnesses. A nurse from the Philippines named Anna was sitting behind a desk in the lobby.

"It's good you're here, Gabriel. Your mother asks for you."

"Sorry I didn't bring any doughnuts tonight."

"I love doughnuts, but they love me too much." Anna touched her plump brown arm. "You must see your mother right now. Very important."

The hospice aides were always washing floors and changing bedsheets, but the building smelled like urine and dead flowers. Gabriel took the stairs to the second floor and walked down the hallway. The fluorescent light fixtures in the ceiling made a soft humming sound.

His mother was asleep when he entered her room. Her body had become a little bump beneath a white sheet. Whenever he visited the hospice, Gabriel tried to remember what his mother was like when he and Michael were boys.

She liked to sing to herself when she was alone, mostly old rock-and-roll songs like "Peggy Sue" or "Blue Suede Shoes." She loved birthdays or any other reason to have a family party. Even though they were living in motel rooms, she always wanted to celebrate Arbor Day or the winter solstice.

Gabriel sat beside the bed and took his mother's hand. It felt cold, so he held it tightly. Unlike the other patients at the hospice, his mother hadn't brought in special pillows or framed photographs to transform the sterile environment into a home. Her only personal gesture was when she asked that the room's television be disconnected and taken away. The TV cable lay coiled on a shelf like a thin black snake. Once a week, Michael sent a new bouquet of flowers to her room. The last delivery of three dozen roses was almost a week old and fallen petals had made a red circle around a white vase.

Rachel Corrigan's eyes fluttered open and she stared at her son. It took her a few seconds to recognize him.

"Where's Michael?"

"He'll be here on Wednesday."

"Not Wednesday. Too late."

"Why is that?"

She let go of his hand and spoke in a calm voice. "I'm going to die tonight."

"What are you talking about?"

"I don't want the pain anymore. I'm tired of my shell."

The shell was his mother's name for her body. Everyone had a shell and it carried around a small portion of something called the Light.

"You're still strong," Gabriel said. "You're not going to die."

"Call Michael and tell him to come."

She closed her eyes and Gabriel went out into the hallway. Anna stood there holding some clean sheets. "What did she say to you?"

"She said she's going to die."

"She told me that same thing when I came on shift," Anna said.

"Who's the doctor tonight?"

"Chatterjee, the one from India. But he went out for dinner."

"Page him. Please. Right now."

Anna went downstairs to the nurse's desk while Gabriel switched on his cell phone. He dialed Michael's number and his brother answered after the third ring. There were crowd noises in the background.

"Where are you?" Gabriel asked.

"Dodger Stadium. Fourth-row seats, right behind home plate. It's great."

"I'm at the hospice. You need to come here right away."

"I'll drop by at eleven o'clock, Gabe. Maybe a little later. When the game's over."

"No. This can't wait."

Gabriel heard more crowd sounds and his brother's muffled voice saying, "Excuse me, excuse me." Michael had probably left his seat to walk up the steps of the baseball stadium.

"You don't understand," Michael said. "This isn't fun. It's business. I paid a lot of money for these seats. These bankers are going to finance half of my new building."

"Mom said she's going to die tonight."

"But what did the doctor say?"

"He left to get dinner."

One of the baseball players must have gotten a hit because the crowd began to cheer. "So find him!" Michael shouted.

"She's made up her mind. I think it might happen. Get here as fast as you can."

Gabriel switched off the phone and returned to his mother's room. Once again he took her hand, but it was several minutes before she opened her eyes.

"Is Michael here?"

"I called. He's on his way."

"I've been thinking about the Leslies . . ."

This was a name he had never heard before. At various times, his mother mentioned different people and told different stories, but Michael was right—none of it ever made sense.

"Who are the Leslies?"

"Friends from college. They were at the wedding. When your father and I went on our honeymoon, we let them stay in our apartment in Minneapolis. Their apartment was being painted . . ." Mrs. Corrigan shut her eyes tightly, as if she were trying to see everything. "Then we came back from the honeymoon and the police were there. Some men had broken into our apartment at night and shot our friends while they were lying in our bed. They meant to kill us and made a mistake."

"They wanted to kill you?" Gabriel tried to sound calm. He didn't want to startle her and stop the conversation. "Did they catch the murderers?"

"Your father made me get in the car and we started driving. That's when he told me who he really was . . ."

"And who was that?"

But then she was gone again, drifting back into a shadow world that was halfway between here and far away. Gabriel continued to hold her hand. She rested awhile, then woke up and asked the same question.

"Is Michael here? Is Michael coming?"

* * *

DR. CHATTERJEE RETURNED to the hospice at eight o'clock and Michael showed up a few minutes later. As usual, he was alert and full of energy. Everyone stood in front of the nurse's desk while Michael tried to find out what was going on.

"My mother says she's going to die."

Chatterjee was a polite little man who wore a white physician's jacket. He studied their mother's medical chart to show that he was aware of the problem. "Cancer patients often say things like this, Mr. Corrigan."

"So what are the facts?"

The doctor made a notation on the chart. "She may die in a few days or a few weeks. It's impossible to say."

"But what about *tonight*?"

"Her vitals haven't changed."

Michael turned away from Dr. Chatterjee and began to walk upstairs. Gabriel followed his brother. It was just the two of them in the stairwell. No one else could hear.

"He called you Mr. Corrigan."

"That's right."

"When did you start using our real name?"

Michael stopped on the landing. "I've been doing it for the last year. I just haven't told you. Right now, I've got a social security number and I'm paying taxes. My new building on Wilshire Boulevard is going to be owned legally."

"But now you're on the Grid."

"I'm Michael Corrigan and you're Gabriel Corrigan. That's who we are."

"You know what Dad said—"

"Goddamnit, Gabe! We can't keep having this same conversation. Our father was crazy. And Mom was so weak that she went along with it."

"Then why did those men attack us and burn down the house?"

"Because of our father. Obviously he did something wrong, something illegal. *We're* not guilty of anything."

"But the Grid—"

"The Grid is just modern life. Everyone has to deal with it." Michael reached out and touched Gabriel's arm. "You're my brother, okay? But you're also my best friend. I'm doing this for both of us. Swear to God. We can't keep acting like cockroaches, hiding in the wall whenever someone turns on the light."

* * *

THE BROTHERS WENT into the room and stood on opposite sides of the bed. Gabriel touched his mother's hand. It felt like all the blood had left her body. "Wake up," he said gently. "Michael's here."

She opened her eyes and smiled when she saw her two sons. "There you are," she said. "I was dreaming about both of you."

"How are you feeling?" Michael looked at her face and body, evaluating her condition. The tension in his shoulders and the quick way he moved his hands showed that he was worried, but Gabriel knew that his brother would never show it. Instead of accepting weakness of any sort, he always pressed forward. "I think you look a little stronger."

"Oh, Michael." She gave him a tired smile as if he'd just left muddy footprints on the kitchen floor. "Please don't be that way. Not tonight. I need to tell you both about your father."

"We've heard all the stories," Michael said. "Let's not get into that tonight. Okay? We need to talk to the doctor and make sure that you're comfortable."

"No. Let her talk." Gabriel leaned over the bed. He felt excited and a little frightened. Maybe this was the moment that it was finally going to be revealed—the reason for his family's pain.

"I know I've told you different stories," Rachel Corrigan said. "I'm sorry. Most of the stories weren't true. I just wanted to protect you."

Michael looked across the bed and nodded triumphantly. Gabriel knew what his brother wanted to say. *See? What did I always tell you: everything was fake.*

"I've waited too long," she said. "It's so difficult to explain. Your father was . . . When he said . . . I didn't . . ." Her lips trembled as if thousands of words were fighting to get out. "He was a Traveler."

She looked up at Gabriel. *Believe me* was the expression on her face. *Please. Believe me.*

"Go on," Gabriel said.

"Travelers can project their energy out of their bodies and cross over into other realms. That's why the Tabula want to kill them."

"Mom, don't talk anymore. It's just going to make you weak." Michael looked disturbed. "We'll get the doctor in here and make you feel better."

Mrs. Corrigan raised her head off the pillow. "Not enough time, Michael. No time at all. You have to *listen*. The Tabula tried to . . ." She began to get confused again. "And then we . . ."

"It's okay. It's okay," Gabriel whispered, almost chanting.

"A Harlequin named Thorn found us when we were living in Vermont. Harlequins are dangerous people, very violent and cruel, but they're sworn to defend Travelers. We were safe for a few years, and then Thorn couldn't protect us from the Tabula. He gave us money and the sword."

Her head fell back onto the pillow. Each word had drained her, taken away little pieces of her life. "I've watched you grow up," she said. "I've watched you both, looking for the signs. I don't know if you can cross over. But if you have the power, you must hide from the Tabula."

She closed her eyes tightly as the pain pushed through her entire body. Desperate, Michael touched her face with his hand. "I'm here. Gabe is here, too. We're going to protect you. I'm going to hire some more doctors, every kind of doctor . . ."

Mrs. Corrigan breathed deeply. Her body stiffened, then relaxed. It felt like the room had suddenly gotten cold, as if some kind of energy had escaped through the little gap beneath the door. Michael turned and ran out of the room, shouting for help. But Gabriel knew that it was over.

* * *

AFTER DR. CHATTERJEE confirmed the death, Michael got a list of local funeral homes from the nurse's desk and called one on his cell phone. He told them the address, asked for a standard cremation, and gave them a credit card number.

"Is all this okay with you?" he asked Gabriel.

"Sure." Gabriel felt numb and very tired. He glanced at the object that was now concealed beneath a sheet. A shell without Light.

They remained beside the bed until two men showed up from the funeral home. The body was slipped into a bag, placed on a stretcher, and carried downstairs to an unmarked ambulance. When the ambulance drove away, the Corrigan brothers stood together beneath the security light.

"When I made enough money I was going to buy her a house with a big garden," Michael said. "I think she would have liked that." He looked around the parking lot as if he had just lost something valuable. "Buying her a house was one of my goals."

"We need to talk about what she told us."

"Talk about what? Can you explain any of it to me? Mom told us stories about ghosts and talking animals, but she never mentioned anyone called a 'Traveler.' The only traveling we ever did was in that goddamn pickup truck."

Gabriel knew Michael was right; their mother's words hadn't made any sense. He had always believed that she was going to give them an explanation for what had happened to their family. Now he would never find out.

"But maybe part of it is true. In some way—"

"I don't want to argue with you. It's been a long night and we're both tired." Michael reached out and hugged his brother. "It's just the two of us now. We've got to back each other up. Get some rest and we'll talk in the morning."

Michael got into his Mercedes and drove out of the parking lot. By the time Gabriel straddled his motorcycle and revved up the engine, Michael was already turning onto Ventura Boulevard.

The moon and stars were concealed by a thick haze. A fragment of ash drifted through the air and stuck to the Plexiglas visor of his helmet. Gabriel kicked into third gear and shot through the intersection. Looking down the boulevard, he saw Michael turn onto the ramp that led to the freeway. Four cars were a few hundred yards behind the Mercedes. They sped up, formed a group, and headed up the ramp.

It all happened very quickly, but Gabriel knew the cars were together and that they were following his brother. He kicked into fourth gear and went faster. He could feel the engine vibration in his legs and arms. Jerk to the left. Now to the right. And then he was on the freeway.

Gabriel caught up with the group of cars about a mile down the road. There were two unmarked vans and two SUVs with Nevada plates. All four vehicles had tinted windows and it was difficult to see who was sitting inside. Michael hadn't changed his driving at all; he seemed oblivious to what was going on. As Gabriel watched, one of the SUVs passed Michael on the left and cut back in front of him while another came up directly behind the Mercedes. The four drivers were in communication—maneuvering, getting ready to make a move.

Gabriel glided into the right lane as his brother approached the transition to the San Diego Freeway. They were all moving so fast now that the lights seemed to streak past them. Lean into the curve. Brake slightly. And now they were gliding out of the curve and heading up the hill to the Sepulveda Pass.

Another mile passed, then the SUV in front of the Mercedes slowed down while the two vans came up on the left and right lanes. Now Michael was trapped by the four cars. Gabriel was close enough so that he could hear his brother beeping his car horn. Michael moved a few inches to the left, but a van driver came back aggressively, slamming against the side of the Mercedes. The four cars began to slow down together as Michael tried to find a way out.

Gabriel's cell phone started ringing. When he answered it, he heard Michael's frightened voice. "Gabe! Where are you?"

"Five hundred yards behind your car."

"I'm in trouble. These guys are boxing me in."

"Just keep going. I'll try to get you clear."

As his motorcycle hit a pothole, Gabriel felt something shift inside his messenger bag. He was still carrying a screwdriver and the adjustable wrench. Holding on to the handlebar with his right hand, he ripped off the Velcro strap, pushed his hand inside the bag, and grabbed the wrench. Gabriel went even faster and cut between his brother's Mercedes and the van in the far right lane.

"Get ready," he told his brother. "I'm right beside you."

Gabriel got close to the van and smashed the wrench at the side window. The glass cracked into intricate lines. He swung the wrench a second time and the window shattered.

For a brief moment, he saw the driver—a young man with an earring and a shaved head. The man looked surprised when Gabriel flung the wrench at his face. The van swerved to the right and hit the guardrail. Metal scraped against metal, sparks spitting out into the darkness. Keep going, Gabriel thought. Don't look back. And he followed his brother off the freeway and down an exit ramp.

1

The four cars didn't turn off the freeway, but Michael drove as if they were still chasing him. Gabriel followed the Mercedes up a steep canyon road where elaborate mansions jutted out into the air, their foundations supported by thin metal pylons. After several quick turns, they ended up in the hills overlooking the San Fernando Valley. Michael turned off the road and stopped in the parking lot of a boarded-up church. Empty bottles and beer cans were scattered across the asphalt.

Gabriel pulled off his motorcycle helmet as his brother got out of the car. Michael looked tired and angry.

"It's the Tabula," Gabriel said. "They knew Mother was dying and that we'd go to the hospice. They waited on the boulevard and decided to capture you first."

"Those people don't exist. They never did."

"Come on, Michael. I saw those men try to force you off the road."

"You don't understand." Michael took a few steps across the parking lot and kicked an empty can. "Remember when I bought that first building on Melrose Avenue? Where do you think I got the money?"

"You said it came from investors on the East Coast."

"It was from people who don't like to pay income taxes. They've got a lot of cash that can't be put into bank accounts. Most of the financing came from a mob guy in Philadelphia named Vincent Torrelli."

"Why would you do business with someone like that?"

"What was I supposed to do?" Michael looked defiant. "The bank refused to give me a loan. I wasn't using my real name. So I took the cash from Torrelli and bought the building. A year ago, I was watching the news and saw that Torrelli got killed outside a casino in Atlantic City. When I didn't hear from his family or his friends, I stopped sending the rent money to a post office box in Philadelphia. Vincent had a lot of secrets. I figure that he hadn't told people about his Los Angeles investments."

"And now they've found out?"

"I think that's what happened. It's not Travelers and all those other crazy stories Mom told us. It's just some mob guys trying to get their money back."

Gabriel returned to his motorcycle. If he looked east, he could see the San Fernando Valley. Distorted by the lens of dirty air, the valley streetlights glowed with a dull orange color. At that moment, all he wanted to do was jump on his bike and ride off to the desert, to some lonely place where he could see the stars as his headlight beam skittered across a dirt road. Lost. Get lost. He would give anything to lose his past, the feeling that he was captive in an enormous prison.

"I'm sorry," Michael said. "Things were finally moving in the right direction. Now it's all screwed up."

Gabriel looked at his brother. Once, when they were living in Texas, their mother had been so distracted that she had forgotten about Christmas. There was nothing in the house on Christmas Eve, but the next morning Michael showed up with a pine tree and some video games he had shoplifted from an electronics store. No matter what happened, they would always be brothers—the two of them against the world.

"Forget about these people, Michael. Let's get out of Los Angeles."

"Give me a day or so. Maybe I can make a deal. Until then, we'll check into a motel. It's not safe to go home."

* * *

GABRIEL AND MICHAEL spent the night at a motel north of the city. The rooms were five hundred yards from the Ventura Freeway and the sound of the passing cars pushed through the windows. When Gabriel woke up at four o'clock in the morning, he heard Michael in the bathroom talking on his cell phone. "I do have a choice," Michael whispered. "You make it sound like there's no choice at all."

In the morning, Michael stayed in bed with the covers pulled over his head. Gabriel left the room, walked to a nearby restaurant, and bought some muffins and coffee. The newspaper in the rack had a photograph of two men running from a wall of flame with a headline that proclaimed HIGH WINDS FAN SOUTHLAND FIRES.

Back in the room, Michael had gotten up and taken a shower. He was polishing his shoes with a damp towel. "Someone is coming here to see me. I think he can solve the problem."

"Who is it?"

"His real name is Frank Salazar, but everyone calls him Mr. Bubble. When he was growing up in East Los Angeles, he ran a bubble machine at a dance club."

While Michael watched the financial news on television Gabriel lay on his bed and stared at the ceiling. Closing his eyes, he put himself and his motorcycle on the top half of the highway that ran up the mountain to Angeles Crest. He was downshifting, leaning into each turn as the green world slipped past him. Michael stayed on his feet, pacing back and forth on the narrow strip of carpet in front of the television.

Someone knocked. Michael peered through the curtains and then opened the door. A huge Samoan with a broad face and bushy black hair stood in the hallway. He wore an unbuttoned Hawaiian shirt over a T-shirt and made no attempt to hide the shoulder holster holding a .45 automatic.

"Hey, Deek. Where's your boss?"

"Down in dah car. Gotta check dis out first."

The Samoan came in and inspected the bathroom and the closet. He slipped his massive hands beneath the bedsheets and picked up the cushions on the chairs. Michael kept smiling as if nothing was unusual. "No weapons, Deek. You know I don't carry anything."

"Safety is dah first priority. Dat's what Mr. Bubble say all day long."

After searching the brothers, Deek left and returned a minute later with a bald Latino bodyguard and an elderly man wearing large tinted glasses and a turquoise golfing shirt. Mr. Bubble had liver spots on his skin, and a pink surgical scar was visible near his neck. "Wait outside," he told the two bodyguards, then closed the door.

Mr. Bubble shook Michael's hand. "Good to see you." He had a soft, wispy voice. "Who's your friend?"

"This is my brother, Gabriel."

"Family is good. Always stick with your family." Mr. Bubble went over and shook Gabriel's hand. "You've got a smart brother. Maybe a little too smart this time."

Mr. Bubble settled himself in the chair next to the television set. Michael sat on the corner of the bed and faced him. Ever since they had run away from the farm in South Dakota, Gabriel had watched his brother convince strangers that they had to buy something or become part of his plan. Mr. Bubble was going to be a hard sell. You could barely see his eyes behind the tinted lenses and he had a slight smile on his lips as if he were about to watch a comedy show.

"Did you talk to your friends in Philadelphia?" Michael asked.

"It will take some time to set that up. I'll protect you and your brother for a few days until the problem is solved. We'll give the Melrose building to the Torrelli family. As payment, I'll take your share of the Fairfax property."

"That's too much for one favor," Michael said. "Then I won't own anything."

"You made a mistake, Michael. And now some people want to kill you. One way or another, the problem has to be solved."

"That may be true, but—"

"Safety is the first priority. You lose control of two office buildings, but you're still alive." Still smiling, Mr. Bubble leaned back in his chair. "Consider this a learning opportunity."

Maya retrieved the video camera and tripod from the Hotel Kampa but left her suitcase and clothes in the room. On the train to Germany, she carefully searched the video equipment but couldn't find any tracer beads. It was clear that her citizen life was over. After the Tabula found the dead taxi driver, they would hunt her down and kill her on sight. She knew that it would be difficult to hide. The Tabula had probably taken her photograph numerous times during her years in London. They might also have her fingerprints, a voice scan, and a DNA sample from the tissues she tossed into the rubbish bin at the office.

When she reached Munich, she approached a Pakistani woman in the train station and got the address of an Islamic clothing store. Maya was tempted to cover herself completely with the blue burqa worn by Afghani women, but the bulky clothing made it difficult to handle weapons. She ended up buying a black chador to cover her Western clothes and some dark sunglasses. Back at the train station, she destroyed her British identification and used a backup passport to become Gretchen Voss, a medical student with a German father and an Iranian mother.

Air travel was dangerous so she took a train to Paris, went to the Gallieni Métro station, and got on the daily charter bus that traveled to England. The bus was filled with Senegalese immigrant workers and North African families carrying bags of old clothes. When the bus reached the English Channel everyone got out and wandered around the enormous ferryboat. Maya watched British tourists buy duty-free liquor, pump coins into slot machines, and stare at a comedy on a television screen. Life was normal—almost boring—when you were a citizen. They didn't seem to realize, or care, that they were being monitored by the Vast Machine.

There were four million closed-circuit television cameras in Britain, about one camera for every fifteen people. Thorn once told her that an average person working in London would be photographed by three hundred different surveillance cameras during the day. When the cameras first appeared, the government put up posters telling everyone that they were SECURE BENEATH THE WATCHFUL EYES. Under the shield of new antiterrorism laws, every industrial country was following the British example.

Maya wondered if citizens made a deliberate choice to ignore the intrusion. Most of them truly believed that the cameras protected them from criminals and terrorists. They assumed that they were still anonymous whenever they walked down the street. Only a few people understood the power of the new facial-scanning programs. The moment your face was photographed by a surveillance camera, it could be transformed into a head shot with a consistent size, contrast, and brightness that could be matched against a driver's license or passport photograph.

The scanner programs identified individual faces, but the government could also use the cameras to detect unusual behavior. These so-called Shadow programs were already being used in London, Las Vegas, and Chicago. The computer analyzed one-second images taken by the cameras and alerted the police if someone left a package in front of a public building or parked a car on the shoulder of a highway. Shadow noticed anyone who strolled through the city observing the world instead of trudging to work. The French had a name for these curious people—*flâneurs*—but as far as the Vast Machine was concerned, any pedestrian who lingered on street corners or paused at construction sites was instantly suspicious. Within a few seconds, images of these people would be highlighted in color and sent to the police.

Unlike the British government, the Tabula weren't encumbered by regulations or civil servants. Their organization was relatively small and well financed. Their computer center in London could hack into any surveillance camera system and sort through the images with a powerful scanning program. Fortunately, there were so many surveillance cameras in North America and Europe that the Tabula were overwhelmed with data. Even if they got an exact match to one of their stored images, they couldn't respond fast enough to arrive at a particular train station or hotel lobby. Never stop, Thorn had told her. They can't catch you if you keep moving.

The danger came from any habitual action that showed a Harlequin taking a daily, predictable route to some location. The facial scanner would eventually discover the pattern and then the Tabula could set up their ambush. Thorn had always been wary of situations he called "channels" or "box canyons." A channel was when you had to travel one particular way and the authorities were watching. Box canyons were channels that led to a place with no way out—such as an airplane or an immigration interrogation room. The Tabula had the advantage of money and technology. The Harlequins had survived because of courage and their ability to cultivate randomness.

When Maya reached London, she took the Underground to the Highbury and Islington station, but didn't return to her flat. Instead she went up the road to a takeout restaurant called Hurry Curry. She gave the delivery boy an exterior door key and asked him to wait two hours, then place a chicken dinner inside her entryway. As it began to get dark, she climbed onto the roof of the Highbury Barn, a pub across the street from her building. Concealed behind an air vent, she watched people stopping to buy wine at the off-license shop on the ground floor of her building. Citizens hurried home carrying briefcases and shopping bags. A white delivery van was parked near the entrance to her flat, but no one was in the front seat.

The Indian boy from Hurry Curry appeared at exactly seven thirty. The moment he unlocked the door that led upstairs to her flat, two men jumped out of the white van and shoved him into the entryway. Perhaps they'd kill the boy or maybe they'd just ask questions and let him live. Maya didn't really care. She was sliding back into Harlequin mentality: no compassion, no attachments, no mercy.

She spent the night at a flat in East London that her father had purchased many years ago. Her mother had lived there, concealed within the East Asian community, until she died from a heart attack when Maya was fourteen. The three-room flat was on the top floor of a shabby building just off Brick Lane. A Bengali travel agency was on the ground floor and some of the men who worked there would arrange work permits and identity cards for a price.

East London had always been outside the walls of the city, a convenient place to do or buy something illegal. For hundreds of years it had been one of the worst slums in the world, the hunting ground for Jack the Ripper. Now crowds of American tourists were led around on nightly Ripper walks, the Old Truman Brewery had become an outdoor pub, and the glass towers of the Bishop's Gate office complex thrust itself into the heart of the old neighborhood.

What used to be a warren of dark passageways was now dotted with art galleries and trendy restaurants, but if you knew where to look you could still find a wide range of products that helped you avoid the scrutiny of the Vast Machine.

Every weekend peddlers appeared on upper Brick Lane near Cheshire Street. The peddlers sold stiletto knives and brass knuckles for street fighting, pirated videos, and SIM chips for cell phones. For a few extra pounds, they would activate the chip with a credit card attached to a shell corporation. Although the authorities had the technology to listen to phone calls, they couldn't trace them back to cell phone owners. The Vast Machine could easily monitor citizens with permanent addresses and bank accounts. Harlequins living off the Grid used an endless supply of disposable phones and identity cards. Almost everything except their swords could be used a few times and tossed away like a candy wrapper.

Maya called her employer at the design studio and explained that her father had cancer and she was going to have to quit work to take care of him. Ned Clark, one of the photographers who worked for the studio, gave her the name of a homeopathic doctor, and then asked if she had tax problems.

"No. Why do you ask?"

"A man from Inland Revenue was in the office asking about you. He talked to the people in accounting and requested information about your tax payments, phone numbers, and addresses."

"And they told him?"

"Well, of course. He's from the government." Clark lowered his voice. "If you've got a place in Switzerland, I'd go there right now. To hell with the bastards. Who wants to pay taxes anyway?"

Maya didn't know if the man from Inland Revenue was a real government employee or just a Tabula mercenary with a fake ID. Either way, they were searching for her. Back at the flat, Maya found the key to a storage locker in a Brixton warehouse. She had gone to the locker with her father when she was a little girl, but hadn't visited it for many years. After watching the warehouse for a few hours, she entered the building, showed her key to the clerk, and was allowed to take an elevator up to the third floor. The locker was a windowless room about the size of a walk-in closet. People stored wine in the warehouse and it was kept fairly cold with air-conditioning units. Maya switched on the overhead lightbulb, locked the door, and began to search through the boxes.

When she was growing up, her father helped her obtain fourteen passports from several different countries. Harlequins acquired the birth certificates of people who had died in car accidents, then used the certificates to apply for legal identification. Unfortunately, most of these fake documents had become obsolete now that the government was gathering biometric information—face scans, iris patterns, and fingerprints—then placing the information on a digital chip attached to each citizen's passport or national ID. When the chip was read by a scanner, the data was compared with the information stored on Britain's National Identity Register. On international flights to America, the passport data had to match the iris and fingerprint scans taken at the airport.

Both the United States and Australia were issuing passports with radio frequency ID chips embedded in the covers. These new passports were convenient for immigration officials, but they also gave the Tabula a powerful tool for hunting down their enemies. A machine called a "skimmer" could read the information on a passport hidden inside a coat pocket or purse. Skimmers were installed in elevators or bus stops, any location where people lingered for a brief amount of time. While a citizen was thinking about lunch, the skimmer was downloading a wide variety of personal information. The skimmer might search for names that suggested a certain race, religion, or ethnicity. It would find out the citizen's age, address, and fingerprint data—as well as where he had traveled in recent years.

The new technology forced Maya to rely on three "facer" passports that matched three different versions of her biometric data. It was still possible to fool the Vast Machine, but you had to be clever and resourceful.

The first thing to disguise was your appearance. Recognition systems focused on the nodal points that comprised each unique human face. The computer analyzed a person's nodal points and transformed them into a string of numbers to create a face print. Tinted contact lenses and different-colored wigs could change your superficial appearance, but only special drugs could defeat the scanners. Maya would have to use steroids to puff up her skin and lips or tranquilizers to relax the skin and make her look older. The drugs had to be injected into her cheeks and forehead before arriving at an airport with scanners. Each of her three facer passports used different doses of drugs and a different sequence of injections.

Maya had seen a Hollywood science-fiction film where the hero got through an iris check showing a dead man's eyeballs to a scanner. In the real world, this wasn't an option. Iris scanners shined a beam of red light at the human eye and a dead man's pupils would fail to contract. Government agencies boasted that iris scanners were a completely reliable means of identification. The unique folds, pits, and pigmentation spots in a person's iris started to develop in the womb. Although a scanner could be confused by long eyelashes or tears, the iris itself stayed the same throughout a person's life.

Thorn and the other Harlequins living in the underground had developed a response to the iris scanner several years before it was used by immigration officials. Opticians in Singapore were paid thousands of dollars to manufacture special contact lenses. The pattern of someone else's iris was etched onto the surface of the flexible plastic. When the pupil was hit by the red light of the scanner, the lens contracted just like human tissue.

The final biometric obstacle was the fingerprint scanner. Although acid or plastic surgery could change someone's fingerprints, the results were permanent and left scars. During a visit to Japan, Thorn discovered that scientists at the University of Yokohama had copied fingerprints left on the surface of drinking glasses and turned them into gelatin coatings that could cover a person's fingertips. These finger shields were delicate and hard to put on, but each of Maya's facer passports had a different set of prints for that false identity.

Searching through the boxes in the storage room, Maya found a leather toiletry bag that contained two hypodermic syringes and a variety of drugs that would change her appearance. Passports. Finger shields. Contact lenses. Yes, it was all there. She worked her way through the other boxes and found knives, guns, and packets of currency from different countries. There was an unregistered satellite phone, a laptop computer, and a random number generator about the size of a café matchbox. The RNG was a true Harlequin artifact, on an equal level with the sword. In earlier times, the knights who defended pilgrims carried dice carved from bone or ivory that could be thrown on the ground before battle. Now all she had to do was press a button and random numbers began to flash on the screen.

A sealed envelope was taped to the sat phone. Maya tore it open and recognized her father's handwriting.

> *When on the Internet, watch out for Carnivore.*
> *Always pretend to be a citizen and use soft language.*
> *Be alert, but not afraid. You always were a strong,*
> *resourceful person even when you were a little girl.*
> *Now that I'm older, I am proud of only one thing in*
> *my life—that you are my daughter.*

Maya hadn't wept for her father when she was in Prague. And during the journey back to London, she had concentrated on her own survival. But now, alone in the storage locker, she sat down on the floor and began to cry. There were still a few surviving Harlequins, but she was basically alone. If she made one mistake, even a small one, the Tabula would destroy her.

As a neuroscientist, Dr. Phillip Richardson had used a variety of techniques to study the human brain. He had examined CAT scans, X-rays, and MRI images that showed the brain thinking and reacting to stimuli. He had dissected brains, weighed them, and held the grayish-brown tissue in his hand.

All these experiences allowed him to observe the activities of his own brain as he gave the Dennison Science Lecture at Yale University. Richardson read his speech from note cards and clicked a button that caused different images to be displayed on the screen behind him. He scratched his neck, shifted his weight to his left foot, and touched the smooth surface of the podium. He could do all this while he counted the audience and placed them in different categories. There were his colleagues from the medical school and about a dozen Yale undergraduates. He had chosen a provocative title for his talk—"God in the Box: Recent Advances in Neuroscience"—and it was gratifying to see that several nonacademics had decided to attend.

"For the last decade, I have studied the neurological basis of the human spiritual experience. I assembled a sample group of individuals who frequently meditated or prayed, then injected them with a radioactive tracer whenever they felt they were in direct connection with God and the infinite universe. The results are as follows . . ."

Richardson pressed the button and a photon-emission image of a human brain appeared on the screen. A few parts of the brain glowed red while other areas showed a faint orange color.

"When the person prays, the prefrontal cortex is focused on the words. Meanwhile the superior parietal lobe at the top of the brain has gone dark. The left lobe processes information about our position in space and time. It gives us the idea that we have a distinct physical body. When the parietal lobe shuts down, we can no longer distinguish between our self and the rest of the world. As a result, the subject believes that he or she is in contact with the timeless and infinite power of God. It feels like a spiritual experience, but it's really just a neurological illusion."

Richardson clicked the button and showed another slide of a brain. "In recent years, I've also examined the brains of people who believe they've had mystical experiences. Note this sequence of images. The individual having a religious vision is actually reacting to flashes of neurological stimulation in the temporal lobe, that area responsible for language and conceptual thinking. In order to duplicate the experience, I've taped electromagnets onto the skulls of my experimental volunteers and have created a weak magnetic field. All of the subjects reported an out-of-body sensation and a feeling that they were in direct contact with a divine power.

"Experiments like these force us to question traditional assumptions concerning the human soul. In the past, these issues were examined by philosophers and theologians. It would have been inconceivable to Plato or Thomas Aquinas that a physician would have been part of the debate. But we have entered a new millennium. While the priests continue to pray and the philosophers continue to speculate, it is the neuroscientists who are closest to answering mankind's fundamental questions. It is my scientific view, verified by experiments, that God lives inside the object concealed by this box."

The neurologist was a tall, shambling man in his forties, but all his awkwardness seemed to disappear as he walked over to a cardboard box on a table next to the podium. The crowd stared at him. Everyone wanted to see. He reached inside the box, hesitated, and then took out a Plexiglas jar containing a brain.

"A human brain. Just a piece of tissue floating in formaldehyde. I have proven with my experiments that our so-called spiritual consciousness is only a cognitive reaction to neurological change. Our sense of the divine, our belief that a spiritual power surrounds us, is created by the brain. Take one last step, judge the implications of the data, and you must conclude that God is also a creation of our neurological system. We have evolved into a consciousness that can worship itself. And that is the true miracle."

* * *

THE DEAD MAN'S brain had provided a dramatic ending to the lecture, but now Richardson had to carry it home. Carefully he placed the jar back in the box and climbed down the steps from the platform. A few friends from the medical school clustered around to offer him their congratulations and a young surgeon escorted him out to the parking lot.

"Whose brain is it?" asked the young man. "Anyone famous?"

"Heavens no. It's got to be more than thirty years old. Some charity patient who signed the release form."

Dr. Richardson placed the brain in the trunk of his Volvo and drove north from the university. After his wife signed the divorce papers and went to live in Florida with a ball-room dance instructor, Richardson had considered selling his Victorian house on Prospect Avenue. His rational mind realized that the house was too large for one person, but he consciously gave in to his emotions and decided to keep the place. Each room in the building was like a portion of the brain. He had a library lined with bookshelves and an upstairs bedroom filled with photographs from his childhood. If he wanted to change his emotional orientation, he just sat in a different room.

Richardson parked his car in the garage and decided to leave the brain in the trunk. Tomorrow morning he would take the brain back to the medical school and return it to its glass display case.

He walked out of the garage and pulled down the overhead door. It was about five o'clock in the evening. The sky showed a dark purple color. Richardson could smell wood smoke coming from his neighbor's chimney. It was going to be cold tonight. Perhaps he'd build a fire in the living-room fireplace after dinner. He could sit in the big green chair while he skimmed through the first draft of a student's dissertation.

A stranger got out of the green SUV parked across the street and walked up the driveway. He appeared to be in his forties, with short hair and steel-rimmed glasses. There was something intense and focused about the way he held his body. Richardson guessed that the man was a bill collector sent by his ex-wife. He had deliberately missed last month's payment after she had sent a certified letter asking for more money.

"Sorry I missed your lecture," the man said. "God in the Box sounded interesting. Did you get a good crowd?"

"Excuse me," Richardson said. "Do I know you?"

"I'm Nathan Boone. I work for the Evergreen Foundation. We gave you a research grant. Correct?"

For the last six years, the Evergreen Foundation had sponsored Richardson's neurological research. It was difficult to get the initial grant. You couldn't actually apply to the foundation; they contacted you. But once you crossed that initial barrier, the renewal was automatic. The foundation never called you on the phone or sent someone to the lab to evaluate your research. Richardson's friends had joked that Evergreen was the closest thing in science to free money.

"Yes. You've supported my work for some time," Richardson said. "Is there something I can do for you?"

Nathan Boone reached inside his parka and pulled out a white envelope. "This is a copy of your contract. I was told to direct your attention to clause 18-C. Are you familiar with this section, Doctor?"

Richardson remembered the clause, of course. It was something unique to the Evergreen Foundation, placed in their grant contracts to guard against waste and fraud.

Boone took the contract out of the envelope and began to read: "Number 18-C. The grant recipient—I guess that's you, Doctor—agrees to meet with a representative of the Foundation at any time to give a description of the ongoing research and a statement concerning the allocation of grant funds. The meeting time will be determined by the Foundation. Transportation will be provided. Refusal to honor this request will cause the grant to be rendered null and void. The grant recipient must return all previously allocated funds to the Foundation."

Boone thumbed through the rest of the contract and reached the final page. "And you signed this, Dr. Richardson? Correct? Is this your notarized signature?"

"Of course. But why do they want to talk to me right now?"

"I'm sure it's just a small problem that needs to be cleared up. Pack some socks and a toothbrush. I'll take you down to our research center in Purchase, New York. They want you to review some data tonight so you can meet with the staff tomorrow morning."

"That's out of the question," Richardson said. "I have to teach my graduate students. I can't leave New Haven."

Boone reached out and grabbed Richardson's right arm. He squeezed slightly so the doctor wouldn't run away. Boone hadn't drawn a gun or made threats, but there was something about his personality that was very intimidating. Unlike most people, he didn't show any doubt or hesitation.

"I know your schedule, Dr. Richardson. I checked it before I drove up here. You don't have any classes tomorrow."

"Let go of me. Please."

Boone released Richardson's arm. "I'm not going to force you to get into the car and come down to New York. I'm not going to force you at all. But if you decide to be irrational, then you should prepare for negative consequences. In this case, I'd always feel regretful that such a brilliant man made the wrong choice."

Like a soldier who had just delivered a message, Boone turned quickly and marched back to his SUV. Dr. Richardson felt like he'd been punched in the stomach. What was this man talking about? Negative consequences.

"Just a minute, Mr. Boone. Please . . ."

Boone stopped at the curb. It was too dark to see his face.

"If I go down to the research center, where am I supposed to stay?"

"We have some very comfortable living quarters for our staff."

"And I'll be back here tomorrow afternoon?"

Boone's voice changed slightly. It sounded as if he was smiling. "You can count on it."

10

Dr. Richardson packed an overnight bag while Nathan Boone waited for him in the downstairs hallway. They left immediately and drove south to New York. When they entered Westchester County, near the town of Purchase, Boone turned onto a two-lane country road. The SUV rolled past expensive suburban homes built of brick and stone. White oak and maple trees dotted the front lawns and the grass was covered with autumn leaves.

It was a few minutes after eight o'clock when Boone turned onto a gravel driveway and reached the entrance of a walled-in compound. A discreet sign announced that they had arrived at a research facility operated by the Evergreen Foundation. The guard in the booth recognized Boone and opened the gate.

They parked in a small lot surrounded by pine trees and got out of the SUV. When they walked up a flagstone path, Richardson saw the five large buildings that filled the compound. There were four glass-and-steel structures placed on the corners of a quadrangle and they were connected to each other by enclosed second-floor walkways. A windowless building with a white marble façade was in the center of the quadrangle. It reminded Dr. Richardson of photographs he had seen of the Kaaba, the Muslim shrine in Mecca where they kept the mysterious black rock that Abraham had received from an angel.

"That's the foundation library," Boone said, pointing at the building on the northern corner of the quadrangle. "Clockwise from that is the genetic research building, the computer research building, and the administrative center."

"What's the white building with no windows?"

"It's called the Neurological Cybernetics Research Facility. They built it about a year ago."

Boone guided Richardson into the administrative center. The lobby was empty except for a surveillance camera mounted on a wall bracket. Two elevators were at the end of the room. As the men walked across the lobby, one of the elevators opened its doors.

"Is someone watching us?"

Boone shrugged his shoulders. "That's always a possibility, Doctor."

"Someone has to be watching us because they just opened these doors."

"I'm carrying a radio frequency identification chip. We call it a Protective Link. The chip tells a computer that I'm in the building and approaching an entrance point."

They stepped into the elevator and the door glided shut. Boone waved his hand at a gray pad built into the wall. There was a faint clicking sound and the elevator began to rise.

"In most buildings, they just use ID cards."

"A few people here still carry cards." Boone raised his arm and Richardson saw a scar on the back of his right hand. "But everyone with a high security clearance has a Protective Link implanted beneath their skin. An implant is a good deal more secure and efficient."

They reached the third floor. Boone escorted Richardson to a suite with a bedroom, bathroom, and sitting room. "This is where you'll spend the night," Boone explained. "Sit down. Make yourself comfortable."

"What's going to happen?"

"It's nothing to worry about, Doctor. Someone wants to talk to you."

Boone left the room and the door clicked softly. This is crazy, Richardson thought. They're treating me like I'm a criminal. For several minutes, the neurologist paced back and forth, and then his anger began to dissipate. Maybe he really had done something wrong. There was that conference in Jamaica and what else? A few meals and hotel rooms that had nothing to do with his research. How could they know about that? Who told them? He thought about his colleagues back at the university and decided that several of them were jealous of his success.

The door swung open and a young Asian man walked in carrying a thick green binder. The man wore a spotless white shirt and narrow black necktie that made him look neat and deferential. Richardson relaxed immediately.

"Good evening, Doctor. I'm Lawrence Takawa, the special projects manager for the Evergreen Foundation. Before we start, I just wanted to say how much I enjoyed reading your books, especially *The Machine in the Skull*. You certainly have come up with some interesting theories regarding the brain."

"I want to know why I was brought here."

"We needed to talk to you. Clause 18-C gives us that opportunity."

"Why are we meeting tonight? I know that I signed the contract, but this is highly unusual. You could have contacted my secretary and arranged an appointment."

"We needed to respond to a particular situation."

"What do you want? A summary of this year's research? I sent you a preliminary report. Didn't anyone read it?"

"You're not here to tell us anything, Dr. Richardson. Instead we want to give you some important information." Lawrence motioned to one of the chairs and the two men sat facing each other. "You've done several different experiments over the last six years, but your research confirms one particular idea: there is no spiritual reality in the universe, human consciousness is simply a biochemical process within our brain."

"That's a simplistic summary, Mr. Takawa. But it's basically correct."

"Your research results support the philosophy of the Evergreen Foundation. The people who run the foundation believe that each human being is an autonomous biological unit. Our brain is an organic computer with its processing capabilities determined by genetic inheritance. During our lifetime, we fill our brain with learned knowledge and conditioned responses to different experiences. When we die, our brain computer is destroyed along with all its data and operating programs."

Richardson nodded. "I think that's clear."

"It's a wonderful theory," Lawrence said. "Unfortunately, it's not true. We've discovered that a fragment of energy exists inside every living thing, independent of the brain or body. This energy enters each plant or animal when they're born. It leaves us when we die."

Richardson tried not to smile. "You're talking about the human soul."

"We call it the Light. It seems to follow the laws of quantum theory."

"Call it whatever you want, Mr. Takawa. I don't particularly care. Let's assume, for a moment, that we do have a soul. It's in us when we're alive. It departs when we die. Even if we accept a soul, it has no relevance to our lives. I mean, we can't *do* anything with the soul. Measure it. Verify it. Take it out and place it in a jar."

"A group of people called the Travelers are able to control their Light and send it out of their body."

"I don't believe in any of that spiritual nonsense. That can't be proven in an experiment."

"Read this and see what you think." Lawrence placed the green binder on the table. "I'll be back in a while."

Takawa walked out and, once again, Richardson was alone. The conversation was so strange and unexpected that the neurologist didn't know how to react. Travelers. The Light. Why was the employee of a scientific organization using such mystical terms? Dr. Richardson lightly touched the cover of the green binder with the tips of his fingers as if the contents could burn him. He took a deep breath, turned to the first page, and began to read.

* * *

THE BOOK WAS divided into five sections, each numbered separately. The first section summarized the experiences of different people who believed that their spirit had left their body, passed through four barriers, and crossed over into another world. These "Travelers" believed that all humans carried energy within their body like a tiger trapped in a cage. Suddenly, the cage door swung open and the Light was free.

Section two described the lives of several Travelers who had appeared during the last thousand years. A few of these people became hermits and went off to live in the desert, but many of the Travelers started movements and challenged the authorities. Because they had stepped outside the world, Travelers saw everything from a different perspective. The author of section two suggested that Saint Francis of Assisi, Joan of Arc, and Isaac Newton had been Travelers. Newton's famous "Dark Journal," kept hidden in a library vault at Cambridge University, revealed that the British mathematician dreamed he had crossed barriers of water, earth, air, and fire.

In the 1930s, Joseph Stalin decided that Travelers were a threat to his dictatorship. Section three described how the Russian secret police arrested more than a hundred mystics and spiritual leaders. A physician named Boris Orlov examined the Travelers held at a special prison camp outside Moscow. When the prisoners crossed over into other realms, their hearts beat once every thirty seconds and they stopped breathing. "They are like dead men," Orlov wrote. "The energy of life has left their bodies."

Heinrich Himmler, head of the German SS, read a translation of Orlov's report and decided that the Travelers would be the source of a secret new weapon that could win the war. Section four of the report described how Travelers captured in occupied countries were sent to a concentration camp research facility under the supervision of the notorious "Death Doctor," Kurt Blauner. The prisoners had sections of their brains removed and they were subjected to electroshock and ice baths. After the experiments failed to come up with a new weapon, Himmler decided that the Travelers were "a degenerate cosmopolitan element" and they became targets of the SS death squads.

Richardson felt no connection to the crude research performed in the past. People who thought they traveled to alternative worlds were suffering from abnormal activity in certain sections of their brains. Teresa of Avila, Joan of Arc, and all the other visionaries were probably epileptics with temporal-lobe seizures. The Nazis were wrong, of course. These people weren't saints or enemies of the state; they simply needed modern tranquilizers and therapy to deal with the emotional stress of their illness.

When Richardson turned to the fifth section of the book, he was glad to see the experimental data was obtained using modern neurological tools like CAT scans and magnetic resonance imaging machines. He wanted to know the names of the scientists, but all that information had been crossed out with a black pen. The first two reports were detailed neurological evaluations of the people who had become Travelers. When these individuals went into a trance, their bodies went into a dormant state. CAT scans during this period showed virtually no neurological activity except for a heartbeat response controlled by the brain stem.

The third report described an experiment at a Beijing medical facility where a Chinese research group had invented something called a neural energy monitor. The NEM measured the biochemical energy produced by the human body. It showed that Travelers had the ability to create short bursts of what Lawrence Takawa had called the Light. This neural power was incredible, up to three hundred times stronger than the weak force that ran through a typical nervous system. The unnamed researchers suggested that the energy was connected with the ability to travel to other worlds.

Still doesn't prove anything, Richardson thought. The energy overwhelms the brain and these people think they've seen angels.

He turned the page to another report and read quickly. In this experiment, the Chinese scientists had placed each Traveler in a plastic box—almost like a coffin—with special devices to monitor energy activity. Every time a Traveler went into a trance, an intense burst of energy was released from his body. The Light triggered the monitors, passed through the box, and escaped. Richardson searched through the footnotes, trying to find the names of the scientists and the Travelers. In each research report, a few words appeared like a casual comment at the end of a long conversation. "Subject returned to protective custody." "Subject no longer cooperative." "Subject deceased."

Dr. Richardson was sweating. It was stuffy in the room; the ventilation didn't seem to be working. Open the window, he thought. Breathe some cold night air. But when he pulled back the heavy curtains, he discovered a blank wall. There were no windows in the suite and the door was locked.

11

A Bengali wedding store was at the south end of Brick Lane. If you walked past the gold saris and pink party decorations, you entered a back room where you could connect to the Internet without being traced. Maya sent coded messages to Linden and Mother Blessing. Using the shop owner's credit card, she placed online obituary notices in Le Monde and The Irish Times.

> *Died in Prague from a sudden illness: H. Lee Quinn, founder of Thorn Security Ltd. Survived by his daughter, Maya. In lieu of flowers, a contribution should be sent to the Traveler's Fund.*

Later that afternoon she got a response on a Harlequin blackboard: a brick wall near the Holborn station where a message could be scrawled like graffiti. Using a piece of orange chalk, someone had left a Harlequin lute, a line of numbers, and the words: Five/ Six/Bush/Green. That was easy to decipher. The numbers gave the time and date. The meeting location was 56 Shepherd's Bush Green.

* * *

MAYA SLIPPED A handgun into her raincoat pocket and slung the sword carrying case over her left shoulder. Number 56 Shepherd's Bush Green turned out to be a discount movie house in an alleyway next to the Empire Theatre. That afternoon, the theater was showing a Chinese kung fu movie and a travel documentary called *Provence: Land of Enchantment.*

Maya bought a ticket from the sleepy young woman in the booth. Someone had scrawled three interlocking Harlequin diamonds near the entrance to theater two, so she walked inside and found a drunk sleeping in the third row. When the lights dimmed and the film started, the man's head flopped backward and he began to snore.

The movie had nothing to do with rural France. Instead, the soundtrack was a scratchy recording of the American jazz singer Josephine Baker singing "J'ai Deux Amours" while the screen showed news footage and historical photographs taken off the Internet. Any citizen who had wandered into the theater would have decided that the movie was visual gibberish, a mix of unconnected images of pain, oppression, and terror. Only Maya realized that the film presented a concise Harlequin view of the world. The conventional history given in schoolbooks was an illusion. Travelers were the only real force of change in the world, but the Tabula wanted to destroy them.

For thousands of years, the killing was done by kings and religious leaders. A Traveler would appear in a traditional society and present a new vision that challenged the powerful. This person would gain a following and then be destroyed. Gradually rulers began to follow a "King Herod strategy." If Travelers were more prevalent in certain ethnic or religious groups, the authorities would slaughter everyone they could find in that group.

By the end of the Renaissance, a small group of men

who called themselves Brethren began to organize these attacks. Using their wealth and connections, they could kill Harlequins or track down Travelers who had fled to other countries. The Brethren served kings and emperors, but they saw themselves as being above the mundane expression of power. What they valued most was stability and obedience: an ordered society where each person knew his place.

In the eighteenth century the British philosopher Jeremy Bentham designed the Panopticon: a model prison where one observer could monitor hundreds of prisoners while remaining unseen. The Brethren used the Panopticon prison design as a theoretical basis for their ideas. They believed that it would be possible to control the entire world as soon as the Travelers were exterminated.

Although the Tabula had money and power, the Harlequins had successfully defended the Travelers for hundreds of years. The introduction of computers and the spread of the Vast Machine changed everything. The Tabula finally had the means to track down and destroy their enemies. After World War II, there were approximately two dozen known Travelers in the world. Now there were none, and the Harlequins were reduced to a handful of fighters. Although the Brethren remained in the shadows, they were confident enough to start a public organization called the Evergreen Foundation.

Any journalist or historian who began to investigate the legends about Harlequins and Travelers was cautioned or dismissed. Web sites about Travelers were infected with computer viruses that got out of control and undermined the rest of the system. Tabula computer experts attacked legitimate Web sites, and then made up false Web sites that connected theories about the Travelers with crop circles, UFOs, and the book of Revelation. Ordinary citizens heard rumors about the secret conflict, but they had no way of knowing if it was true.

* * *

JOSEPHINE BAKER CONTINUED to sing. The drunk continued to snore. Up on the screen, the killing continued. Maya watched television news footage of top officials in different governments, all of them older men with dead eyes and smug smiles who controlled armies of soldiers and policemen. They were the Brethren or their supporters. We're lost, Maya thought. Lost forever.

Halfway through the film, a man and woman entered the theater and sat down in the front row. Maya slipped the automatic out of her coat pocket and clicked off the safety. She got ready to defend herself, and then the man pulled down his zipper and the prostitute leaned over the armrest and began servicing him. Josephine Baker and the images of Traveler destruction had had no effect on the drunk, but now he woke up and noticed the intruders. "You should be ashamed!" he told them with a slurred voice. "There are places for that, you know!"

"Sod off," said the woman, and there was a loud argument that ended with the couple leaving and the drunk tagging along after them.

Maya sat alone in the theater. The movie froze on an image of the president of France shaking hands with the American secretary of state. When the door to the projection booth creaked open she stood up, raised her automatic, and got ready to fire. A large man with a shaved head came out of the booth and climbed down a short ladder. Like Maya, he carried his Harlequin sword in a metal tube slung over his shoulder.

"Don't shoot," Linden said. "It would ruin my day."

Maya lowered her weapon. "Were those people working for you?"

"No. They were just some drones. I thought they'd never leave. Did you like the film, Maya? I created it last year when I was living in Madrid."

Linden walked down the aisle and embraced Maya. He had powerful arms and shoulders and she felt protected by his bulk and strength. "I'm sorry about your father," Linden said. "He was a great man. The bravest person I've ever known."

"My father said that you have an informant working for the Tabula."

"That's right."

They sat down beside each other and Maya touched Linden's arm. "I want you to find out who killed my father."

"I've already asked the informant," Linden said. "It was probably an American named Nathan Boone."

"So how do I find him?"

"Killing Boone is not our immediate objective. Your father called me three days before you came to Prague. He wanted you to go to the States and help Shepherd."

"He asked me to do that. I turned him down."

Linden nodded. "Now I'm asking you again. I'll buy the plane ticket. You can leave tonight."

"I want to find the man who killed my father. I'm going to kill him and then I'm going to disappear."

"Many years ago your father discovered a Traveler named Matthew Corrigan. This man lived in the United States with his wife and two sons. When it was clear that they were in danger, your father gave Corrigan a suitcase full of money and a sword once owned by Sparrow. Thorn was given the sword when he helped Sparrow's fiancée leave Japan."

Maya was impressed with her father's gift. A sword used by a famous Harlequin like Sparrow was a precious object. But her father had made the right choice. Only a Traveler could fully use the power of a talisman.

"Father said that the Corrigans went underground."

"Yes. But the Tabula caught up with them in South Dakota. We heard that mercs had killed everyone, but apparently the mother and the sons got away. They were lost for a long time until one of the brothers, Michael Corrigan, gave his true name to the Vast Machine."

"Do the sons know if they can cross over?"

"I don't think so. The Tabula plan to capture the two brothers and turn them into Travelers."

"That can't be true, Linden. The Tabula have never done that before."

The Frenchman stood up quickly, towering over Maya. "Our enemies have developed something called a quantum computer. They've made an important discovery using the computer, but our informant can't get access to that information. Whatever the Tabula learned caused them to change their strategy. Instead of killing Travelers, they want to use their power."

"Shepherd should do something."

"Shepherd has never been a very good fighter, Maya. Whenever I see him, he's always talking about some new scheme for making money. I've thought about flying to the States myself, but the Tabula know too much about me. No one can find Mother Blessing. She's shut down her communication channels. We still have contacts with a few reliable mercenaries, but they're not capable of dealing with this kind of problem. Someone has to find the Corrigans before they're captured."

Maya stood up and walked to the front of the theater. "I killed someone in Prague, but that was just the beginning of the nightmare. When I returned to my father's flat, I found him lying on the bedroom floor. I could barely recognize him—just those old knife scars on his hands. Some kind of animal had mutilated his body."

"A Tabula research team is creating genetically altered animals. The scientists call them 'splicers' because different strands of DNA are cut apart and spliced together. Perhaps they used one of these animals to attack your father." Linden's massive hands became fists as if he was confronting his enemies. "The Tabula have gained this power without thought of consequences. The only way we can defeat them is to find Michael and Gabriel Corrigan."

"I don't give a damn about the Travelers. I still remember my father telling me that most Travelers don't even like us. They're floating off to other realms and we're trapped in this world—forever."

"You're Thorn's daughter, Maya. How can you refuse his last request?"

"No," she said. "No." But her voice betrayed her.

12

Lawrence Takawa sat at his desk watching Dr. Richardson on the screen of his computer monitor. Four surveillance cameras were hidden in the guest suite. They had photographed Richardson for the last twelve hours as he read about Travelers, slept, and took a shower.

A security guard had just entered the suite to remove the breakfast tray. Lawrence moved his cursor to the top of the screen. He pressed a "plus" sign and camera two zoomed in on the neurologist's face.

"When am I going to meet with the foundation staff?" Richardson asked.

The security guard was a large man from Ecuador named Immanuel. He wore a navy blue blazer, gray slacks, and a red necktie. "I don't know, sir."

"Is it going to be this morning?"

"No one told me anything."

Holding the tray with one hand, Immanuel opened the door to the outer hallway.

"Don't lock the door," Richardson said. "It's not necessary."

"We're not locking you in, sir. We're locking you out. You

don't have the security clearance necessary to walk around this building."

When the lock clicked shut, Richardson swore loudly. He jumped up as if he was going to do something decisive, then began to pace around the room. It was easy to look at Richardson's face and know what he was thinking. He appeared to alternate between two principal emotions: anger and fear.

* * *

LAWRENCE TAKAWA HAD learned how to conceal his emotions when he was a sophomore at Duke University. Although he was born in Japan, his mother had brought him to America when he was six months old. Lawrence hated sushi and samurai movies. Then a touring group of Noh actors arrived at the university and he saw a day of performances that changed his life.

At first, Noh drama seemed exotic and difficult to understand. Lawrence was fascinated by the stylized motions of the actors on the stage, the men playing women, and the eerie sound of the *nohkan* flute and three drums. But the Noh masks were the true revelation. Carved wooden masks were worn by the principal characters, the women characters, and the old people. Ghosts, demons, and crazy people had garish masks that showed one strong emotion, but most actors wore a mask with a deliberately neutral expression. Even the middle-aged men acting without masks tried not to move their faces. Each gesture on the stage, each statement and reaction was a conscious choice.

Lawrence had just joined a fraternity that had drinking parties and elaborate hazing rituals. Whenever he glanced at his reflection, he saw insecurity and confusion: a young man who wasn't going to fit in. A living mask solved the problem. Standing in front of the mirror in his bathroom, he practiced masks of happiness, admiration, and enthusiasm. By his senior year of college he was voted president of his fraternity and his professors gave him strong recommendations for graduate school.

* * *

THE PHONE ON his desk buzzed softly and Lawrence turned away from the computer screen. "How's our new guest reacting?" Boone asked.

"He seems agitated and somewhat frightened."

"There's nothing wrong with that," Boone said. "General Nash just arrived. Get Richardson and put him in the Truth Room."

Lawrence took the elevator down to the third floor. Like Boone, he had a Protective Link inserted beneath his skin. He waved his hand at the door sensor. The lock clicked open and he walked into the suite.

Dr. Richardson spun around and approached Lawrence. He jabbed at the air with his index finger. "This is outrageous! Mr. Boone said that I was going to meet with your staff. Instead, I've been kept locked in here like a prisoner."

"I apologize for the delay," Lawrence said. "General Nash just arrived and he's eager to talk to you."

"You mean Kennard Nash? Your executive director?"

"That's right. I'm sure you've seen him on television."

"Not for several years." Richardson lowered his voice and relaxed slightly. "But I remember when he was a presidential adviser."

"The general has always been involved in public service. So it was a natural transition for him to join the Evergreen Foundation." Lawrence reached into his suit-coat pocket and took out a hand-held metal detector—the sort of thing that security guards use in airports. "For security reasons, we'd like you to leave all metal objects in the room. That includes your wristwatch, coins, and belt. It's standard procedure at our research facility."

If Lawrence had given him a direct order, Richardson might have refused. Instead, he had to deal with the bland assumption that taking off his wristwatch was the normal thing to do when meeting an important person. He placed his possessions on the table and then Lawrence passed the detector over the neurologist's body. The men left the room and walked down the hallway to the elevator.

"Did you read all the materials last night?"

"Yes."

"I hope you found them interesting."

"It's incredible. Why haven't these recent studies been published? I've never read anything about the Travelers."

"At this time, the Evergreen Foundation wants to keep this information secret."

"That's not how science works, Mr. Takawa. Major discoveries occur because scientists all over the world have access to the same data."

They took the elevator to the basement and walked down a corridor to a white door without handles or knobs. When Lawrence waved his hand, the door glided open. He motioned Dr. Richardson forward and the scientist entered a windowless room where there was no furniture except for a wooden table and two wooden chairs.

"This is a special security room," Lawrence explained. "Everything said here is confidential."

"So where's General Nash?"

"Don't worry. He'll be here in a few minutes."

* * *

LAWRENCE WAVED HIS right hand and the door closed, locking Richardson inside the Truth Room. For the last six years, the Evergreen Foundation had funded a secret research effort to find out when someone was lying. This wasn't done with a voice analyzer or a polygraph machine that recorded a person's breathing rate and blood pressure.

Fear could distort the results of such tests and a good actor could suppress these secondhand signs of deceit.

Ignoring outward physical changes, the Evergreen Foundation scientists looked directly inside the brain using magnetic resonance imaging. The Truth Room was simply a large MRI chamber in which a person could talk, eat, and move about. The man or woman being questioned didn't have to know what was going on, which allowed for a wider range of reactions.

While watching a person's brain as he answered questions, it was possible to see how different sectors of tissue reacted to what was being said. The foundation scientists discovered that it was easier for the brain to tell the truth. When a person was lying, his left prefrontal cortex and the anterior cingulate gyrus lit up like red patches of molten lava.

* * *

LAWRENCE CONTINUED DOWN the corridor to another unmarked door. A lock clicked open and he entered a shadowy room. Four television monitors were set in a wall opposite a bank of computers and a long table that contained the control panel. A plump, bearded man sat at the table and typed instructions on a computer keyboard. Gregory Vincent had built and installed the equipment that was being used today.

"Did you get rid of all his metal?" Vincent asked.

"Yes."

"Why didn't you go in? Afraid that you might say something while I was watching?"

Lawrence rolled an office chair over to the control panel and sat down. "I was just following instructions."

"Yeah. Sure." Vincent scratched his stomach. "Nobody wants to go into the Truth Room."

Looking up at the monitors, Lawrence saw that Richardson's body had become a hazy image made up of different patches of light. The light changed color and intensity as Richardson breathed, swallowed, and thought about his predicament. He was a digital man who could be quantified and analyzed by the computers behind them.

"Looks good," Vincent said. "This is going to be easy." He glanced up at a small security monitor hanging from the ceiling. A bald man was coming down the hallway. "Perfect timing. Here comes the general."

Lawrence created the appropriate mask. Studious. Intent. He stared at the monitors as Kennard Nash entered the Truth Room. The general was in his sixties; he had a blunt nose and straight-backed military posture. Lawrence admired the way that Nash concealed his toughness with the amiable style of a successful athletic coach.

Richardson stood up and Nash shook his hand. "Dr. Richardson! Good to meet you. I'm Kennard Nash, the executive director of the Evergreen Foundation."

"It's an honor to meet you, General Nash. I remember when you used to be in the government."

"Yes. That was a real challenge, but it was time to move on. It's been exciting to run Evergreen."

Both men sat down at the table. In the monitoring room, Vincent typed in commands to the computer. Different images of Richardson's brain appeared on the monitors.

"I understand you've read what we call the 'Green Book.' It summarizes everything we know about Travelers."

"The information is incredible," Richardson said. "Is it true?"

"Yes. Certain people have the ability to project their neural energy out of their bodies. It's a genetic abnormality that can be passed from parent to child."

"And where does the energy go?"

Kennard Nash unclasped his hands and hid them under the table. He stared at Richardson for a few seconds, his eyes moving slightly as he examined the doctor's face. "As our reports indicate, they go to another dimension and then they return."

"That's not possible."

The general looked amused. "Oh, we've known about other dimensions for years. It's one of the foundations of modern quantum theory. We always had the mathematical proof, but not the means to make the journey. It was a surprise to discover these individuals have been doing it for centuries."

"You should release your data. Scientists all over the world would start experiments to verify this discovery."

"That's exactly what we don't want to do. Our country is under attack by terrorists and subversives. Both the foundation and our friends around the world are worried that certain groups might use the Travelers' power to destroy the economic system. Travelers have the tendency to be antisocial."

"You need more data about these people."

"That's why we're developing a new research project here at the center. Right now, we're getting the equipment ready and finding a cooperative Traveler. Perhaps we'll obtain two of them—brothers. We need a neurologist with your background to implant sensors into their brains. Then we can use our quantum computer to track where the energy is going."

"To the other dimensions?"

"Yes. How to get there and how to get back. The quantum computer will enable us to follow whatever happens. You don't need to know how the computer works, Doctor. You just have to plant the sensors and set our Travelers on their way." General Nash raised both hands as if he were invoking the Deity. "We are on the verge of a great discovery that will change our civilization. I don't have to tell you how exciting this is, Dr. Richardson. I'd be honored if you joined our team."

"And everything would be secret?"

"In the short run. For security reasons, you'd move to the research center and use our staff. If we're successful, then you'd be allowed to publish your research. Verifying the existence of different worlds would mean an automatic Nobel Prize, but you can see that it's much more than that. It would be a discovery on the same level as the work of Albert Einstein."

"And what if we fail?" Richardson asked.

"Our security arrangements will protect us from media scrutiny. If the experiment is unsuccessful, then no one needs to hear about it. The Travelers can go back to being folk legends with no scientific verification."

Richardson's brain showed a bright red color as he analyzed the possibilities. "I think I'd feel more comfortable working at Yale."

"I know what goes on at most university laboratories," Nash said. "You're forced to deal with review committees and endless paperwork. At our research center there's no bureaucracy. If you want a piece of equipment, it will be delivered to your lab within forty-eight hours. Don't worry about cost. We're paying for everything—plus we'd like to give you a significant honorarium for your personal contribution."

"At the university I have to fill out three allocation forms to receive a box of test tubes."

"That sort of nonsense is a waste of your intelligence and creativity. We want to give you everything you need to make an important discovery."

Richardson's body relaxed. His frontal lobe displayed little pink patches of activity. "All of this is very tempting . . ."

"We're under some time pressure, Doctor. I'm afraid that I need a decision right now. If you're hesitant, then we'll contact other scientists. I think that your colleague Mark Beecher is on the list."

"Beecher doesn't have the clinical background," Richardson said. "You need a neurologist who has also trained as a neurosurgeon. Who else did you have in mind?"

"David Shapiro up at Harvard. Apparently he's done some important experiments with the cortex."

"Yes, but only with animals." Richardson tried to look reluctant, but his brain was very active. "I guess I'm the logical person for this project."

"Wonderful! I knew we could count on you. Go back to New Haven and start making arrangements to leave the university for a few months. You'll discover that the Evergreen Foundation has many high-level contacts at the university, so taking time off won't be a problem. Lawrence Takawa is your contact person." General Nash stood up and shook Richardson's hand. "We're going to change the world forever, Doctor. And you're going to be part of the effort."

* * *

LAWRENCE WATCHED AS General Nash's luminous body left the room. One of the monitors continued to show Dr. Richardson as he fidgeted in his chair. The other screens showed digital recordings of different segments of the previous conversation. A framework of green lines was superimposed over the neurologist's skull. It analyzed his brain reactions while he made different statements.

"I don't see a deception pattern in any of Dr. Richardson's statements," Vincent said.

"Good. That's what I expected."

"The only deception came from General Nash. Take a look . . ." Vincent typed a command and one of the monitors showed a digital recording of Kennard Nash's brain. A close-up of the cortex showed that the general was concealing something during most of the conversation.

"For technical reasons, I always take images of both people in the Truth Room," Vincent said. "It shows me if there are any problems with the sensors."

"That wasn't authorized. Please remove all images of General Nash from the system."

"Of course. No problem." Vincent typed a new command and Nash's deceitful brain disappeared from the screen.

* * *

A SECURITY GUARD escorted Dr. Richardson out of the building. Five minutes later, the neurologist was sitting in the back of a stretch limousine as it carried him to New Haven. Lawrence returned to his office and sent an e-mail to one of the Brethren who had contacts at the Yale Medical School. He started a file on Richardson and typed in the doctor's personal information.

The Brethren placed all of their employees in one of ten security levels. Kennard Nash was a level one and had full knowledge of all operations. Dr. Richardson had been given a level five clearance; he knew about the Travelers, but would never learn about the Harlequins. Lawrence was a trusted level-three employee; he was able to access a vast amount of information, but he would never learn about the Brethren's grand strategies.

* * *

SURVEILLANCE CAMERAS FOLLOWED Lawrence as he left his office, passed down the corridor, and took the elevator down to the underground parking lot beneath the administrative center. When Lawrence drove out the gates of the compound, his movements were tracked by a global positioning satellite and the information was sent to an Evergreen Foundation computer.

During his time at the White House, General Nash proposed that every American citizen wear or carry a Protective Link, or "PL device." The government's Freedom from Fear program stressed both national security and the practical aspects of the program. Coded a certain way, the PL device could be a universal credit card and debit card. It could access all of your medical information in case you were in an accident. If all loyal, law-abiding Americans wore a PL device, street crime might disappear within a few years. In one magazine ad, two young parents wearing PL devices tucked in a sleeping daughter whose Protective Link ID card was being held by her teddy bear. The ad slogan was simple but effective: Fighting Terrorism While You Sleep.

Radio frequency ID chips had already been inserted beneath the skin of thousands of Americans—mostly the elderly or people with serious medical conditions. Similar ID card devices were tracking employees who worked for large companies. Most Americans seemed positive about a device that would protect them from unknown dangers and help them get through the checkout line at their local grocery store. But the Protective Link had been attacked by an unusual alliance of left-wing civil liberties groups and right-wing libertarians. After losing support from the White House, General Nash was forced to resign.

When Nash took over the Evergreen Foundation, he immediately set up a private Protective Link system. Employees could keep their ID in their shirt pocket or hang it from a cord around their neck, but all the top employees had the chip inserted beneath their skin. The scar on the back of their right hand indicated their high status in the foundation. Once a month, Lawrence had to lay his hand on a plug-in charger. He felt a warm, tingling sensation as the chip gained enough power to continue transmitting.

Lawrence wished he had known how the Protective Link worked during the beginning of the program. A global positioning satellite tracked one's movements and the computer established a frequent destination grid for each employee. Like most people, Lawrence spent ninety percent of his life in the same destination grid. He shopped at certain stores, worked out at the same gym, and traveled back and forth between his town house and the office. If

Lawrence had known about the grid, he would have done a few unusual things during the first month.

Whenever he deviated from his frequent destination grid, a list of questions immediately appeared on his computer: *Why were you in Manhattan on Wednesday at 2100 hours? Why did you go to Times Square? Why did you travel down 42nd Street to Grand Central Terminal?* The questions were computer generated, but you had to respond to each one. Lawrence wondered if his answers went promptly to a file that no one read or if they were scanned and evaluated by another program. Working for the Brethren, you never knew when you were being watched—so you had to assume that it was all the time.

* * *

WHEN LAWRENCE ENTERED his town house, he kicked off his shoes, removed his necktie, and tossed his briefcase on the coffee table. He had bought all his furniture with the help of a decorator hired by the Evergreen Foundation. The woman announced that Lawrence was a "spring" personality, so all the furniture and wall art were color coordinated in matching pastel blues and greens.

Lawrence followed the same ritual whenever he was finally alone—he screamed. Then he walked over to a mirror and smiled and frowned and shouted like a madman. After his tension was released, he took a shower and put on a robe.

A year ago Lawrence had constructed a secret room in the closet of his home office. It had taken months to wire the room and conceal it behind a bookcase that rested on hidden rollers. Lawrence had been in the room three days ago, and it was time for another visit. He pushed back the case a few feet, slipped inside, and switched on the light. On a small Buddhist altar he displayed two snapshots of his parents taken at a hot spring in Nagano, Japan. In one of the photographs, they were smiling at each other and holding hands. His father sat alone in the second photograph, looking off at the mountains with a sad expression on his face. On the table in front of him were two ancient Japanese swords: one with a handle that had a jade fitting, the other with fittings made of gold.

Lawrence opened an ebony wood box and took out a satellite phone and a laptop computer. A minute later he was online and wandering through the Web until he found the French Harlequin named Linden in a chat room dedicated to trance musik.

"Sparrow Son here," Lawrence typed.

"Safe?"

"I think so."

"News?"

"We've found a doctor who has agreed to implant sensors into the subject's brain. The treatment will start soon."

"Any other news?"

"I think the computer team has made another breakthrough. They seemed very happy in the dining room during lunch. I still don't have access to their research."

"Have they found the two most important elements of the experiment?"

Lawrence stared at the monitor screen, and then typed rapidly. "They're looking for them right now. Time is running out. You must find the brothers."

13

The front entrance to the four-story building that contained Mr. Bubble's clothing factory was framed by two stone obelisks set into the red brick wall. Plaster sculptures of Egyptian tomb figures were in the ground-floor reception area and hieroglyphics were on the walls of the staircases. Gabriel wondered if they had found a professor to write real hieroglyphic messages or if the symbols had been copied out of an encyclopedia. When he was walking around the empty building at night, he would touch the hieroglyphics and trace their shapes with his forefinger.

Each weekday morning workers began to arrive at the factory. The ground floor was for shipping and receiving, and it was run by young Latino men who wore loose slacks and white T-shirts. Incoming fabric was sent up the freight elevator to the cutters on the third floor. Right now they were making lingerie and the cutters stacked layers of satin and rayon fabric on large wooden tables and sliced through the fabric with electric scissors. The seamstresses on the second floor were illegal immigrants from Mexico and Central America. Mr. Bubble paid them thirty-two cents for each piece they sewed. They worked hard in the dusty room, but always seemed to be laughing about something or talking to one another. Several of them had framed photographs of the Virgin Mary taped to their sewing machines and the Holy Mother watched over them while they stitched together red bustiers with little gold hearts dangling from the back zipper.

Gabriel and Michael had spent the last few days living on the fourth floor, a storage place for empty boxes and old office furniture. Deek had purchased sleeping bags and folding cots from a sporting goods store. There weren't any showers in the building, but at night the brothers went downstairs and took sponge baths in the employee restroom. They ate doughnuts or bagels for breakfast. A catering truck was parked outside the factory during lunch and one of the bodyguards would bring them egg burritos or turkey sandwiches in Styrofoam containers.

Two El Salvadorans watched them during the daytime. After the workers went home, Deek arrived with the bald Latino man—a former nightclub bouncer named Jesús Morales. Jesús spent most of his time reading car magazines and listening to ranchero music on the radio.

If Gabriel got bored and wanted a conversation, he went downstairs and talked to Deek. The big Samoan got his nickname because he was a deacon in a fundamentalist church in Long Beach.

"Each man is responsible for his own soul," he told Gabriel. "If someone goin' to hell, then there's more room for dah righteous in heaven."

"What if you end up in hell, Deek?"

"Ain't gonna happen, brutha. I'm goin' upstairs to the good place."

"But what if you had to kill someone?"

"Depends on the person. If he was a real sinner, den I'm makin' dah world a better place. Trash goes in dah trash can. Know what I'm tellin' you, brutha?"

Gabriel had brought his Honda motorcycle and a few books up to the fourth floor. He spent his time dismantling the bike, cleaning each part, and putting it back together. When he was tired of doing that, he read old magazines or a paperback translation of *The Tale of Genji*.

Gabriel missed the feeling of release that came to him whenever he raced his motorcycle or jumped out of a plane. Now he was trapped in the factory. He kept having dreams about fire. He was inside an old house watching a rocking chair burn with an intense yellow flame. Breathe deep. Wake up in darkness. Michael lay a few feet away, snoring, while a garbage truck outside the building loaded a dumpster.

During the day, Michael paced around the fourth floor while he talked on the cell phone. He was trying to hold together his purchase of the office building on Wilshire Boulevard, but couldn't explain his sudden disappearance to the bank. The deal was falling apart as he pleaded for more time.

"Let it go," Gabriel said. "You can find another building."

"That might take years."

"We could always move to another city. Start a different life."

"This is my life." Michael sat down on a packing crate. He pulled a handkerchief out of his pocket and tried to wipe off a grease mark on the toe of his right shoe. "I've worked hard, Gabe. Now it feels like everything is about to disappear."

"We've always survived."

Michael shook his head. He looked like a boxer who had just lost a championship fight. "I wanted to protect us, Gabe. Our parents didn't do that. They just tried to hide. Money buys protection. It's a wall between yourself and the rest of the world."

14

The plane chased the darkness as it headed west across the United States. When the cabin attendants switched on the lights, Maya raised the little plastic shutter and peered out the window. A bright line of sunlight on the eastern horizon illuminated the desert below. The plane was passing over Nevada or Arizona; she wasn't quite sure. A cluster of lights glimmered from a small town. In the distance, the dark line of a river slithered across the land.

She refused breakfast and the free champagne but accepted a hot scone, served with strawberries and clotted cream. Maya could still remember when her mother used to bake scones for afternoon tea. It was the only time during the day that she felt like a normal child, sitting at the little table reading a comic book while her mother bustled around the kitchen. Indian tea with plenty of cream and sugar. Fish fingers. Rice pudding. Fairy cakes.

When they were an hour away from landing, Maya walked back to the airplane toilet and locked the door. She opened the passport she was using, taped it to the toilet mirror, and compared the image in the photograph to her current appearance. Maya's eyes were now brown because of the special contact lenses. Unfortunately, the plane had left Heathrow three hours late and her facer drugs were beginning to wear off.

She opened her purse and took out the syringe and diluted steroids used for a touch-up. The steroids were disguised as insulin supplies and the kit contained an official-looking physician's letter that stated that she was a diabetic. Watching her face in the mirror, Maya coaxed the needle deep into her cheek muscle and injected half a syringe.

When she was finished with the steroids, she filled up the sink, took a test tube out of her purse, and emptied a finger shield into the cold water. The gelatin shield was grayish white, thin, and fragile; it resembled a segment of an animal's intestine.

Maya took a fake perfume bottle from her purse and sprayed adhesive on her left index finger. She reached into the water, slipped the finger into the shield, and quickly removed her hand. The shield covered her fingerprint with another print for the digital scan at immigration. Before the plane landed, she would use an emery board to scrape away the portion covering her fingernail.

Maya waited two minutes for the first shield to dry, and then opened up a second test tube for the shield that went on her right index finger. The airplane hit a patch of turbulence and began to bounce around in the air. A red warning sign went on in the toilet. PLEASE RETURN TO YOUR SEAT.

Concentrate, she told herself. You can't make a mistake. As she slipped her finger into the shield, the airplane lurched downward and she tore the fragile tissue.

Maya fell back against the wall, feeling sick to her stomach. She had only one backup shield and if that didn't work, there was a good chance that she would be arrested when she landed in America. The Tabula had probably obtained her fingerprints when she was working for the design firm in London. It would be easy for them to insert false information into the United States immigration computer that would be triggered by a fingerprint scan. *Suspicious person. Terrorist contacts. Detain immediately.*

Maya opened a third test tube and poured her only backup shield into the sink water. Once again, she sprayed the adhesive on her right index finger. She took a deep breath and reached into the water.

"Excuse me!" The cabin attendant knocked on the toilet door. "Please return to your seat immediately!"

"Just one minute."

"The pilot has switched on the seat-belt light! Regulations require all passengers to return to their seats!"

"I'm—I'm feeling sick," Maya said. "Give me one minute. That's all."

Sweat trickled down her neck. This time she breathed slowly, filling her lungs with air, then slipped her finger into the shield and removed her hand from the water. Still wet, the gelatin shield glistened on her finger.

The cabin attendant, an older woman, glared at Maya as she returned to her seat. "Didn't you see the light?"

"I *am* sorry," Maya whispered. "But I feel sick to my stomach. I'm sure you understand."

The plane jumped again as she buckled her seat belt and prepared her mind for battle. A Harlequin who arrived in a strange country for the first time was supposed to be met by a local contact who would hand over guns, money, and identification. Maya was carrying her sword and knives concealed in the camera tripod. Both the weapons and the tripod had been manufactured in Barcelona by a Catalan sword maker who tested everything with his own X-ray machine.

Shepherd had promised to meet her at the airport, but the American Harlequin was showing his usual incompetence. During the three days before Maya left London, Shepherd changed his mind several times, then sent an e-mail saying that he was being followed and had to be careful about his movements. Shepherd contacted a Jonesie, and this person was going to be at the terminal.

"Jonesie" was the nickname for a member of the Divine Church of Isaac T. Jones. They were a small group of African Americans who believed that a Traveler named Isaac Jones was the greatest prophet who had ever walked the earth. Jones was a cobbler who lived in Arkansas in the 1880s. Like many Travelers he started out preaching a spiritual message, and then began to spread ideas that challenged the ruling structure. In southern Arkansas, both black and white sharecroppers were controlled by a small group of powerful landowners. The prophet told these poor farmers to break the contracts that kept them in economic slavery.

In 1889, Isaac Jones was falsely accused of touching a white woman who had come to his shop to pick up some shoes. He was arrested by the town sheriff and killed that night by a lynch mob that broke down the door of his cell. On the night that Jones was martyred, a traveling salesman named Zachary Goldman had gone to the jail cell. When the mob broke in, Goldman killed three men with the sheriff's shotgun and two others with a crowbar. The mob overwhelmed Goldman and the young man was castrated, then burned alive in the same bonfire that consumed Isaac Jones.

Only the true believers knew the real story: that Zachary Goldman was a Harlequin named Lion of the Temple who had gone to Jackson City with enough money to bribe the sheriff and get the Prophet out of town. When the sheriff fled, Goldman remained at the jail and died defending the Traveler.

The church had always been a Harlequin ally, but the relationship had changed during the last decade. A few Jonesies believed that Goldman wasn't really at the jail, but that the Harlequins had made up the story for their own advantage. Others believed that the church had done so many favors for the Harlequins that Goldman's deed had been repaid years ago. It bothered them that other Travelers existed in the world, because new revelations should never supplant the teachings of the Prophet. Only a handful of stubborn Jonesies called themselves DNPs—an abbreviation for "Debt Not Paid." A Harlequin had died with the Prophet during his martyrdom and it was their duty to honor that sacrifice.

At the Los Angeles airport, Maya picked up her clothing bag, camera case, and tripod, then passed through immigration with her German passport. The contact lenses and finger shields worked perfectly.

"Welcome to the United States," said the man in the uniform, and Maya smiled politely. She followed the green sign for passengers with nothing to declare and walked up a long ramp to the reception area.

Hundreds of people were pushed against a steel railing, waiting for arriving passengers. A limousine driver held a cardboard sign for someone named J. Kaufman. A young woman wearing a tight skirt and clattery high heels ran forward and embraced an American soldier. The woman was laughing and weeping like a fool for her scrawny boyfriend, but Maya felt a twinge of jealousy. Love made you vulnerable; if you gave your heart to another, they could leave you or die. And yet visions of love surrounded her. People hugged each other near the doorway and waved homemade signs. WE LOVE YOU, DAVID! WELCOME HOME!

She had no idea how she was supposed to find the Jonesie. Acting like she was looking for a friend, Maya strolled through the terminal. Damn Shepherd, she thought. His grandfather was a Latvian who had saved hundreds of lives during World War II. The grandson had assumed this honored Harlequin name, but he had always been a fool.

Maya reached the exit, turned around, and headed back to the security barrier. Maybe she should leave and try to find the backup contact that Linden had given her: a man named Thomas who lived south of the airport. Her father had spent a lifetime doing this, going to strange countries where he hired mercenaries and searched for Travelers. Now she was on her own, feeling unsure of herself and a little scared.

She gave herself a five-minute deadline, and then noticed a young black woman wearing a white dress standing by the information booth. The woman held a small bouquet of roses as a welcome gift. Three glittery cardboard diamonds—a Harlequin sign—were mixed with the flowers. As Maya approached the booth, she saw that the young woman had a small photograph of a solemn-looking black man pinned to the bodice of her dress. It was the only picture ever taken of Isaac T. Jones.

15

Holding the roses, Victory From Sin Fraser stood in the middle of the terminal. Like most of the members of her church, she had met Shepherd during his occasional trips to Los Angeles. The man seemed so conventional, with his genial smile and stylish clothes, that Vicki found it difficult to believe that he was a Harlequin. In her fantasy, the Harlequins were exotic warriors who could walk up walls and catch bullets in their teeth. Whenever she saw someone acting cruelly she wanted a Harlequin to smash through a window or jump down from a roof to deliver instant justice.

Vicki turned away from the booth and saw a woman approaching her. The woman carried a canvas travel bag, a black tube with a shoulder strap, a video camera, and a tripod. She wore dark sunglasses and had short brown hair. Although the woman's body was slender, her face was puffy and unattractive. As she got closer, Vicki realized that there was something fierce and dangerous about this person, a barely controlled intensity.

The woman stopped in front of Vicki and gave her an appraising look. "Are you looking for me?" She spoke with a slight British accent.

"I'm Vicki Fraser. I'm waiting here for someone who knows a friend of our church."

"That must be Mr. Shepherd."

Vicki nodded. "He told me to take care of you until he finds a safe meeting place. Right now, people are watching him."

"All right. Let's get out of here."

They left the international terminal in a crowd and crossed a narrow road to a four-level parking structure. The woman refused to let Vicki carry her luggage. She kept glancing over her shoulder as if she expected to be followed. As they climbed the concrete stairs, she grabbed Vicki's arm and twisted her around.

"Where are we going?"

"I—I parked on the second floor."

"Go back downstairs with me."

They returned to the ground level. A Latino family chattering in Spanish pushed past them and went up the staircase. The Harlequin turned quickly, looking in every direction. Nothing.

They went back upstairs and Vicki walked over to a Chevrolet sedan with a bumper sticker in the rear window: "Learn the Truth! Isaac T. Jones Died for YOU!"

"Where's my shotgun?" the woman asked.

"What shotgun?"

"You were supposed to supply me with weapons, money, and American identification. That's standard procedure."

"I'm sorry Miss—Miss Harlequin. Shepherd didn't say anything about that. He just told me to carry a diamond shape and meet you at the terminal. My mother didn't want me to do this, but I came anyway."

"Open the boot—the trunk—whatever you call it."

Vicki fumbled with her keys and opened the trunk. It was filled with aluminum cans and plastic bottles that she was taking to a recycling station. She felt embarrassed that the Harlequin had seen them.

The young woman placed her camera case and tripod inside the trunk. She glanced around. No one was looking. Without a word of explanation, she snapped open the hiding places in the tripod and pulled out two knives and a sword. All of this was much too harsh. Vicki remembered the imaginary Harlequins in her dreams who carried golden swords and swung through the air on ropes. The weapon in front of her was a real sword that looked very sharp. Not knowing what to say, she remembered a passage of scripture from *The Collected Letters of Isaac T. Jones*.

"When the Final Messenger comes, the Evil One will fall into the Darkest Realm and swords will be transformed into Light."

"Sounds wonderful." The Harlequin slipped her sword into a carrying tube. "But until that happens, I'm keeping my own blade sharp."

They got into the car and the Harlequin adjusted the right side mirror so that she could see if anyone was behind them. "Let's get out of here," she said. "We need to go someplace where there aren't any cameras."

They left the parking structure, followed the airport traffic circle, and turned onto Sepulveda Boulevard. It was November, but the air was warm and sunlight was reflected off every windshield and pane of glass. They were driving through a commercial district of two- and three-story structures, modern office buildings facing immigrant grocery stores, and fingernail salons. Only a few people were on the sidewalk: the poor, the elderly, and a crazy man with matted hair who looked like John the Baptist.

"There's a park a few miles from here," Vicki said. "It doesn't have surveillance cameras."

"Are your sure about that or just guessing?" The Harlequin kept looking at the side mirror.

"Guessing. But it's a logical guess."

Her answer seemed to amuse the young woman. "All right. Let's see if logic works any better in America."

The park was a small strip of land with a few trees across the street from Loyola University. No one was in the parking lot and there didn't appear to be any surveillance cameras. The Harlequin examined the area carefully, and then removed her sunglasses, tinted contact lenses, and brown wig. The young woman's real hair was thick and black, and her eyes were very pale—with only a hint of blue color. Her puffy appearance came from some kind of drug. As it began to wear off, she looked much stronger and even more aggressive.

Vicki tried not to stare at the sword case. "Are you hungry, Miss Harlequin?"

The young woman stuffed the wig into her travel bag. Once again, she glanced at the side mirror. "My name is Maya."

"My church name is Victory From Sin Fraser. But I ask most people to just call me Vicki."

"That's a wise choice."

"Are you hungry, Maya?"

Instead of answering her, Maya reached into her shoulder purse and took out a small electronic device about the size of a matchbox. She pressed a button and numbers flashed on a narrow screen. Vicki didn't understand what the numbers meant, but the Harlequin used them to make a decision. "Okay. Let's have lunch," Maya said. "Take me to a place where we can buy food and eat in the car. Park facing out, toward the street."

They ended up at a Mexican-food stand called Tito's Tacos. Vicki carried sodas and burritos back to the car. Maya remained silent and picked at the beef filling with a little plastic fork. Not knowing what else to do, Vicki watched the people come and go in the parking lot. An old woman with the stocky physique and Indian features of a Guatemalan peasant. A middle-aged Filipino husband and wife. Two young Asian men—probably Korean—wearing the flashy clothes and gold jewelry of black rappers.

Vicki faced the Harlequin and tried to sound confident. "Can you tell me why you're in Los Angeles?"

"No."

"Is this about a Traveler? The pastor of my church says that the Travelers don't exist anymore. They've all been hunted down and killed."

Maya lowered her can of soda. "Why didn't your mother want you to meet me?"

"The Divine Church of Isaac T. Jones doesn't believe in violence. Everyone in the church knows that Harlequins . . ." Vicki stopped talking and looked embarrassed.

"Kill people?"

"I'm sure that the people you fight are wicked and cruel." Vicki dumped the rest of her food into a paper bag and looked straight at Maya. "Unlike my mother and her friends, I believe in the Debt Not Paid. We must never forget that the Lion of the Temple was the only person brave enough to defend the Prophet on the night of his martyrdom. He died with the Prophet and was burned in the same fire."

Maya rattled the ice in her cup. "So what do you do when you're not picking up strange people at airports?"

"I graduated from high school this summer and now Mother wants me to take the exam for the post office. Many of the Faithful here in Los Angeles are postal carriers. It's a good job with lots of benefits. At least, that's what they say."

"And what do you want to do?"

"It would be wonderful to travel around the world. There are so many places I've only seen in books or on television."

"So do it."

"I don't have money and plane tickets like you. I've never even been to a nice restaurant or a nightclub. Harlequins are the freest people in the world."

Maya shook her head. "You don't want to be a Harlequin. If I was free, I wouldn't be in this city."

The cell phone in Vicki's purse began playing the theme from Beethoven's *Ode to Joy*. Vicki hesitated, then answered the phone and heard Shepherd's cheerful voice.

"Did you get the package at the airport?"

"Yes, sir."

"Let me talk to her."

Vicki passed the phone over to Maya and listened to the Harlequin say "yes" three times. She switched off the phone and dropped it on the seat of the car.

"Shepherd has my weapons and identification. You're supposed to go to 489 Southwest—whatever that means."

"It's a code. He told me to be careful talking on the cell phone."

Vicki got a Los Angeles phone book from the backseat and turned to page 489. In the lower left corner—the southwest section of the page—she found an ad for a business called Resurrection Auto Parts. The address was in Marina del Rey, a few miles from the ocean. They left the parking lot and drove west on Washington Boulevard. Maya stared out the window as if she were trying to find landmarks that she could remember.

"Where's the center of Los Angeles?"

"Downtown, I guess. But not really. There's no center here, just little communities."

The Harlequin reached beneath the sleeve of her sweater and adjusted one of her knives. "Sometimes my father would recite a poem by Yeats when we were walking around London." She hesitated, then spoke softly: *"Turning and turning in the widening gyre, the falcon cannot hear the falconer; things fall apart, the centre cannot hold . . ."*

They drove past shopping malls and gas stations and residential areas. Some of the neighborhoods were poor and shabby with little Spanish-style houses or ranch houses that had flat roofs covered with gravel. In front of each house was a strip of Bermuda grass and a tree or two, usually a palm or a Chinese elm.

Resurrection Auto Parts was on a narrow side street between a T-shirt factory and a tanning salon. On the front of the windowless building someone had painted a cartoon version of God's hand from the Sistine Chapel. Instead of giving life to Adam, the hand was hovering over a muffler.

Vicki parked across the street. "I can wait for you here. I don't mind."

"That's not necessary."

They got out of the car and unloaded the luggage. Vicki expected Maya to say "goodbye" or "thank you very much," but the Harlequin was already focused on this new environment. She glanced up and down the street, evaluating each driveway and parked car, then picked up her bag, camera, and tripod and began to walk away.

"Is that all?"

Maya stopped and glanced over her shoulder. "What do you mean?"

"We're not going to see each other again?"

"Of course not. You've done your job, Vicki. It's best if you never mention this to anyone."

Carrying all the luggage with her left hand, Maya crossed the street to Resurrection Auto Parts. Vicki tried not to feel insulted, but angry thoughts pushed through her mind. When she was a little girl, she had heard stories about the Harlequins, about how they were brave defenders of the righteous. Now she had met two Harlequins: Shepherd was an ordinary person, and this young woman, Maya, was selfish and rude.

It was time to go home and prepare dinner for Mother. The Divine Church had prayer service tonight at seven o'clock. Vicki got back in her car and returned to Washington Boulevard. When she stopped at a red light, she thought about Maya walking across the street with the luggage in her left hand. That kept the right hand free. Yes, that was it. Free to draw the sword and kill someone.

16

Maya avoided the front door of Resurrection Auto Parts. She entered the parking lot and began to circle the building. There was an unmarked emergency door near the back with a diamond Harlequin mark scrawled on the rusty metal. She pulled the door open and entered the building. Smell of oil and cleaning solvent. Sound of distant voices. She was in a room filled with racks of used carburetors and exhaust pipes. Everything was stacked and sorted by make and model. Pulling her sword out a little farther, she moved toward the light. A door was open a few inches, and when she peered through the crack she saw Shepherd and two other men standing around a small table.

They looked surprised when Maya came through the door. Shepherd reached beneath his jacket for a gun, then recognized her and grinned. "There she is! All grown up and very attractive. This is the famous Maya I've been telling you about."

She had seen Shepherd six years ago, when he visited her father in London. The American had a plan to make millions of dollars from pirated Hollywood movies, but Thorn refused to finance the operation. Although Shepherd was in his late forties, he looked a good deal younger. His blond hair was cut in a spiky style and he wore a gray silk shirt and a tailored sports jacket. Like Maya, he carried his sword in a case slung over his shoulder.

The other two men looked like brothers. They were both in their twenties with bad teeth and bleached blond hair. The older one had smudged prison tattoos on his arms. Maya decided that they were taints—Harlequin slang for low-class mercenaries—and she decided to ignore them.

"What's going on?" she asked Shepherd. "Who's been following you?"

"That's a conversation for later," Shepherd said. "Right now I want you to meet Bobby Jay and Tate. I've got your money and identification. But Bobby Jay is providing the weapons."

Tate, the younger brother, was staring at her. He wore warm-up pants and an extra-large football jersey that probably concealed a handgun. "She's got a sword like yours," he said to Shepherd.

Shepherd smiled indulgently. "It's a useless thing to carry around, but it's kind of like being in a club."

"What's your sword worth?" Bobby Jay asked Maya. "You want to sell it?"

Annoyed, she turned to Shepherd. "Where did you find these taints?"

"Relax. Bobby Jay buys and sells weapons of all kinds. He's always looking for a deal. Pick out your gear. I'll pay for it and they'll go."

A steel suitcase was on the table. Shepherd opened it and displayed five handguns lying on a foam pad. As Maya stepped closer, she saw that one of the weapons was made of black plastic with a cartridge mounted at the top of the frame.

Shepherd picked up the plastic weapon. "Ever seen one of these? It's a Taser that delivers an electric shock. You'd carry a real gun, of course, but this would give you the choice of not killing the other person."

"Not interested," Maya said.

"I'm serious about this. Swear to god. I carry a Taser. If you shoot someone with a gun, the police are going to get involved. This gives you more options."

"The only option is to attack or not attack."

"All right. Fine. Have it your way . . ."

Shepherd grinned and pulled the trigger. Before she could react, two darts attached to wires flew out of the barrel and hit her in the chest. A massive electric jolt knocked her to the floor. As she struggled to stand up she was hit with another shock and then another that brought darkness.

17

General Nash called Lawrence on Saturday morning and said that Nathan Boone was going to have a teleconference with the Brethren's executive committee at four o'clock that afternoon. Lawrence drove immediately from his town house to the research center in Westchester County and gave an entry list to the guard at the front gate. He dropped by his own office to check e-mails, and then went up to the third floor to prepare for the meeting.

Nash had already typed in the command allowing Lawrence to enter the conference room. When Lawrence approached the door, his Protective Link was detected by a scanner and the lock clicked open. The conference room contained a mahogany wood table, brown leather chairs, and a wall-sized television screen. Two video cameras photographed different angles of the room so that the Brethren living overseas could watch the discussion.

Alcohol was never allowed at committee meetings, so Lawrence placed bottled water and drinking glasses on the table. His primary job was to make sure that the closed-circuit television system was working. Using the control panel placed in one corner, he connected with a video camera set up at a rented office suite in Los Angeles. The camera showed a desk and an empty chair. Boone would sit there when the meeting started and give a report about the Corrigan brothers. Within twenty minutes, four small squares appeared at the bottom of the television screen, and the control panel indicated that Brethren living in London, Tokyo, Moscow, and Dubai would be joining the discussion.

Lawrence was trying to appear diligent and respectful, but he was glad that no one else was in the room. He was frightened and his usual mask wasn't concealing his emotions. A week earlier, Linden had mailed him a tiny battery-operated video camera called a spider. Concealed in Lawrence's pocket, the spider felt like a time bomb that could explode at any moment.

He double-checked the water glasses, making sure they were clean, and then headed for the door. Can't do it, he thought. Too dangerous. But his body refused to leave the room. Lawrence began praying silently. *Help me, Father. I'm not as brave as you.*

The anger he felt at his own cowardice suddenly overpowered his survival instinct. First he switched off the closed-circuit camera that would be used during the discussion, then he bent down and pulled off his shoes. Moving quickly, he stepped onto one of the chairs and stood in the middle of the table. Lawrence inserted the spider into a ceiling air-conditioning vent, made sure that the holding magnets were in contact with the metal, and jumped back onto the floor. Five seconds had gone by. Eight seconds. Ten seconds. Lawrence turned on the closed-circuit camera and began to adjust the chairs.

*　*　*

WHEN HE WAS growing up, Lawrence never suspected that his father was Sparrow, the Japanese Harlequin. His mother told him that she had gotten pregnant when she was a student at Tokyo University. Her wealthy lover refused to marry her and she didn't want to have an abortion. Instead of bringing up an illegitimate child in Japanese society, she immigrated to America and raised her son in Cincinnati, Ohio. Lawrence accepted this story completely. Although his mother taught him to read and speak Japanese, he never felt the desire to fly to Tokyo and track down some selfish businessman who had abandoned a pregnant college girl.

Lawrence's mother died of cancer during his third year of college. In an old pillowcase hidden in the closet, he found letters from her relatives in Japan. The friendly, affectionate letters surprised him. His mother had told him that her family had thrown her out of the house when she became pregnant. Lawrence wrote to the family members and his aunt Mayumi flew to America for the funeral.

After the ceremony, Mayumi stayed to help her nephew pack up everything in the house and transfer it to a storage warehouse. It was during this time that they found the belongings that Lawrence's mother had brought from Japan: an antique kimono, some old college textbooks, and a photo album.

"That's your grandmother," Mayumi said, pointing to an old woman smiling at the camera. Lawrence turned the page. "And that's your mother's cousin. And her school friends. They were such pretty girls."

Lawrence turned the page again and two photographs fell out. One showed his young mother sitting next to Sparrow. The other photograph showed Sparrow alone with the two swords.

"And who's this?" Lawrence asked. The man in the photograph looked calm and very serious.

"Who is this person? Please tell me." He stared at his aunt and she began to cry.

"It's your father. I met him only once, with your mother, at a restaurant in Tokyo. He was a very strong man."

Aunt Mayumi knew only a few things about the man in the photographs. He called himself Sparrow, but occasionally used the name Furukawa. Lawrence's father was involved in something dangerous. Perhaps he was a spy. Many years ago, he was killed with a group of Yakuza gangsters during a gunfight at the Osaka Hotel.

After his aunt flew back to Japan, Lawrence spent all his free time on the Internet looking for information about his father. It was easy to find out about the Osaka Hotel incident. Articles about the massacre appeared in all the Japanese newspapers as well as the international press. Eighteen Yakuza had died. A gangster named Hiroshi Furukawa was listed as one of the dead, and a Japanese magazine printed a morgue photograph of his father. It seemed strange to Lawrence that none of the articles gave a definitive reason for the incident. Usually the reporter called it a "gangland dispute" or a "clash over illegal profits." Two wounded Yakuza had survived, but they refused to answer questions.

At Duke University, Lawrence had learned how to write computer programs that could handle a large amount of statistical data. After graduation, he worked for a game Web site run by the U.S. Army that analyzed the responses of the teenagers who formed online teams and fought each other in a bombed-out city. Lawrence helped create a program that generated a psychological profile of each player. The computer-created profiles had a high correlation with the face-to-face evaluations performed by the army's recruiters. The program determined who was a future master sergeant, who should operate the radio, and who would volunteer for high-risk missions.

The army job led to a job in the White House and Kennard Nash. The general felt that Lawrence was a good administrator and that he shouldn't waste his talents writing computer programs. Nash had a relationship with the CIA and the National Security Agency. Lawrence realized that working for Nash would help him obtain a high-level security rating that would give him access to secret data about his father. He had studied the photograph of his father with the two swords. Sparrow didn't have the elaborate tattoos of a typical Yakuza.

Eventually General Nash called Lawrence into his office and gave him what the Brethren called "the Knowledge." He was told the most basic version: that there was a terrorist group called the Harlequins who protected heretics called Travelers. For the health of society, it was important to destroy the Harlequins and control the visionaries. Lawrence went back to his workstation with his first Brethren access codes, typed his father's name into the information database, and received his revelation. NAME: *Sparrow.* AKA: *Hiroshi Furukawa.* SUMMARY: *Known Japanese Harlequin.* RESOURCES: *Level 2.* EFFECTIVENESS: *Level 1.* CURRENT STATUS: *Terminated—Osaka Hotel—1975.*

As Lawrence was given more of the Knowledge and a larger range of access codes, he discovered that most of the Harlequins had been destroyed by Brethren mercenaries. Now he was working for the forces that had murdered his father. The evil surrounded him, but like a Noh actor he kept his mask on at all times.

When Kennard Nash left the White House, Lawrence followed him to a new job at the Evergreen Foundation. He was allowed to read the Green, Red, and Blue books that described the Travelers and Harlequins and that gave a short history of the Brethren. In this new age, the Brethren rejected the brutal totalitarian control of Stalin and Hitler for the more sophisticated Panopticon system developed by the eighteenth-century British philosopher Jeremy Bentham.

"You don't need to watch everyone if everyone believes they're being watched," Nash explained. "Punishment isn't necessary, but the inevitability of punishment has to be programmed into the brain."

Bentham had believed that the soul didn't exist and there was no reality other than the physical world. Upon his death, he promised to leave his fortune to the University of London if his body was preserved, dressed in his favorite clothes, and placed in a glass case. The philosopher's body was a private shrine for the Brethren, and they all made a point to see it whenever they were visiting London.

A year ago, Lawrence had flown to Amsterdam for a meeting with one of the Brethren's Internet monitoring teams. He had a one-day layover in London and took a taxi to the University College London. Entering from Gower Street, he walked across the main quadrangle. It was late in the summer and quite warm. Students wearing shorts and T-shirts were sitting on the white marble steps of the Wilkins Building and Lawrence felt jealous of their casual freedom.

Bentham sat on a chair inside a glass-and-wood display case at the entrance to the south cloister. His skeleton had been stripped of flesh, padded with straw and cotton wool, and then dressed in the philosopher's clothes. The philosopher's head had been kept in a container placed at his feet, but students had stolen it for football games on the quadrangle. Now the head was gone, stored in the university's vault. A wax face had been substituted, and it had a pale, ghostly appearance.

Normally a college security guard sat in an identical wood-and-glass case about twenty feet away from the philosopher. Brethren paying homage to the inventor of the Panopticon used to joke that it was impossible to know who was more dead—Jeremy Bentham or the obedient drone who watched his body. But that particular afternoon, the guard had vanished and Lawrence was alone in the hall. Slowly he approached the display case and stared at the wax face. The French sculptor who had created the face had done a particularly good job, and the slight upward curve of Bentham's lip suggested that he was quite satisfied with the progress of the new millennium.

After staring at the preserved body for a few seconds, Lawrence stepped to the left to study a small exhibit about

Bentham's life. He glanced down and saw graffiti scrawled with a red grease pencil on the tarnished brass molding at the bottom edge of the case. It was an oval shape and three straight lines; Lawrence knew from his research that it was a Harlequin's lute.

Was it a gesture of contempt? A defiant statement from the opposition? Crouching down, he studied the mark closer and saw that one of the lines was an arrow pointing toward Bentham's padded skeleton. A sign. A message. He looked down the cloister hallway at a distant tapestry. A door slammed somewhere in the building, but no one appeared.

Do something, he thought. This is your only chance. The door of the display case was fastened with a small brass padlock, but he pulled it hard and ripped off the latch. When the door squeaked open, he reached inside and searched the outer pockets of Bentham's black coat. Nothing. Lawrence opened the coat, touched cotton padding, then found an inside pocket. Something was there. A card. Yes, a postcard. He concealed the prize within his briefcase, shut the glass door, and walked quickly away.

An hour later he sat in a pub near the British Museum, examining a postcard of La Palette, a café on the rue de Seine in Paris. A green awning. Sidewalk tables and chairs. An X had been drawn on one of the tables in the photograph, but Lawrence didn't understand what that meant. On the other side of the postcard, someone had written in French: *When the temple fell*.

Lawrence studied the postcard when he returned to America and spent hours doing research on the Internet. Had a Harlequin left the card as a clue, a ticket to a certain destination? What temple had collapsed? He could think of only the original Jewish temple in Jerusalem. Ark of the Covenant. Holy of Holies.

One evening at his town house, Lawrence drank an entire bottle of wine and realized that the ancient order of the Templars was connected to the Harlequins. The Templars' leaders had been arrested by the King of France and eventually burned at the stake. When did that happen? Using his laptop computer, he went on the Internet and found out immediately. October 1307. Friday the thirteenth.

There were two Friday the thirteenths this year and one of them was a few weeks away. Lawrence changed his vacation schedule and flew to Paris. On the morning of the thirteenth, he went to La Palette wearing a sweater with a Harlequin diamond pattern. The café was situated on a side street of small art galleries that was near Pont Neuf. Lawrence sat outside at one of the little tables and ordered a café crème from the waiter. He was tense and excited, ready for an adventure, but an hour went by and nothing happened.

Studying the postcard one more time, he saw that the X mark was on a particular table at the extreme left edge of the restaurant's sidewalk area. When a young French couple finished reading the newspaper and left for work, he moved to the chosen table and ordered a baguette with ham. He waited until noon, when an elderly waiter wearing a white shirt and black vest walked over to his table.

The man spoke French. Lawrence shook his head. The waiter tried English. "You are looking for someone?"

"Yes."

"And who is that?"

"I can't say. But I'll know this person when they arrive."

The old waiter reached beneath his waistcoat, took out a cell phone, and handed it to Lawrence. Almost immediately the phone rang, and Lawrence answered it. A deep voice spoke in French, German, and then English.

"How did you find this place?" asked the voice.

"A postcard in a dead man's pocket."

"You have encountered an access point. We have seven of these points around the world to gain allies and contact mercenaries. This is only an access point. It doesn't mean that you'll be allowed to enter."

"I understand."

"So tell me—what happened today?"

"The Templar order was rounded up and destroyed. But some survived."

"Who survived?"

"The Harlequins. One of them was my father, Sparrow."

Silence. And then the man on the phone laughed softly. "Your father would have enjoyed this moment. He savored the unexpected. And who are you?"

"Lawrence Takawa. I work for the Evergreen Foundation."

Again, silence. "Ahhh yes," the voice whispered. "The public façade of the group that calls themselves the Brethren."

"I want to find out about my father."

"Why should I trust you?"

"That's your choice," Lawrence said. "I'll sit at this table for ten more minutes, then I'm leaving."

He clicked off the cell phone and waited for it to explode, but nothing happened. Five minutes later, a large man with a shaved head marched down the sidewalk, stopped in front of the table. The man had a black metal tube slung over his shoulder and Lawrence realized that he was looking at a Harlequin carrying a hidden sword. "*Apportez-moi une eau-de-vie, s'il vous plaît,*" the man said to the waiter and sat down in a wicker chair. The Harlequin thrust his right hand in the pocket of his trench coat as if he was grabbing a handgun. Lawrence wondered if the Harlequin was going to execute him immediately or if he would wait for his drink to arrive.

"Switching off the phone was a decisive action, Mr. Takawa. I like that. Maybe you really are the son of Sparrow."

"I've got a photograph of my parents sitting together. You can see it if you want."

"Or I could kill you first."

"That's another choice."

The Frenchman smiled for the first time. "So why are you risking your life to meet me?"

"I want to know why my father died."

"Sparrow was the last Harlequin left in Japan. When the Tabula hired Yakuza gangsters to kill three known Travelers, he defended these people and kept them alive for almost eight years. One of the Travelers was a Buddhist monk living in a Kyoto temple. The Yakuza sent several teams of men to assassinate this monk, but the killers kept disappearing. Sparrow caught them, of course, and cut them down like tall weeds in a garden. Unlike many modern Harlequins, he actually preferred using a sword."

"What happened? How did they catch him?"

"He met your mother at a bus stop near Tokyo University. They started to see each other and fell in love. When your mother became pregnant, the Yakuza found out about it. They kidnapped your mother and took her to a banquet room at the Osaka Hotel. She was tied up, hanging from a rope. The Yakuza planned to get drunk and rape her. They couldn't kill Sparrow, so they were going to defile the only important person in his life."

A waiter served a glass of brandy and the big man removed his hand from his coat pocket. The traffic noise, the sound of conversations around them faded away. All that Lawrence could hear was the man's voice.

"Your father walked into the banquet room disguised as a waiter. He reached under a serving cart and pulled out a sword and a twelve-round rotary-drum shotgun. Sparrow attacked the Yakuza, killed some and wounded the rest. Then he freed your mother and told her to run away."

"Did she obey him?"

"Yes. Sparrow should have fled with your mother, but his honor had been violated. He walked around the banquet room with his sword, executing the Yakuza. While he was doing this, one of the wounded men pulled out a handgun and shot him in the back. The local police were bribed to obscure the facts, and the newspapers said it was a gang war."

"What about the Travelers?"

"With no one to protect them, they were destroyed in a few weeks. A German Harlequin named Thorn flew to Japan, but it was already too late."

Lawrence stared down at his coffee cup. "And that's what happened . . ."

"Like it or not, you're the son of a Harlequin and you work for the Tabula. The only question is: What are you going to do about that?"

* * *

AN INTENSE FEAR returned to Lawrence as the meeting time got closer. He locked his office door, but anyone with a higher security rating—like Kennard Nash—would be allowed to enter. At 3:55 PM, he took out the receiver device that Linden mailed with the spider and plugged it into the cable port of his laptop computer. Hazy red lines appeared on the monitor, and then suddenly he saw the conference room and heard voices on his headset.

Kennard Nash was standing by the long table and greeting the Brethren as they arrived for the meeting. A few of the men were wearing golf clothes and had spent the afternoon at a local Westchester country club. The Brethren shook hands firmly with one another, made jokes, and gossiped about the current political situation. An uninformed observer might have decided that this group of well-dressed older men ran a charitable foundation with a yearly banquet and honorary awards.

"All right, gentlemen," Nash said. "Take your seats. It's time for our conversation."

Typing instructions into his computer, Lawrence focused the spider's lens. He watched as Nathan Boone appeared on the conference-room video screen. The small squares at the bottom of the screen showed head shots of the Brethren in other countries.

"Hello, everyone." Boone spoke calmly, like a financial officer discussing current revenue. "I wanted to give you a summary of the current situation regarding Michael and Gabriel Corrigan.

"A month ago, I started a surveillance program to watch these two men. Temporary staff was hired in Los Angeles and some employees were brought in from other cities. Our men were told to observe the brothers and obtain information about their personal characteristics. They were supposed to detain the Corrigans only if it became clear that they were going to flee the area."

The television screen showed an image of a run-down two-story building. "Several nights ago, the two brothers met at the hospice facility where their mother is staying. Our team did not have a thermal imaging device, but they did have an audio scanner. Rachel Corrigan said the following to her sons . . ."

The faint voice of the dying woman came out of the television speakers. "Your father . . . was a Traveler . . . A Harlequin named Thorn found us . . . If you have the power, you must hide from the Tabula."

Boone's face reappeared on the screen. "Rachel Corrigan died that night and the brothers left the facility. Mr. Prichett was in charge of the team. He made the decision to capture Michael Corrigan. Unfortunately, Gabriel followed his brother onto the freeway and attacked one of our vehicles. The Corrigans escaped."

"Where are they now?" Nash asked.

Lawrence watched as a new image appeared on the screen. A large man who looked like he was from the South Sea Islands and a bald Latino man carrying a shotgun guarded the Corrigan brothers as they left a small house.

"The next morning, one of our surveillance teams saw two bodyguards and Gabriel at his house. A half hour later, the same group dropped by Michael's apartment and picked up articles of clothing.

"The four men drove south of Los Angeles to a clothing factory in the City of Industry. The factory is owned by a man named Frank Salazar. He made money through illegal activities, but now owns several legitimate businesses. Salazar was an investor in one of Michael's office buildings. His men are currently guarding both brothers."

"And they're still in the factory?" Nash asked.

"That's correct. I request permission to attack the building tonight and take control of the brothers."

The men around the conference table were quiet for a few seconds, and then the bald representative in Moscow began speaking. "Is this factory in a public area?"

"That's correct," Boone said. "Two apartment buildings are about five hundred yards away."

"The committee decided several years ago that we would avoid actions that might gain attention from the police."

General Nash leaned forward. "If this was a routine execution, I would ask Mr. Boone to pull back and wait for a better opportunity. But the situation has changed very quickly. Because of the quantum computer, we have been given the opportunity to acquire an ally of great power. If the Crossover Project is successful, then we will finally have the technology necessary to control the general population."

"But we need a Traveler," said one of the men at the table.

General Nash tapped his finger on the table. "Yes. And as far as we know the Travelers don't exist anymore. These two young men are the sons of a known Traveler and that means they might have inherited his gift. We've got to take control of them. There's no alternative."

18

Maya sat quietly and watched the three men. It had taken her a while to recover from the electric shock, and she still had a burning sensation in her chest and left shoulder. While she was unconscious, the men had cut apart an old fan belt and used it to tie her legs together. Her wrists were chained with a pair of handcuffs passed beneath the chair. At that moment, she was trying to control her anger and find the calm place within her heart. Think of a stone, her father used to tell her. A smooth black stone. Pull it out of a cold mountain stream and hold it in your hand.

"Why isn't she talking?" Bobby Jay asked. "If I was her, I'd be calling you a bastard."

Shepherd glanced at Maya and laughed. "She's trying to figure out a way to cut your throat. Her father taught her how to kill people when she was a little girl."

"Intense."

"No, it's insane," Shepherd said. "Another Harlequin, this Irishwoman named Mother Blessing, went to a town in Sicily and murdered thirteen people in ten minutes. She was trying to rescue a Catholic priest who was kidnapped by some local mafiosi working as mercenaries. The priest was shot and bled to death in a car, but Mother Blessing escaped. And now, swear to god, there's an altar at a roadside chapel north of Palermo that includes a painting of Mother Blessing as the Angel of Death. To hell with that. She's a goddamn psychopath, that's what she is."

Chewing gum and scratching himself, Tate walked to the chair and leaned forward so that his mouth was a few inches away from her face. "Is that what you're doing, sweet face? Thinking about killing us? Now that's not nice."

"Keep away from her," Shepherd said. "Just leave her on the chair. Don't unlock the handcuffs. Don't give her any food or water. I'll be back as soon as I find Prichett."

"Traitor." Maya should have stayed silent—there was no advantage in conversation—but the word seemed to come out of her mouth.

"That word implies betrayal," Shepherd said. "But you know what? I've got nothing to betray. The Harlequins don't exist anymore."

"We can't let the Tabula take control."

"I've got some news for you, Maya. The Harlequins are out of a job because the Brethren aren't killing the Travelers anymore. They're going to capture them and use their power. That's what we should have done years ago."

"You don't deserve your Harlequin name. You've betrayed the memory of your family."

"Both my grandfather and my father only cared about Travelers. Neither of them ever thought twice about me. We're the same, Maya. We both grew up with people who worshipped a lost cause."

Shepherd turned to Bobby Jay and Tate. "Watch her at all times," he said, and walked out of the room.

Tate went over to the table and picked up Maya's throwing knife. "Take a look at this," he said to his brother. "It's perfectly balanced."

"We're going to get the knives, her Harlequin sword, and some bonus money when Shepherd comes back."

Maya flexed her arms and legs slightly, waiting for an opportunity. When she was much younger, her father took her to a club in Soho where they played three-cushion billiards. It taught her how to think ahead and organize a quick sequence of actions: the white ball would strike the red ball, and then bounce off the rubber cushions.

"Shepherd is way too scared of her." Holding the knife, Tate walked over to Maya. "The Harlequins have got this big reputation, but there's nothing backing it up. Look at her. She's got two arms and two legs just like anybody else."

Tate began to push the point of the knife against Maya's cheek. The skin flexed and gave way. He pushed harder and a little dot of blood appeared. "Now look at that. They bleed, too." Carefully, like an artist shaping wet clay, Tate made a shallow cut from the side of Maya's neck to her collarbone. She felt blood oozing out of the wound and trickling across her skin.

"See. Red blood. Just like you and me."

"Stop fooling around," said Bobby Jay. "You're going to get us in trouble."

Tate grinned and returned to the table. For a few seconds, his back was turned and he blocked his brother's view. Maya fell forward, onto her knees, and pulled her arms as far back as possible. When she was free of the chair, she slipped her arms beneath her pelvis and legs. Now her hands were in front of her.

Maya stood up—wrists, ankles still bound—and leaped past Tate. She somersaulted over the table, grabbed her sword, and landed in front of Bobby Jay. Startled, he fumbled inside his leather jacket for a gun. Maya swung the sword with two hands and slashed open his neck; blood sprayed out from the cut artery. Bobby Jay started to fall, but she had already forgotten about him. Sliding the sword down behind the black rubber fan belt, she cut her legs free.

Move faster. Now. She stepped around the table toward Tate while he reached beneath his oversized shirt and grabbed an automatic. As he raised the weapon, Maya moved to the left, swung down hard, and chopped off his forearm. Tate screamed and staggered backward, but she was on him immediately, slashing back and forth across his neck and chest.

Tate dropped to the floor and Maya stood over his body, clutching her sword. The world became smaller at that moment, collapsing like a dark star into one small point of fear and rage and exultation.

19

The Corrigan brothers had been living upstairs at the clothing factory for four days. That afternoon Mr. Bubble called Michael and assured him that his negotiations with the Torrelli family in Philadelphia were proceeding smoothly. In a week or so Michael would have to sign some transfer-of-ownership documents and then they would be free.

Deek showed up in the evening and ordered Chinese food. He sent Jesús downstairs to wait for the delivery van and started a chess game with Gabriel. "Lotta chess in prison," Deek explained. "But the bruthas there play chess the same way. They attack and keep on attacking until somebody's king goesdown."

It was very quiet in the factory when the sewing machines were switched off and the workers went home to their families. Gabriel heard a car come down the street and stop in front of the building. He peered out the fourth-floor window and saw a Chinese driver get out of his car with two bags of food.

Deek stared at the chessboard, considering his next move. "Somebody gonna get angry when Jesús pays them.

That driver come a long way and cheap Jesús give him a one-dollah tip."

The driver got the money from Jesús and began to walk back to his car. Suddenly the driver reached beneath his warm-up jacket and pulled out a handgun. He caught up with Jesús, raised the weapon, and blew off the top of the bodyguard's head. Deek heard the gunshot. He hurried over to the window as two cars roared up the street. A crowd of men jumped out and followed the Chinese man into the building.

Deek punched a number on his cell phone and spoke quickly. "Get some bruthas over here, fast time. Six men, with guns, comin' through the door." He switched off the phone, picked up his M-16 rifle, and motioned to Gabriel. "You go find Michael. Stay with him 'til Mr. Bubble come and help us out."

The big man moved cautiously toward the staircase. Gabriel hurried down the hallway and found Michael standing beside the folding cots.

"What's going on?"

"They're attacking the building."

They heard a burst of gunfire, muffled by the walls. Deek was in the stairwell, firing down at the attackers. Michael seemed confused and frightened. Standing in the doorway, he watched Gabriel pick up the rusty shovel.

"What are you doing?"

"Let's get out of here."

Gabriel cracked the shovel through the lower part of a window frame and pried the window open. Tossing the shovel away, he forced the window up with his hands and looked outside. A four-inch-wide concrete molding ran around the side of the factory. The roof of another building was six feet across the alleyway, one floor lower than where they were trapped.

Something exploded inside the building and the power went off. Gabriel went over to the corner and grabbed his father's Japanese sword. He thrust its hilt down into his backpack so that only the tip of the scabbard was sticking out. More gunshots. Then Deek screamed with pain.

Gabriel put on the backpack and returned to the open window. "Let's go. We can jump to the other building."

"I can't do that," Michael said. "I'll screw up and miss."

"You have to try. If we stay here, we'll get killed."

"I'll talk to them, Gabe. I can talk to anybody."

"Forget it. They don't want to make a deal."

Gabriel climbed out of the window and stood on the molding with his left hand holding on to the window frame. There was enough light from the street to see the roof, but the alleyway between the two buildings was a patch of darkness. He counted to three, then pushed off and fell through the air to the tar-paper surface of the roof. Scrambling to his feet, he looked up at the factory building.

"Hurry up!"

Michael hesitated, made a move like he was going to climb out the window, and then pulled away.

"You can do it!" Gabriel realized that he should have stayed with his brother and helped him go first. "Remember what you've always said. We've got to stick together. It's the only way."

A helicopter with a mounted spotlight roared across the sky. The beam cut through the darkness, briefly touched the open window, and continued across the top of the factory.

"Come on, Michael!"

"I can't! I'm going to find someplace to hide."

Michael reached into his coat pocket, took something out, and threw it to his brother. When the object fell onto the roof Gabriel saw that it was a gold money clip holding a credit card and a wad of twenty-dollar bills.

"I'll meet you at Wilshire Boulevard and Bundy at noon," Michael said. "If I'm not there, wait twenty-four hours and try again."

"They're going to kill you."

"Don't worry. I'll be all right."

Michael disappeared into the darkness and Gabriel stood alone. The helicopter flew back over the building and hovered in the air, its engine roaring, the big propeller stirring up dust and bits of trash. A spotlight beam hit Gabriel's eyes; it was like staring at the sun. Half blinded from the glare, he stumbled across the roof to a fire escape, grabbed a steel ladder, and let gravity pull him down.

20

Maya stripped off her blood-splattered clothes and stuffed them into a plastic garbage bag. The two dead bodies were only a few feet away and she tried not to think about what had happened. Stay in the present, she told herself. Concentrate on each action. Scholars and poets had written about the past—admired it, longed for it, regretted it—but Thorn had taught his daughter to avoid these distractions. The sword blade itself was the proper model as it flashed through the air.

Shepherd had left to meet someone named Prichett, but he could return at any moment. Although Maya wanted to stay and kill the traitor, her first objective was to track down Gabriel and Michael Corrigan. Perhaps they've already been captured, she thought. Or maybe they didn't have the power to become Travelers. There was only one way to answer those questions: she had to find the brothers as quickly as possible.

Maya got some spare clothes out of her suitcase and pulled on jeans, a T-shirt, and a blue cotton sweater. She wrapped her hands with strips of plastic bags, sorted through Bobby Jay's handguns, and picked out a small German-made

automatic with an ankle holster. A combat shotgun with a
pistol grip and a folding stock was in the long metal suitcase
and she decided to take it along with her. When she was
ready to go she tossed an old newspaper on the bloody floor
and stood on it while she searched the brothers' pockets.
Tate was carrying forty dollars and three plastic vials filled
with rock cocaine. Bobby Jay had more than nine hundred
dollars in cash rolled up with a rubber band. Maya took the
money and left the drugs beside Tate's body.

Carrying the shotgun case and her other equipment, she
left through the emergency door, walked a few blocks west,
and tossed the bloody clothes into a dumpster. Now she was
standing on Lincoln Boulevard, a four-lane street lined with
furniture stores and fast-food restaurants. It was hot and she
felt as if the splattered blood was still sticking to her skin.

Maya had only one backup contact. Several years ago,
Linden had visited America to obtain false passports and
credit cards. He had set up a mail drop with a man named
Thomas who lived in Hermosa Beach.

She used a pay phone to call a taxi. The driver was an
elderly Syrian man who barely spoke English. He opened a
map book, examined it for a long time, and then said he
could take her to the address.

Hermosa Beach was a small town south of the Los
Angeles airport. There was a central tourist area with restaurants and bars, but most of the buildings were little one-
story cottages a few blocks from the ocean. The taxi driver
got lost twice. He stopped, flipped through his map book
again, and finally managed to find the house on Sea Breeze
Lane. Maya paid the driver and watched the cab disappear
down the street. Perhaps the Tabula were already there,
waiting inside the house.

She climbed onto the front porch and knocked on the
door. No one answered, but she could hear music coming
from the backyard. Maya opened a side gate and found herself in a passageway between the house and a concrete wall.

In order to free her hands, she left all her bags near the gate. Bobby Jay's automatic was in a breakaway holster strapped to her left ankle. The sword case hung from her shoulder. She took a deep breath, prepared herself for combat, and went forward.

A few pine trees grew near the wall, but the rest of the backyard was stripped of vegetation. Someone had dug a shallow pit in the sandy ground and covered it with a five-foot-high wicker dome of sticks lashed together with rope. While a portable radio played country and western music, a bare-chested man covered the dome with blackened squares of tanned cattle hide.

The man saw Maya and stopped working. He was Native American, with long black hair and a flabby stomach. When he smiled, he showed a gap in his back teeth. "It's tomorrow," he said.

"Excuse me?"

"I changed the date for the sweat lodge ceremony. All the regulars got an e-mail, but I guess you're one of Richard's friends."

"I'm looking for someone named Thomas."

The man leaned down and turned off the radio. "That's me. I'm Thomas Walks the Ground. And who am I talking to?"

"Jane Stanley. I just flew in from England."

"I went to London once to give a talk. Several people asked me why I didn't wear feathers in my hair." Thomas sat down on a wooden bench and began to pull on a T-shirt. "I said I was one of the Absaroka, the bird people. You whites call us the Crow tribe. I don't need to pluck an eagle to be an Indian."

"A friend told me that you know a great many things."

"Maybe I do or maybe I don't. That's for you to decide."

Maya kept looking around the yard; no one else was in the area. "And now you build sweat lodges?"

"That's right. I usually have one going every weekend.

For the last few years, I've organized sweat lodge weekends for divorced men and women. After two days of sweating and pounding a drum, people decide they don't hate their ex-spouse anymore." Thomas smiled and gestured with his hands. "It's not a big thing, but it helps the world. All of us fight a battle every day, but we just don't know it. Love tries to defeat hatred. Bravery destroys fear."

"My friend said you could tell me how the Tabula got their name."

Thomas glanced at a portable cooler and a folded-up sweatshirt on the dirt. That was where the weapon was hidden. Probably a handgun.

"The Tabula. Right. I might have heard something about that." Thomas yawned and scratched his stomach as if she had just asked him about a group of Boy Scouts. "Tabula comes from the Latin phrase tabula rasa—which means 'a blank slate.' The Tabula think the human mind is a blank slate when you're born. That means the men in power can fill up your brain with selected information. If you do this to large numbers of people you can control most of world's population. The Tabula hate anyone who can show that there's a different reality."

"Like a Traveler?"

Once again, Thomas looked at his hidden weapon. He hesitated, and then seemed to decide that he couldn't grab it in time to save himself.

"Listen, Jane—or whatever your name is—if you want to kill me, go ahead. I don't give a damn. One of my uncles was a Traveler, but I don't have the power to cross over. When my uncle came back to this world, he tried to organize the tribes so that we would turn away from alcohol and take control of our lives. The men in power didn't like that. Land was involved. Oil leases. Six months after my uncle started preaching, someone ran him down on the road. You made it look like an accident, didn't you? A hit-and-run driver and no witnesses."

"Do you know what a Harlequin is?"

"Maybe . . ."

"You met a French Harlequin named Linden several years ago. He used your address to obtain fake passports. Right now, I'm in trouble. Linden said that you could help me."

"I'm not fighting for the Harlequins. That's not who I am."

"I need a car or a truck, some kind of vehicle that can't be tracked by the Vast Machine."

Thomas Walks the Ground stared at her for a long time, and she felt the power in his eyes. "All right," he said slowly. "I can do that."

G abriel walked up the drainage ditch that ran alongside the San Diego Freeway. It was almost dawn. A thin line of orange sunlight glowed on the eastern horizon. Cars and trailer trucks raced past him, heading south.

Whoever had attacked Mr. Bubble's clothing factory was probably waiting for him to return to the house in West Los Angeles. Gabriel had left his Honda back at the factory and needed another bike. In New York or Hong Kong—any vertical city—he could lose himself on the subway or in the crowd. But only homeless people and illegal immigrants walked in Los Angeles. If he were on a motorcycle, he would be absorbed by the traffic that flowed from the surface streets into the anonymous confusion of the freeways.

An old man named Foster lived two doors down from Gabriel's house. Foster had a toolshed with an aluminum roof in his backyard. Gabriel climbed up on the concrete wall that separated the freeway from the houses on his street, and then jumped onto the toolshed. Looking over the rooftops, he saw that a repair truck from the power company was parked across the street. He stood there for a few minutes, wondering what to do, and a yellow flame flashed inside the truck cab. Someone sitting in the shadows had just lit a cigarette.

Gabriel jumped off the shed and scrambled over the wall to the freeway. Now the sun was up, emerging like a dirty balloon from behind a line of warehouses. Better do it now, he thought. If they've been waiting all night, they're probably half asleep.

He returned to the wall, grabbed the top, and pulled himself over to his weed-filled backyard. Without hesitation, he ran to the garage and kicked in the side door. His Italian-made Moto Guzzi was parked in the middle of the garage. Its large engine, black fuel tank, and short racing handlebars had always reminded him of a fighting bull waiting for a toreador.

Gabriel slammed his fist on the button that activated the electric garage-door opener, straddled the motorcycle, and kick-started the engine. The metal garage door made a grinding sound as it rolled upward. The moment Gabriel saw five feet of clearance, he gunned the accelerator.

Three men jumped out of the truck and sprinted toward him. As Gabriel roared down the driveway, a man wearing a blue jacket raised a weapon that looked like a shotgun with a grenade attached to the muzzle. Gabriel bumped across the sidewalk to the street and the man fired his weapon. The grenade turned out to be a thick plastic bag filled with something heavy. It hit the side of the motorcycle and the bike lurched sideways.

Don't stop, Gabriel thought. Don't slow down. He jerked the handlebars to the left, recovered his balance, and roared down the street to the end of the block. Glancing over his shoulder, he saw the three men running to the repair truck.

Gabriel turned the corner at a steep angle, the Guzzi's back wheel spitting up gravel. He gunned the engine and a burst of speed pulled him back on the seat. His body seemed to become part of the machinery, an extension of its power, as he held on tightly and raced through a red light.

*   *   *

HE STAYED ON surface streets, traveling south to Compton, then turned around and rode back to Los Angeles. At noon, he cruised past the corner of Wilshire and Bundy, but Michael wasn't there. Gabriel rode his motorcycle north to Santa Barbara and spent the night in a run-down motel several miles from the beach. He returned to Los Angeles the following day, but Michael still wasn't at the street corner.

Gabriel bought several newspapers and read every article. There was no mention of the shooting at the clothing factory. He knew that newspapers and television announcers reported on a certain level of reality. What was happening to him was on another level, like a parallel universe. All around him, different societies were growing larger or being destroyed, forming new traditions or breaking the rules while citizens pretended that the faces shown on television were the only important stories.

For the rest of the day, he stayed on the motorcycle, stopping only once for fuel and drinking water. Gabriel knew that he should find a hiding place, but a nervous energy kept him moving. As he got tired, Los Angeles broke apart into fragments: isolated images with no tissue connecting them. Dead palm fronds in the gutter. A giant plaster chicken. The wanted poster for a lost dog. Signs were everywhere: PRICES SLASHED! NO OFFER REFUSED! WE WILL DELIVER! An old man reading the Bible. A teenage girl chattering on her cell phone. Then the stoplight clicked green and he raced off to nowhere.

Gabriel had gone out with several women in Los Angeles, but the relationships rarely lasted more than one or two months. They wouldn't know how to help if he showed up at their apartments looking for shelter. He had a few male friends who liked skydiving and others who raced motorcycles, but there wasn't a strong bond between them. In order to avoid the Grid, he had cut himself off from everyone but his brother.

Riding east on Sunset Boulevard, he thought about Maggie Resnick. She was an attorney and he trusted her; she would know what to do. Turning off Sunset, he followed the winding road that led up through Coldwater Canyon.

Maggie's house was built on the side of a steep slope. A garage door was at the base of the house, then three glass-and-steel floors of diminishing size were stacked on top of each other like the tiers of a wedding cake. It was almost midnight, but the lights were still on inside. Gabriel rang the bell and Maggie opened the door wearing a red flannel bathrobe and fuzzy slippers.

"I hope you're not here to offer me a motorcycle ride. It's cold and dark and I'm tired. I've got to read three more depositions."

"I need to talk to you."

"What happened? Are you in trouble?"

Gabriel nodded.

Maggie stepped away from the doorway. "Then come on in. Virtue is admirable, but boring. I guess that's why I practice criminal law."

Although Maggie hated to cook, she had told her architect to design an extra-large kitchen. Copper pots hung from ceiling hooks. Crystal wineglasses were in a wood rack on the shelf. There was a huge stainless-steel refrigerator that held four bottles of champagne and a takeout carton of Chinese food. While Maggie brewed some tea, Gabriel sat at the kitchen counter. Just his being here might be dangerous for her, but he desperately needed to tell someone what had happened. Now that everything was so volatile, memories from his childhood began to force their way into his thoughts.

Maggie poured him a cup of tea, then sat on the opposite side of the counter and lit a cigarette. "All right. At this moment, I'm your lawyer. That means that everything you say to me is confidential unless you're contemplating a future crime."

"I haven't done anything wrong."

She waved her hand and a line of cigarette smoke drifted through the air. "Of course you have, Gabriel. We've all committed crimes. The first question is: Are the police looking for you?"

Gabriel gave her a brief description of his mother's death, and then described the men who had attacked Michael on the freeway, the meeting with Mr. Bubble, and the incident at the clothing factory. For the most part, Maggie just let him talk, but occasionally she asked how he knew a certain fact.

"I thought Michael might get you into trouble," she said. "People who hide their money from the government are usually involved in other kinds of criminal activity. If Michael stopped paying them rent on his office building, they wouldn't contact the police. They'd hire some muscle to track him down."

"It might be something else," Gabriel said. "When we were growing up in South Dakota, men came looking for my father. They burned down our house and my father disappeared, but we never learned why it happened. My mother told us this wild story before she died."

Gabriel had avoided telling anyone about his family, but now he couldn't stop talking. He gave a few details about their life in South Dakota and described what his mother had said on her deathbed. Maggie had spent most of her life listening to her clients explain their crimes. She had trained herself not to reveal any skepticism until the story was finished.

"Is that all, Gabriel? Any other details?"

"That's all I can remember."

"You want some cognac?"

"Not right now."

Maggie took out a bottle of French cognac and poured herself a drink. "I'm not going to discount what your mother told you, but it doesn't relate to what I know. People usually get into trouble because of sex, pride, or money. Sometimes it's all three things at the same time. This gangster Michael told you about—Vincent Torrelli—was killed in Atlantic City. From what you've told me about Michael, I think he might be tempted to accept some illegal financing and then figure out a way not to pay it back."

"Do you think Michael's all right?"

"Probably. They need to keep him alive if they want to protect their investment."

"What can I do to help him?"

"You can't do much of anything," Maggie said. "So the question is—am I going to get involved in this? I don't suppose you have any money?"

Gabriel shook his head.

"I do like you, Gabriel. You've never lied to me and that's been a pleasure. I spend most of my time dealing with professional liars. It gets tiring after a while."

"I just wanted some advice, Maggie. I'm not asking you to get involved with something that could be dangerous."

"Life is dangerous. That's what makes it interesting." She finished her brandy and made a decision. "All right. I'll help you. It's a mitzvah, and I can display my unused maternal instincts." Maggie opened a kitchen cabinet and took out a pill container. "Now humor me and take some vitamins."

22

When Victory From Sin Fraser was eight years old, a cousin visiting Los Angeles told her about the brave Harlequin who had sacrificed himself for the Prophet. The story was so dramatic that she felt an immediate connection to this mysterious group of defenders. As Vicki grew older, her mother, Josetta, and her pastor, Reverend J. T. Morganfield, had tried to guide her away from an allegiance to Debt Not Paid. Vicki Fraser was usually an obedient servant of the church, but she refused to change her views on this one issue. Debt Not Paid became her substitute for drinking alcohol and sneaking out at night; it was her only real act of rebellion.

Josetta was furious when her daughter confessed that she had met a Harlequin at the airport. "You should be ashamed," she said. "The Prophet said that it's a sin to disobey your parents."

"The Prophet also said that one can disobey small rules when following the larger will of God."

"Harlequins have nothing to do with the will of God," Josetta said. "They'll slit your throat, then get angry because you're bleeding on their shoes."

The day after Vicki went to the airport, a truck from the electric power company appeared on their street. A black man and his two white partners began climbing poles and checking transmission lines, but Josetta wasn't fooled. The fake employees took two-hour lunches and never seemed to finish their work. Throughout the day, one of them was always standing around, watching the Frasers' house. Josetta ordered her daughter to stay inside and away from the telephone. Reverend Morganfield and other members of the church put on their best clothes and began to drop by the house for prayer meetings. No one was going to bust down the door and kidnap this maiden of the Lord.

Vicki was in trouble because she had helped Maya, but she didn't regret it. People rarely listened to her, and now the whole congregation was talking about what she had done. Since she couldn't go out, she spent most of her time thinking about Maya. Was the Harlequin safe? Had someone killed her?

Three days after her act of disobedience she was looking out the back window when Maya leaped over the fence. For a moment Vicki felt as if she had conjured up the Harlequin from her dreams.

As Maya walked across the lawn, she pulled an automatic pistol out of her coat pocket. Vicki pushed open the sliding glass door and waved her hand. "Be careful," she said. "Three men are working out on the street. They act like they're with the power company, but we think they're Tabula."

"Have they been inside the house?"

"No."

Maya took off her sunglasses when she moved from the living room into the kitchen. The handgun disappeared into her pocket, but her right hand touched the top of the metal sword case hanging from her shoulder.

"Are you hungry?" Vicki asked Maya. "Can I make you breakfast?"

The Harlequin stood by the sink, her eyes scanning every object in the room. And Vicki saw the kitchen differently, as if for the first time in her life. The avocado green pots and pans. The plastic wall clock. The cute little farm girl standing at the ceramic well. Everything was ordinary and safe.

"Shepherd was a traitor," Maya said. "He's working for the Tabula. And you helped him. Which means you might be a traitor, too."

"I didn't betray you, Maya. I swear that in the name of the Prophet."

The Harlequin looked tired and vulnerable. She kept glancing around the kitchen as if someone was going to attack her at any moment. "I don't really trust you, but I don't have many options at this point. I'm willing to pay for your assistance."

"I don't want Harlequin money."

"It guarantees some loyalty."

"I'll help you for free, Maya. Just ask me."

Looking at Maya's eyes, Vicki realized that she was asking for something that was very difficult for a Harlequin to give. To ask for another person's help required some degree of humility and an acknowledgment of your own weakness. The Harlequins were sustained by pride and their unshakable confidence.

Maya mumbled a few words, and then tried again, speaking very precisely. "I want you to help me."

"Yes. I'd be glad to. Do you have a plan?"

"I have to find these two brothers before the Tabula capture them. You won't have to touch a gun or a knife. You won't have to hurt anyone. Just help me hire a mercenary who won't betray me. The Tabula are very powerful in this country and Shepherd is helping them. I can't do this alone."

"Vicki?" Her mother had heard their voices. "What's going on? Do we have visitors?"

Josetta was a big woman with a broad face. That morning she wore a forest green pants suit and the heart locket that held her deceased husband's photograph. She entered the doorway, and then stopped when she saw the stranger. The two women glared at each other and, once again, Maya touched the sword case.

"Mother, this is—"

"I know who she is—a murderous sinner who has brought death into our lives."

"I'm trying to find two brothers," Maya said. "They might be Travelers."

"Isaac T. Jones was the last Traveler. There are no others."

Maya touched Vicki's arm. "The Tabula are watching this house. Sometimes they have equipment that allows them to look through walls. I can't stay here any longer. It's dangerous for all of us."

Vicki stood between her mother and the Harlequin. So much of her life had seemed hazy and vague until that moment, like an out-of-focus photograph in which blurry figures ran away from the camera. But now, right now, she had a real choice in her life. Walking is easy, said the Prophet. But it requires faith to find the right path.

"I'm going to help her."

"No," Josetta said. "I don't give my permission."

"I don't need permission, Mother." Vicki grabbed her purse and walked out into the backyard. Maya caught up with her when she reached the edge of the grass.

"Just remember one thing," Maya said. "We're working together, but I still don't trust you."

"All right. You don't trust me. So what's the first thing we have to do?"

"Grab the top of the fence and jump."

*   *   *

THOMAS WALKS THE GROUND had given Maya a Plymouth delivery van. It had no side windows, so she could sleep in the back if necessary. When Vicki got into the van, Maya told her to take off all her clothes.

"Why should I do that?"

"Have you and your mother stayed in the house for the last two days?"

"Not all the time. We went to see Reverend Morganfield."

"The Tabula entered your house and searched it. They probably put tracer beads in your clothes and luggage. Once you leave the area, a satellite will track you down."

Feeling a little embarrassed, Vicki got in the back and removed her shoes, blouse, and slacks. A stiletto appeared in Maya's hand and she used the weapon to probe every hem and seam. "Did you get these shoes repaired recently?" she asked.

"No. Never."

"Someone's used a hammer on this." Maya thrust the point of the knife beneath the heel and pried it off. A little pocket was carved into the heel. She turned the shoe upside down and a white tracer bead fell into the palm of her hand.

"Wonderful. Now they know you've left the house."

Maya tossed the bead out the window and drove to a Korean neighborhood on Western Avenue. They bought a new pair of shoes for Vicki, then dropped by a Seventh-day Adventist church and picked up a dozen religious pamphlets. Pretending to be an Adventist missionary, Vicki visited Gabriel's house near the freeway and knocked on the door. No one was home, but she felt like she was being watched.

The two women drove to the parking lot of a warehouse store and sat in the back of the van. While Vicki watched, Maya attached a laptop computer to a satellite phone and typed in a phone number.

"What are you doing?"

"Going on the Internet. It's dangerous because of Carnivore."

"What's that?"

"The name of an Internet surveillance program developed by your FBI. The National Security Agency has developed even more powerful tools, but my father and his Harlequin friends kept using the word 'Carnivore.' The old name reminded them to be careful when using the Internet. Carnivore is a packet sniffer program that looks at everything that comes through a particular network. It's aimed at specific Web sites and e-mail addresses, but it also detects certain trigger words and phrases."

"And the Tabula know about this program?"

"They have unauthorized access through their Internet monitoring operation." Maya began to type on her computer. "You can get around Carnivore by using soft language that avoids trigger words."

Vicki sat in the front seat of the van and looked out at the parking lot while Maya searched for another Harlequin. Citizens came out of the warehouse store with extra-large shopping baskets piled high with food, clothing, and electronic equipment. The baskets were heavy with all these things, and the citizens had to lean forward to push them to their cars. Vicki remembered reading in high school about Sisyphus, the Greek king doomed forever to push a stone up a mountain.

After searching through several Web sites and typing in different code words, Maya found Linden. Vicki looked over Maya's shoulder as she sent instant messages using soft language. The traitor Harlequin, Shepherd, became "the grandson of a good man" who "joined a competing firm" and destroyed "our possible business venture."

"You healthy?" Linden asked.

"Yes."

"Problems with the negotiation?"

"Cold meat times two," Maya typed.

"Enough tools?"

"Adequate."

"Physical condition?"

"Tired, but no damage."

"Have assistance?"

"One local employee from Jones and Company. Hiring a professional today."

"Good. Funds available."

The screen was blank for a second, then Linden typed. "Last heard from my friend forty-eight hours ago. Suggest you look . . ."

Linden's informant inside the Evergreen Foundation had provided him with six addresses for finding Michael and Gabriel Corrigan. There were short notes such as: "Plays golf with M." or "Friend of G."

"Thanks."

"Will try for more data. Good luck."

Maya wrote down the addresses and shut off the computer. "We have some more locations to check out," she told Vicki. "But I need to hire a mercenary—someone who can back me up."

"I know one person."

"Is he in a tribe?"

"What does that mean?"

"Some of the people who reject the Vast Machine come together in groups that live in various levels of the underground. Some tribes reject Machine-grown food. Some reject Machine music and clothing styles. Some tribes try to live by faith. They reject the Machine's fear and bigotry."

Vicki laughed. "Then the Church of Isaac T. Jones is a tribe."

"That's right." Maya started the van and began to drive out of the enormous parking lot. "A fighting tribe is a group that can defend itself, physically, from the Machine. Harlequins use them as mercenaries."

"Hollis Wilson isn't part of any group. But he definitely knows how to fight."

As they drove to South Los Angeles, Vicki explained that the Divine Church realized that their young followers might be tempted by the flashy materialism of New Babylon. Teenagers were encouraged to be church missionaries in South Africa or the Caribbean. It was seen as a good way to channel youthful energy.

Hollis Wilson was part of a well-known church family, but he refused to become a missionary and began to hang out with the gang members in his neighborhood. His parents prayed for him and locked him in his room. Once he came home at two in the morning and found a Jonesie minister waiting to exorcise the demon in the young man's heart. When Hollis was arrested in the vicinity of a stolen car, Mr. Wilson took his son to a karate class at the local Police Athletic League. He thought the karate teacher might be able to add some structure to Hollis's scattered life.

The disciplined world of martial arts was the true power that pulled Hollis away from the church. After receiving a fourth-degree black belt in karate, Hollis followed one of his teachers to South America. He ended up in Rio de Janeiro and lived there for six years, becoming an expert in a Brazilian style of martial arts called capoeira.

"Then he came back to Los Angeles," Vicki said. "I met him at his sister's wedding. He started a martial arts school in South Central."

"Describe him to me. What's he look like? Big? Small?"

"Broad shoulders, but slender. Nappy hair, like a Rastafarian."

"And what's his personality?"

"Confident, and vain. He thinks he's God's gift to women."

Hollis Wilson's martial arts school was on Florence Avenue, wedged between a liquor store and a video rental outlet. Someone had painted words on the sidewalk window in garish reds and yellows. DEFEND YOURSELF! KARATE, KICK-BOXING, AND BRAZILIAN CAPOEIRA. NO CONTRACTS. BEGINNERS WELCOME.

They heard drumming as they approached the school and the sound got louder when they opened the front door.

Hollis had taken sheets of plywood and built a reception area with a desk and folding chairs. Pinned to a bulletin board was a class schedule and posters advertising local karate tournaments. Maya and Vicki walked past two small dressing rooms with old bedspreads hung in place of doors and looked into a long windowless room.

An old man was playing a conga drum in one corner and the sound bounced off the concrete walls. Wearing T-shirts and white cotton pants, the capoeiristas stood in a circle. They clapped their hands in rhythm with the drum and watched two people fighting. One of the fighters was a short Latino man wearing a *Think Critically!* T-shirt. He was trying to defend himself against a black man in his twenties who was giving instructions between the kicks. The black man glanced at the visitors and Vicki touched Maya's arm. Hollis Wilson had long legs and muscular arms. His braided dreadlocks came down to his shoulders. After watching for a few minutes, Maya turned and whispered to Vicki, "That's Hollis Wilson?"

"Yes. With the long hair."

Maya nodded. "He'll do."

Capoeira was a peculiar mixture of grace and violence that looked like a ritualized dance. After Hollis and the Latino stopped sparring, two other people entered the circle. They began lunging at each other, mixing in cartwheels and punches and spinning kicks. If one person went down, he knew how to kick upward with his hands flat on the floor. The motion was continuous, and everyone's T-shirt was damp with sweat.

They passed around the circle once, Hollis cutting in to attack or defend. The drummer beat faster and each person fought a second time and then a final series of matches that emphasized leg sweeps and lightning-fast side kicks. Hollis nodded to the drummer and the fighting was over.

Exhausted, the students sat on the floor. They stretched their legs and took deep breaths. Hollis didn't look tired at all. He paced back and forth in front of them, speaking in the cadence of a Jonesie preacher.

"There are three kinds of human responses: the deliberate, the instinctive, and the automatic. Deliberate is when you think about your actions. Instinctive is when you just react. Automatic is when you do something from habit because you've done it before."

Hollis paused and stared at the students sitting in front of him. He seemed to be evaluating their strengths and weaknesses. "In New Babylon, many of the people you know think they're being deliberate when they're just on automatic. Like a bunch of robots, they drive their car down the freeway, go to work, get a paycheck in exchange for sweat and pain and humiliation, then drive back home to listen to fake laughter coming from the television set. They're already dead. Or dying. But they don't know it.

"Then there's another group of people—the party boys and girls. Smoke some weed. Drink some malt liquor. Try to hook up for a little quick sex. They think they're connecting with their instincts, their natural power, but you know what? They're on automatic, too.

"The warrior is different. The warrior uses the power of the brain to be deliberate and the power of the heart to be instinctive. Warriors are never automatic except when they're brushing their teeth."

Hollis paused and spread his hands. "Try to think. Feel. Be real." He clapped his hands together. "That's all for today."

The students bowed to their teacher, grabbed gym bags, slipped rubber flip-flop sandals on their bare feet, and left the school. Hollis wiped some sweat off the floor with a towel and turned to smile at Vicki.

"Now this is a real surprise," he said. "You're Victory From Sin Fraser—Josetta Fraser's daughter."

"I was a little girl when you left the church."

"I remember. Wednesday night prayer service. Friday night youth group. Sunday night potluck social. I always liked the singing. There's good music in the church. But it was a little too much praying for me."

"Obviously you weren't a believer."

"I believe in a lot of things. Isaac T. Jones was a great prophet, but he's not the final one." Hollis walked over to the doorway. "So why are you here and who's your friend? Beginner classes are Wednesday, Thursday, and Friday night."

"We're not here to learn how to fight. This is my friend, Maya."

"And what are you?" he asked Maya. "A white convert?"

"That's a foolish comment," Vicki said. "The Prophet accepted all races."

"I'm just trying to get the facts, Little Miss Victory From Sin. If you're not here for lessons, then you're here to invite me to some church function. I guess Reverend Morganfield thought he'd get a better reaction sending two pretty women to talk to me. That might be true, but it still doesn't work."

"This has nothing to do with the church," Maya said. "I want to hire you as a fighter. I'm assuming that you have weapons or access to them."

"And who the hell are you?"

Vicki glanced at Maya, asking for permission. The Harlequin moved her eyes slightly. Tell him.

"This is Maya. She's a Harlequin who's come to Los Angeles to search for two unborn Travelers."

Hollis looked surprised, and then laughed loudly. "Right! And I'm the Goddamn King of the World. Don't give me this garbage, Vicki. There aren't any Travelers or Harlequins left. They've all been hunted down and killed."

"I hope everyone thinks that," Maya said calmly. "It's easier for us if no one believes we exist."

Hollis stared at Maya, raising his eyebrows as if questioning her right to be in the room. Then he spread his legs into a fighting stance and snapped off a punch at half speed. Vicki screamed, but Hollis continued the attack with a head punch and crossing kick. As Maya stumbled backward, the sword carrying case fell off her shoulder and rolled a few inches across the tile floor.

Hollis went into a cartwheel that ended in a crossing kick and Maya managed to block it. He moved faster, attacking with full power and speed. Using kicks and punches, he pushed Maya toward the wall. She knocked his fists away with her hands and forearms, shifted her weight onto the right foot, and aimed a front kick at Hollis's groin. Hollis fell backward, rolled across the floor, and jumped up with another combination.

They were fighting hard now, trying to hurt each other. Vicki shouted for them to stop, but neither person seemed to hear her. Now that Maya had recovered from her initial surprise, her face was calm, her eyes intense and focused. She moved in close, throwing quick punches and kicks that tried to achieve maximum damage.

Hollis danced away from her. Even in this situation, he had to show everyone that he was a graceful and inventive fighter. With roundhouse punches and spinning back kicks, he began to push Maya across the room. The Harlequin stopped when the sword case touched her shoe.

She faked a punch at Hollis's head, reached down, and grabbed the case. And then the sword was out, the hilt clicking into place, as she lunged toward her attacker. Hollis lost his balance, fell backward, and Maya stopped moving. The point of the sword blade was two inches away from Hollis Wilson's neck.

"Don't!" Vicki shouted, and the spell was broken. The violence and anger vanished from the room. Maya lowered her sword as Hollis got to his feet.

"You know, I've always wanted to see one of those Harlequin swords."

"The next time we fight like this, you'll be dead."

"But we're not going to fight. We're on the same side." Hollis turned his head and winked at Vicki. "So how much are you pretty women going to pay me?"

23

Hollis drove the blue delivery van and Vicki sat in the passenger seat. Maya crouched in back, away from the window. As they cut through Beverly Hills, she saw scattered images of the city. Some of the homes were built in the Spanish style with red tile roofs and courtyards. Others looked like modern versions of Tuscan villas. Several of the houses were simply big, lacking any identifiable style; they had elaborate porticos over the front door and fake Romeo-and-Juliet balconies. It was strange to see so many buildings that were both grandiose and bland.

Hollis crossed Sunset Boulevard and began to drive up Coldwater Canyon. "Okay," he said. "We're getting close."

"They may be watching the place. Slow down and park before we get there."

Hollis pulled over a few minutes later and Maya came forward to peer through the windshield. They were parked on a hillside residential street where the homes were built close to the curb. A Department of Water and Power truck had stopped a few feet away from Maggie Resnick's house. A man in an orange jumpsuit was climbing a power pole while two other workers watched him from below.

"Seems okay," Hollis said.

Vicki shook her head. "They're looking for the Corrigan brothers. A truck just like that has been outside my house for the last two days."

Crouched on the floor of the van, Maya took the combat shotgun out of its case and loaded it with shells. The shotgun had a metal stock and she folded it down so that the weapon resembled a large pistol. When she returned to the front seat area, an SUV had parked behind the phone truck. Shepherd got out, nodded to the fake repairmen, and climbed the wooden steps that led to the entrance of the two-story house. He rang the bell and waited until a woman came to the door.

"Start the van," Maya said. "And drive up to the house."

Hollis didn't obey her. "Who's the guy with the blond hair?"

"He's a former Harlequin named Shepherd."

"What about the other two men?"

"Tabula mercs."

"How do you want to handle this?" Hollis asked.

Maya didn't say anything. It took a few seconds for the others to realize that she was going to destroy Shepherd and the mercs. Vicki looked horrified, and the Harlequin saw herself in the young woman's eyes.

"You're not killing anybody," Hollis said quietly.

"I hired you, Hollis. You're a mercenary."

"I gave you my conditions. I'll help you and protect you, but I won't let you walk up to some stranger and blow him away."

"Shepherd is a traitor," Maya said. "He's working for . . ."

Before she could finish her explanation, the garage door rolled open and a man came out riding a motorcycle. As he bumped over the curb, one of the telephone repairmen spoke into a handheld radio.

Maya touched Vicki's shoulder. "That's Gabriel Corrigan," she said. "Linden said that he rides a motorcycle."

Gabriel turned right onto Coldwater Canyon Drive and headed up the hill toward Mulholland. A few seconds later, three motorcycle riders wearing black helmets shot past the van and chased after him.

"Looks like some other people were waiting for him." Hollis started the engine and slammed his foot on the accelerator. Fishtailing on its worn tires, the delivery van headed up the canyon. A few minutes later, they were turning onto Mulholland Drive, the two-lane road that followed the ridge of the Hollywood hills. If you looked to the left you could see a brown haze covering a valley filled with homes, light-blue swimming pools, and office buildings.

Maya traded places with Vicki and sat by the passenger window with her shotgun. The four motorcycles were already well ahead of them and they lost sight of the pack for a few seconds when the van went into a curve. The road straightened out again. Maya watched one of the riders pull out a weapon that looked like a flare gun. He approached Gabriel, fired the weapon at the motorcycle, and missed. The bullet hit the thin asphalt near the edge of the road and the pavement exploded.

"What the hell was that?" Hollis shouted.

"He's shooting a Hatton round," Maya said. "The slug is a mixture of wax and metal powder. They're trying to take out the back tire."

Immediately the Tabula rider fell behind while his two companions continued the chase. A pickup truck came from the opposite direction. The terrified driver honked his horn and waved his hands, trying to warn Hollis about what he had just seen.

"Don't kill him!" shouted Vicki as they approached the first rider.

Staying near the edge of the road, the Tabula loaded another shell into his flare gun. Maya stuck the barrel of her shotgun out of the open window and fired, blowing away the motorcycle's front tire. The bike jerked to the right, slammed into a concrete retaining wall, and the rider was thrown sideways.

Maya pumped a new round into the shotgun's firing chamber. "Keep going!" she shouted. "We don't want to lose them!"

The delivery van was shuddering like it couldn't go any faster, but Hollis pressed the gas pedal to the floor. They heard a booming sound, and when they came around the next curve, they saw that a second rider had fallen back to load a new shell into his flare gun. He snapped the barrel shut and turned onto the road before they could reach him.

"Faster!" Maya shouted.

Hollis gripped the steering wheel as they skidded into another turn. "I can't. One of these tires is going to break apart."

"Faster!"

The second rider was holding the flare gun in his right hand while he gripped the handlebar with his left. He hit a pothole and almost lost control of his bike. When the rider slowed down, the van caught up with him. Hollis cut around to the left. Maya shot out the bike's back tire and the rider was flung over the handlebars. The van kept moving and hit another turn. A large green sedan came toward them, honking its horn and swerving. Turn back, the driver gestured, turn back.

They passed the turn to Laurel Canyon, honking and swerving around other cars as they ran through a red light. Maya heard a third booming sound, but she couldn't see Gabriel and the third rider. Then they came out of a curve and looked down the narrow road. Gabriel's back tire had been hit, but the bike continued moving. Smoke rose up from the shredded tire and there was a raspy sound of steel grinding on asphalt.

"Here we go!" shouted Hollis. He steered the van into the middle of the road and came up on the left of the rider.

Maya leaned out the window, the butt of her shotgun pressed against the van's door, and squeezed the trigger. Shotgun pellets hit the motorcycle's fuel tank and it exploded like a gasoline bomb. The Tabula was thrown into a ditch.

Five hundred yards up the road, Gabriel turned into a driveway. He stopped his motorcycle, jumped off, and began running. Hollis turned into the driveway and Maya leaped out of the van. She was too far from Gabriel. He was going to get away. But she sprinted after him and shouted the first thing that passed through her mind. "My father knew your father!"

Gabriel stopped on the edge of the hillside. In a few steps, he would be falling down a steep slope of chaparral.

"He was a Harlequin!" Maya shouted. "His name was Thorn!"

And those words—her father's name—reached Gabriel. He looked startled and desperate to know. Ignoring the shotgun in Maya's hands, he took one step toward her.

"Who am I?"

24

Nathan Boone looked down at Michael as the private jet headed east over the squares and rectangles of Iowa farmland. Before they left Long Beach Airport, the young man appeared to be sleeping. Now his face was slack and unresponsive. Perhaps the drugs were too strong, Boone thought. There could be permanent brain damage.

He swiveled around in the leather seat and faced the physician sitting behind him. Dr. Potterfield was just another mercenary, but he kept acting like he had special privileges. Boone enjoyed ordering him around.

"Check the patient's vital signs."

"I did that fifteen minutes ago."

"Do it again."

Dr. Potterfield knelt beside the stretcher, touched Michael's carotid artery, and took his pulse. He listened to Michael's heart and lungs, pulled back his eyelid and studied the iris. "I wouldn't recommend keeping him under for another day. His pulse is strong, but his breathing is getting shallow."

Boone glanced at his watch. "What about four more

hours? It'll take us that long to land in New York and get him to the research center."

"Four hours won't change anything."

"I expect you to be there when he wakes up," Boone said. "And if there's any problem, I'm sure you'll be glad to take full responsibility."

Potterfield's hands trembled slightly as he took a digital thermometer out of his black bag and slipped the sensor into Michael's ear. "There won't be any long-term problems, but don't expect him to climb a mountain right away. This is just like recovering from general anesthesia. The patient is going to be confused and weak."

Boone swiveled back to the small table in the middle of the plane. He was annoyed that he had to leave Los Angeles. One of his employees, a young man named Dennis Prichett, had interviewed the injured motorcycle riders who chased after Gabriel Corrigan. It was clear that Maya had acquired allies and captured the young man. The team in Los Angeles needed direction, but Boone's instructions were clear. The Crossover Project had highest priority. The moment he obtained control of either of the brothers, Boone was supposed to personally escort him back to New York.

He had spent most of the flight using his computer to search for Maya. All these efforts were channeled through the Brethren's Internet monitoring center located in an underground site in central London.

Privacy had become a convenient fiction. Kennard Nash once lectured on that subject to a group of Evergreen Foundation employees. The new electronic monitoring had changed society; it was as if everyone had been moved into a traditional Japanese house with interior walls constructed of bamboo and paper. Although you could hear people sneezing, talking, and making love, the social assumption was that you shouldn't pay attention to it. You had to pretend the walls were solid and soundproof. People felt the same way when they walked past a surveillance camera or used a cell phone. These days the authorities were using special X-ray machines at Heathrow Airport that could see through passengers' clothes. It was disturbing to realize that different organizations were watching you, listening to your conversations, and tracking your purchases—so most people pretended that it wasn't true.

Government officials who supported the Brethren had provided access codes to crucial databases. The largest source was the Total Information Awareness system, established by the American government after the passage of the United States Patriot Act. The TIA database was designed to process and analyze every computer-connected transaction in the country. Whenever a person used a credit card, checked out a library book, transferred money overseas, or went on a trip, the information was entered into the centralized database. A few libertarians objected to this intrusion, so the government transferred control of the program to the intelligence community and changed its name to the Terrorism Information Awareness system. Once the word "Total" was replaced by the word "Terrorism," all the criticism stopped.

Other countries were passing new security laws and setting up their own versions of TIA. In addition, a variety of privately owned companies were collecting and selling personal information. If the Tabula employees at the computer center in London couldn't obtain the access codes, they had software programs called Peephole, Hacksaw, and Sledgehammer that allowed them to break through firewalls and enter every database in the world.

Boone felt that the most promising weapons in the battle against the Brethren's enemies were the new computational immunology programs. The CI programs had originally been developed to monitor the Royal Mail's computer system in England. The Brethren's programs were even more powerful. They treated the entire Internet as if it were an enormous human body. The programs acted like electronic lymphocytes that targeted dangerous ideas and information.

During the last few years, CI programs had been released onto the Internet by the Brethren's computer team. The self-contained programs wandered unnoticed through thousands of computer systems. Sometimes they lingered like a lymphocyte in a person's home computer, waiting for an infectious idea to appear. If they found something suspicious, the program would return to the host computer in London for further instructions.

The Brethren scientists were also experimenting with a new interactive program that could actually punish the Brethren's enemies, like a cluster of white blood cells dealing with an infection. The CI program identified people who mentioned the Travelers or the Harlequins in their Internet communications. Once that was done, the program automatically placed a data-destroying virus in the owner's computer. A small proportion of the most dangerous computer viruses on the Internet had been created by the Brethren or their government allies. It was easy to place the blame on a seventeen-year-old computer hacker living in Poland.

Maya had been tracked down using both computational immunology and a conventional data scan. Three days earlier, the Harlequin had entered an automobile parts warehouse and killed some mercenaries. When Maya fled the area, she'd either had to walk, get a ride from someone, buy a car, or find public transportation. The computer center in London had sorted through Los Angeles police reports involving a young woman in the target area. When that wasn't successful, they entered taxi company computer systems to discover what passengers hired cabs during the four-hour period after the murders. These pickup and drop-off addresses were matched against information obtained by the CI programs. The central computer had the names and addresses of thousands of people who might help the Travelers or the Harlequins.

Five years ago, the Brethren's psychological evaluation team had plugged into the computers of the shopping clubs run by American grocery stores. Whenever a person bought something and used their discount card, the purchases were entered into a general database. During the initial study, the Brethren's psychologists attempted to match a person's food and alcohol consumption with their political affiliation. Boone had seen some of the statistical correlations and they were fascinating. Women living in northern California who bought more than three kinds of mustard were usually political liberals. Men who bought expensive bottled beer in East Texas were usually conservative. With a home address and data from a minimum of two hundred grocery-store purchases, the psychological evaluation team could accurately predict a person's attitude toward a mandatory citizen ID card.

Boone found it interesting to see what kind of people resisted social discipline and order. Opposition sometimes came from antitechnology tree huggers who ate organic food and shunned the factory food manufactured by the Vast Machine. But equally troublesome groups were organized by the high-technology freaks that ate candy bars for dinner and searched the Internet for rumors about the Travelers.

By the time Boone's plane flew over Pennsylvania, the monitoring center had sent a message to Boone's computer. *Drop-off address corresponds to residence of Thomas Walks the Ground—nephew of a terminated Native American Traveler. Computational immunology picked up negative remarks concerning the Brethren placed by this individual on a Crow tribe Web site.*

The jet plane banked steeply as they approached a regional airport near the Evergreen Foundation's research center. Boone switched off his computer and glanced over at Michael. The Brethren had found this young man and saved him from the Harlequins, but he might refuse to cooperate. It annoyed Boone that people still refused to recognize the truth. There was no need to worry about religion or philosophy; the truth was determined by whoever was in power.

* * *

THE CORPORATE JET landed at the Westchester County Airport and taxied to a private hangar. A few minutes later, Boone climbed down the steps of the plane. The sky was gray with clouds and there was a cold autumn feeling in the air.

Lawrence Takawa was waiting beside the ambulance that would transport Michael to the Evergreen Foundation Research Center. He gave orders to a team of paramedics, and then walked over to Boone.

"Welcome back," Takawa said. "How's Michael?"

"He'll be all right. Is everything ready at the center?"

"We were prepared two days ago, but we've had to make some last-minute adjustments. General Nash contacted the psychological evaluation team and they've given us a new strategy for dealing with Michael."

There was a slight tension in Lawrence Takawa's voice and Boone glanced at the young man. Every time he saw Nash's assistant, Lawrence was carrying something—a clipboard, a folder, a piece of paper—an object that proclaimed his authority.

"Do you have a problem with that?" Boone asked.

"The new strategy does seem rather *aggressive*," Lawrence said. "I don't know if that's necessary."

Boone turned on his heel and looked back at the jet. Dr. Potterfield supervised a team of paramedics as they eased the stretcher onto the tarmac. "Everything has changed now that the Harlequins have taken control of Gabriel. We have to make sure that Michael is working for our side."

Lawrence glanced at his clipboard. "I've read the preliminary reports about the two brothers. It sounds like they have a close relationship."

"Love is just another means of manipulation," Boone said. "We can use that emotion like we use hatred and fear."

Michael's stretcher was placed on a steel gurney and

pushed across the tarmac to the ambulance. Still looking worried, Dr. Potterfield remained with his patient.

"Do you understand our objective, Mr. Takawa?"

"Yes, sir."

Boone made a quick motion with his right hand that seemed to take in the plane and the ambulance and all the employees working for the Brethren. "This is our army," he said. "And Michael Corrigan has become our new weapon."

25

Vicki Fraser watched Hollis and Gabriel grab the motorcycle and lift it into the back of the van. "You drive," Hollis said as he tossed the keys to Vicki. He and Gabriel crouched beside the motorcycle while Maya remained in the front passenger seat with the shotgun on her lap.

They turned west and got lost on the narrow residential streets that cut through the Hollywood hills. Gabriel kept asking Maya questions about his family's background; he seemed desperate to find out everything as quickly as possible.

Vicki knew only a few facts about the Travelers and the Harlequins, and she listened carefully to the conversation. The ability to cross over into other realms seemed to be genetic, inherited from a parent or a relative, but occasionally new Travelers appeared without a family connection. Harlequins keep elaborate lineages of past Travelers and this was how Thorn had known about Gabriel's father.

Hollis lived a few blocks away from his storefront capoeira school. The single-family homes in the area had front yards and flower beds, but gang graffiti was spray-painted with dripping lines on the walls and billboards. When they turned off Florence Avenue, Hollis told Maya to move to the back of the van. Sitting up front, he instructed Vicki to slow down whenever they saw groups of young men wearing extra-large clothes and blue bandannas. Each time they stopped beside these gang members, Hollis would shake hands with the young men and use their street names.

"Some people might come around and ask about me," he told them. "Tell 'em they're in the wrong neighborhood."

The driveway of Hollis's two-bedroom house was blocked by a chain-link gate woven with plastic strips. Once they drove the van down the driveway and closed the gate, the vehicle was concealed from the street. Hollis unlocked the back door and they went into the house. Each room was clean and uncluttered, and Vicki didn't see any signs of a girl-friend. The curtains were made out of bedsheets, oranges were stored in a clean automobile hubcap, and one bedroom had been filled with barbells and turned into a gym.

Vicki sat down at the kitchen table with Gabriel and Maya. Hollis took an assault rifle out of a broom closet, snapped in an ammunition clip, and placed the weapon on the counter. "We'll be safe here," he said. "If someone attacks the house, I'll keep them busy. You jump over the wall to my neighbor's backyard."

Gabriel shook his head. "I don't want anyone to risk their life for me."

"I'm getting paid for this," Hollis said. "Maya is the one who's doing it for free."

Everyone watched as Hollis filled up a kettle and boiled water for tea. He opened the refrigerator and took out bread, cheese, strawberries, and two ripe mangos. "Is everybody hungry?" he asked. "I think I've got enough food."

Vicki decided to make a fruit salad while Hollis made grilled-cheese sandwiches. She liked standing at the counter and slicing up the strawberries. It was uncomfortable to sit next to Maya. The Harlequin looked exhausted, but she couldn't seem to relax. Vicki thought that it would be painful to go through life always being ready to kill, always expecting to be attacked. She remembered the letter that Isaac T. Jones had written to his congregation about Hell. There was a real Hell, of course. The Prophet had seen it with his own eyes. *But my brothers and sisters, your main concern should be the Hell you create within your own hearts.*

"You told me a few things about the Travelers when we were in the van," Gabriel said to Maya. "But what about the rest of it? Tell me about the Harlequins."

Maya adjusted the cord on her sword's carrying case. "Harlequins protect Travelers. That's all you need to know."

"Are there leaders and rules? Did someone order you to come to America?"

"No. It was my own decision."

"But why didn't your father come with you?"

Maya's eyes were focused on the salt shaker in the middle of the table. "My father was killed a week ago in Prague."

"The Tabula did it?" Hollis asked.

"Correct."

"What happened?"

"That's not your concern." Maya's voice was controlled, but her body was almost rigid with anger. Vicki felt like the Harlequin was ready to jump up and destroy all of them. "I've accepted an obligation to protect Gabriel and his brother. When that's done, I'm going to hunt down the man who killed my father."

"Did Michael and I have anything to do with this?" Gabriel asked.

"Not really. The Tabula have been hunting my father for most of his life. He was almost killed two years ago in Pakistan."

"I'm sorry—"

"Don't waste your emotions," Maya said. "We feel nothing for the rest of the world and expect nothing in return. When I was a child, my father used to tell me: *Verdammt durch das Fleisch. Gerettet durch das Blut.* It means: Damned by the flesh. Saved by the blood. Harlequins are condemned to fight a battle without end. But maybe the Travelers will save us from Hell."

"And how long have they been fighting this battle?" Hollis asked.

Maya pushed the hair away from her face. "My father said that we are an unbroken line of warriors that has lasted for thousands of years. On Passover, he would light candles and read from chapter eighteen in the book of John. After Jesus spends the night in the garden at Gethsemane, Judas shows up with Roman soldiers and officers sent by the chief priest."

"I know that passage in the Bible," Hollis said. "Actually, it's kind of a strange detail. Jesus is supposed to be the Prince of Peace. Throughout the New Testament, no one has ever mentioned weapons or bodyguards, but suddenly one of the disciples—"

"It's Peter," Vicki said.

"Right. Now I remember. Anyway, Peter draws a sword and cuts off the ear of the high priest's servant, a man named . . ."

This time Hollis glanced at Vicki, knowing that she would have the answer.

"Malchus."

"Right again." Hollis nodded. "So the bad guy is standing there in the garden with only one ear."

"Some scholars feel that Peter was a member of the Zealots," Maya said. "But my father believed that he was the first Harlequin to be mentioned in a historical document."

"Are you telling us that Jesus was a Traveler?" Vicki asked.

"Harlequins are fighters, not theologians. We don't make pronouncements about which Traveler is the true embodiment of the Light. The most important Traveler could be Jesus or Muhammad or the Buddha. Or it could be an obscure Hasidic rabbi who was killed in the Holocaust. We defend Travelers, but we don't judge their holiness. That's up to the faithful."

"But your father quoted from the Bible," Gabriel said.

"I come from the European branch of Harlequins and we have close ties with Christianity. In fact, some Harlequins read farther in the book of John. After Jesus was taken away, Peter—"

"—backed out on Jesus." Hollis turned away from the stove. "He was a disciple, but he denied his Lord three times."

"The legend is that Harlequins are damned by this. Because Peter didn't stay loyal at that moment, we must defend the Travelers until the end of time."

"Sounds like you don't buy that," Hollis said.

"It's just a story in the Bible. I don't accept it for myself, but I do believe that there is a secret history of the world. There have always been warriors defending pilgrims or other spiritual seekers. During the Crusades, a group of Christian knights began to protect the pilgrims traveling to the Holy Land. Baldwin II, the crusader king of Jerusalem, let these knights occupy part of the former Jewish temple. They began to call themselves the Poor Knights of Christ and Knights of the Temple of Solomon."

"Weren't they usually called the Templars?" Gabriel asked.

"Yes, that's the common name. The Templars became a rich, powerful order that controlled churches and castles throughout Europe. They owned ships and would lend money to European kings. Eventually the Templars stopped occupying the Holy Land and started to defend people who made spiritual journeys. They developed connections with heretical groups, the Bogomils in Bulgaria and the Cathars in France. These people were Gnostics who believed that the soul is trapped within the body. Only individuals given a secret knowledge are able to escape this prison and enter into different realms."

"Then the Templars were destroyed," Gabriel said.

Maya nodded slowly, as if reminding herself of a story she had learned long ago. "King Philip of France feared their power and wanted to seize their treasury. In 1307, he sent his troops into the Templar headquarters and arrested them for heresy. The grand master of the Templars was burned at the stake and the order ceased to exist—publicly. But only a few Templars were killed. Most of them went underground and continued their activities."

"Lunchtime," Hollis said. He set a plate of sandwiches on the table and Vicki finished making the fruit salad. Everyone sat down and began eating. Maya had relaxed slightly, but it was still an uncomfortable atmosphere. The Harlequin stared at Gabriel as if she was trying to decide if he had the power to cross over. Gabriel seemed to know what she was thinking. He looked down at his plate and picked at his food.

"But why are you called Harlequins?" Hollis asked Maya. "Isn't that some kind of actor with a painted face, like a clown?"

"We took that name in the seventeenth century. The Harlequin is one of the characters in Italian commedia dell'arte, usually a clever servant. The Harlequin character wears a costume with diamond shapes. Sometimes he plays the lute or carries a wooden sword. The Harlequin always wears a mask, concealing his identity."

"But that's an Italian name," Hollis said. "I was told that Harlequins used to be in Japan and Persia and just about every other place in the world."

"In the seventeenth century, the European Harlequins began to contact warriors from other cultures who were also defending Travelers. Our first alliance was with the Sikhs living in the Punjab. Like the Harlequins, devout Sikhs carry a ritual sword called a kirpan. Around the same time, we also made alliances with Buddhist and Sufi warriors. In the eighteenth century, we were joined by an order of Jewish fighters in Russia and Eastern Europe that defended rabbis who studied the Kabbalah."

Vicki turned to Gabriel. "Lion of the Temple, the Harlequin who defended the Prophet, came from a Jewish family."

Hollis looked amused. "You know, I've been in that town in Arkansas where they lynched Isaac Jones. Thirty years ago, the NAACP and some Jewish group got together and put up a plaque in honor of Zachary Goldman. They make it like a peace-and-love brotherhood thing because this Harlequin killed two racist bastards with a crowbar."

"Was there ever a Harlequin gathering?" Gabriel asked. "Did the different groups ever meet in one room?"

"That would never happen. Harlequins respect the randomness of battle. We don't like rules. Harlequin families are connected to each other by marriage, tradition, and friendship. Some families have been allies for hundreds of years. We don't have elected leaders or a constitution. There's just a Harlequin way of looking at the world. Some Harlequins fight because it's our destiny. Some of us fight to defend freedom. I'm not talking about the opportunity to buy fourteen different kinds of toothpaste or the insanity that drives a terrorist to blow up a bus. True freedom is tolerant. It gives people the right to live and think in new ways."

"I still want to know about 'Damned by the flesh, saved by the blood,'" Hollis said. "Whose blood are you talking about? The Tabula, the Harlequins, or the Travelers?"

"Take your pick," Maya said. "Maybe it's everyone."

*   *   *

THERE WAS ONLY one bedroom in the house. Hollis proposed that the two women share the bed while he and Gabriel sleep in the living room. Vicki could tell that Maya didn't like the idea. Now that she had found Gabriel, she seemed uncomfortable when he wasn't in her sight.

"It'll be okay," Vicki whispered. "Gabriel is only a few feet away. We can leave the door open if you want. Besides, Hollis has the rifle."

"Hollis is a mercenary. I don't know how much he's willing to sacrifice."

Maya walked several times from the living room to the bedroom as if she was memorizing the position of the doorways and walls. Then she went into the bedroom and slid the blades of her two knives between the box spring and the mattress. Both handles were sticking out. If she dropped her hand down, she could instantly pull a knife from its sheath. Finally she got into bed, and Vicki lay on the other side of the mattress.

"Good night," Vicki said, but Maya didn't answer her.

Vicki had slept with her older sister and various cousins during vacations and was used to their restless movements. Maya was different in every way. The Harlequin lay flat on her back with her hands clenched into fists. It looked as if an immense weight was pushing down on her body.

26

When Maya woke up the next morning she saw a black cat with a white throat sitting on the dresser. "What do you want?" she whispered, but didn't get an answer. The cat jumped down onto the floor, glided through the doorway, and left her alone.

She heard voices and peered out the bedroom window. Hollis and Gabriel were standing in the driveway, inspecting the damaged motorcycle. Buying a new tire meant a monetary transaction and contact with a business that was connected to the Vast Machine. The Tabula would know all about the damaged bike and activate their computer search programs to monitor motorcycle tire sales in the Los Angeles area.

Considering her next move, she went into the bathroom and took a quick shower. The finger shields that had gotten her through United States immigration were starting to peel off her index fingers like dead skin. She got dressed, strapped both knives onto her arms, and checked her other weapons. The black cat reappeared when she left the bathroom and led her into the hallway. Vicki was washing dishes in the sink.

"I see you met Garvey."

"Is that his name?"

"Yes. He doesn't like to be touched, and he doesn't purr. I don't think that's normal."

"I wouldn't know," Maya said. "I never had a pet."

There was a coffeemaker on the counter. Maya poured coffee into a bright yellow mug and mixed in some cream.

"I just made some corn bread. Are you hungry?"

"Definitely."

Vicki cut a thick slice of corn bread and placed it in a bowl. The two young women sat together at the table. Maya smeared some butter on the corn bread, and then added a spoonful of blackberry jam. The first bite was delicious and she felt a moment of unexpected pleasure. Everything in the kitchen was clean and organized. Patches of sunlight glowed on the green linoleum floor. Although Hollis had broken away from the church, a framed photograph of Isaac T. Jones hung on the wall beside the refrigerator.

"Hollis is going to buy some motorcycle parts," Vicki said. "But he wants Gabriel to keep out of sight and stay here."

Maya nodded as she swallowed her corn bread. "That's a good plan."

"So what are you going to do?"

"I'm not quite sure. I need to contact my friend in Europe."

Vicki picked up the dirty dishes and took them over to the sink. "Do you think the Tabula know that Hollis was driving yesterday?"

"Maybe. It depends what those three riders saw as we passed them."

"And what will happen if they learn about Hollis?"

Maya's voice was deliberately flat and unemotional. "They'll try to capture him, torture him for information, and kill him."

Vicki turned with a dish towel in her hand. "That's what I told Hollis, but he made a joke about it. He said he's always looking for new sparring partners."

"I think Hollis can protect himself, Vicki. He's a very good fighter."

"He's much too confident. I think he should . . ."

The screen door squeaked open and Hollis strolled in. "Okay. I've got my shopping list." He smiled at Vicki. "Why don't you come with me? We'll buy a new tire and pick up some food for lunch."

"Do you need money?" Maya asked.

"You got any?"

Maya reached into her pocket and pulled out some twenty-dollar bills. "Use cash. After you buy the tire, leave the store right away."

"No reason to hang around."

"Avoid stores with surveillance cameras in the parking lot. The cameras are able to photograph license plate numbers."

Maya watched Vicki and Hollis leave. Gabriel was still outside in the driveway, pulling the tire off the motorcycle's wheel rim. Maya made sure the gate was closed, concealing Gabriel from anyone driving down the street. She thought about discussing the next step with him, but decided that she needed to talk to Linden first. Gabriel had seemed overwhelmed by everything she had told him yesterday. He probably needed some time to think it over.

Maya returned to the bedroom, switched on her laptop computer, and got onto the Internet with her satellite phone. Linden was either asleep or away from his computer. It took her an hour to find him and follow him to a safe conversation room. Using soft language that wouldn't trigger Carnivore, she described what had happened.

"Our business competitors responded with aggressive marketing tactics. Right now I'm at my employee's house with our new associate." Maya used a code based on random prime numbers and gave Linden the address to the house.

The French Harlequin didn't answer and after a few minutes she typed: "Understand?"

"Does our new associate have the ability to travel to distant locations?"

"Not at this time."

"Do you see any indications of that ability?"

"No. He's just an ordinary citizen."

"You must introduce him to a teacher who can evaluate his power."

"Not our responsibility," Maya typed. Harlequins were only supposed to find and protect Travelers. They didn't get involved in anyone's spiritual journey.

Once again, there was a delay of several minutes as Linden appeared to be considering his response. Finally words began to appear on the computer screen. "Our competitors have gained control of the older brother and have flown him to a research facility near New York City. They plan to evaluate his ability and train him. At this point, we don't know their larger objective. But we must use all our resources to oppose them."

"And our new associate is our main resource?"

"Correct. A race has started. At this moment, our competitors are winning."

"What if he won't cooperate?"

"Use any means necessary to change his mind. A teacher is living in the southwestern United States, protected by a community of friends. Take the associate to this location in three days. During this time, I will contact our friends and tell them that you're coming. Your destination is . . ." Another pause and then a long set of coded numbers appeared on the screen.

"Confirm transmission," Linden typed.

Maya didn't answer.

The words appeared again, this time in capital letters that demanded her agreement. "CONFIRM TRANSMISSION."

Don't answer him, Maya told herself. She considered leaving the house and taking Gabriel across the border into Mexico. That was the safe thing to do. A few seconds passed, then she placed her fingers on the computer keyboard and typed slowly. "Information received."

The screen went blank and Linden's presence disappeared. Maya decoded the numbers with her computer and discovered that she was supposed to travel to a town called San Lucas in southern Arizona. And what will happen there? New enemies? Another confrontation? She knew that the Tabula would be looking for them using the full power of the Vast Machine.

She returned to the kitchen and opened the screen door. Gabriel sat on the driveway next to the motorcycle. He had found a coat hanger, straightened it out, and bent one end of the metal rod. Now he was using this improvised tool to make sure the rear wheel axle was properly aligned.

"Gabriel, I'd like to look at the sword you're carrying."

"Go ahead. It's sticking out of my knapsack. I left it next to the couch in the living room."

She remained in the doorway, not knowing what to say. He didn't seem to realize the disrespect he was showing toward his weapon.

Gabriel stopped working. "What's wrong?"

"This particular sword is very special. It's best if you handed it to me yourself."

He looked surprised, then smiled and shrugged his shoulders.

"Sure. If that's what you want. Give me a minute."

Maya brought her suitcase into the living room and sat on the couch. She heard water running through the plumbing as Gabriel washed the grease off his hands in the kitchen. When he entered the living room, he stared at her as if she were a crazy person who might attack him. Maya realized that the outline of her knives was visible beneath the sleeves of the cotton pullover.

Thorn had warned her about the awkward relationship between Harlequins and Travelers. Just because Harlequins risked their lives to defend Travelers didn't mean the two groups liked each other. People who crossed over into different realms usually became more spiritual. But Harlequins would always remain earthbound, tainted by the death and violence of the Fourth Realm.

When Maya was fourteen years old, she traveled through Eastern Europe with Mother Blessing. The moment the Irish Harlequin gave a command, both citizens and drones jumped to obey her. *Yes, madam. Of course, madam. We hope there aren't any problems.* Mother Blessing had stepped over some kind of line, and people sensed it immediately. Maya realized that she still wasn't strong enough to have that kind of power.

Gabriel went to the knapsack and took out the sword— still in its black lacquer scabbard. He presented it to Maya with two hands.

She felt the sword's perfect balance and knew immediately that it was a special weapon. The ray-skin hilt was wrapped in thread with a fitting of dark green jade.

"My father passed this on to your father when you were a child."

"I don't remember that," Gabriel said. "It was always around when I was growing up."

Holding the scabbard on her knee, Maya drew the sword slowly, then held it up and stared down the length of the blade. This was a tachi-style sword, a weapon meant to be worn with the edge downward. The shape was perfect, but the real beauty was shown in the hamon, the border between the tempered edge of the blade and the untempered metal of the rest of the sword. The bright areas of the steel, called the nie, contrasted with a soft pearl-white haze. It reminded Maya of patches of ground among a light spring snow.

"Why is this sword so important?" Gabriel asked.

"It was used by Sparrow, a Japanese Harlequin. He was the only Harlequin left in Japan: the last survivor of a noble tradition. Sparrow was known for his courage and resourcefulness. Then he allowed a weakness in his life."

"What was that?"

"He fell in love with a young college student. Yakuza working for the Tabula found out and kidnapped this woman. When Sparrow tried to rescue her, he was killed."

"Then how did the sword get to America?"

"My father tracked down the college student. She was pregnant and hiding from the Yakuza. He helped her flee to America and she allowed him to take the sword."

"If this particular thing was so important, then why didn't your father keep it?"

"It's a talisman. That means that it's very old and contains its own power. A talisman can be an amulet or a mirror—or a sword. Travelers can take talismans with them when they cross over to another realm."

"So that's why we ended up owning it."

"You can't own a talisman, Gabriel. Its power exists independently of human greed and desire. We can only use a talisman or pass it on to someone else." Maya looked again at the edge of the sword. "This particular talisman needs to be cleaned and oiled. If you don't mind . . ."

"Sure. Go ahead." Gabriel looked embarrassed. "I didn't spend time polishing it."

Maya had brought along supplies to maintain her own sword. Reaching into her suitcase, she picked up a piece of soft *hosho* paper made from the inner bark of a mulberry tree. Willow had taught her how to treat a weapon with respect. She tilted the sword slightly and began to wipe the dirt and smudge marks off the blade.

"I've got some bad news, Gabriel. A few minutes ago I contacted another Harlequin through the Internet. My friend has a spy inside the Tabula organization and he confirms that they've captured your brother."

Gabriel leaned forward in his chair. "What can we do?" he asked. "Where are they holding him?"

"He's being kept at a guarded research facility near New York City. Even if I knew the location, it would be difficult to free him."

"Why can't we contact the police?"

"The average policeman might be honest, but that doesn't help our cause. Our enemies are able to manipulate the Vast Machine—the worldwide system of computers that monitors and controls our society."

Gabriel nodded. "My parents called it the Grid."

"The Tabula can break into police computers and insert false reports. They've probably placed a message into the system that you and I are wanted for murder."

"All right, forget about the police. Let's go to where they're keeping Michael."

"I'm just one person, Gabriel. I've hired Hollis to fight, but I don't know if he's reliable. My father used to call fighters 'swords.' It's just a different way to count up the people on your side. Right now, I don't have enough swords to attack a research facility defended by the Tabula."

"We've got to help my brother."

"I don't think they'll kill him. The Tabula have a plan that involves something called a quantum computer and the use of a Traveler. They want to train your brother to cross over into other realms. All this is new. I don't know how they're going to do it. Travelers are usually taught by someone called a Pathfinder."

"What's that?"

"Give me a minute and I'll explain . . ."

Maya checked the blade again and saw a few small scratches and pits in the metal. Only a Japanese expert called a *togishi* could sharpen this weapon. All she could do was cover the blade with oil so that it wouldn't rust. Picking up a small brown bottle, she poured oil of cloves on some cotton gauze. The sweet smell of cloves filled the room as she gently wiped the blade. For a second, she knew something with complete certainty. This sword was very powerful. It had killed and would kill again.

"A Pathfinder is a special kind of teacher. Usually it's a person with spiritual training. Pathfinders aren't Travelers—they can't cross over into other realms—but they can help someone who has the gift."

"And where do you find them?"

"My friend has given me the location of a Pathfinder living in Arizona. This person will find out if you have the power."

"What I really want to do is fix my motorcycle and get out of here."

"That would be foolish. Without my protection, the Tabula would eventually find you."

"I don't need anybody's protection, Maya. I've stayed off the Grid for most of my life."

"But now they're looking for you with all their resources and power. You don't understand what they can do."

Gabriel looked angry. "I saw what happened to my father. The Harlequins didn't save us. Nobody did."

"I think you should come with me."

"Why? What's the point?"

Still holding the sword, she spoke slowly, remembering what Thorn had taught her. "Some people believe that the natural tendency of mankind is to be intolerant, hateful, and cruel. The powerful want to hold on to their position and they will destroy anyone who challenges them."

"That seems pretty clear," Gabriel said.

"The urge to control others is very strong, but the desire for freedom and the ability to show compassion will always survive. Darkness is everywhere, but Light still appears."

"And you believe this is because of the Travelers?"

"They appear in every generation. The Travelers leave this world and then return to help others. They inspire humanity, give us new ideas, and lead us forward—"

"Maybe my father was one of these people, but that doesn't mean that Michael and I have the same ability. I'm not going to Arizona to meet this teacher. I want to find Michael and help him escape."

Gabriel glanced at the doorway as if he'd already decided to leave. Maya tried to find the calmness she felt when fighting. She had to say the right thing or he would run away.

"Perhaps you'll find your brother in another realm."

"You don't know that."

"I can't promise anything. If you're both Travelers, it could happen. The Tabula are going to teach Michael how to cross over."

Gabriel looked her straight in the eyes. For a moment, she was startled by his courage and strength. Then he lowered his head and, once again, became an ordinary young man wearing jeans and a faded T-shirt.

"Maybe you're lying to me," he said quietly.

"You'll just have to take that risk."

"If we go to Arizona, are you sure we're going to find this Pathfinder?"

Maya nodded. "He lives near a town called San Lucas."

"I'll go there and meet this person. Then I'll decide what I'm going to do."

He stood up quickly and left the room. Maya remained on the couch with the jade sword. The blade was oiled perfectly and the steel flashed as she swung the sword through the air. Put it away, she told herself. Hide its power in the darkness.

* * *

VOICES CAME FROM the kitchen. Stepping softly so that the wooden floor wouldn't creak, Maya entered the dining room and peered through a crack in the door. Hollis and Vicki had returned. They were preparing lunch while they gossiped about their church. Apparently two old women had argued about who could bake the best wedding cake, and the congregation had taken sides.

"So when my cousin picked Miss Anne to bake her cake, Miss Grace came to the reception and pretended to get sick eating it."

"That doesn't surprise me. But I am surprised she didn't slip a dead cockroach into the cake batter."

They both laughed at the same time. Hollis smiled at Vicki, and then looked away quickly. Maya made the floor creak to let them know she was in the next room, waited a few seconds, and entered the kitchen. "I talked to Gabriel. He'll put the new tire on and we'll leave tomorrow morning."

"Where are you going?" Hollis asked.

"Away from Los Angeles. That's all you need to know."

"Okay. That's your choice." Hollis shrugged his shoulders. "Can you give me any information at all?"

Maya sat down at the kitchen table. "It's a security risk to use checks or make bank account transfers. The Tabula have gotten very skillful at monitoring things like that. In a few days, you'll get a magazine or a catalog in an envelope with a German postmark. Hundred-dollar bills will be hidden in the pages. It might take two or three deliveries, but we'll pay you $5,000."

"That's too much money," Hollis said. "It was a thousand dollars a day and I've only been helping you for two days."

Maya wondered if Hollis would have said the same thing without Vicki watching him. If you liked another person, that made you foolish and vulnerable. Hollis wanted to look noble in front of this young woman.

"You helped me find Gabriel. I'm paying you for your services."

"And that's it?"

"Yes. The contract is canceled."

"Come on, Maya. The Tabula aren't going to give up. They'll keep looking for you and Gabriel. If you really want to confuse them, you should give out some false information. Make it look like you're still in Los Angeles."

"And how would you do that?"

"I've got a few ideas." Hollis glanced at Vicki. Yes, she was watching him. "You Harlequins are paying me $5,000. So I'll give you three more days of work."

27

The next morning, Vicki woke early and made coffee and biscuits for everyone. After eating, they went outside and Hollis inspected Maya's van. He poured a quart of oil into the crankcase and switched the van's license plates with those of a broken-down car owned by a neighbor. Then he rummaged through his closets and came up with supplies: plastic water bottles and extra clothes for Gabriel, a long cardboard box to hide the shotgun, and a road map that would guide them to southern Arizona.

Maya proposed that they carry the motorcycle in the back of the van—at least until they got out of California— but Gabriel rejected the idea. "You're overreacting," he told her. "Right now, there are more than a hundred thousand vehicles traveling on the Los Angeles freeways. I don't see how the Tabula could find me."

"A human isn't doing the searching, Gabriel. The Tabula can access the surveillance cameras that are attached to the freeway signs. Right now, a computer scanning program is processing images, looking for your motorcycle's license plate."

After five minutes of arguing, Hollis found some nylon

cord in his garage and attached Gabriel's knapsack to the back of the motorcycle. It appeared to be a casual, improvised way to carry the knapsack, but it also concealed the license plate. Gabriel nodded and kick-started the bike as Maya climbed into the van. She rolled down the side window and nodded to Vicki and Hollis.

By now, Vicki was used to Harlequin manners. Maya found it difficult to say "thank you" or "goodbye." Perhaps her behavior was just rudeness or pride, but Vicki had decided that there was another reason. Harlequins had accepted a powerful obligation: to defend Travelers with their lives. To acknowledge a friendship with anyone outside their world would be an additional burden. That's why they preferred mercenaries who could be used and thrown away.

"From now on, you should be very careful," Maya told Hollis. "The Tabula have developed a tracking system for electronic transactions. They're also experimenting with splicers—genetically altered animals that can be used to kill people. Your best strategy is to be disciplined but unpredictable. Tabula computers find it difficult to calculate an equation involving randomness."

"You just send the money," Hollis said. "Don't worry about me."

Hollis pushed open the driveway gate. Gabriel went out first, and Maya followed him. The van and the motorcycle cruised slowly down the street, turned the corner, and then they were gone.

"What do you think?" Vicki asked. "Will they be safe?"

Hollis shrugged his shoulders. "Gabriel has been living a very independent life. I don't know if he's going to accept orders from a Harlequin."

"So what do you think of Maya?"

"On the fighting circuit down in Brazil, you walk out to the middle of the ring at the beginning of a match and the referee makes the introduction and you stare at your opponent's eyes. Some people think the fight is already over at that point. One man is just pretending to be brave while the winner is looking through the obstacle to the other side."

"And Maya is like that?"

"She accepts the possibility of death and it doesn't seem to frighten her. That's a big advantage for a warrior."

* * *

VICKI HELPED HOLLIS wash the dishes and clean up the kitchen. Hollis asked if she wanted to go with him to his school and take the beginning capoeira class at five o'clock, but Vicki said no, thank you very much. It was time to go home.

They didn't talk in the car. Hollis kept glancing at her, but she didn't look back. When Vicki had taken a shower that morning, she had given in to her curiosity and searched the bathroom like a detective. In the bottom drawer of the sink cabinet, she found a clean nightgown, a can of hair spray, sanitary napkins, and five new toothbrushes. She didn't expect Hollis to be celibate, but the five toothbrushes, each in a plastic case, suggested an endless series of women pulling off their clothes and lying down on his bed. In the morning Hollis would make coffee, drive the woman home, throw away the used toothbrush, and start again.

When they reached her street in Baldwin Hills, Vicki told Hollis to park at the corner. She didn't want her mother to see them in the car and come running out of the house. Josetta would assume the worst about Hollis—that her daughter's rebellion had been caused by a secret relationship with this man.

She turned to Hollis. "How are you going to convince the Tabula that Gabriel is still in Los Angeles?"

"I don't have an exact plan, but I'll come up with something. Before Gabriel left, I recorded his voice with my tape recorder. If they hear him talking on a local phone call, they'll assume he's still in the city."

"And when that's over, what will you do next?"

"Take the money and fix up my school. We need an air-conditioning system and the landlord won't buy one."

She must have shown her disappointment because Hollis looked annoyed. "Come on, Vicki. Don't act like a church girl. For the last twenty-four hours you haven't been that way at all."

"And what way is that?"

"Always making judgments. Quoting Isaac Jones every chance you get."

"Yes. I forgot. You don't believe in anything."

"I believe in seeing things clearly. And it seems obvious to me that the Tabula have all the money and the power. There's a good chance they're going to find Gabriel and Maya. She's a Harlequin so she won't surrender . . ." Hollis shook his head. "I predict she'll be dead in a couple of weeks."

"And you're not going to do anything about it?"

"I'm not an idealist. I left the church a long time ago. Like I said, I'll finish this job. But I'm not going to fight for a lost cause."

Vicki took her hand off the door handle and faced him. "What is your training for, Hollis? To make money? Is that all? Shouldn't you be fighting for something that helps others? The Tabula want to capture and control anyone who could be a Traveler. They want the rest of us to act like little robots, obeying the faces we see on television, hating and fearing people we've never met."

Hollis shrugged his shoulders. "I'm not saying you're wrong. But that doesn't change anything."

"And if a great battle takes place, which side will you be on?"

She grabbed the door handle again, getting ready to go, but Hollis reached out and touched her left hand. With just a little tug, he pulled her toward him, then leaned over and kissed her on the lips. It felt as if light was flowing through both of them, only to be united for a moment. Vicki pulled away and opened the door.

"Do you like me?" he asked. "Admit that you like me."

"Debt Not Paid, Hollis. Debt Not Paid."

Vicki hurried down the sidewalk and cut across a neighbor's lawn to her front door. Don't stop, she told herself. Don't look back.

28

Maya studied the map and saw that an interstate highway led straight from Los Angeles to Tucson. If they followed this thick green line they would be there in six or seven hours. A direct route was efficient, but also more dangerous. The Tabula would be looking for them on the main highways. Maya decided to cross the Mojave Desert into southern Nevada, then take local roads through Arizona.

The freeway system was confusing, but Gabriel knew where to go. He rode his motorcycle in front of her like a police escort, gesturing with his right hand to tell her to slow down, change lanes, take this ramp. At first they followed the interstate into Riverside County. About every twenty miles, they'd pass a shopping center with massive warehouse stores. Clustered around the stores were residential communities of identical houses with red tile roofs and bright green lawns.

All these cities had names that appeared on the road signs, but to Maya they were as artificial as the plywood sets on an opera stage. She couldn't believe that anyone had traveled to these locations in a covered wagon to plow the land

and build a schoolhouse. The freeway cities looked willful, deliberate, as if some Tabula corporation had designed the entire community and the citizens had followed the plan: buying homes, getting jobs, having children, and giving them up to the Vast Machine.

When they reached a town called Twentynine Palms, they got off the main highway and turned onto a two-lane asphalt road that led across the Mojave Desert. This was a different America from the freeway communities. At first the landscape was flat and barren, and then they began to pass piles of red rocks—each hill as separate and distinct as the pyramids. There were yucca plants with sword-shaped leaves and Joshua trees with twisted branches that reminded her of upraised arms.

Now that they were off the freeway, Gabriel began to enjoy the journey. He leaned from side to side, making graceful S curves down the middle of the empty road. All of a sudden, he began to go much faster. Maya stepped on the accelerator, trying to keep up, but Gabriel kicked into fifth gear and roared ahead of her. Furious, she watched him grow smaller and smaller until bike and rider disappeared into the horizon.

She began to get worried when Gabriel didn't return. Had he decided to forget about the Pathfinder and go off alone? Or had something bad happened? Maybe the Tabula had captured him and now they were waiting for her to appear. Ten minutes passed. Twenty minutes. When she was almost frantic, a tiny dot appeared on the road in front of her. It grew larger, and finally Gabriel emerged from the haze. He was going very fast when he blew past her in the opposite direction, smiling and waving his hand. Fool, she thought. Damn fool.

Glancing in the rearview mirror, she watched Gabriel turn around and race to catch up with her. When he passed her again, she honked the horn and flashed the headlights. Gabriel pulled out into the opposite lane and drifted alongside the van as Maya rolled down the window.

"You can't do that!" she shouted.

Gabriel did something to the motorcycle so that it got even louder. He pointed to his ear and shook his head. Sorry. Can't hear you.

"Slow down! You've got to stay with me!"

He grinned like a mischievous boy, pulled back on the accelerator, and raced away from her. Once again, he headed down the road and was absorbed by the haze. A mirage appeared on a dry lake bed. The false water sparkled and flowed beneath the white sun.

* * *

WHEN THEY REACHED the town of Saltus, Gabriel stopped at a combination general store and restaurant that was designed to look like a pioneer's log cabin. He filled up his motorcycle's fuel tank and went into the building.

Maya pumped some gasoline into the van, paid the old man running the general store, and passed through an open doorway into the restaurant. The room was decorated with farm tools and wagon-wheel light fixtures. The stuffed heads of deer and mountain sheep hung on the walls. It was late in the afternoon and no other customers were there.

She sat in a booth opposite Gabriel and they spoke to a bored waitress wearing a stained apron. The food came quickly. Gabriel wolfed down his hamburger and ordered a second one while Maya picked at her mushroom omelet.

People who crossed over into different realms often became spiritual leaders, but Gabriel Corrigan didn't show any sign of spirituality. Most of the time he acted like an ordinary young man who liked motorcycles and put too much ketchup on his food. He was just another citizen—that's all—and yet Maya felt uncomfortable being around him. The men she had known in London loved the sound of their own voice. They listened to you with one ear while they waited for their turn to speak. Gabriel was different.

He watched her carefully, focused on what she was saying, and seemed to respond to her different moods.

"Is your name really Maya?" he asked.

"Yes."

"So what's your last name?"

"I don't have one."

"Everyone has a last name," Gabriel said. "Unless you're a rock star or a king or something like that."

"In London, I called myself Judith Strand. I entered this country with a passport that said I'm a German citizen named Siegrid Kohler. I'm carrying backup passports from three different countries. But 'Maya' is my Harlequin name."

"What does that mean?"

"Harlequins pick one special name when we're twelve or thirteen years old. There's no ritual to follow. You simply decide on a name and tell your family. Names don't always have an obvious meaning. The French Harlequin who calls himself 'Linden' is named after a tree with a heart-shaped leaf. A very fierce Harlequin from Ireland calls herself Mother Blessing."

"So why are you called Maya?"

"I picked a name that would annoy my father. Maya is another name for the goddess Devi, the consort of Shiva. But it also means illusion, the false world of the senses. That's what I wanted to believe in—the things I could see and hear and feel. Not the Travelers and the different realms."

Gabriel looked around at the dingy little restaurant. WE TRUST IN GOD, said a sign. ALL OTHERS, PAY CASH.

"What about your brothers and sisters? Are they also running around with swords looking for Travelers?"

"I was an only child. My mother came from a Sikh family that had lived in Britain for three generations. She gave me this . . ." Maya raised her right wrist and displayed the steel bracelet. "This is called a *kara*. It reminds you not to do anything that could cause shame or disgrace."

Maya wanted to finish the meal and leave the restaurant.

If they were outside, then she could put her sunglasses back on and conceal her eyes.

"What was your father like?" Gabriel asked.

"You don't need to know about him."

"Was he crazy? Did he beat you?"

"Of course not. He was usually in some other country trying to save a Traveler. My father never told us where he was going. We never knew if he was alive or dead. He would miss my birthday or Christmas, and then would show up at some unexpected moment. Father always acted like everything was normal, that he had just been around the corner for a pint of beer. I missed him, I guess. But I also didn't want him to come home. That meant we had to resume my lessons."

"And he taught you how to use a sword?"

"That was just one part of it. I also had to learn karate, judo, kickboxing, and how to fire different kinds of guns. He tried to make me think a certain way. If we shopped at a store, he'd suddenly ask me to describe every person we had seen. If we were riding in the Underground together, he'd tell me to look at everyone in the car and determine the sequence of battle. You're supposed to attack the strongest person first and work your way down."

Gabriel nodded as if he understood what she was talking about. "What else did he do?"

"When I got older, Father would hire thieves or drug addicts to follow me through the streets after school. I had to notice them and figure out a way to escape. My training was always out on the street, as dangerous as possible."

She was about to describe the fight in the Underground with the football thugs, but fortunately the waitress arrived with the second hamburger. Gabriel ignored it and tried to continue the conversation.

"It sounds like you didn't want to become a Harlequin."

"I tried to live a citizen life. It wasn't possible."

"Are you angry about that?"

"We can't always choose our path."

"You seem angry at your father."

The words slipped beneath her guard and touched her heart. For a second, she thought she was going to start crying so hard that it would shatter the world that surrounded them. "I—I respected him," she stammered.

"That doesn't mean you can't be angry."

"Forget about my father," Maya said. "He has nothing to do with our current situation. Right now the Tabula are looking for us and I'm trying to protect you. Stop racing up the road on your motorcycle. I need to keep you in sight the whole time."

"We're in the middle of the desert, Maya. No one is going to see us."

"The Grid still exists even if you don't see the lines." Maya stood up and slung the sword carrier over her shoulder. "Finish your meal. I'll be outside."

*   *   *

FOR THE REST of the day, Gabriel rode in front of her and matched the speed of the van. The sun went down and melted into the horizon as they continued traveling northeast. About forty miles from the Nevada border she saw the green-and-blue neon sign of a small motel.

Maya reached into her purse and pulled out the random number generator. An even number meant keep driving. An odd number meant stop here. She pressed the button. The RNG showed 88167, so she flashed her headlights and turned off into the gravel courtyard. The motel was shaped like a U. Twelve rooms. An empty swimming pool that had grass growing on the bottom.

Maya got out of the van and walked over to Gabriel. They needed to share a room so that she could watch him, but Maya decided not to mention that fact. Don't push him, she thought. Make up an excuse.

"We don't have a lot of money. It's cheaper if we share a room."

"That's okay," Gabriel said, and followed her into the lighted office.

The hotel owner was a chain-smoking old woman who smirked when Maya wrote *Mr. and Mrs. Thompson* on a little white card. "We'll pay cash," Maya said.

"Yes, dear. That's fine. And try not to break anything."

Two saggy beds. A small table and two plastic chairs. There was an air conditioner in the room, but Maya decided to leave it off. Noise from the fan would muffle the sound of anyone approaching. She slid open the window above the beds, then went into the bathroom. Tepid water trickled out of the shower head. It had a flat, alkaline smell, and it was difficult to rinse her thick hair. She came out wearing a T-shirt and athletic shorts and Gabriel took his turn.

Maya pulled the blanket off her bed, and then slipped beneath the sheet with her sword lying a few inches from her right leg. Five minutes later, Gabriel stepped out of the bathroom with wet hair, wearing a T-shirt and underwear. He walked slowly across the worn carpet and sat down on the edge of his bed. Maya thought he was going to say something, but he changed his mind and crawled under the covers.

Lying faceup, Maya began to catalog all the sounds around her. The wind lightly pushing against the screen. An occasional truck or car passing down the highway. She was falling asleep, half in a dream, and then she was a child again, standing alone in the Underground tunnel as the three men attacked her. No. Don't think about that.

Opening her eyes, she turned her head slightly and looked across the room at Gabriel. His head was on the pillow and his body was a soft form beneath the sheet. Maya wondered if he had lots of girlfriends back in Los Angeles who flattered him and said "I love you." She was suspicious of the word *love*. They kept using it in songs and television commercials. If love was a slippery, deceitful word—a word for citizens—then what was the most intimate thing a Harlequin could say to another person?

Then the phrase came back to her, the last thing she had heard her father say in Prague: *I would die for you.*

There was a creaking noise as Gabriel moved restlessly on his bed. A few minutes passed, and then he propped his head up on two pillows. "You got angry when we were eating lunch this afternoon. Maybe I shouldn't have asked all those questions."

"You don't need to know about my life, Gabriel."

"I didn't have a normal childhood either. My parents were suspicious of everything. They were always hiding or running away."

Silence. Maya wondered if she should say something. Were Harlequins and the people they protected supposed to have personal conversations?

"Did you ever meet my father?" she asked. "Do you remember him?"

"No. But I do remember seeing the jade sword for the first time. I was probably eight years old."

He remained silent and she didn't ask any more questions. Some memories were like scars that you kept hidden from other people. A trailer truck passed the motel. A car. Another truck. If a vehicle turned into the courtyard, she would hear tires crunching across the loose gravel.

"I can forget about my family when I'm jumping out of a plane or riding my bike." Gabriel's voice was quiet, the words absorbed by the darkness. "Then I slow down and it comes back again . . ."

29

"All of my early memories are about riding in our car or pickup truck. We were always packing our bags and leaving. I guess that's why Michael and I were obsessed with having a home.

"If we lived in one place for more than a few weeks, we'd pretend we were going to be there forever. Then a car would drive by our motel more than twice or a gas station attendant would ask Father an unusual question. Our parents would start whispering to each other and they'd wake us up at midnight and we'd have to get dressed in the darkness. Before the sun came up, we'd be back on the road, driving to nowhere."

"Did your parents ever give you an explanation?" Maya asked.

"Not really. And that's what made it so scary. They'd just say 'It's dangerous here' or 'Bad men are looking for us.' And then we'd pack and leave."

"And you never complained about this?"

"Not in front of my father. He always wore shabby clothes and work boots, but there was something about him—a look in his eyes—that made him seem very powerful and wise. Strangers were always telling secrets to my father as if he could help them."

"What was your mother like?"

Gabriel was silent for minute. "I keep thinking about the last time I saw her before she died. It's hard to get that out of my mind. When we were little she was always so positive about everything. If our truck broke down on a country road, she'd take us out into the fields and we'd start looking for wildflowers or a lucky four-leaf clover."

"And how did you behave?" Maya asked. "Were you a good child or mischievous?"

"I was pretty quiet, always keeping things to myself."

"What about Michael?"

"He was the confident older brother. If we needed a storage locker or extra towels from the hotel manager, my parents sent Michael to deal with it.

"Being on the road was okay, sometimes. We seemed to have enough money even though Father didn't work. My mother hated television, so she was always telling us stories or reading books out loud. She liked Mark Twain and Charles Dickens, and I remember how excited we were when she read us *The Moonstone* by Wilkie Collins. My father taught us how to tune a car engine, how to read a map, and how not to get lost in a strange city. Instead of studying school textbooks, we stopped at every historical marker on the highway.

"When I was eight and Michael was twelve, our parents sat us down and told us they were going to buy a farm. We'd stop in little towns, read the newspaper, and drive out to farms that had 'for sale' signs on the lawn. Every place seemed okay to me, but Father always came back to the truck shaking his head and telling Mom that 'The terms weren't right.' After a few weeks of this, I started to think that 'the terms' were a group of mean old women who liked to say 'no.'

"We drove up to Minnesota, and then turned west toward South Dakota. At Sioux Falls, Father learned about a farm for sale in a town called Unityville. It was a nice area with rolling hills and lakes and fields of alfalfa. The farm was half a mile from the road, concealed by a grove of spruce trees. There was a big red barn, a few toolsheds, and a rickety two-story house.

"After a lot of haggling, Father bought the property from a man who wanted cash and we moved in two weeks later. Everything seemed normal until the end of the month, when the electric power went off. At first, Michael and I thought that something was broken, but our parents called us into the kitchen and told us that electric power and a telephone connected us to the rest of the world."

"Your father knew you were being hunted," Maya said. "He wanted to live apart from the Vast Machine."

"Father never mentioned that. He just said that we were going to call ourselves 'Miller' and everyone was going to pick a new first name. Michael wanted to call himself Robin, the Boy Wonder, but Father didn't like that idea. After a lot of talk, Michael decided to be David and I picked the name Jim, after Jim Hawkins in *Treasure Island*.

"That was the same night Father brought out all the weapons and showed us where each one was going to be stored. The jade sword was in our parents' bedroom and we weren't allowed to touch it without permission."

Maya smiled to herself, thinking about the valuable sword hidden in a closet. She wondered if it had been propped up in a corner, next to some old shoes.

"An assault rifle was behind the couch in the front parlor and the shotgun was stored in the kitchen. Father kept his .38 in a shoulder holster beneath his jacket when he was working. This wasn't a big issue when Michael and I were growing up. The guns were just another fact that we accepted. You said that my father was a Traveler. Well, I never saw him float away or disappear or anything like that."

"A person's body stays in this world," Maya said. "It's the Light within you that crosses the barriers."

"Twice a year, Father would get in the pickup truck and go away for a few weeks. He always told us that he was fishing, but he never came back with any fish. When he was home, he would make furniture or weed the garden. Usually he'd stop working around four o'clock in the afternoon. He'd take Michael and me into the barn and teach us judo and karate and kendo with bamboo swords. Michael hated practicing. He thought it was a waste of time."

"Did he ever say that to your father?"

"We didn't dare challenge him. Sometimes my father would just look at you and know exactly what you were thinking. Michael and I believed that he could read our minds."

"What did your neighbors think of him?"

"We didn't know a lot of people. The Stevenson family lived on a farm that was farther up the hill, but they weren't very friendly. An older couple named Don and Irene Tedford lived on the other side of the stream and they came over one afternoon with two apple pies. They were surprised that we didn't have electricity, but it didn't seem to bother them. I remember Don saying that television was a big waste of time.

"Michael and I started going to the Tedfords every afternoon to eat homemade doughnuts. My father always stayed home, but sometimes Mother would take a load of laundry over to their place and wash it in their machine. The Tedfords had a son named Jerry who had died in a war and his picture was all over the house. They talked about him like he was still alive.

"Everything was okay until Sheriff Randolph came up the driveway in his squad car. He was a big man in a uniform and he was carrying a gun. I was scared when he arrived. I thought that he was from the Grid and that Father would have to kill him—"

Maya interrupted. "Once I was in a car with a Harlequin named Libra and we were stopped for speeding. I thought that Libra was going to cut the constable's throat."

"That's how it felt," Gabriel said. "Michael and I didn't know what was going to happen. My mother made iced tea for Sheriff Randolph and all of us sat on the front porch. At first Randolph just said a lot of nice things about the way we had fixed up the place, and then he began talking about the local property tax. Because we weren't connected to the power line, he thought we might refuse to pay the tax for political reasons.

"Father didn't say anything at first, but he kept staring at Randolph, really concentrating on him. All of a sudden, he announced that he'd be glad to pay the tax and everyone relaxed. The only person who didn't look happy was Michael. He went over to the sheriff and said he wanted to go to school with all the other kids.

"When the sheriff drove away, Father brought us into the kitchen for a family discussion. He told Michael that school was dangerous because it was part of the Grid. Michael said that we needed to learn things like math and science and history. He said that we couldn't defend ourselves from our enemies if we weren't educated."

"So what happened?" Maya asked.

"We didn't talk about it for the rest of the summer. Then Father said okay, we could go to school—but we had to be careful. We couldn't tell people our real name and we couldn't mention the weapons.

"I was nervous about meeting other kids, but Michael was happy. On the first day of school, he woke up two hours early to pick out the clothes he was going to wear. He told me that all the boys in town wore blue jeans and flannel shirts. And we had to dress that way, too. So we'd look just like everyone else.

"Mother drove us into Unityville and we got registered at the school under our fake names. Michael and I spent two hours in the office being tested by the assistant principal, Mrs. Batenor. We were both advanced readers, but I wasn't so good at math. When she took me into a classroom, the other students stared at me. It was the first time I really understood how different our family was and how other people saw us. All the kids started whispering until the teacher told them to be quiet.

"At recess, I found Michael on the playground and we stood around watching the other boys play football. Just like he'd said, they were all wearing jeans. Four older boys left the football game and came over to talk to us. I can still remember the look on my brother's face. He was so excited. So happy. He thought the boys were going to ask us to join the football game and then we'd become their friends.

"One of the boys, the tallest one, said, 'You're the Millers. Your parents bought Hale Robinson's farm.' Michael tried to shake his hand, but the boy said, 'Your parents are crazy.'

"My brother kept smiling for a few seconds as if he couldn't believe that the boy had said that. He had spent all those years on the road creating this fantasy about school and friends and a normal life. He told me to stay back and then he punched the tallest boy in the mouth. Everybody jumped him, but they didn't have a chance. Michael was using spinning back-kicks and karate punches on farm boys. He beat them to the ground and would have kept on punching them if I hadn't pulled him off."

"So you never made any friends?"

"Not really. The teachers liked Michael because he knew how to talk to adults. We spent all of our free time at the farm. That was okay. We always had some project going, like building a tree house or training Minerva."

"Who was Minerva? Your dog?"

"She was our owl security system." Gabriel smiled at the memory. "A few months after we started going to school, I found a baby owl near the stream that ran through Mr. Tedford's property. I couldn't see a nest anywhere, so I wrapped her in my T-shirt and took her back to the house.

"When she was little we kept her in a cardboard box and fed her cat food. I decided to name her Minerva because I had read this book that said the goddess kept an owl as a helper. When Minerva got bigger, Father cut a hole in the kitchen wall, then built a platform on both sides with a little trapdoor. We taught Minerva how to push through the door and enter the kitchen.

"Father placed Minerva's cage in a thicket of spruce trees at the bottom of the driveway. The cage had a trigger weight that would open the cage door, and the weight was attached to some fishing line that was stretched across our driveway. If a car turned off the road, they would hit the fishing line and open the cage. Minerva was supposed to fly up to the house and tell us that we had visitors."

"That was a clever idea."

"Maybe it was, but I didn't think so at the time. When we were living in motels, I had seen spy movies on television and I remembered all the high-tech devices. If bad people were searching for us, then I thought we should have better protection than an owl.

"Anyway, I pulled the fishing line, the cage door opened and Minerva flew up the hill. When Father and I reached the kitchen, the owl had come through the trapdoor and was eating her cat food. We carried Minerva down the driveway, tested the cage a second time, and she flew back to the house.

"That was when I asked my father why people wanted to kill us. He said he'd explain everything when we got a little older. I asked him why we couldn't go to the North Pole or some other distant location where they could never find us.

"My father just looked tired and sad. 'I could go to a place like that,' he told me. 'But you and Michael and your mother couldn't come along. I won't run away and leave you alone.'"

"Did he tell you he was a Traveler?"

"No," Gabriel said. "Nothing like that. We went through a couple of winters and everything seemed all right. Michael stopped having fights at school, but other kids thought he was a big liar. He'd tell them about the jade sword and Father's assault rifle, but he also said we had a swimming pool in the basement and a tiger in the barn. He told so many stories nobody realized that some of them were true.

"One afternoon when we were waiting for the school bus to take us home, another boy mentioned a concrete bridge that ran over the interstate highway. A water pipe ran underneath the bridge and a couple years back some kid named Andy used the pipe to cross the road.

"'That's easy,' Michael told them. 'My little brother could do that in his sleep.' Twenty minutes later I was on the embankment beneath the bridge. I jumped up and grabbed onto the pipe and started to cross the interstate while Michael and the other boys watched. I still think I could have done it, but when I was halfway across the pipe broke and I fell onto the highway. I hit my head and broke my left leg in two places. I remember raising my head, looking down the interstate, and seeing a tractor-trailer truck coming directly toward me. I passed out and, when I woke up, I was in a hospital emergency room with a cast on my leg. I'm pretty sure I heard Michael telling the nurse that my name was Gabriel Corrigan. I don't know why he did that. Maybe he thought I'd die if he didn't give the right name."

"And that's how the Tabula found you," Maya said.

"Maybe, but who knows? A few more years went by and nothing happened to us. When I was twelve and Michael was sixteen, we were sitting in the kitchen doing our homework after dinner. It was January and real cold outside. Then Minerva came through the trapdoor and sat there hooting and blinking at the light.

"This had happened a couple of times before when the Stevensons' dog hit the trip line. I got on my boots and went outside to find the dog. I came around the corner of the house, looked down the hill, and saw four men come out of the spruce trees. All of them wore dark clothes and carried rifles. They talked to each other, split apart, and began walking up the hill."

"Tabula mercenaries," Maya said.

"I didn't know who they were. For a few seconds I couldn't move, then I ran into the house and told my family. Father went upstairs to the bedroom and came down with a duffel bag and the jade sword. He gave the sword to me and the duffel bag to my mother. Then he handed the shotgun to Michael and told us to go out the back door and hide in the root cellar.

" 'What about you?' we asked.

" 'Just go to the cellar and stay there,' he told us. 'Don't come out until you hear my voice.'

"Father grabbed the rifle and we went out the back door. He told us to walk by the fence so we wouldn't leave footprints in the snow. I wanted to stay and help him, but Mother said we had to go. When we reached the garden, I heard a gunshot and a man shouting. It wasn't my father's voice. I'm sure about that.

"The root cellar was just a dumping place for old tools. Michael pulled the door open and we climbed down the staircase to the cellar. The door was so rusty that Michael couldn't shut it all the way. The three of us sat there in the darkness, on a concrete ledge. For a while we heard gunfire and then it was quiet. When I woke up, sunlight was coming through the crack around the door.

"Michael pushed the door open and we followed him out. The house and barn had burned down. Minerva was flying above us as if she was searching for something. Four dead men lay in different places—twenty or thirty yards away from each other—and their blood had melted the snow around them.

"My mother sat down, wrapped her arms around her legs, and began crying. Michael and I checked what was left of the house, but we didn't find any trace of our father. I told Michael that the men didn't kill him. He ran away.

"Michael said, 'Forget that. We better get out of here. You've got to help me with Mom. We'll go over to the Tedfords and borrow their station wagon.'

"He went back into the root cellar and returned with the jade sword and the duffel bag. We looked inside the duffel and saw that it was filled with packets of one-hundred-dollar bills. Mother was still sitting in the snow, crying and whispering to herself like a crazy woman. Carrying the weapons and the bag, we took her across the fields to the Tedfords' farm. When Michael pounded on the front door, Don and Irene woke up and came downstairs in their bathrobes.

"I'd heard Michael lie hundreds of times at school, but no one ever believed his stories. This time, he sounded like he believed what he was saying. He told the Tedfords that our father had been a soldier and he had run away from the army. Last night, government agents had burned down our house and killed him. The whole thing sounded crazy to me, but then I remembered that the Tedfords' son had been killed in the war."

"A skillful lie," Maya said.

"You're right. It worked. Don Tedford loaned us his station wagon. Michael had already been driving for a couple of years on the farm. We loaded up the weapons and the duffel bag, then headed down the road. Mother lay on the backseat. I covered her with a blanket and she went to sleep. When I looked out the side window, I saw Minerva flying through the smoke up in the sky . . ."

Gabriel stopped talking and Maya stared at the ceiling. A truck came down the highway and its headlights cut through the window blinds. Darkness again. Silence. The shadows that surrounded them seemed to gain substance and weight. Maya felt like they were lying together at the bottom of a deep pool.

"And what happened after that?" she asked.

"We spent a few years driving around the country, and then we got fake birth certificates and lived in Austin, Texas. When I was seventeen, Michael decided that we should move to Los Angeles and start a new life."

"Then the Tabula found you and now you're here."

"Yes," Gabriel said softly. "Now I'm here."

30

Boone didn't like Los Angeles. It was ordinary enough on the surface, but there was an impulse toward anarchy. He remembered watching a video of a riot in the ghetto neighborhoods. Smoke rising to a sunny sky. A palm tree bursting into flames. There were a great many street gangs in Los Angeles and most of the time they just tried to kill each other. That was acceptable. But a visionary leader, like a Traveler, could stop the drugs and direct the anger outward.

He took the freeway south to Hermosa Beach, left his car in a public lot, and walked over to Sea Breeze Lane. A power company repair van was parked across the street from the Indian's house. Boone knocked on the van's rear door, and Prichett pulled up the shade that covered the window. He smiled and nodded eagerly—glad you're here. Boone opened the door and climbed inside.

The three Tabula mercenaries were sitting in low beach chairs set up in the back of the van. Hector Sanchez was a former Mexican *federale* who had gotten involved in a bribery scandal. Ron Olson was an ex–military policeman who had been accused of rape.

The youngest of the group was Dennis Prichett. He had short brown hair, a chubby face, and a polite but earnest manner that made him seem like a young missionary. Prichett went to church three times a week and never used foul language. During the last few years, the Brethren had started to hire true believers from different religions. Although they were paid like mercenaries, they joined the Brethren for moral reasons. As far as they were concerned, the Travelers were false prophets who challenged whatever they considered to be the true faith. These new employees were supposed to be more dependable and ruthless than the regular mercenaries, but Boone distrusted them. He understood greed and fear much better than religious zeal.

"Where is our suspect?" he asked.

"On the back porch," Prichett said. "Here. Take a look."

He got out of his chair and Boone sat in front of the monitor screen. One of the more pleasurable aspects of his job was that it gave him the technology to look through walls. For the Los Angeles operation, the van had been equipped with a thermal imaging device. The special camera gave you a black-and-white image of any surface that produced or reflected heat. There was a white patch in the garage: that was the water heater. Another patch was in the kitchen: probably a coffeemaker. A third object—a human being—was sitting on the back porch.

The surveillance team had been scanning the house for three days, monitoring phone calls and using the Carnivore program to track e-mails. "Any messages sent or received?" Boone asked.

"He's had two calls this morning about a weekend sweat lodge," Sanchez said.

Olson glanced at a computer monitor. "Nothing in his e-mail but spam."

"Good," Boone said. "Let's get going. Does everyone have a badge?"

The three men nodded. They had been given fake FBI badges when they arrived in Los Angeles.

"Okay. Hector and Ron, you go through the front door. If there's any resistance, the Brethren have given us permission to close this man's file. Dennis, you come with me. We'll go down the driveway."

The four men got out of the van and quickly crossed the street. Olson and Sanchez climbed onto the front porch of the cottage. Boone opened the wooden gate and Prichett followed him down the driveway. A crude hut constructed of sticks and patches of rawhide was in the backyard.

They came around the corner of the house and saw Thomas Walks the Ground sitting at a small wooden table set up on the porch. The Indian had taken apart a broken garbage disposal and was putting the pieces back together. Boone glanced at Prichett and saw that the younger man had drawn his 9-mm automatic. Tight grip. White knuckles. A loud cracking sound came from the front of the house as the other two mercenaries kicked in the door.

"It's okay," Boone told Prichett. "There's nothing to worry about." He reached into his jacket, pulled out a fake federal warrant, and went up to the back porch.

"Good afternoon, Thomas. I'm Special Agent Baker and this is Special Agent Morgan. We have a warrant to search your house."

Thomas Walks the Ground stopped tightening a bolt on the garbage disposal. He put down his socket wrench and studied the two visitors. "I don't think you're real police officers," he said. "And I don't think that's a real warrant. Unfortunately, I left my gun in the kitchen, so I'm going to accept this particular reality."

"That's a wise choice," Boone said. "Good for you." He turned to Prichett. "Go back to the van and run communications. Tell Hector to suit up and use the sniffer. Ron stays on the front porch."

"Yes, sir." Prichett slipped the gun back in his shoulder holster. "And what about the suspect, sir?"

"We'll be okay right here. I'm going to have a conversation with Thomas about his various options."

Determined to do a good job, Prichett hurried back down the driveway. Boone pulled out a bench and sat at the table. "What's wrong with the garbage disposal?" he asked.

"It jammed up and burned out the motor. You know what the problem was?" Thomas pointed to a small black object on the table. "A plum pit."

"Why not buy a new disposal?"

"Too expensive."

Boone nodded. "That's right. We've examined your bank account and your credit card balance. You're out of money."

Thomas Walks the Ground continued his work, rummaging through the parts scattered across the table. "I'm very glad that a pretend police officer is concerned about my pretend finances."

"Don't you want to keep this house?"

"It's not important. I can always go back to my tribe in Montana. I've stayed too long in this place."

Boone reached into the inside pocket of his leather jacket, pulled out an envelope, and placed it on the table. "This is twenty thousand dollars in cash. It's all yours in exchange for an honest conversation."

Thomas Walks the Ground picked up the envelope but didn't open it. He held it in the palm of his hand as if he was judging the weight. Then he dropped it on the table. "I'm an honest man, so I'll give you the conversation for free."

"A young woman took a taxi to this address. Her name is Maya, but she probably used a false name. She's in her twenties. Black hair. Pale blue eyes. She was raised in Britain and has an English accent."

"A lot of people visit me. Maybe she came to my sweat lodge." Thomas smiled at Boone. "There are still a few openings for this weekend's ceremony. You and your men should join us. Pound on a drum. Sweat out your poison. When you step into the cold air, you feel completely alive."

Sanchez walked down the driveway carrying a white bio-hazard suit and the sniffer equipment. The sniffer resembled a hand-held vacuum cleaner attached to a shoulder power pack. There was a radio transmitter attached to the pack that sent the data directly to the computer in the van. Sanchez placed the sniffer on a lawn chair. He stepped into the suit and then pulled it over his legs, arms, and shoulders.

"What's that for?" Thomas asked.

"We have a DNA sample from this young woman. The equipment on the chair is a genetic data collection device. It uses a microarray chip to match the suspect's DNA with the DNA found inside your house."

Thomas found three matching screws and smiled. He placed them next to a new electric motor. "As I said, I've had many visitors."

Sanchez pulled the suit over his head and began to breathe through the air filter. Now his own DNA wouldn't interfere with the sample. The mercenary opened the back door, entered the house, and began to work. The best samples were found on bed linen, toilet seats, and the backs of upholstered furniture.

The two men watched each other as they listened to the muffled whirring sound that came from the sniffer. "So tell me," Boone said, "did Maya visit your house?"

"Why is this important to you?"

"She's a terrorist."

Thomas Walks the Ground began searching for three steel washers to match his three screws. "There are real terrorists in this world, but a small group of men uses our fear of them to increase their power. These men hunt down shamans and mystics . . ." Thomas smiled again. "And people called Travelers."

The whirring sound continued from inside the house. Boone knew that Sanchez was moving from room to room scraping the nozzle of the sniffer on various objects.

"All terrorists are the same," Boone said.

Thomas leaned back in his lawn chair. "Let me tell you about a Paiute Indian named Wovoka. In the 1880s, he began to go off into other worlds. After Wovoka returned, he talked to all the tribes and started a movement called the Ghost Dance. His followers would dance in circles, singing special songs. When you weren't dancing, you were supposed to live a righteous life. No drinking alcohol. No stealing. No prostitution.

"Now you would think that the whites who ran the reservations would admire this. After years of degradation, the Indian was becoming moral and strong again. Unfortunately, the Lakota weren't becoming obedient. Dancers started the ritual at the Pine Ridge Reservation in South Dakota and the whites in the area got very frightened. A government agent named Daniel Royer decided that the Lakota didn't need freedom or their own land. They needed to learn baseball. He tried to teach the warriors how to pitch and swing a bat, but they weren't distracted from the Ghost Dance.

"And the whites said to one another, 'The Indians are becoming dangerous again.' So the government sent soldiers to a Ghost Dance ceremony at Wounded Knee Creek and they fired their rifles and slaughtered 290 men, women, and children. The soldiers dug pits and tossed the bodies into the frozen ground. And my people went back to alcohol and confusion . . ."

The noise stopped. A minute later, the back door squeaked open and Sanchez came out. He removed the mouth filter and pulled off the hood of the white suit. His face glistened with sweat. "We've got a match," he said. "There was a strand of her hair on the couch in the living room."

"Good. You can go back to the van."

Sanchez removed the suit and went back down the driveway. Once again, Boone and Thomas were alone.

"Maya was here," Boone said.

"According to this machine."

"I want to know what she said and did. I want to know if you gave her money or a ride somewhere. Was she wounded? Has she changed her appearance?"

"I won't help you," Thomas said calmly. "Leave my house."

Boone drew his automatic, but kept it flat on his right leg. "You don't really have a choice, Thomas. I just need you to accept that fact."

"I have the freedom to say no."

Boone sighed like a parent with a stubborn child. "Freedom is the biggest myth ever created. It's a destructive, unachievable goal that has caused a great deal of pain. Very few people can handle freedom. A society is healthy and productive when it's under control."

"And you think that's going to happen?"

"A new age is on its way. We're approaching a time where we will have the technology necessary to monitor and supervise vast numbers of people. In the industrial nations, the structure is already in place."

"And you'll be in control?"

"Oh, I'll be watched, too. Everyone will be watched. It's a very democratic system. And it's inevitable, Thomas. There's no way it can be stopped. Your sacrifice for some Harlequin is completely meaningless."

"You're welcome to your opinion, but I will decide what gives meaning to my life."

"You're going to help me, Thomas. There's no negotiation here. No compromise. You need to deal with the reality of the situation."

Thomas shook his head sympathetically. "No, my friend. It's you who are out of touch with reality. You look at me and see an overweight Crow Indian with a broken garbage disposal and no money. And you think: 'Ahhh, he's just an ordinary man.' But I'm telling you that ordinary men and women will see what you're doing. And we will stand up, rip open the door, and leave your electronic cage."

Thomas got out of the chair, stepped off the porch, and headed for the driveway. Boone swiveled around on the bench. Holding the automatic with two hands, he blew away his enemy's right kneecap. Thomas collapsed, rolled onto his back, and stopped moving.

Still holding the gun, Boone walked over to the body. Thomas was conscious, but breathing quickly. His leg was almost severed from the knee down and dark red blood pulsed from the cut artery. As Thomas began to go into shock, he looked up at Boone and spoke slowly. "I'm not frightened of you . . ."

An intense anger overcame Boone. He pointed his gun at Thomas's forehead as if he wanted to destroy all the other man's thoughts and memories, then his finger squeezed the trigger.

The second gunshot seemed unbearably loud, the sound waves expanding out into the world.

31

Michael was being kept in a windowless suite of four rooms. Occasionally he heard muffled noises and the sound of water going through pipes, so he assumed that there were other people in the building. There was a bathroom, a bedroom, a living room, and an outer guardroom where two silent men wearing navy blue blazers blocked him from leaving. He wasn't sure if he was in America or a foreign country. None of the rooms had a clock and he never knew if it was daytime or night.

The only person who talked to him was Lawrence Takawa, a young Japanese American man who always wore a white shirt and a black necktie. Lawrence was sitting beside Michael's bed when he woke up from his drugged sleep. A doctor came in a few minutes later and gave Michael a quick physical examination. He whispered something to Lawrence and then never returned.

From that first day, Michael started asking questions. Where am I? Why are you keeping me here? Lawrence smiled pleasantly and always gave the same set of answers. This is a safe place. We're your new friends. Right now, we're looking for Gabriel so he can be safe, too.

Michael knew he was a prisoner and they were the enemy. But Lawrence and the two guards spent most of their time making sure he was comfortable. The living room had an expensive television and a rack of DVDs. Cooks were on duty twenty-four hours a day in the building, and they would prepare whatever he wanted to eat. When Michael first got out of bed, Lawrence led him to a walk-in closet and showed him thousands of dollars' worth of clothes, shoes, and accessories. The dress shirts were made of silk or Egyptian cotton and had his initials discreetly monogrammed on the pocket. The sweaters were woven from the softest cashmere. There were dress shoes, athletic shoes, and slippers—everything in his size.

He asked for exercise equipment. A treadmill and a set of free weights appeared in the living room. If he wanted to read a certain book or magazine, he gave his request to Lawrence and it appeared a few hours later. The food was excellent and he could order from a list of French and domestic wines. Lawrence Takawa assured him that eventually there would be women, too. He had everything he wanted except the freedom to leave. Lawrence said the short-term objective was to make him fit and healthy after his ordeal. Michael was going to meet a very powerful man and this person would tell him what he wanted to know.

Late one afternoon, after Michael took a shower, he left the bathroom and discovered that someone had picked out his clothes and placed them on the bed. Shoes and socks. Gray wool pleated pants and a black knit shirt that fit perfectly. He went into the next room in the suite and found Lawrence drinking a glass of wine while he listened to a jazz CD.

"How are you, Michael? Sleep well?"

"Okay."

"Any dreams?"

Michael had dreamed that he was flying over an ocean, but there was no reason to describe what had happened. He didn't want them to know what was going on in his mind. "No dreams. Or, at least, I don't remember them."

"This is what you've been waiting for. In a few minutes, you're going to meet Kennard Nash. Do you know who he is?"

Michael recalled a face from a news program on television. "Didn't he used to be in the government?"

"He was a brigadier general. Since leaving the army, he's worked for two American presidents. Everyone respects him. Right now, he's executive director of the Evergreen Foundation."

"For all generations," Michael said, quoting the slogan the foundation used when it sponsored programs on television. Their logo was very distinct. There was a film clip of two children, a boy and a girl, bending over a pine seedling, and then everything morphed into a stylized symbol of a tree.

"It's about six o'clock in the evening. You're in the administrative building of the foundation's national research center. The building is in Westchester Country—about a forty-five-minute drive from New York City."

"So why did you bring me here?"

Lawrence put down his wineglass and smiled. It was impossible to know what he was thinking. "We're going upstairs to see General Nash. He'll be glad to answer all your questions."

The two security men were waiting for them in the guardroom. Without saying a word, they escorted Michael and Lawrence out of the room and down a hallway to a row of elevators. There was a window a few feet away from where they were standing, and Michael realized it was night. When the elevator came, Lawrence motioned him inside. He waved his right hand across a sensor and punched the floor button.

"Listen carefully to General Nash, Michael. He's a very knowledgeable man." Lawrence stepped back into the hallway and Michael traveled alone to the top floor.

The elevator opened directly onto a private office. It was a large room that had been decorated to resemble the library of a British men's club. Oak shelves holding sets of leather-bound books lined the walls, and there were easy chairs and little green reading lamps. The only unusual detail was that three surveillance cameras were mounted on the ceiling. The cameras moved slowly back and forth, monitoring the entire room. They're watching me, Michael thought. Someone is always watching.

He stepped around the furniture and lamps, trying not to touch anything. In one corner of the room, pinpoint spotlights illuminated an architectural model set on a wooden pedestal. There were two parts to the miniature building: a central tower surrounded by a ring-shaped building. The outer structure was divided into small identical rooms, each with one barred window on the outside wall and another window set in the top half of the entrance door.

It looked as if the tower was a solid monolith, but when Michael moved to the other side of the pedestal, he saw a cross section of the building. It was a maze of doorways and staircases. Strips of balsa wood covered the windows like Venetian blinds.

Michael heard a door squeak open and saw Kennard Nash enter the room. Bald head. Wide shoulders. When Nash smiled, Michael remembered the various times he had seen the general on television talk shows.

"Good evening, Michael. I'm Kennard Nash."

General Nash walked quickly across the room and shook Michael's hand. One of the surveillance cameras turned slightly as if to take in the scene.

"I see you've found the Panopticon." Nash approached the architectural model.

"What is it? A hospital?"

"I suppose it could be a hospital or even an office building, but it's a prison designed by the eighteenth-century philosopher Jeremy Bentham. Although he sent his plans to everyone in the British government, it was never actually constructed. The model is based on Bentham's drawings."

Nash stepped closer to the model and studied it carefully. "Each room is a cell with thick enough walls so there can't be communication between the prisoners. Light comes from the outside so the prisoner is always backlit and visible."

"And the guards are in the tower?"

"Bentham called it an inspection lodge."

"Looks like a maze."

"That's the cleverness of the Panopticon. It's designed so that you can never see the face of your guard or hear him moving about. Think of the implications, Michael. There can be twenty guards in the tower or one guard or no guards at all. It doesn't make a difference. The prisoner must assume that he's being watched all the time. After a while, that realization becomes part of the prisoner's consciousness. When the system is working perfectly the guards can leave the tower for lunch—or a three-day weekend. It doesn't make a difference. The prisoners have accepted their condition."

General Nash walked over to a bookcase. He opened a false wall of books, revealing a bar stocked with glasses, an ice bucket, and bottles of liquor. "It's six thirty. I usually have a glass of scotch around this time. We've got bourbon, whiskey, vodka, and wine. Or I can order you something more elaborate."

"I'll have malt whiskey with a little bit of water."

"Excellent. Good choice." Nash began pulling corks out of bottles. "I'm part of a group called the Brethren. We've been around for quite a long time, but for hundreds of years we were just reacting to events, trying to reduce the chaos. The Panopticon was a revelation to our members. It changed our way of thinking.

"Even the most casual student of history realizes that human beings are greedy, impulsive, and cruel. But Bentham's prison showed us that social control was possible with the right sort of technology. There was no need to have a policeman standing on every corner. All you need is a Virtual Panopticon that monitors your population. You aren't required to literally watch them all the time, but the masses have to accept that possibility and the inevitability of punishment. You need the structure, the system, the implicit threat that becomes a fact of life. When people discard their notions of privacy, they permit a peaceful society."

The general carried two glasses over to a couch and some chairs clustered around a low wood table. He placed Michael's drink on the table and the men sat opposite each other.

"So here's to the Panopticon." Nash raised his glass to the model on the pedestal. "It was a failed invention, but a great insight."

Michael sipped some of the whiskey. It didn't taste like it was drugged, but he couldn't be sure. "You lecture about philosophy if you want," he said, "but I don't really care. All I know is that I'm a prisoner."

"Actually, you know a good deal more than that. Your family lived under an assumed name for several years until a group of armed men attacked your home in South Dakota. We did that, Michael. Those men were our employees and they were following our old strategy."

"You killed my father."

"Did we?" Kennard Nash raised his eyebrows. "Our staff searched what was left of the house, but we never found his body."

The casual tone of Nash's voice was infuriating. You bastard, Michael thought. How can you sit there and smile? A wave of anger surged through his body and he thought about flinging himself across the table and grabbing Nash by the throat. Finally there would be payback for the destruction of his family.

General Nash didn't seem to realize that he was on the verge of being attacked. When his cell phone rang, he put down his drink and pulled the phone out of his suit-coat pocket. "I asked not to be disturbed," he told the caller. "Yes. Is that so? How very interesting. Well, why don't I just ask him?"

Nash lowered the phone and frowned at Michael. He resembled a bank official who had just found a small problem in a loan application. "Lawrence Takawa is on the phone. He says that you're either going to attack me or try to escape."

Michael stopped breathing for a few seconds while his hands gripped the edge of his chair. "I—I don't know what you're talking about," he said.

"Please, Michael, don't waste your time being deceitful. Right now you're being monitored by an infrared scanner. Lawrence says that you show an increased heart rate, elevated skin galvanic response, and heat signals around the eyes. All this data is a clear indication of a fight-or-flight reaction. Which leads me back to my original question: Are you going to attack me or run away?"

"Just tell me why you wanted to kill my father."

Nash studied Michael's face, and then decided to continue the conversation. "Don't worry," he said to Takawa. "I think we're making progress here." The general switched off the cell phone and dropped it back into his pocket.

"Was my father a criminal?" Michael asked. "Did he steal something?"

"Remember the Panopticon? The model works perfectly if all humanity lives inside the building. It doesn't work if one individual can open a door and stand outside the system."

"And my father could do that?"

"Yes. He's what we call a 'Traveler.' Your father was able to project his neural energy out of his body and travel to other realities. Our world is the Fourth Realm. There are fixed barriers one must pass through to enter the other realms. We don't know if your father explored all of them." Nash stared directly at Michael. "The ability to leave this world appears to have a genetic origin. Perhaps you could do it, Michael. You and Gabriel might have the power."

"And you're the Tabula?"

"That name is used by our enemies. As I told you, we call ourselves the Brethren. The Evergreen Foundation is our public institution."

Michael stared down at his drink while he tried to figure out a strategy. He was still alive because they wanted something. *Perhaps you could do it, Michael*. Yes. That was it. His father had disappeared and they needed a Traveler.

"All I know about your foundation is the commercials I've seen on public television."

Nash stood up and walked over to the window. "The Brethren are true idealists. We want what is best for everyone: peace and prosperity for all. The only way to achieve this goal is to establish social and political stability."

"So you put everyone in a giant prison?"

"Don't you understand, Michael? These days people are frightened of the world around them, and that fear is easily encouraged and maintained. People *want* to be in our Virtual Panopticon. We'll watch over them like good shepherds. They'll be monitored, controlled, protected from the unknown.

"Besides, they rarely recognize the prison. There's always some distraction. A war in the Middle East. A scandal involving celebrities. The World Cup or the Super Bowl. Drugs, both illegal and prescribed. Advertisements. A novelty song. A change of fashion. Fear may induce people to enter our Panopticon, but we keep them amused while they're inside."

"Meanwhile you're killing Travelers."

"As I said, that's an outdated strategy. In the past, we responded like a healthy body rejecting different viruses. All the basic laws have been written down, in a multitude of languages. The rules are clear. Mankind just has to learn how to obey. But whenever a society was close to some degree of stability, a Traveler came along with new ideas and a desire to change everything. While the wealthy and the wise were trying to build a vast cathedral, the Travelers kept undermining the foundation—causing trouble."

"So what's changed?" Michael asked. "Why haven't you killed me?"

"Our scientists started working on something called a quantum computer and received unexpected results. I'm not going to give you the details this evening, Michael. All you need to know is that a Traveler can help us achieve an incredible breakthrough in technology. If the Crossover Project works, history will be changed forever."

"And you want me to become a Traveler?"

"Yes. Exactly."

Michael got up from the couch and approached General Nash. By now he had recovered from his reaction to the infrared scanner. Perhaps these people could read his heart rate and skin temperature, but that wasn't going to change anything.

"A few minutes ago you said that your organization attacked my family's house."

"I had nothing to do with that, Michael. It was a regrettable incident."

"Even if I agreed to forget about the past and help you, that doesn't mean that it's possible. I don't know how to 'travel' anywhere. My father didn't teach us anything but sword fighting with bamboo sticks."

"Yes, I'm aware of that. Have you seen our research center?" Nash motioned with his hand and Michael looked out the window. Security lights illuminated the guarded compound. Nash's office was on the top floor of a modern office building connected to three other buildings by covered walkways. In the middle of the quadrangle was a fifth building that looked like a white cube. The marble walls of the cube were thin enough so that the interior light made the building glow from within.

"If you have the potential to be a Traveler, then we have the staff and technology necessary to help you achieve this power. In the past, Travelers have been instructed by heretical priests, dissenting ministers, and rabbis trapped in the ghetto. The whole process was dominated by religious faith and mysticism. Sometimes it didn't work. As you can see, there's nothing disorganized about our operation."

"Okay. It's clear that you've got some big buildings and a lot of money. That still doesn't mean I'm a Traveler."

"If you succeed, you'll help us change history. Even if you fail, we'll set you up in a comfortable environment. You'll never have to work again."

"And what if I refuse to cooperate?"

"I don't think that's going to happen. Don't forget, I know all about you, Michael. Our staff has been investigating you for several weeks. Unlike your brother, you're the ambitious one."

"Leave Gabriel out of this," Michael said sharply. "I don't want anybody looking for him."

"We don't need Gabriel. We have you. And now I'm offering you a great opportunity. You're the future, Michael. You're going to be the Traveler who will truly bring peace to the world."

"People will still keep fighting."

"Remember what I told you? It's all just fear and distraction. Fear will get people into our Virtual Panopticon and then we'll keep them happy. People will be free to take antidepressant drugs, go into debt, and stare at their television sets. Society might seem disorganized, but it will be very stable. Every few years we'll pick a different mannequin to give speeches from the White House Rose Garden."

"But who's really in control?"

"The Brethren, of course. And you'll be part of our family, guiding us forward."

Nash put his hand on Michael's shoulder. It was a friendly gesture as if he were a kind uncle or a new stepfather. *Guide us forward*, Michael thought. *Part of our family*. He stared out the window at the white building.

General Nash turned away from him and walked over to the bar. "Let me pour you another drink. We'll order dinner—sirloin or sushi, whatever you wish. And then we'll talk. Most people go through life never knowing the truth about the major events of their time. They're watching a farce performed at the edge of the stage while the real drama is going on behind the curtain.

"Tonight I'll raise the curtain and we'll walk backstage and see how the props work and what's behind the set and how the actors behave in the dressing room. Half the things you've been taught in school are just convenient fictions. History is a puppet show for childish minds."

32

Gabriel woke up in the motel room and saw that Maya was gone. Without making a sound, she had left her bed and gotten dressed. He found it strange that she had neatly tucked in the blanket and folded the two pillows into the frayed cotton bedspread. It was as if she wanted to erase all signs of her presence, the fact that the two of them had spent the night in the same space.

He sat up in bed and leaned against the creaky headboard. Ever since they had left Los Angeles, he had thought about what it meant to be a Traveler. Was everyone just a biological machine? Or was there something eternal within each living thing, a spark of energy that Maya called the Light? Even if that was true, it didn't mean that he had the power.

Gabriel tried to think about another world, but he found himself overcome by random thoughts. He couldn't control his mind. It jumped around like a chattering monkey in a cage, throwing up images of old girlfriends, motorcycle races down a mountain, and lyrics from a song. He heard a buzzing sound and opened his eyes. A fly was bashing itself against the windowpane.

Angry with himself, he walked into the bathroom and splashed water on his face. Maya, Hollis, and Vicki had risked their lives for him, but they were going to be disappointed. Gabriel felt like a gate crasher at a party who was pretending to be someone important. The Pathfinder—if he existed—would laugh at his pretensions.

When he returned to the main room, he saw that Maya's travel bag and laptop computer were sitting beside the door. That meant that she was somewhere nearby. Had she taken the van and gone to buy food? Not possible. There were no restaurants or grocery stores in the area.

Gabriel got dressed and stepped out into the courtyard parking area. The old lady who ran the motel had switched off the neon sign and her office was dark. The dawn sky was a lavender color with thin silvery clouds. He walked around the south wing of the motel and saw Maya standing on a concrete slab in the middle of some sagebrush. The concrete looked like the foundation for a house that had been abandoned to the desert.

Maya must have found a steel rod at the construction site. Holding it like a sword, she ran through a series of ritual forms and combinations, similar to the ones he had seen in his kendo school. Parry. Thrust. Defend. Each motion glided gracefully into another.

From a distance, he could observe Maya and stay detached from her single-minded intensity. Gabriel had never met anyone like this Harlequin. He knew she was a warrior who would kill without hesitation, but there was also something pure and honest in the way she faced the world. Watching her practice, Gabriel wondered if she cared about anything other than this ancient obligation, the violence that had claimed her life.

A discarded broom was lying beside the motel's dumpster. He broke off the broom section and carried the stick over to the concrete slab. When Maya saw him, she stopped moving and lowered her improvised weapon.

"I've taken a few kendo lessons, but you look like an expert," he said. "Do you want to practice sparring?"

"Harlequins must never fight Travelers."

"I might not be a Traveler, okay? We should accept that possibility." Gabriel waved the broomstick around. "And this isn't exactly a sword."

He gripped the stick with both hands, and then attacked her at half speed. Maya parried gently and swung her weapon around to his left side. The soles of his motorcycle boots made a faint scraping sound as they moved across the concrete rectangle. For the first time, he felt like Maya was looking at him, treating him as an equal. She even smiled a few times when he blocked her attack and tried to surprise her with an unexpected move. Fighting with grace and precision, they moved beneath the enormous sky.

It began to get hot as they crossed the state border into Nevada. The moment they left California, Gabriel pulled off his motorcycle helmet and tossed it into the van. He slipped on some sunglasses and roared ahead of Maya. She watched the wind touch his shirtsleeves and the cuffs of his jeans. Turning southeast, they headed toward the Colorado River and the crossing point at Davis Dam. Red rocks. Saguaro cactus. Waves of hot air shimmering on the blacktop. Near a town called Searchlight, Maya saw a series of hand-lettered signs by the side of the road. PARADISE DINER. FIVE MILES. LIVE COYOTE! SHOW THE KIDS! THREE MILES. PARADISE DINER. EAT!

Gabriel gestured with his hand—let's have breakfast—and when the Paradise Diner appeared he turned into the dirt parking lot. The diner was a flat-topped building that looked like a railroad boxcar with windows. A large air-conditioning unit was installed on the roof. Holding the sword carrying case, Maya got out of the van and studied the building before she decided to go inside. Front entrance. Back entrance. A battered red pickup truck was parked in front of the diner and a second pickup with a camper shell was parked on the side.

Gabriel strolled over to her. He shifted his shoulders around, relaxing his knotted muscles. "I don't think we need that," he said and motioned to the sword case. "We're just eating breakfast, Maya. It's not World War Three."

She saw herself in Gabriel's eyes. Harlequin craziness. Constant paranoia. "My father trained me to carry weapons at all times."

"Relax," Gabriel said. "It'll be all right." And she saw, in some new way, his face and eyes and brown hair.

Turning away from him, Maya took a deep breath and placed the sword inside the van. Don't worry, she told herself. Nothing's going to happen. But she checked the two knives that were strapped to her arms.

The coyote was kept in a chain-link cage built near the front of the restaurant. Sitting on a concrete slab dotted with piles of scat, the captive panted from the heat. This was the first time Maya had ever seen a coyote. He looked like a mongrel dog with a wolf's head and teeth. Only his dark brown eyes were wild; they watched Maya intently as she raised her hand.

"I hate zoos," she told Gabriel. "They remind me of prisons."

"People like to see animals."

"Citizens want to kill wild creatures or put them into cages. It helps them forget that they're also prisoners."

The diner was a long, narrow room with booths near the windows, a counter with stools, and a small kitchen. Three slot machines were near the front door and each one had a garish theme. Circus of Jackpots. Big Winner. Happy Daze. A pair of Mexicans wearing cowboy boots and dusty work clothes sat at the counter eating scrambled eggs and corn tortillas. A young waitress with bleached blond hair and a pinafore apron was emptying one ketchup bottle into another. Maya saw a face peering through the kitchen serving window: an old man with bleary eyes and a scruffy beard. The cook.

"Sit anywhere you want," the waitress said, and Maya picked the best defensive position—last booth down, facing the entrance. As she sat down, she stared at the silverware on the Formica table and tried to visualize the room in her mind. This was a good place to stop. The two Mexicans looked harmless and she could see any car that approached the building from the road.

The waitress came over with glasses of ice water. "Mornin'. You two want coffee?" She had a chirpy little voice.

"Just some orange juice," Gabriel said.

Maya stood up. "Where's the restroom?"

"You got to walk outside to the back. Plus, it's locked. Come on. I'll take you there."

The waitress—whose name tag read "Kathy"—led Maya around the diner to an unmarked door fastened with a padlock and latch. She kept chattering as she searched through her pockets for the key. "Daddy's worried about people coming in and stealing all his toilet paper. He's the cook and the dishwasher and everything else around here."

Kathy unlocked the door and switched on the light. The room was filled with cardboard boxes of canned food and other supplies. She bustled around, checking the paper-towel dispenser and wiping out the sink.

"You got a real cute boyfriend," Kathy said. "I'd like to drive around with a good-looking man like that, but I'm stuck at the Paradise until Daddy sells this place."

"You're a bit isolated here."

"Nothing but us and that ol' coyote. Plus a few people driving down from Vegas. You been to Vegas?"

"No."

"I've been six times."

When she finally left the room, Maya locked the door and sat on a stack of cardboard boxes. It bothered her that she might feel any kind of attachment to Gabriel. Harlequins weren't allowed to become friends with the Travelers they protected. The proper attitude was to feel somewhat superior to the Travelers, as if they were little children who were innocent of the wolves in the forest. Her father always said there was a practical reason for this emotional distance. Surgeons rarely operated on family members. It might cloud their judgment. The same rules applied to Harlequins.

Maya stood in front of the sink and stared into the cracked mirror. Look at yourself, she thought. Tangled hair. Bloodshot eyes. Dark, drab clothing. Thorn had turned her into a killer without attachments, someone who lacked the drone desire for comfort and the citizen desire for security. Travelers might be weak and confused, but they could cross over and escape from this worldly prison. Harlequins were trapped in the Fourth Realm until they died.

When Maya returned to the diner, the two Mexicans had finished their meals and driven away. She and Gabriel ordered breakfast, then he leaned back in the booth and watched her carefully.

"Let's assume that people really can cross over into other realms. What's it like there? Is it dangerous?"

"I don't know that much about it. That's why you need a Pathfinder to help you. My father did tell me about two possible dangers. When you cross over, your shell—your body—stays here."

"And what's the second danger?"

"Your Light, your spirit, whatever you want to call it, can be killed or injured in another realm. If that happens, then you're trapped there forever."

Voices. Laughter. Maya watched the door as four young men entered the restaurant. Out in the parking lot, the desert sun gleamed on their dark blue SUV. Maya evaluated each person in the group and gave them nicknames. Big Arms, Shaved Head, and Fat Boy all wore a mixture of sports team jerseys and workout pants. They looked as if they had just run from an athletic club fire and had grabbed their clothes randomly from different lockers. Their leader—the smallest man, but the one with the loudest voice—wore cowboy boots to make himself look taller. Call him Mustache, she thought. No. Silver Buckle. The buckle was part of an elaborate cowboy belt.

"Sit anywhere you want," Kathy said.

"Hell yes," Silver Buckle told her. "We were going to do that anyway."

Their loud voices, their desire to be recognized, made Maya nervous. She ate quickly, finishing her breakfast, while Gabriel smoothed some strawberry jam onto his toast. The four young men got the restroom key from Kathy and gave their breakfast orders, changing their minds and demanding extra bacon. They told Kathy they were driving back to Arizona after watching a boxing match in Las Vegas. They had lost a large bet on the challenger, plus additional money at the blackjack tables. Kathy took their order and retreated behind the counter. Fat Boy exchanged a twenty-dollar bill for some singles and began to play the slot machines.

"You finished eating?" Maya asked Gabriel.

"In a minute."

"Let's get out of here."

Gabriel looked amused. "You don't like those guys."

She rattled the ice in her water glass and lied. "I don't pay any attention to citizens unless they're in my way."

"I thought you liked Vicki Fraser. You two were acting like friends . . ."

"This is a goddamn cheat!" Fat Boy pounded his fist on one of the slot machines. "I just put in twenty bucks and I didn't even get one back."

Silver Buckle was sitting across from Shaved Head in a booth. He stroked his mustache and grinned. "Wise up, Davey. It's set to never pay off. They don't make enough money from this bad coffee so they rip off a few more bucks from the tourists who play those machines."

Kathy came out from behind the counter. "It pays off, sometimes. A trucker got a jackpot about two weeks ago."

"Don't lie to me, honey. Just give my friend his twenty dollars back. It's gotta be a law, or something, that you're supposed to pay a percentage out."

"Can't do that. We don't even own those machines. We just lease them from Mr. Sullivan."

Big Arms came back inside from the restroom. He stood near the slot machine and listened to the conversation. "We don't care about that," he said. "The whole damn state of Nevada is just one big rip-off. Give us the money or a free meal."

"Yeah," said Shaved Head. "I'll go for a free meal."

"The food doesn't have anything to do with the slot machines," Kathy said. "If you ordered a meal, then—"

Fat Boy took three steps over to the counter and grabbed Kathy's arm. "Hell, I'll take something other than a free meal."

His three friends howled their approval. "You sure about that?" Big Arms asked. "Think she's worth twenty dollars?"

"If she does the four of us, it's five dollars apiece."

The door to the kitchen popped open and Kathy's father came out with a baseball bat. "Let go of her! Right now!"

Silver Buckle looked amused. "Are you threatening me, old man?"

"You're damn right! Now get your stuff and go!"

Silver Buckle reached across the table and picked up the heavy glass sugar container next to the little red bottle of Tabasco sauce. He sat up slightly and flung the container as hard as possible. Kathy's father jerked back, but the container hit his left cheek and cracked open. Sugar sprayed everywhere and the old man staggered back.

Shaved Head slid out of the booth. He grabbed the end of the baseball bat, twisted it out of the old man's hands, and held him in a neck lock. Using the butt end of the bat, Shaved Head struck the old man again and again. The old man went limp and Shaved Head let his victim drop onto the floor.

Maya touched Gabriel's hand. "Go out through the kitchen."

"No."

"This has nothing to do with us."

Gabriel looked at her with contempt and Maya felt as if she'd been slashed with a knife. She didn't move—couldn't move—as Gabriel stood up and took a few steps toward the men.

"Get out of here."

"And who the hell are you?" Silver Buckle slid out of his booth. Now all four men were standing near the counter. "You're not telling us nothing."

Shaved Head kicked Kathy's father in the ribs. "First thing we're going to do is lock this old bastard up with that coyote."

Kathy tried to get away, but Fat Boy held her tightly. "Second thing we do is inspect the merchandise."

Gabriel showed the uncertainty of someone who had only practiced fighting at a karate school. He stood there, waiting for the attack. "You heard what I said."

"Yeah. We heard." Shaved Head waved the baseball bat like a policeman's nightstick. "You got five seconds to get lost."

Maya slid out of the booth. Her hands were open and she felt relaxed. *Our kind of fighting is like diving into the ocean*, Thorn once told her. Falling, but graceful. Pulled by gravity, but controlled.

"Don't touch him," Maya said. The men laughed and she took a few steps forward, moving into the killing zone.

"What country are you from?" Silver Buckle asked. "Sounds like England or something like that. Around here, women let their men do their own fighting."

"Hey, I want her involved," said Big Arms. "She's got a nice little body."

Maya felt the Harlequin coldness overcome her heart. Instinctively, her eyes measured distances and trajectories between herself and the four targets. Her face was dead—unemotional—but she tried to make her words as clear and distinct as possible. "If you touch him, I will destroy you."

"Oh, I'm real scared."

Shaved Head glanced at his friend and grinned. "You're in big trouble, Russ! Little Missy looks mad! Better watch out!"

Gabriel turned to Maya. And, for the first time, he seemed to be in control of their relationship: like a Traveler commanding his Harlequin. "No, Maya! Do you hear me? I order you not to—"

He was half turned toward her, ignoring the danger, and Shaved Head raised the baseball bat. Maya jumped on a stool, then onto the counter. With two long steps, she ran past the ketchup and mustard containers, jabbed her right leg forward, and kicked Shaved Head in the throat. He spat and made a gurgling sound, but still held the bat. Maya grabbed the end of it and jumped down, wrenching it out of his hand with one motion, then swinging the bat at his head with a second motion. There was a loud cracking sound and he fell forward.

At the edge of her vision, she saw Gabriel fighting with Silver Buckle. She ran toward Kathy, holding the bat with her right hand and pulling out the stiletto with her left hand. Fat Boy looked terrified. He raised his arms like a soldier surrendering in battle and she drove the point of the stiletto through his palm, pinning his hand to the wooden paneling. The citizen gave a high-pitched scream, but she ignored him and continued toward Big Arms. Fake to the head, but swing lower. Break the right knee. Crack. Splinter. Then follow through to the head. Her target fell forward and she spun around. Silver Buckle was on the floor, unconscious. Gabriel had finished him off. Fat Boy was whimpering as she marched toward him.

"No," he said. "Please, God. No." And with one swing of the bat, she took him out. As he fell facedown, he ripped the knife out of the wall.

Maya dropped the bat, leaned over, and pulled out the stiletto. It was stained with blood, so she wiped it off on Fat

Boy's shirt. When she straightened up, the extreme clarity of combat began to fade away. Five bodies lay on the floor. She had defended Gabriel, but no one was dead.

Kathy stared at Maya as if she were a ghost. "You go away," she said. "Just go away. Because I'm calling the sheriff in one minute. Don't worry. If you go south, I'll say you went north. I'll change your car and everything."

Gabriel went out the door first and Maya followed him. As she passed the coyote, she undid the latch and opened the door of the cage. At first the animal didn't move, as if he had lost his memory of freedom. Maya kept walking and glanced over her shoulder. He was still in his prison. "Go ahead!" she shouted. "It's your only chance!"

As she started up the van, the coyote walked cautiously out of the cage and surveyed the dirt parking lot. The loud roar of Gabriel's motorcycle startled the animal. He jumped to one side, recovered his nonchalant attitude, and trotted past the diner.

Gabriel didn't look at Maya as he turned back onto the road. There were no more smiles and waves, no graceful S curves across the broken white line. She had protected Gabriel—saved him—but somehow her actions seemed to push them farther apart. At that moment she knew with absolute certainty that no one would ever love her or heal her pain. Like her father, she would die surrounded by enemies. Die alone.

37

Wearing a surgical mask and gown, Lawrence Takawa stood in one corner of the operating room. The new building at the center of the research quadrangle still wasn't equipped for a medical procedure. A temporary installation had been set up in the basement of the library.

He watched as Michael Corrigan lay down on the surgical table. Miss Yang, the nurse, came over with a heated blanket and folded it around his legs. Earlier that day, she had shaved all the hair off Michael's head. He looked like an army recruit who had just started basic training.

Dr. Richardson and Dr. Lau, the anesthesiologist brought in from Taiwan, finished preparing for the operation. A needle was inserted into Michael's arm, and the plastic IV tube was attached to a sterile solution. They had already taken X-ray and MRI images of Michael's brain at a private clinic in Westchester County that was controlled by the Brethren. Miss Yang clipped the film to light boxes at one end of the room.

Richardson looked down at his patient. "How are you feeling, Michael?"

"Is this going to be painful?"

"Not really. We're using anesthesia for safety reasons. During the procedure, your head needs to be completely immobile."

"What if something goes wrong and this injures my brain?"

"It's just a minor procedure, Michael. There's no reason for concern," Lawrence said.

Richardson nodded to Dr. Lau and the IV tube was attached to a plastic syringe. "All right. Here we go. Start counting backward from a hundred."

In ten seconds, Michael was unconscious and breathing evenly. With the nurse's help, Richardson attached a steel clamp to Michael's skull and tightened the padded screws. Even if Michael's body went into convulsions, his head wouldn't move.

"Map time," Richardson told the nurse. Miss Yang handed him a flexible steel ruler and a black felt-tip pen, and the neurologist spent the next twenty minutes drawing a grid on the top of Michael's head. He checked his work twice, then marked eight separate spots for an incision.

For several years neurologists had been placing permanent electrodes into the brains of patients suffering from depression. This deep-brain stimulation allowed doctors to turn a knob, inject a small amount of electricity into the tissue, and instantly change a person's mood. One of Richardson's patients—a young baker named Elaine—preferred setting two on the electronic meter when she was home watching television, but liked to turn her brain up to setting five if she was working hard to create a wedding cake. The same technology that helped scientists stimulate the brain would be used to track Michael's neural energy.

"Did I tell him the truth?" Lawrence asked.

Dr. Richardson glanced across the room. "What do you mean?"

"Can the procedure damage his brain?"

"If you want to monitor someone's neurological activity with a computer, then you have to insert sensors into the brain. Electrodes attached to the outside of the skull wouldn't be as effective. In fact, they might give you conflicting data."

"But won't the wires destroy his brain cells?"

"We all have millions of brain cells, Mr. Takawa. Perhaps the patient will forget how to pronounce the word Constantinople or he might lose the name of the girl who sat next to him in a high-school math class. It's not important."

When he was satisfied with the incision points, Dr. Richardson sat on a stool beside the operating table and studied the top of Michael's head. "More light," he said, and Miss Yang adjusted the surgical lamp. Dr. Lau stood a few feet away, watching a monitor screen and tracking Michael's vital signs.

"Everything okay?"

Dr. Lau checked Michael's heartbeat and respiration. "You can proceed."

Richardson lowered a bone drill attached to an adjustable arm and carefully cut a small hole in Michael's skull. There was a high-pitched grinding noise; it sounded like the machinery in a dentist's office.

He pulled the drill away. A tiny dot of blood appeared on the skin and began to grow larger, but Miss Yang wiped it away with a cotton swab. A neuropathic injector device was mounted on a second arm that hung from the ceiling. Richardson placed it over the tiny hole, squeezed the trigger, and a Teflon-coated copper wire the width of a human hair was pushed directly into Michael's brain.

The wire was attached to a cable that fed data to the quantum computer. Lawrence was wearing a radio headset with a direct link to the computer center. "Begin the test," he told one of the technicians. "The first sensor is in his brain."

Five seconds passed. Twenty seconds. Then a technician confirmed that they were picking up neural activity.

"The first sensor is working," Lawrence said. "You may proceed."

Dr. Richardson slid a small electrode plate down the length of the wire, glued it to the skin, and trimmed off the excess wire. Ninety minutes later, all the sensors had been inserted into Michael's brain and attached to the plates. From a distance, it looked like eight silver coins were glued to his skull.

* * *

MICHAEL WAS STILL unconscious, so the nurse remained beside him while Lawrence followed the two doctors into the next room. Everyone pulled off their surgical gowns and tossed them into a bin.

"When will he wake up?" Lawrence asked.

"In about an hour."

"Will he have any pain?"

"Minimal."

"Excellent. I'll ask the computer center when we can start the experiment."

Dr. Richardson looked nervous. "Perhaps you and I should talk."

The two men left the library and walked across the quadrangle to the administrative center. It had rained the night before and the sky was still gray. The roses were cut back and the irises were dry stalks. The Bermuda grass that bordered the walkway was dying. Everything looked vulnerable to the passage of time except for the windowless white building at the center of the courtyard. The official name for the building was the Neurological Cybernetics Research Facility, but the younger members of the staff called it "the Tomb."

"I've been reading more data concerning the Travelers," Richardson said. "Right now, I can anticipate some problems. We have a young man who may—or may not—be able to cross over to another realm."

"That's correct," Lawrence said. "We won't know until he tries."

"The research materials indicate that Travelers can learn how to cross over on their own. It can occur because of long-term stress or a sudden shock. But most people have some kind of teacher to instruct them."

"They're called Pathfinders," Lawrence said. "We've been looking for someone to perform that function, but we haven't been successful."

They paused at the entrance to the administrative center. Lawrence noticed that Dr. Richardson disliked looking at the Tomb. The neurologist stared at the sky and then at a concrete planter filled with English ivy—anything but the white building.

"What happens if you can't find a Pathfinder?" Richardson asked. "How is Michael going to know what to do?"

"There's another approach. The support staff is investigating different drugs that could act as a neurological catalyst."

"This is my field and I can tell you that no such drug has been developed. Nothing you take into your body is going to cause a rapid intensification of neural energy."

"The Evergreen Foundation has a great many contacts and sources. We're doing everything we can."

"It's clear that I'm not being told everything," Richardson said. "Let me tell you something, Mr. Takawa. That attitude is not conducive to a successful experiment."

"And what else do you need to know, Doctor?"

"It's not just the Travelers, is it? They're only part of a much larger objective—something that involves the quantum computer. So what are we really looking for? Can you tell me?"

"We've hired you to get a Traveler into another realm," Lawrence said. "And all you need to understand is that General Nash does not accept failure."

* * *

BACK IN HIS office, Lawrence had to deal with a dozen urgent phone messages and more than forty e-mails. He talked to General Nash about the surgical operation and confirmed that the computer center had picked up neural activity from every section of Michael's brain. During the next two hours, he wrote a carefully worded message that was e-mailed to the scientists who had received grants from the Evergreen Foundation. Although he couldn't mention the Travelers, he asked for explicit information about psychotropic drugs that gave people visions of alternative worlds.

At six o'clock in the evening the Protective Link device tracked Lawrence as he left the research center and drove back to his town house. Locking the front door, he stripped off his work clothes, pulled on a black cotton robe, and entered his secret room.

He wanted to give Linden an update on the Crossover Project, but the moment he got on the Internet a small blue box began flashing on the top left-hand corner of his screen. Two years ago, after Lawrence was given a new access code to the Brethren's computer system, he designed a special program to search for data about his father. Once the program was released, it scurried through the Internet like a ferret hunting for rats in an old house. Today it had found information about his father in the evidence files of the Osaka Police Department.

Two swords were displayed in Sparrow's photograph: one with a gold handle and another with jade fittings. Back in Paris, Linden explained that Lawrence's mother had given the jade sword to a Harlequin named Thorn who passed it on to the Corrigan family. Lawrence guessed that Gabriel Corrigan was still carrying the weapon when Boone and his mercenaries attacked the clothing factory.

A jade sword. A gold sword. Perhaps there were others. Lawrence had learned that the most famous sword maker in

Japanese history was a priest named Masamune. He had forged his blades during the thirteenth century; when the Mongols attempted to invade Japan. The ruling emperor had ordered a series of prayer rituals at Buddhist temples, and many famous swords were created as religious offerings. Masamune himself had forged a perfect sword with a diamond in its handle to inspire his ten students, the Jittetsu. As they learned how to hammer steel, each of the students had created one special weapon to present to their master.

Lawrence's computer program had found the Web site of a Buddhist priest living in Kyoto. The site gave the names of the ten Jittetsu and their special swords.

	SMITH	SWORD
I.	Hasabe Kinishige	Silver
II.	Kanemitsu	Gold
III.	Go Yoshihiro	Wood
IV.	Naotsuna	Pearl
V.	SaBone	
VI.	Rai Kunitsugu	Ivory
VII.	Kinju	Jade
VIII.	Shizu Kaneuji	Iron
IX.	Chogi	Bronze
X.	Saeki Norishige	Coral

A jade sword. A gold sword. The other Jittetsu swords had disappeared—probably lost in earthquakes or wars—but the doomed line of Japanese Harlequins had protected two of these sacred weapons. Now Gabriel Corrigan was carrying one of these treasures and the other was used to kill Yakuza in a blood-splattered banquet hall.

The search program moved through the lists of police evidence and translated the Japanese characters into English. *Antique tachi (long sword). Gold handle. Criminal investigation 15433. Evidence missing.*

Not missing, he thought. Stolen. The Brethren must have taken the gold sword from the Osaka police. It could be in Japan or America. Maybe it was stored at the research center, just a few feet away from his desk.

Lawrence Takawa was ready to jump up and drive back to the center. He controlled his emotions and switched off his computer. When Kennard Nash first told him about the Virtual Panopticon, it was just a philosophical theory, but now he actually lived inside the invisible prison. After one or two generations, every citizen in the industrial world would have to make the same assumption: that they were being tracked and monitored by the Vast Machine.

I'm alone, Lawrence thought. Yes. Completely alone. But he assumed a new mask that made him look alert, diligent, and ready to obey.

35

Sometimes Dr. Richardson felt like his old life had completely disappeared. He dreamed of his return to New Haven like a ghost from Dickens's *A Christmas Carol*, standing on the street in the cold darkness while his former friends and colleagues were inside his own house laughing and drinking wine.

It was clear that he never should have agreed to live at the research compound in Westchester County. He thought it would take weeks to arrange his departure from Yale, but the Evergreen Foundation appeared to wield extraordinary power at the university. The dean of the Yale Medical School had personally agreed to Richardson's sabbatical at full salary, and then asked if the foundation might be interested in funding the new genetic research lab. Lawrence Takawa hired a Columbia University neurologist who agreed to drive up every Tuesday and Thursday to finish teaching Richardson's classes. Five days after his interview with General Nash, two security men showed up at Richardson's house, helped him pack, and drove him to the compound.

His new world was comfortable, but very restricted. Lawrence Takawa had given Dr. Richardson a clip-on

Protective Link ID, and this determined his access to the different parts of the facility. Richardson could enter the library and the administrative center, but he was denied access to the computer area, the genetic research center, and the windowless building called the Tomb.

During his first week at the facility, he worked in the library basement practicing his surgical skills on the brains of dogs and chimpanzees as well as a fat cadaver with a white beard that the staff called Kris Kringle. Now that the Teflon-coated wires had been successfully inserted in Michael Corrigan's brain, Richardson spent most of his time in his small apartment at the administrative center or in a cubicle at the library.

The Green Book gave a summary of the extensive neurological research performed on Travelers. None of the reports had been published, and thick black lines disguised the names of the various research teams. The Chinese scientists had apparently used torture on Tibetan Travelers; the footnotes described chemical and electric-shock treatments. If a Traveler died during a torture session a discreet asterisk would be placed beside the case number of the subject.

Dr. Richardson felt like he understood the key aspects of a Traveler's brain activity. The nervous system produced a mild electric charge. When the Traveler was going into a trance state, the charge became stronger and showed a distinctive pulsing pattern. Suddenly everything seemed to switch off in the cerebrum. Respiration and cardiovascular activity was minimal. Except for a low-level response in the medulla oblongata, the patient was technically brain-dead. During this time, the Traveler's neurological energy was in another realm.

Most Travelers showed a genetic link to a parent or relative who had the power, but this wasn't always true. A Traveler could appear in the middle of rural China, born to a peasant family that had never traveled to another realm. A research team at the University of Utah was currently preparing a secret genealogy database involving all known Travelers and their ancestors.

Dr. Richardson wasn't sure what information was restricted and what could be shared with the rest of the staff. His anesthesiologist, Dr. Lau, and the surgical nurse, Miss Yang, had been flown in from Taiwan for the experiment. When the three of them ate together at the cafeteria, they talked about practical matters or Miss Yang's passion for old-fashioned American musicals.

Richardson didn't want to discuss *The Sound of Music* or *Oklahoma*. He was worried about the possible failure of the experiment. There was no Pathfinder to guide Michael, and his team hadn't received any special drugs that would force the Traveler's Light out of his body. The neurologist sent a general e-mail asking for help from other research teams working at the facility. Twelve hours later, he received a lab report from the genetic research building.

The report described an experiment involving cell regeneration. Richardson had studied the concept many years ago in his undergraduate biology class. He and his lab partner had cut a flatworm into twelve different pieces. A few weeks later, there were twelve identical versions of the original creature. Certain amphibians, such as salamanders, could lose a leg and grow a new one. The Research Project Agency of the United States Defense Department had spent millions of dollars on regeneration experiments with mammals. The Defense Department said it wanted to grow new fingers and arms for injured veterans, but there were rumors of more ambitious attempts at regeneration. One government scientist told a congressional panel that the future American soldier would be able to sustain a major bullet wound, heal himself, and continue fighting.

Apparently the Evergreen Foundation had gone far beyond that initial research in regeneration. The lab report described how a hybrid animal called a "splicer" could stop bleeding from a serious wound in one to two minutes and could regenerate a severed spinal nerve in less than a week. How these scientists had achieved these results was never described. Richardson was reading the report a second time when Lawrence Takawa appeared in the library.

"I just found out that you received some unauthorized information from our genetic research team."

"I'm glad it happened," Richardson said. "This data is very promising. Who's in charge of the program?"

Instead of responding, Lawrence took out his cell phone and dialed a number. "Could you send someone over to the library," he said. "Thank you."

"What's going on?"

"The Evergreen Foundation isn't ready to publish its discoveries. If you mention the report to anyone, Mr. Boone will see it as a security violation."

A security guard entered the library and Richardson felt sick to his stomach. Lawrence stood beside the cubicle with a bland expression on his face.

"Dr. Richardson needs to replace his computer," Lawrence announced as if there had been some kind of equipment failure. The guard immediately disconnected the computer, picked it up, and carried the machine out of the library. Lawrence glanced at his watch. "It's almost one o'clock, Doctor. Why don't you go have lunch."

Richardson ordered a chicken salad sandwich and a cup of barley soup, but he was too tense to finish the meal. When he returned to the library, a new computer had been placed in his cubicle. The lab report wasn't on the new hard disk, but the foundation's computer staff had downloaded a sophisticated chess simulator. The neurologist tried not to think of negative consequences, but it was difficult to control his thoughts. He nervously played endgames for the rest of the day.

*　　*　　*

ONE NIGHT AFTER dinner Richardson remained in the employee cafeteria. He tried to read a *New York Times* article about something called the New Spirituality while a group of young computer programmers sat at a nearby table and made loud jokes about a pornographic video game.

Someone touched his shoulder and he turned around to find Lawrence Takawa and Nathan Boone. Richardson hadn't seen the security man for several weeks and had decided that his previous fear was an irrational reaction. Now that Boone was staring at him, the fear returned. There was something about the man that was very intimidating.

"I have some wonderful news," Lawrence said. "One of our contacts just called about a drug we've been investigating called 3B3. We think it might help Michael Corrigan cross over."

"Who developed the drug?"

Lawrence shrugged his shoulders as if this wasn't important. "We don't know."

"Can I read the lab reports?"

"There aren't any."

"When can I get a supply of this drug?"

"You're coming with me," Boone said. "We're going to look for it together. If we find a source, you need to make a quick evaluation."

* * *

THE TWO MEN left immediately, driving down to Manhattan in Boone's SUV. Boone wore a telephone headset and he answered a series of calls—never saying anything specific or mentioning anybody's name. Listening to scattered comments, Richardson concluded that Boone's men were searching for someone in California who had a dangerous female bodyguard.

"If you find her, watch her hands and don't let her get near you," Boone told someone. "I would say eight feet is the approximate safety zone."

There was a long pause and Boone received some more information.

"I don't think the Irish woman is in America," he said. "My European sources tell me she's completely dropped out of sight. If you see her, respond in an extreme manner. She has no restraint whatsoever. Highly dangerous. Do you know what happened in Sicily? Yes? Well, don't forget."

Boone switched off his phone and concentrated on the road. Light from the car's instrument panel was reflected off the lenses of his eyeglasses. "Dr. Richardson, I've heard reports that you gained access to unauthorized information from the genetic research team."

"It was just an accident, Mr. Boone. I wasn't trying to—"

"But you didn't see anything."

"Unfortunately I did, but . . ."

Boone glared at Richardson as if the neurologist were a stubborn child. "You didn't see anything," he repeated.

"No. I guess I didn't."

"Good." Boone glided into the right lane and took the turn for New York City. "Then there isn't a problem."

* * *

IT WAS ABOUT ten o'clock in the evening when they reached Manhattan. Richardson stared out the window at a homeless man searching through a trash can and a group of young women laughing as they left a restaurant. After the quiet environment of the research center, New York seemed noisy and uncontrolled. Had he really visited this city with his ex-wife, gone to plays and restaurants? Boone drove over to the east side and parked on Twenty-eighth Street. They got out and walked toward the dark towers of Bellevue Hospital.

"What are we doing here?" Richardson asked.

"We're going to meet a friend of the Evergreen Foundation." Boone gave Richardson a quick, appraising look. "Tonight you'll discover how many new friends you have in this world."

Boone handed a business card to the bored woman at the reception desk and she allowed them to take the elevator up to the psychiatric ward. On the sixth floor, a uniformed hospital guard sat behind a Plexiglas barrier. The guard didn't look surprised when Boone pulled an automatic pistol out of his shoulder holster and placed the gun in a little gray locker. They entered the ward. A short Hispanic man wearing a white lab coat was waiting for them. He smiled and extended both hands as if they had just arrived for a birthday party.

"Good evening, gentlemen. Which one of you is Dr. Richardson?"

"That's me."

"A pleasure to meet you. I'm Dr. Raymond Flores. The Evergreen Foundation said you'd be dropping by tonight."

Dr. Flores escorted them down the hallway. Even though it was late, a few male patients wearing green cotton pajamas and bathrobes wandered around. All of them were drugged and they moved slowly. Their eyes were dead and their slippers made little hissing sounds as they touched the tile floor.

"So you work for the foundation?" Flores asked.

"Yes. I'm in charge of a special project," Richardson said.

Dr. Flores passed several patient rooms, then stopped at a locked door. "Someone from the foundation named Takawa asked me to look for admits picked up under the influence of this new street drug, 3B3. No one's made a chemical analysis yet, but it seems to be a very potent hallucinogen. The people taking it think they've been given a vision of different worlds."

Flores unlocked the door and they entered a detention cell that smelled of urine and vomit. The only light came from a single bulb protected by a mesh screen. A young man wrapped in a canvas straitjacket lay on the green tile floor. His head was shaved, but a faint haze of blond hair was beginning to appear on his skull.

The patient opened his eyes and smiled at the three men standing over him. "Hello, everyone. Why don't you take out your brains and make yourselves comfortable?"

Dr. Flores smoothed the lapels of his lab coat and smiled pleasantly. "Terry, these gentlemen want to learn about 3B3."

Terry blinked twice and Richardson wondered if he was going to say anything at all. Suddenly he began pushing with his legs, wiggling across the floor to a wall, then forcing himself up to a sitting position. "It's not really a drug. It's a revelation."

"Do you shoot it, snort it, inhale it, or swallow it?" Boone's voice was calm and deliberately neutral.

"It's a liquid, light blue, like a summer sky." Terry closed his eyes for a few seconds, then opened them again. "I swallowed it at the club and then I was cracking out of this body and flying, passing through water and fire to a beautiful forest. But I couldn't stay for more than a few seconds." He looked disappointed. "The jaguar had green eyes."

Dr. Flores glanced at Richardson. "He's told this story many times, and he always ends up with the jaguar."

"So where can I find 3B3?" Richardson asked.

Terry closed his eyes again and smiled serenely. "Do you know what he charges for one dose? Three hundred and thirty-three dollars. He says it's a magic number."

"And who's making that kind of money?" Boone asked.

"Pius Romero. He's always at the Chan Chan Room."

"It's a midtown dance club," Dr. Flores explained. "We've had several patients who have overdosed there."

"This world is too small," Terry whispered. "Do you realize that? It's a child's marble dropped into a pool of water."

They followed Flores back out into the corridor. Boone walked away from the two doctors and immediately called someone with his cell phone.

"Have you examined other patients who have used this drug?" Richardson asked.

"This is the fourth admit in the last two months. We put them on a combination of Fontex and Valdov for a few days until they're catatonic, then we lower the dosage and bring them back to reality. After a while, the jaguar disappears."

*   *   *

BOONE ESCORTED RICHARDSON back to the SUV. He received two more phone calls, said "yes" to each person, then switched off the cell.

"What are we going to do?" asked Richardson.

"Next stop is the Chan Chan Room."

Limousines and black town cars were double parked outside the club entrance on Fifty-third Street. Held behind a velvet rope, a crowd of people waited for the bouncers to search them with hand-held metal detectors. The women standing in line wore short dresses or flimsy skirts with slits up the side.

Boone drove past the crowd, then stopped beside a sedan parked halfway down the block. Two men got out of the car and walked up to Boone's side window. One of the men was a short African American wearing an expensive suede car coat. His partner was white and as big as a football lineman. He wore an army surplus jacket and looked like he wanted to pick up a few pedestrians and throw them down on the street.

The black man grinned. "Hey, Boone. It's been a while." He nodded at Dr. Richardson. "Who's your new friend?"

"Dr. Richardson, this is Detective Mitchell and his partner, Detective Krause."

"We got your message, drove here, and talked to the club bouncers." Krause had a deep, growly voice. "They say this Romero guy came in an hour ago."

"You two go around to the fire door," Mitchell said. "We'll bring him out."

Boone rolled up the window and drove down the street. He parked two blocks away from the club, then reached under the front seat and found a black leather glove. "You come with me, Doctor. Mr. Romero might have some information."

Richardson followed Boone to an alleyway at the rear exit of the Chan Chan Room. A rhythmic, thumping music pushed through the steel fire door. A few minutes later the door popped open and Detective Krause threw a skinny Puerto Rican man onto the asphalt. Still looking cheerful, Detective Mitchell strolled over to the man and kicked him in the stomach.

"Gentlemen, we'd like you to meet Pius Romero. He was sitting in the VIP room drinking something fruity with a little umbrella. Now that's not fair, is it? Krause and I are dedicated public servants and we never get invited to the VIP room."

Pius Romero lay on the asphalt, gasping for breath. Boone pulled on the black leather glove. He gazed at Romero as if the young man was an empty cardboard box. "Listen carefully, Pius. We're not here to arrest you, but I want some information. If you lie about anything, my friends will track you down and give you a great deal of pain. Do you understand that? Show me that you understand."

Pius sat up and touched his scraped elbow. "I ain't doing nothing wrong."

"Who supplies your 3B3?"

The name of the drug made the young man sit up a little straighter.

"Never heard of it."

"You sold it to several people. Who sold it to you?"

Pius scrambled to his feet and tried to run away, but Boone caught him. He threw the drug dealer against the wall and began slapping him with his right hand. The leather glove made a smacking sound every time it hit Romero's face. Blood trickled out of his nose and mouth.

Dr. Richardson knew this violence was real—very real—but he didn't feel attached to what was happening. It was like he was one step back from what was going on, watching a movie on a television screen. As the beating continued, he glanced at the two detectives. Mitchell was smiling while Krause nodded like a basketball fan who had just seen a perfect three-point shot.

Boone's voice was calm and reasonable. "I've broken your nose, Pius. Now I'm going to strike upward and crush the nasal turbinate bones beneath your eyes. These bones will never heal successfully. Not like a leg or arm. You're going to feel pain for the rest of your life."

Pius Romero raised his hands like a child. "What do you want?" He whimpered. "Names? I'll give you names. I'll give you everything . . ."

*   *   *

AROUND TWO O'CLOCK in the morning, they found the address near JFK airport in Jamaica, Queens. The man who manufactured 3B3 lived in a white clapboard house with aluminum lawn chairs chained to his porch. It was a quiet, working-class neighborhood, the kind of place where people swept their sidewalks and placed concrete statues of the Virgin Mary on their tiny front lawns. Boone parked his SUV and told Dr. Richardson to get out. They walked over to the detectives sitting in their car.

"You want help?" Mitchell asked.

"Stay here. Dr. Richardson and I are going to go inside. If there's trouble, I'll call you on my cell phone."

The sense of detachment that had protected Richardson when Boone was beating Pius Romero had disappeared during the ride out to Queens. The neurologist felt tired and scared. He wanted to run away from the three men, but he knew that would be useless. Shivering from the cold, he followed Boone across the street. "What are you going to do?" he asked.

Boone stood on the sidewalk and gazed up at a light

coming from a third-floor window. "I don't know. First I have to assess the problem."

"I hate violence, Mr. Boone."

"So do I."

"You almost killed that young man."

"I didn't even come close." Puffs of white breath came out of Boone's mouth as he talked. "You need to study history, Doctor. All great changes are based on pain and destruction."

The two men walked down the driveway to the back door of the house. Boone stood on the porch and touched the door frame with the tips of his fingers. All of a sudden, he took one step back and kicked just above the knob. There was a cracking sound and the door flew open. Richardson followed him inside.

The house was very warm and smelled harsh and foul, like someone had spilled a bottle of ammonia. The two men passed through the dark kitchen, and Richardson accidentally stepped on a water dish. Creatures were moving around the kitchen and on the counters. Boone flicked on the switch for the overhead light.

"Cats," Boone said, almost spitting out the word. "I hate cats. You can't teach them anything."

There were four cats in the kitchen and two more in the hallway. They moved quietly on soft paws as the inner layer of their eyes reflected the dim light and turned gold and pink and dark green. Their tails curved up like little question marks while their whiskers tasted the air.

"There's a light upstairs," Boone said. "Let's see who's home." Single file, they climbed up the wooden stairs to the third floor. Boone opened a door and they entered an attic that had been turned into a laboratory. There were tables and chemical glassware. A spectrograph. Microscopes and a Bunsen burner.

An old man sat in a wicker chair with a white Persian cat on his lap. He was clean-shaven and neatly dressed, and wore bifocal eyeglasses tilted downward on the end of his nose. He didn't seem surprised by the intrusion.

"Good evening, gentlemen." The man spoke very precisely, enunciating each syllable. "I knew that you'd show up here eventually. In fact, I predicted it. Newton's third law of motion states that for every action there's an equal and opposite reaction."

Boone watched the old man as if he were about to run away. "I'm Nathan Boone. What's your name?"

"Lundquist. Dr. Jonathan Lundquist. If you're the police, you can leave right now. I haven't done anything illegal. There's no law against 3B3 because the government doesn't know that it exists."

A tortoiseshell cat tried to rub against Boone's leg, but he kicked it away. "We're not policemen."

Dr. Lundquist looked surprised. "Then you must be—yes, of course—you work for the Brethren."

Boone looked like he was going to slip on his black leather glove and break the old man's nose. Richardson shook his head slightly. No need for that. He walked over to the old man and sat down on a folding chair. "I'm Dr. Phillip Richardson, a research neurologist with Yale University."

Lundquist looked pleased to be meeting another scientist. "And now you're working for the Evergreen Foundation."

"Yes. On a special project."

"Many years ago, I applied for a grant from the foundation, but they didn't even answer my letter. That was before I learned about the Travelers from renegade Web sites on the Internet." Lundquist laughed softly. "I thought it was best if I worked on my own. No forms to fill out. No one looking over my shoulder."

"Were you trying to duplicate the Traveler's experience?"

"It's much more than that, Doctor. I was trying to answer some fundamental questions." Lundquist stopped stroking the Persian cat and it jumped off his lap. "A few years ago I was at Princeton, teaching organic chemistry . . ." He glanced at Richardson. "I had a respectable career, but nothing flashy. I was always interested in the big picture. Not just chemistry but other areas of science. So one afternoon I went to a graduate seminar in the physics department about something called brane theory.

"Physicists have a serious problem these days. The concepts that explain the universe, such as Einstein's theory of general relativity, aren't compatible with the subatomic world of quantum mechanics. Some physicists have gotten around this contradiction with string theory, the idea that everything is composed of tiny subatomic objects that are vibrating in multidimensional space. The math makes sense, but the strings are so small that you can't prove much experimentally.

"Brane theory goes large and tries to give a cosmological explanation. 'Brane' is short for 'membrane.' The theorists believe that our perceivable universe is confined to a sort of membrane of space and time. The usual analogy is that our galaxy is like pond scum—a thin layer of existence floating on a much larger bulk of something. All matter, including our own bodies, is trapped in our brane, but gravity can leak off into the bulk or subtly influence our own physical phenomenon. Other branes, other dimensions, other realms— use any word you wish—can be very near to us, but we would be totally unaware of them. That's because neither light nor sound nor radioactivity can break free of its own particular dimension."

A black cat approached Lundquist and he scratched behind the animal's ears. "That's the theory at least, in a very simplified form. And I had the theory in my mind when I went to hear a lecture in New York given by a monk from Tibet. I'm sitting there, listening to him talk about the six different realms of Buddhist cosmology, and I realize that he's describing the branes—the different dimensions and the barriers that separate them. But there's one crucial difference: my associates at Princeton can't conceive of going to these different places. For a Traveler, it's quite possible. The body can't do it, but the Light within us can."

Lundquist leaned back in his chair and smiled at his guests. "This connection between spirituality and physics made me view science in a new way. Right now we're smashing atoms and ripping apart chromosomes. We're going to the bottom of the ocean and looking up into space. But we're not really investigating the region within our skull except in the most superficial way. People are using MRI machines and CAT scans to view the brain, but it's all very small and physiological. No one seems to realize how immense consciousness really is. It ties us to the rest of the universe."

Richardson glanced around the room and saw a tabby cat sitting on a leather folder crammed with sheets of stained paper. Trying not to alarm Lundquist, he stood up and took a few steps toward the table. "So you started your experiment?"

"Yes. First, at Princeton. Then I retired and moved here to save money. Remember, I'm a chemist, not a physicist. So I decided to search for a substance that would break our Light free of our body."

"And you came up with a formula . . ."

"It's not a cake recipe." Lundquist sounded annoyed. "3B3 is a living thing. A new strain of bacterium. When you swallow the liquid solution, it's absorbed into your nervous system."

"Sounds dangerous."

"I've taken it dozens of times. And I can still remember to take out my garbage cans on Thursday and pay my electric bill."

The tabby cat purred and walked over to Richardson when he reached the table. "And 3B3 allows you to see different realms?"

"No. It's a failure. You can swallow all you want, but it won't turn you into a Traveler. The journey is very short, a brief contact instead of a real landing. You stay long enough to get one or two images, then you have to leave."

Richardson opened the folder and glanced at the stained graphs and scribbled notes. "What if we took your bacterium and gave it to someone?"

"Be my guest. Some of it is in the petri dish right in front of you. But you'd be wasting your time. As I told you, it doesn't work. That's why I started giving it away to this young man named Pius Romero who used to shovel the snow off my driveway. I thought that perhaps there was something wrong with my own consciousness. Perhaps other people could take 3B3 and cross over to another place. But it wasn't me. Whenever Pius comes back for more, I insist that he give me a full report. People have visions of another world, but they can't remain."

Richardson picked up the petri dish on the table. A blue-green bacterium was growing in a graceful curve on the agar solution. "This is it?"

"Yes. The failure. Go back to the Brethren and tell them to check into a monastery. Pray. Meditate. Study the Bible, the Koran, or the Kabbalah. There's no quick way to escape our shabby little world."

"But what if a Traveler took 3B3?" Richardson asked. "It would start him on the journey, then he could finish on his own."

Dr. Lundquist leaned forward and Richardson thought that the old man might jump out of the chair. "That's an interesting idea," he said. "But aren't all the Travelers dead? The Brethren have spent a great deal of money slaughtering them. But who knows? Maybe you can find one hiding out in Madagascar or Kathmandu."

"We've found a cooperative Traveler."

"And you're using him?"

Richardson nodded.

"I can't believe it. Why are the Brethren doing this?"

Richardson picked up the folder and the petri dish. "This is a wonderful discovery, Dr. Lundquist. I just want you to know that."

"I'm not looking for compliments. Just an explanation. Why have the Brethren changed their strategy?"

Boone approached the table and spoke with a soft voice, "Is that what we came for, Doctor?"

"I think so."

"We're not coming back. You better be sure."

"This is all we need. Listen, I don't want anything negative happening to Dr. Lundquist."

"Of course, Doctor. I understand how you feel. He's not a criminal like Pius Romero." Boone placed a gentle hand on Richardson's shoulder and guided him to the doorway. "Go back to the car and wait. I need to explain our security concerns to Dr. Lundquist. It won't take long."

Richardson stumbled down the staircase, passed through the kitchen, and went out the back door. A blast of cold air made his eyes tear up as if he was crying. As he stood on the porch he felt so weary that he wanted to lie down and curl up in a ball. His life had changed forever, but his body still pumped blood, digested food, and took in oxygen. He wasn't a scientist anymore, writing papers and dreaming of the Nobel Prize. Somehow he had become smaller, almost insignificant, a tiny piece of a complex mechanism.

Still holding the petri dish, Richardson shuffled down the driveway. Apparently Boone's conversation with Dr. Lundquist didn't take very long. He caught up with the neurologist before he reached the car.

"Is everything all right?" Richardson asked.

"Of course," Boone said. "I knew there wouldn't be a problem. Sometimes it's best to be clear and direct. No extra words. No false diplomacy. I expressed myself firmly and got a positive response."

Boone opened the door to the car and made a mocking bow like an insolent chauffeur. "You must be tired, Dr. Richardson. It's been a long night. Let me take you back to the research center."

36

Hollis drove past Michael Corrigan's apartment complex at nine o'clock in the morning, two o'clock in the afternoon, and seven o'clock in the evening. He looked for Tabula mercenaries sitting in parked cars and on park benches, men pretending to be power company employees or city workers. After each drive-by, he would park in front of a beauty salon and write down everything he had seen. *Old lady pushing a shopping cart. Man with a beard loading a child's car seat.* When he came back five hours later, he compared his notes and saw no similarities. That only meant that the Tabula weren't waiting outside the building. Perhaps they were sitting in the apartment across the hall from Michael's apartment.

He thought up a plan after teaching his evening capoeira class. The next day, he put on a blue cotton jumpsuit and picked up the mop and the bucket on wheels that he used when he was washing the floor of his school. Michael's apartment complex occupied an entire city block on Wilshire Boulevard near Barrington. There were three skyscrapers, an attached four-level parking structure, and a large inner courtyard with a pool and tennis courts.

Be deliberate, Hollis thought. You don't want to fight the Tabula, just play with their minds. He parked his car two blocks away from the entrance, filled the bucket on wheels with soapy water from two plastic jugs, set the mop into the water, and began to push everything up the sidewalk. As he approached the entrance, he tried to think like a janitor—play that role.

Two old ladies were leaving the building when he arrived. "Just cleaned the sidewalk," he told them. "Now somebody messed up one of the hallways."

"People need to learn some manners," one of the women said. Her friend held the door open so that Hollis could push the bucket inside the foyer.

Hollis nodded and smiled as the old ladies walked away. He waited for a few seconds, then went over to the elevators. When the next elevator arrived, he rode alone up to the eighth floor. Michael Corrigan's apartment was at the end of the hallway.

If the Tabula were hiding in the opposite apartment, watching him through the security peephole, then he would have to start lying right away. Mr. Corrigan pays me to clean up his place. Yes, sir. I do it once a week. Is Mr. Corrigan gone? I didn't know he was gone, sir. He hasn't paid me for a month.

Using the key that Gabriel had given him, Hollis unlocked the door and went inside. He was alert, ready to defend himself against an attack, but no one appeared. The apartment had a hot, dusty smell. A two-week-old copy of the *Wall Street Journal* was still on the coffee table. Hollis left the bucket and mop near the door and hurried into Michael's bedroom. He found the telephone, pulled out a small tape recorder, and dialed Maggie Resnick's home number. She wasn't home, but Hollis didn't want to talk to her anyway. He was sure that the Tabula were monitoring the phone lines. After Maggie's answering machine came on, Hollis switched on the tape recorder and held it up to the telephone handset.

"Hey, Maggie. This is Gabe. I'm going to get out of Los Angeles and find someplace to hide. Thanks for everything. Bye."

Hollis hung up the phone, switched off the tape recorder, and quickly left the apartment. He felt tense pushing the bucket down the hallway, but then the elevator arrived and he stepped inside. Okay, he thought. That was easy enough. Don't forget, you're still the janitor.

When the elevator reached the lobby, Hollis pushed the bucket out and nodded to a young couple with a cocker spaniel. The entrance door clicked open and three Tabula mercs hurried into the lobby. They looked like police officers who were doing this for money. One man wore a denim jacket and his two pals were dressed as painters. The painters carried towels and drop cloths that concealed their hands.

Hollis ignored the Tabula as they pushed past him. He was five feet away from the door when an older Latino man pushed open the door that led to the swimming pool area. "Hey, what's going on?" the man asked Hollis.

"Somebody dropped a bottle of cranberry juice on the fifth floor. I just cleaned it up."

"I didn't see that in the morning report."

"It just happened." Hollis was at the door now, almost touching the knob.

"Besides, isn't that Freddy's job? Who are you working for?"

"I was just hired by—"

But before Hollis could finish the sentence he sensed movement behind him. And then the hard point of a gun muzzle was pushed against the small of his back.

"He's working for us," said one of the men.

"That's right," said another man. "And he's not done."

The two men dressed as painters stood beside Hollis. They made him turn around and guided him back to the elevator. The man with the denim jacket was talking to the maintenance man, showing him a letter that described some kind of official permission.

"What's going on?" Hollis tried to look surprised and frightened.

"Don't talk," whispered the larger man. "Don't say one damn thing at all."

Hollis and the two painters stepped into the elevator. Just before the door closed, Denim Jacket slipped in and punched the button for the eighth floor.

"Who are you?" Denim asked.

"Tom Jackson. I'm the janitor here."

"Don't bullshit us," said the smaller painter. He was the one with the weapon. "That guy out there didn't know who you were."

"I just got hired here two days ago."

"What's the name of the company that hired you?" Denim asked.

"It was Mr. Regal."

"I asked you the name of the company."

Hollis shifted slightly so that he was away from the barrel of the gun. "I'm sorry, sir. I'm real sorry. But all I know is that Mr. Regal hired me and I was told to—"

He made a half turn, grabbed the gunman's wrist, and thrust it outward. With his right hand he punched the man in the Adam's apple. The gun went off with a loud cracking sound in the small space and the other painter was shot. He screamed as Hollis whipped around, smashing his elbow into Denim's mouth. Hollis twisted the gunman's arm downward and the Tabula merc dropped the weapon.

Turn. Attack. Spin around and punch again. Within a few seconds, all three men were lying on the floor. The door opened. Hollis flipped the red switch to stop the elevator and stepped out. He ran down the hallway, found the fire exit, and ran down the stairs two at a time.

37

When Michael was growing up on the road he had an automatic response to his mother's wild stories and Gabriel's impractical schemes for making money. *It's time to go to Reality Town,* he told them, which meant that someone in the family had to be objective about their problems. Michael considered himself to be the Mayor of Reality Town—not a pleasant location, perhaps, but at least you knew where you stood.

Living at the research center, he found it difficult to be objective. There was no question that he was a prisoner. Even if he discovered a way to get out of his locked room, the security guards would never let him stroll through the gates and catch a bus to New York City. Perhaps he had lost his freedom—but that fact didn't trouble him. For the first time in his life people seemed to be giving him the right amount of respect and deference.

Every Tuesday, Michael would join Kennard Nash for drinks and dinner in the oak-paneled office. The general dominated the conversation, explaining the hidden objectives behind what appeared to be random occurrences. One night Nash described the RFID chip hidden in American passports, and showed photographs of a device called a "skimmer" that could read passports from a distance of sixty-five feet. When the new technology was first proposed, a few experts had called for a "contact" passport that had to be pushed through a slot like a credit card, but the Brethren's friends in the White House had insisted on the radio frequency chip.

"Is the information encrypted?" Michael asked.

"Of course not. That would make it difficult to share the technology with other governments."

"But what if terrorists use the skimmers?"

"It would certainly make their job easier. Let's say a tourist was walking through the marketplace in Cairo. A skimmer could read his passport—find out if he was American and if he had visited Israel. By the time this American reached the end of the street, an assassin could be stepping out of a nearby doorway."

Michael sat for a moment and studied Nash's bland smile. "None of this makes sense. The government says it wants to protect us, but it's doing something that makes us more vulnerable."

General Nash looked as if his favorite nephew had just made an innocent mistake. "Yes, it's unfortunate. But you have to weigh the loss of a few lives against the power given to us by this new technology. This is the future, Michael. No one can stop it. In a few years, it won't just be passports. Everyone will carry a Protective Link device that tracks them all the time."

*   *   *

IT WAS DURING one of these weekly conversations that Nash mentioned what had happened to Gabriel. Apparently, Michael's brother had been captured by a fanatical woman who worked for a terrorist group called the Harlequins. She had killed several people before they fled from Los Angeles.

"My staff is going to keep looking," Nash said. "We don't want anyone to harm your brother."

"Let me know when you find him."

"Of course." Nash smeared some cream cheese and caviar onto a cracker and squeezed on a drop of lemon juice. "The reason I'm mentioning this is because the Harlequins might be training Gabriel to become a Traveler. If you both have the ability, there's a possibility that you could meet in another realm. You'll need to ask him the location of his physical body. Once we know that, we can rescue him."

"Forget it," Michael said. "Gabe would only go to another realm if he could ride there on a motorcycle. Maybe the Harlequins will realize that and let him go."

*　　*　　*

ON THE MORNING of the experiment, Michael woke up early and took a shower, wearing a swimming cap so that the silver plates on the top of his skull wouldn't get wet. He pulled on a T-shirt, drawstring pants, and rubber flip-flops. No breakfast this morning. Dr. Richardson didn't think it was a good idea. Michael was sitting on the couch, listening to music, when Lawrence knocked softly on the door and entered the room. "The research team is ready," he said. "It's time."

"And what if I decide not to do it?"

Lawrence looked startled. "That's your choice, Michael. Obviously the Brethren wouldn't be pleased by this decision. I'd have to call General Nash and—"

"Relax. I haven't changed my mind."

He pulled a knit wool cap over his shaved head and followed Lawrence out into the hallway. Two security men were there wearing their usual black neckties and navy blue blazers. They formed a sort of honor guard—one man in front, the other behind. The little group passed through a locked door to the courtyard.

Michael was surprised to see that everyone involved in the Crossover Project—secretaries, chemists, and computer programmers—had come out to watch him enter the Tomb. Although most of the staff didn't understand the true nature of the Crossover Project, they had been told that it would help protect America from its enemies and that Michael was an important part of the plan.

He nodded slightly, like an athlete acknowledging the crowd, and sauntered across the courtyard to the Tomb. All these buildings had been constructed and all these people had been assembled for this moment. Bet it cost a lot of money, he thought. Bet it cost millions. Michael had always felt that he was special, destined for greatness, and now he was being treated like a movie star in a high-budget film that had only one role, a single face on the screen. If he really could travel to another realm, then they should give him their respect. It wasn't luck that he was here. It was his birthright.

*   *   *

A STEEL DOOR slid open and they entered a vast, shadowy room. A glass-enclosed gallery, about twenty feet above the smooth concrete floor, ran around all four walls. Light from control panels and computer monitors glowed inside the gallery and Michael saw that several technicians were looking down at him. The air was cold and dry and he could hear a faint humming sound.

A steel surgical table with a small pillow for his head was in the middle of the room. Dr. Richardson stood near the table. The nurse and Dr. Lau were checking the monitoring equipment and the contents of a steel rack that held test tubes filled with different colored liquids. Eight wires connected to silver-colored electrode plates lay beside the little white pillow. The separate wires were spliced together into a thick black cable that slithered off the table and disappeared into the floor.

"You okay?" Lawrence asked.

"So far."

Lawrence lightly touched Michael's arm and remained near the door with the two security men. They were acting like he was going to run out of the building, jump over the wall, and hide in the forest. Michael walked to the center of the Tomb, pulled off his knit cap, and handed it to the nurse. Wearing only a T-shirt and the drawstring pants, he lay faceup on the table. The room was cold, but he felt ready for anything, like an athlete about to play an important game.

Richardson leaned over him and taped the eight sensor wires to the eight electrode plates on his skull. Now his brain was directly connected to the quantum computer, and the technicians up in the gallery could monitor his neurological activity. Richardson looked nervous, and Michael wished that the doctor's face was concealed with a surgical mask. To hell with him. It wasn't his brain that was skewered with little copper wires. It's my life, thought Michael. My risk.

"Good luck," Richardson said.

"Forget luck. Let's just do it and see what happens."

Richardson nodded and slipped on a radio headset so he could talk to the technicians in the gallery. He was responsible for Michael's brain while Dr. Lau and the nurse were in charge of the rest of the body. They taped sensors to his chest and neck so they could track his vital signs. The nurse swabbed topical anesthetic on his arm, then slipped an intravenous needle through his skin. The needle was attached to a plastic tube and a saline solution began to drip into his veins.

"Are you getting a wave range?" Richardson whispered into the microphone. "Good. Yes. That's very good."

"We need a baseline to start out," he told Michael. "So we're going to give the brain different kinds of stimuli. Nothing to think about here. You'll just react."

The nurse went to the steel cabinet and came back with several test tubes. The first batch contained tastes: salty, sour, bitter, sweet. Then different smells: rose, vanilla, and something that reminded Michael of burned rubber. Richardson kept murmuring into the headset as he took a special flashlight and aimed colored lights at Michael's eyes. They played sounds at various volumes and touched his face with a feather, a block of wood, and a rough piece of steel.

Satisfied with the sensory data, Richardson asked Michael to count backward, add numbers, and describe the dinner served to him last night. Then they went into deep memory and Michael had to tell them about the first time he saw the ocean and the first time he saw a naked woman. Did you have your own room when you were a teenager? What did it look like? Describe the furniture and the posters on the wall.

Finally Richardson stopped asking him questions and the nurse squirted some water into his mouth. "Okay," Richardson told the technicians. "I think we're ready."

The nurse reached into the cabinet and took out an IV bag filled with a diluted mixture of the drug they called 3B3. Kennard Nash had called Michael to talk about the drug. He explained that 3B3 was a special bacterium developed in Switzerland by a top scientific team. The drug was very expensive and difficult to manufacture, but the toxins created from the bacterium seemed to increase neural energy. As the nurse raised the bag higher, the viscous turquoise-blue liquid sloshed around in the IV bag.

She took away the neutral saline solution, attached the IV bag, and a thread of 3B3 raced down the plastic tube to the needle in his arm. Richardson and Dr. Lau stared at him as if he were going to float off into another dimension.

"How do you feel?" Richardson asked.

"Normal. How long does it take for this stuff to kick in?"

"We don't know."

"Heart rate slightly elevated," Dr. Lau informed them. "Respiration unchanged."

Trying not to show his disappointment, Michael gazed at the ceiling for a few minutes, then closed his eyes. Maybe he wasn't really a Traveler, or perhaps the new drug didn't work. All this effort and money had led to failure.

"Michael?"

He opened his eyes. Richardson was staring at him. The room was still cool, but there were beads of sweat on the doctor's forehead.

"Start counting backward from one hundred."

"We already did that."

"They want to return to a neurological baseline."

"Forget it. This isn't going to . . ."

Michael moved his left arm and saw something extraordinary. A hand and wrist composed of little points of light emerged from his flesh hand like a ghost pushing through a locked cabinet. Lifeless, his flesh hand flopped back down onto the table while the ghost hand remained.

He knew instantly that this thing—this apparition—had always been part of him, inside his body. The ghost hand reminded him of the simple drawings made of constellations like the Twins or the Archer. His hand was composed of tiny stars that were connected by thin, almost imperceptible lines of light. He couldn't move this ghost hand like the rest of the body. If he thought—move thumb, clench fingers— nothing happened. He had to think of what he wanted the hand to do in the future and, after a brief interval, it responded to his vision. It was tricky. Everything operated with a slight delay, like moving your body underwater.

"What do you think?" he asked Richardson.

"Start counting backward please."

"What do you think of my hand? Can't you see what's going on?"

Richardson shook his head. "Both of your hands are lying on the examination table. Can you describe what you see?"

Michael was finding it difficult to talk. It wasn't just moving his lips and tongue; it was the awkward, laborious effort to conceptualize ideas and come up with words for them. The mind was faster than words. Much faster.

"I—think—that . . ." He paused for what felt like a long time. "This is not a hallucination."

"Describe, please."

"This was always inside me."

"Describe what you are seeing, Michael."

"You—are—blind."

Michael's annoyance grew stronger, twisting into anger, and he pushed with his forearms to sit up on the table. He felt as if he were cracking his way out of something old and brittle, a capsule of yellowed glass. Then he realized that the upper part of his ghost body was vertical while his flesh body remained behind. Why couldn't they see this? It was all very clear. But Richardson continued to stare at the body on the table as if it was an equation that would suddenly produce its own answer.

"All vital signs have stopped," Lau said. "He's dead or—"

"What are you talking about?" Richardson snapped.

"No. There's a heartbeat. A single heartbeat. And his lungs are moving. He's in some kind of dormant state, like someone who's been buried beneath the snow." Lau studied the monitor screen. "Slow. Everything is very slow. But he's still alive."

Richardson leaned down so his lips were only a few inches away from Michael's left ear. "Can you hear me, Michael? Can you . . ."

And the human voice was so difficult to listen to—so attached to regret and weakness and fear—that Michael ripped the rest of his ghost body from his flesh and floated above them. He felt awkward in this position, like a child learning to swim. Floating up. Floating down. He watched the world, but was detached from its nervous commotion.

Although he couldn't see anything visible, he felt as if there were a small black opening in the floor of the room, like a drain at the bottom of a swimming pool. It was pulling him downward with a gentle force. No. Stay away. He could resist it and keep back if he wanted to. But what was there? Was this part of becoming a Traveler?

Time passed. It could have been a few seconds or several minutes. As his luminous body drifted lower, the power—the attractive force—gained strength, and he started to get frightened. He had a vision of Gabriel's face and felt an intense desire to see his brother again. They should face this together. Everything was dangerous when you were alone.

Closer. Very close now. And he gave up struggling and felt his ghost body collapse into a globe, a point, a concentrated essence that was pulled into the dark hole. No lungs. No mouth. No voice. Gone.

* * *

MICHAEL OPENED HIS eyes and found himself floating in the middle of a dark green ocean. Three small suns were above him in a triangular arrangement. They glowed white-hot in a straw-yellow sky.

He tried to stay relaxed and assess the situation. The water was warm and there was a gentle swell. No wind. Pushing his legs beneath the water, he bobbed up and down like a cork and surveyed the world around him. He saw a dark, hazy line that marked a horizon, but no sign of land.

"Hello!" he shouted. And, for a moment, the sound of his voice made him feel powerful and alive. But the word disappeared into the infinite expansion of the sea. "I'm here!" he shouted. "Right here!" But no one answered him.

He remembered the transcripts from the interrogated Travelers that Dr. Richardson had left in his room. There were four barriers that blocked his access to the other realms: water, fire, earth, air. There was no particular order to the barriers, and Travelers encountered them in different ways. You had to find a way out of each barrier, but the Travelers used different words to describe the ordeal. There was always a door. A passageway. One Russian Traveler had called it *a slash in a long black curtain*.

Everyone agreed that you could escape to another barrier or back to your starting place in the original world. But no one had left an instruction book on how to manage this trick. *You find a way*, a woman explained. *Or it finds you*. The various explanations annoyed him. Why couldn't they just say: walk eight feet, turn right. He wanted a road map, not philosophy.

Michael swore loudly and splashed with his hands, just to hear a sound. Water struck his face and trickled down his cheek to his mouth. He expected a harsh, salty taste, like the ocean, but the water was completely neutral, without taste or smell. Scooping up some of the water in his palm, he examined it closely. Little particles were suspended in the liquid. It could be sand or algae or fairy dust; he had no way of knowing.

Was this just a dream? Could he really drown? Looking up at the sky, he tried to remember news stories of lost fishermen or tourists who had fallen from cruise ships and floated in the ocean until they were rescued. How long had they survived? Three or four hours? A day?

He dropped his head beneath the surface, came up, and spat out the water that had leaked into his mouth. Why were three suns in the sky above him? Was this a different universe with different rules for life and death? Although he tried to consider these ideas, the situation itself, the fact that he was alone without sight of land, asserted itself in his mind. Don't panic, he thought. You can last for a long time.

Michael remembered old rock-and-roll songs and sang them out loud. He counted backward and chanted nursery rhymes—anything to give him the feeling that he was still alive. Breathe in. Breathe out. Splash. Turn. Splash some more. But each time, when he was done, the little waves and ripples were absorbed by the stillness around him. Was he dead? Perhaps he was dead. Richardson could be laboring over his limp body at this exact moment. Maybe he was almost dead and, if he allowed himself to go under, the last fragment of life would be washed from his body.

Frightened, he picked a direction and began to swim. He did a basic crawl, then a backstroke when his arms got tired. Michael had no way of gauging how much time had passed. Five minutes. Five hours. But when he stopped and bobbed around again he saw the same line on the horizon. The same three suns. The yellow sky. He let himself go under, and then came up quickly, spitting out water and shouting.

Michael lay faceup, arched his back, and closed his eyes. The sameness of his surroundings, its static nature, implied a creation of the mind. And yet his dreams had always featured Gabriel and the other people he knew. The absolute solitude of this place was something strange and disturbing. If this was his dream, then it should have included a pirate ship or a flashy speedboat filled with women.

Suddenly he felt something touch his leg with a quick slithery motion. Michael began to swim frantically. Kick. Reach forward. Grasp the water. His only thought was to go as fast as possible and get away from the thing that touched him. Water filled his nostrils, but he forced it out. He shut his eyes and swam blind, with a pawing, desperate motion. Stop. Wait. Sound of his own breathing. Then the fear passed through him and, once again, he was swimming nowhere, toward the endlessly receding horizon.

Time passed. Dream time. Space time. He wasn't sure about anything. But he stopping moving and lay on his back, exhausted and gasping for air. All thoughts disappeared from him except for the desire to breathe. Like a single piece of living tissue, he concentrated on this action that had seemed simple and automatic in his past life. More time passed and he became aware of a new sensation. He felt as if he were moving in a particular direction, pulled toward one part of the horizon. Gradually the current grew stronger.

Michael heard water flowing past his ears and then a faint roaring sound, like a distant waterfall. Moving into a vertical position, he forced his head up and tried to see where he was going. In the distance a fine mist was rising into the air and small waves broke the surface of the ocean. The current was powerful now and it was difficult to swim against it. A roaring sound grew louder and louder until his own voice was overpowered by the noise. Michael raised his right arm into the air as if a gigantic bird or an angel could reach down and save him from destruction. The current pulled him on until the sea appeared to collapse in front of him.

For an instant he was underwater, and then he forced himself toward the light. He was on the side of an immense whirlpool that was as big as a crater on the moon. The green water was swirling around and around to a dark vortex. And he was pushed along by the current as it dragged him deeper, away from the light. Keep moving, Michael told himself. Don't give up. Something within him would be destroyed forever if he allowed the water to fill his mouth and lungs.

Halfway to the bottom of this green bowl, he saw a small black shadow about the size and shape of a ship's porthole. The shadow was something independent from the whirlpool. It vanished beneath the spray and foam, like a dark rock hidden in a river, only to reappear again in the same position.

Kicking and thrusting with his hands, Michael fell downward toward the shadow. Lost it. Found it again. And then he threw himself into its dark core.

38

Most of the glass-enclosed gallery that ran around the interior of the Tomb was used by the technical staff, but the north side of the building could be entered only through a guarded door. This private viewing area was carpeted and filled with a sectional couch and stainless-steel floor lamps. Small black tables and straight-backed suede chairs were set beside the tinted windows.

Kennard Nash sat alone at one of the tables while his bodyguard, an ex–Peruvian policeman named Ramón Vega, poured Chardonnay into a wineglass. Ramón had once murdered five copper miners foolish enough to organize a strike, but Nash valued the man for his skill as a valet and a waiter.

"What's for dinner, Ramón?"

"Salmon. Garlic mashed potatoes. Green beans and almonds. They'll bring it over from the administrative center."

"Excellent. Make sure the food doesn't get cold."

Ramón went back to the anteroom near the security door and Nash sipped his wine. One of the lessons Nash had learned from twenty-two years in the army was the necessity for officers to remain separate from enlisted men. You were their leader, not their friend. When he worked in the White House, the staff followed the same procedure. Every few weeks, the President would be brought out of seclusion to throw a baseball or light the national Christmas tree, but for the most part he was protected from the dangerous randomness of unscripted events. Although Nash was a military man, he had particularly warned the President against attending any soldier's funeral. An emotionally unstable wife might weep and scream. A mother could throw herself on the coffin while a father demanded a reason for his son's death. The philosophy of the Panopticon taught the Brethren that true power was based on control and predictability.

Because the Crossover Project had an unpredictable outcome, Nash hadn't informed the Brethren that the experiment was actually going on. There were simply too many variables to guarantee success. Everything was dependent on Michael Corrigan, the young man whose body now lay on the table in the middle of the Tomb. Many of the young men and women who took 3B3 had ended up in mental hospitals. Dr. Richardson complained that he couldn't gauge the correct dosage of the drug or predict its effect on a possible Traveler.

If this had been a military operation, Nash would have given full responsibility to a junior officer and stayed away from the battle. It was easier to avoid blame if you weren't in the same area. Nash knew that basic rule—had followed it throughout his career—but he found it impossible to stay away from the research center. The design of the quantum computer, the construction of the Tomb, and the attempt to create a Traveler were all his decisions. If the Crossover Project was successful, he would change the direction of history.

Already the Virtual Panopticon was taking control of the workplace. Sipping his wine, Kennard Nash allowed himself the pleasure of a grand vision. In Madrid a computer was counting the keystrokes of a tired young woman inputing credit card information. The computer program that monitored her work created an hourly chart that showed if she had achieved her quota. Messages would automatically tell her *Good work, Maria* or *I'm concerned, Miss Sanchez. You're falling behind*. And the young woman would bend forward and type faster, even faster, so that she wouldn't lose her job.

Somewhere in London a surveillance camera was focusing on the faces in a crowd, transforming a human being into a string of numbers that could be matched with a digitized file. In Mexico City and Jakarta electronic ears were overhearing phone calls and the constant chatter of the Internet was being monitored. Government computers knew that a certain book was bought in Denver while another book was being checked out of a library in Brussels. Who bought one book? Who read the other? Track the names. Cross-reference. Track again. Day by day, the Virtual Panopticon was watching its prisoners, becoming part of their world.

Ramón Vega slipped back into the room and bowed slightly. Nash assumed that something had gone wrong with dinner.

"Mr. Boone is at the door, General. He said you wanted to see him."

"Yes, of course. Send him in right away."

Kennard Nash knew that if he had been sitting in the Truth Room, the left side of his cortex would have glowed a deceitful red color. He disliked Nathan Boone and felt nervous when the man was around. Boone had been hired by Nash's predecessor, and he knew a great deal about the inner workings of the Brethren. During the last few years, Boone had established his own separate relationships with the other members of the executive board. Most of the Brethren thought Mr. Boone was brave and resourceful: the perfect head of security. It bothered Nash that he wasn't in complete control of Boone's activities. He recently discovered that the head of security had disobeyed a direct order.

Ramón escorted Boone into the gallery, and then left the two men alone. "You wanted to see me?" Boone asked. He stood with his legs spread slightly, his hands behind his back.

Nash was supposed to be the leader, the man in charge, yet both men knew that Boone could walk across the room and break the general's neck in a few seconds. "Sit down, Mr. Boone. Have a glass of Chardonnay."

"Not right now." Boone strolled over to the window and gazed down at the surgical table. The anesthesiologist was adjusting a heart sensor on Michael's chest. "How's it going?"

"Michael is in a trance state. Weak pulse. Limited breathing. I'm hoping that he's become a Traveler."

"Or maybe he's half dead. The 3B3 could have fried his brain."

"Neural energy has left his body. Our computers seem to be tracking the movement fairly well."

Both men were silent for moment, staring out the window. "Let's assume that he really is a Traveler," Boone said. "Can he die at this moment?"

"The person lying on the examination table can cease to be biologically alive."

"But what would happen to his Light?"

"I don't know," Nash said. "But it couldn't return to his body."

"Can he die in another realm?"

"Yes. We believe that if you're killed in another realm, you're trapped there forever."

Boone turned away from the window. "I hope this works."

"We need to anticipate all possibilities. That's why it's crucial that we find Gabriel Corrigan. If Michael dies, we'll need an immediate substitute."

"I understand."

General Nash lowered his wineglass. "According to my sources, you pulled back our field agents in California. This was the team looking for Gabriel."

Boone didn't seem disturbed by the accusation. "Electronic

surveillance continues. I also have a team searching for the Harlequin mercenary who placed a false clue in Michael Corrigan's apartment. I think it's a martial arts instructor who used to be affiliated with the Church of Isaac Jones."

"But no one is actually looking for Gabriel," Nash said. "You've disobeyed a direct command."

"It is my responsibility to protect our organization and help us achieve our goals."

"At this point, the Crossover Project is our primary goal, Mr. Boone. There's nothing more important."

Boone stepped closer to the table like a police officer about to confront a suspect. "Perhaps this issue should be discussed by the executive board."

General Nash looked down at the table and considered his options. He had avoided giving Boone all the facts about the quantum computer, but it had become impossible to keep the secret.

"As you know, we now have a working quantum computer. This isn't the time to discuss the technological aspects of this device, but it involves suspending subatomic particles in an energy field. For an extremely brief period of time these particles disappear from the force field and then they return. And where do they go, Mr. Boone? Our scientists tell me that they travel to another dimension—another realm."

Boone looked amused. "They travel with the Travelers."

"These particles have returned to our computer with messages from an advanced civilization. At first, we received simple binary codes and then information of increasing complexity. This civilization has given our scientists new discoveries in physics and computers. They've shown us how to make genetic modifications in animals and create the splicers. If we can learn more of this advanced technology, we'll be able to establish the Panopticon in our lifetime. The Brethren will finally have the power to watch and control an immense group of people."

"And what does this civilization want in exchange?" Boone asked. "No one gives anything for free."

"They want to come into our world and meet us. And that's what we need Travelers for—to show them the way. The quantum computer is tracking Michael Corrigan as he moves between the different realms. Do you understand, Mr. Boone? Is it all quite clear?"

For once, Boone looked impressed. Nash allowed himself to enjoy the moment as he refilled his glass. "That's why I asked you to find Gabriel Corrigan. And I'm not happy about your refusal to follow orders."

"I pulled back the field agents for one reason," Boone said. "I think there's a traitor in this organization."

Nash's hand trembled slightly as he put down the wine-glass. "Are you sure about this?"

"Thorn's daughter, Maya, is in the United States. But I haven't been able to capture her. The Harlequins have antic-ipated all of our actions."

"And you think that a field agent has betrayed us?"

"It is the philosophy of the Panopticon that everyone should be watched and evaluated—even those in charge of the system."

"Are you saying that I have something to do with this?"

"Not at all," Boone said, but he stared at the general as if he had considered the possibility. "Right now I'm using the Internet team to track everyone who has a connection to this project."

"And who will examine your own activities?"

"I've never had any secrets from the Brethren."

Don't look at him, Nash thought. Don't let him see your eyes. He peered out the window at Michael's body.

Dr. Richardson paced nervously beside his motionless patient. Somehow, a white moth had slipped into the climate-controlled environment of the Tomb. The doctor looked startled as it emerged from the shadows and flut-tered in and out of the light.

39

Maya and Gabriel passed through the town of San Lucas around one o'clock in the afternoon and headed south on a two-lane highway. As each new mile clicked on the van's odometer, Maya tried to ignore her growing tension. Back in Los Angeles, the message from Linden was quite clear. *Drive to San Lucas, Arizona. Follow Highway 77 south. Look for green ribbon. Name of contact—Martin.* Perhaps they had missed the ribbon or the desert wind had blown it away. Linden could have been tricked by the Tabula's Internet group and they could be walking into an ambush.

Maya was used to vague directions that led to safe houses or access points, but guarding a possible Traveler like Gabriel changed everything. Ever since the fight at the Paradise Diner, he had kept his distance from her, saying only a few words when they stopped for gasoline and looked at the map. He acted like a man who had agreed to climb a dangerous mountain and was prepared to tolerate obstacles along the way.

She rolled down the window of the van and the desert air dried the sweat on her skin. Blue sky. A hawk riding a

thermal. Gabriel was a mile in front of her and suddenly he
turned and raced back down the road. He pointed to the left
and signaled with the palm of his hand. Found it.

Maya saw a length of green ribbon tied around the steel
base of a mileage marker. A dirt road—no wider than two
wheel ruts—touched the highway at that point, but there
was no sign indicating where it would lead them. Gabriel
pulled off his motorcycle helmet and it dangled from the
bike's handlebars as they followed the road. They were passing through the high desert—a flat, arid land with cactus,
clumps of dead grass, and cat's-claw acacia that scraped
against the sides of the van. There were two junctions in the
dirt road, but Gabriel found the green ribbons that guided
them east. As they gained elevation, mesquite and gray oak
trees began to appear and there were holly-green bushes
with little yellow flowers that attracted honeybees.

Gabriel led them to the top of a low hill and stopped for
a minute. What had looked like a line of mountains from the
highway was actually a plateau that extended two enormous
arms around a sheltered valley. Even from a distance you
could see a few box-shaped houses half hidden in the pine
trees. Far above this community, at the edge of the plateau,
were three wind turbines. Each steel tower supported a
rotor with three blades that was spinning like a massive airplane propeller.

Gabriel wiped the dust off his face with a bandanna, and
then continued up the dirt road. He traveled slowly, glancing from side to side, as if he expected someone to jump out
of the undergrowth and surprise them.

The combat shotgun was lying on the floor of the van,
covered with an old blanket. Maya picked up the weapon,
pumped a round into the firing chamber, and placed it on
the passenger seat beside her. She wondered if a Pathfinder
were really living in this place or if he had been hunted
down and killed by the Tabula.

The road turned directly toward the valley and crossed a

stone bridge that arched over a narrow stream. On the other side of the stream, she saw figures moving in the undergrowth and slowed down.

Four—no, five—children were carrying large stones down the path to the stream. Perhaps they were building some kind of dam or swimming hole. Maya couldn't be sure. But they all stopped and stared at the motorcycle and the van. A thousand feet up the road, they passed a small boy carrying a plastic bucket and he waved at them. They still hadn't seen any adults, but the children appeared quite happy to be on their own. For a few seconds, Maya envisioned a kingdom of children growing up without the constant influence of the Vast Machine.

As they got closer to the valley, the road became paved with brownish-red brick, slightly darker than the surrounding soil. They passed three long greenhouses with glazed windows, and then Gabriel pulled into the courtyard of a vehicle maintenance area. Four dusty pickup trucks were parked inside an open pavilion that was used as a repair garage. A bulldozer, two jeeps, and an ancient school bus were lined up near a wooden shed filled with tools. Brick steps led up the slope to a large pen filled with white chickens.

Maya left the shotgun concealed beneath the blanket, but slung the sword carrier over her shoulder. When she shut the door of the van, she saw a ten-year-old girl sitting on top of a brick retaining wall. The girl was Asian and had long black hair that touched her narrow shoulders. Like the other children, she wore jeans, a T-shirt, and a solid pair of work boots. A large hunting knife with a horn handle and a sheath was hanging from her belt. The weapon and long hair made the girl look like a knight's squire, ready to grab their horses as they arrived at a castle.

"Hello there!" the girl said. "Are you the people from Spain?"

"No, we're from Los Angeles." Gabriel introduced himself and Maya. "And who are you?"

"Alice Chen."

"Does this place have a name?"

"New Harmony," Alice said. "We picked that name two years ago. Everyone had a vote. Even the kids."

The girl jumped down from the wall and went over to inspect Gabriel's dusty motorcycle. "We're waiting for two possibles from Spain. Possibles live here for three months and then we can vote them in." She turned away from the motorcycle and stared at Maya. "If you're not possibles, then what are you doing here?"

"We're looking for someone named Martin," Maya explained. "Do you know where he is?"

"I think you better talk to my mom first."

"That's not necessary—"

"Follow me. She's in the community center."

The little girl led them across another bridge where the stream tumbled over red rocks and swirled around in pools. Large houses built in the Southwestern style were on both sides of the road. The houses had stucco outer walls, small windows, and flat roofs that could be used as patios on hot nights. Most of the houses were quite large, and Maya wondered how the builders had trucked in tons of brick and concrete over the narrow dirt road.

Alice Chen kept glancing over her shoulder as if she expected the visitors to run away from her. As they walked past a house painted pastel green, Gabriel caught up with Maya. "Weren't these people expecting us?"

"Apparently not."

"Who is Martin? The Pathfinder?"

"I don't know, Gabriel. We'll find out soon enough."

They walked through a grove of pine trees and reached a compound of four white buildings around a courtyard with a stone fountain placed in the center. "This is the community center," Alice told them as she pulled open a heavy wooden door.

They followed her down a short hallway to a schoolroom

filled with toys. A young teacher sat on a throw rug with five children and read from a picture book. She nodded at Alice, then stared at the strangers as they walked past the doorway.

"Little kids have school all day long," Alice explained. "But I get out at two o'clock in afternoon."

They left the school, passed through the courtyard, and entered the second building. This contained three window-less offices filled with computers. In one of the rooms, peo-ple sat in separate cubicles, studying the images on computer screens while they talked on phone headsets. "Turn the mouse over," said a young man. "Can you see a red light? That means . . ." He stopped for a few seconds and stared at Maya and Gabriel.

They kept moving, passing back through the courtyard and into a third building with more desks and computers. A Chinese woman wearing a white physician's jacket came out of a back room. Alice ran up to the woman and whispered to her.

"Good afternoon," the woman said. "I'm Alice's mother, Dr. Joan Chen."

"She's Maya and that's Gabriel. They're not from Spain."

"We're looking for—"

"Yes. I know why you're here," Joan said. "Martin men-tioned you at the council meeting. But there was no agree-ment. We didn't vote on the issue."

"We just want to talk to Martin," Gabriel said.

"Yes. Of course." Joan touched her daughter's shoulder. "Take them up the hill to see Mr. Greenwald. He's helping build the new house for the Wilkins family."

Alice ran ahead of them as they left the clinic and con-tinued up the road. "I wasn't expecting a welcome commit-tee when we showed up here," Gabriel said. "But your friends don't seem to be very hospitable."

"Harlequins don't have friends," Maya said. "We have obligations and alliances. Don't say anything until I can eval-uate the situation."

Bits of straw littered the road. A few hundred yards later, they reached a stack of straw bales placed next to a busy construction site. Steel rods had been embedded into the concrete foundation of a new house and the bales were being skewered on the rods like giant yellow bricks. About twenty people of all ages were working on the house at the same time. Teenagers wearing sweat-stained T-shirts were hammering rods into the bales with sledgehammers while three older people pinned a galvanized steel mesh to the outer walls. Two carpenters wearing tool belts were building a wood frame to support the home's roof beams. Maya realized that all the buildings in the valley had been built in the same simple way. The community didn't need massive amounts of brick and concrete, just plywood boards, wood beams, waterproof plaster, and a few hundred bales of straw.

A muscular Latino man in his forties was kneeling in the dirt, measuring a piece of plywood. He wore shorts, a stained T-shirt, and a well-worn tool belt. When he saw the two strangers, he stood up and approached them.

"Can I help you?" he asked. "Are you looking for someone?"

Before Maya could come up with an answer, Alice stepped through the doorway of the house with a stocky older man who wore thick eyeglasses. The man hurried over to them and forced a smile.

"Welcome to New Harmony. I'm Martin Greenwald. And this is my friend, Antonio Cardenas." He turned to the Latino man. "These are the visitors we discussed at the council meeting. I was contacted by our friends in Europe."

Antonio didn't look happy to see them. His shoulders tensed up and he spread his legs slightly as if he was getting ready to fight. "Do you see what's hanging from her shoulder? Know what that means?"

"Keep your voice down," Martin said.

"She's a goddamn Harlequin. The Tabula wouldn't be happy if they knew she was here."

"These people are my guests," Martin said firmly. "Alice will take them down to the Blue House. Around seven o'clock, they can come over to the Yellow House and we'll have dinner." He turned to Antonio. "And you're invited too, my friend. We'll talk about it over a glass of wine."

Antonio hesitated for a few seconds, then returned to the construction site. Acting as tour guide, Alice Chen escorted her visitors back to the parking area. Maya wrapped her weapons in the blanket and Gabriel slung the jade sword over his shoulder. They followed Alice back up the valley to a blue house on a side road near the stream. It was fairly small—a kitchen, one bedroom, a living room with a sleeping loft. A pair of French doors opened onto a walled garden with rosemary bushes and wild mustard.

The bathroom had a high ceiling and an old-fashioned claw-foot tub with green stains on the faucets. Maya stripped off her dirty clothes and took a bath. The water smelled faintly like iron, as if it came from deep in the earth. When the tub was half full, she lay back and tried to relax. Someone had placed a wild rose in a dark blue bottle above the sink. For a moment she forgot about the dangers around them and concentrated on this single point of beauty in the world.

If Gabriel turned out to be a Traveler, then she could continue to protect him. If the Pathfinder decided that Gabriel was just another ordinary soul, then she would have to leave him forever. Sliding beneath the surface of the water, she pictured Gabriel remaining at New Harmony, falling in love with a pleasant young woman who liked to bake bread. Gradually, her imagination pulled her down a darker path and she saw herself standing outside a house at night, staring through a window while Gabriel and his wife prepared dinner. Harlequin. Blood on your hands. Stay away.

She washed and rinsed her hair, found a bathrobe in the cabinet, and slipped down the hallway to the bedroom. Gabriel was sitting on the bed in the sleeping loft that occupied a half ledge in the living room. A few minutes later he got up quickly and she heard him swear to himself. More time passed and then the wooden ladder creaked as he climbed down to take a bath.

* * *

AT SUNSET, SHE rummaged through her travel bag and found a blue tank top and an ankle-length cotton skirt. When she looked in the mirror, she was pleased to see how ordinary she looked—just like any young woman Gabriel might have known in Los Angeles. Then she pulled up the skirt and strapped the two knives onto her legs. The other weapons were hidden under the quilt that covered the bed.

She came out into the living room and found Gabriel standing in the shadows. He was peering through a crack in the curtains. "Someone is hiding in the bushes about twenty yards up the hill," he said. "They're watching the house."

"It's probably Antonio Cardenas or one of his friends."

"So what are we supposed to do about it?"

"Nothing. Let's go find a yellow house."

Maya tried to look relaxed as they walked back down the road, but she couldn't be sure if someone was following them. The air was still warm and the pine trees seemed to have captured little patches of darkness. A large yellow house was near one of the bridges. Oil lamps glowed from the roof patio and they heard people talking.

They entered the house and found eight children of different ages eating dinner at a long table. A short woman with frizzy red hair was working in the kitchen. She wore a denim skirt and a T-shirt with the cartoon image of a surveillance camera and a red bar slashed across it. This was a resistance symbol against the Vast Machine. Maya had seen the symbol on the floor of a Berlin dance club and spray-painted on a wall in the Malasaña district of Madrid.

Still holding her spoon, the woman stepped forward to greet them. "I'm Rebecca Greenwald. Welcome to our home."

Gabriel smiled and gestured to the children. "You got a lot of kids here."

"Only two of them are ours. Antonio's three children are eating with us plus Joan's daughter, Alice, plus two friends from other families. The children in this community are constantly eating dinner at someone else's house. After the first year, we had to make a rule: the child has to tell at least two adults by four o'clock in the afternoon. I mean, that's the rule, but it can get a little frantic. Last week, we were making road bricks so we had seven muddy kids here plus three teenage boys who eat double. I cooked a lot of spaghetti."

"Is Martin . . . ?"

"My husband is up on the roof patio with the others. Just climb the stairs. I'll be there in a few minutes."

They walked through the dining room to a walled-in garden. As they climbed the outer staircase to the roof, Maya heard voices arguing.

"Don't forget about the children in this community, Martin. We've got to protect our children."

"I'm thinking about kids growing up all over the world. They're taught fear and greed and hatred by the Vast Machine . . ."

The conversation stopped the moment Maya and Gabriel appeared. A wooden table had been placed on the roof patio and lit with vegetable-oil lamps. Martin, Antonio, and Joan sat around the table drinking wine.

"Welcome again," Martin said. "Sit down. Please."

Maya made a quick assessment of the logical direction of an attack and sat next to Joan Chen. From that position, she could see whoever was coming up the staircase. Martin bustled around them, making sure they had silverware and pouring two glasses of wine from a bottle with no label.

"This is a Merlot that we buy directly from a winery," he explained. "When we were first thinking about New Harmony, Rebecca asked me what my vision was and I said that I wanted to drink a decent glass of wine in the evening with good friends."

"Sounds like a modest goal," Gabriel said.

Martin smiled and sat down. "Yes, but even a small wish like that has implications. It means a community with free time, a group with enough income to buy the Merlot, and a general desire to enjoy the small pleasures of life." He smiled and raised his glass. "In this context, a glass of wine becomes a revolutionary statement."

Maya knew nothing about wine, but it had a pleasant taste that reminded her of cherries. A light breeze came down the canyon and the flames on the three lamp wicks fluttered slightly. Thousands of stars were above them in the clear desert sky.

"I want to apologize to both of you for the inhospitable welcome," Martin said. "And I also want to apologize to Antonio. I mentioned you at the council meeting, but we never voted. I didn't think you'd arrive so soon."

"Just tell us where the Pathfinder is," Maya said, "and we'll leave right now."

"Maybe the Pathfinder doesn't exist," Antonio growled. "And maybe you're spies sent by the Tabula."

"This afternoon, you were angry that she was a Harlequin," Martin said. "And now you're accusing her of being a spy."

"Anything's possible."

Martin smiled as his wife came up the staircase carrying a tray of food. "Even if they are spies, they're our guests and they deserve a good meal. I say, eat first. Let's talk on a full stomach."

Platters and bowls of food were passed around the table. Salad. Lasagna. A crusty wheat bread cooked in the community oven. As they ate dinner, the four members of New

Harmony began to relax and talk freely about their responsibilities. A water pipe was leaking. One of the trucks needed an oil change. A convoy was going to San Lucas in a few days and they needed to leave very early because one of the teenagers was taking a college entrance exam.

Past the age of thirteen, the children were guided by a teacher in the community center, but their instructors were from all over the world—mostly university graduate students who taught on the Internet. Several colleges had offered full scholarships to a girl who had graduated last year from the New Harmony school. They were impressed by a student who had studied calculus and could translate Molière's plays, but was also capable of digging a water well and fixing a broken diesel engine.

"What's the biggest problem here?" Gabriel asked.

"There's always something, but then we deal with it," Rebecca explained. "For example, most homes have at least one fireplace, but the smoke used to hang over the valley. Children were coughing. You could barely see the sky. So we met and decided that no one could have a wood fire unless a blue flag was flying at the community center."

"And are you all religious?" Maya asked.

"I'm a Christian," Antonio said. "Martin and Rebecca are Jewish. Joan is a Buddhist. We've got a whole spectrum of beliefs here, but our spiritual life is a private matter."

Rebecca glanced at her husband. "All of us were living in the Vast Machine. But everything began to change when Martin's car broke down on the freeway."

"I guess that was the starting point," Martin said. "Eight years ago, I was living in Houston, working as a real estate consultant for wealthy families that owned commercial property. We had two houses and three cars and—"

"He was miserable," Rebecca said. "When he came home from work, he'd go down to the basement with a bottle of scotch and watch old movies until he fell asleep on the couch."

Martin shook his head. "Human beings have an almost unlimited capacity for self-delusion. We can justify any amount of sadness if it fits our own particular standard of reality. I probably would have trudged down the same road for the rest of my life, but then something happened. I took a business trip to Virginia and it was an awful experience. My new clients were like greedy children without any sense of responsibility. At one point in the meeting, I suggested that they give one percent of their yearly income to charities in their community and they complained that I wasn't tough enough to deal with their investments.

"Everything got worse after that. There were hundreds of police officers at the Washington airport because of some kind of special alert. I got searched twice passing through security and then I saw a man have a heart attack in the waiting lounge. My plane was delayed six hours. I spent my time drinking and staring at a television in the airport bar. More death and destruction. Crime. Pollution. All the news stories were telling me to be frightened. All the commercials were telling me to buy things that I didn't need. The message was that people could only be passive victims or consumers.

"When I got back to Houston, it was about 110 degrees with 90 percent humidity. Halfway home, my car broke down on the freeway. No one stopped, of course. No one wanted to help me. I remember getting out of the car and looking up at the sky. It was a dirty brown color because of all the pollution. Trash everywhere. The noise of the traffic surrounding me. I realized that there was no reason to worry about hell in the afterlife because we've already created hell on earth.

"And that's when it happened. This pickup truck stopped behind my car and a man got out. He was about my age, wearing jeans and a work shirt, and he was carrying an old ceramic cup—no handle—like something you'd use for the tea ceremony in Japan. He walked up to me and he didn't introduce himself or ask about my car. He looked in my eyes and I felt like he knew me, that he understood what I was feeling at that moment. Then he offered me the cup and said 'Here's some water. You must be thirsty.'

"I drank the water and it was cold and it tasted good. The man pulled up the hood of my car, tinkered with the engine, and got it going in a few minutes. Now, normally, I would have just given this man some money and been on my way, but that didn't feel right, so I asked him home for dinner. Twenty minutes later, we got back to my house."

Rebecca shook her head and smiled. "I thought that Martin had gone out of his mind. He met a man on the freeway, and now this stranger is eating dinner with our family. My first thought was that he was a homeless person. Maybe a criminal. When we finished eating, he cleared the dishes and started washing them while Martin put the children to bed. The stranger asked me about my life and, for some reason, I began telling him everything. How unhappy I was. How I was worried about my husband and my children. How I had to take pills to go to sleep at night."

"Our guest was a Traveler," Martin said, looking straight across the table at Gabriel and Maya. "I don't know how much you know about their power."

"I'd like to hear anything you can tell me," Gabriel said.

"Travelers have gone outside our world and then they've come back," Martin said. "They have a different way of looking at everything."

"Because they've been outside this prison we live in, Travelers can see things clearly," Antonio said. "That's why the Tabula are scared of them. They want us to believe that the Vast Machine is the only true reality."

"At first, the Traveler didn't say very much," Rebecca said. "But when you were with him it felt like he could look inside your heart."

"I took off work for three days," Martin said. "Rebecca and I just talked to him, trying to explain how we had ended up in this situation. After the three days were over, the Traveler checked into a motel in downtown Houston. Every night, he would come out to the house and we started to invite some of our friends over."

"I was the contractor who built the new bedroom in the Greenwalds' house," Antonio said. "When Martin called me, I thought he wanted me to meet some kind of preacher. I went over there one night and that's when I met the Traveler. There were a lot of people in the living room and I was hiding in the corner. The Traveler looked at me for about two seconds and it changed my life. It felt like I had finally met someone who truly understood all my problems."

"We learned about Travelers much later," Joan said. "Martin contacted other people through the Internet and found out about the secret Web sites. The crucial thing to know is that every Traveler is different. They come from different religions and cultures. Most of them only visit one or two realms. When they return to this world, they have different interpretations of their experiences."

"Our Traveler had visited the Second Realm of the hungry ghosts," Martin explained. "What he saw there made him realize why people are desperate to feed the hunger in their souls. They keep looking for new objects and experiences that can only satisfy them for a short time."

"The Vast Machine keeps us dissatisfied and frightened," Antonio said. "It's just another way to make us obedient. I gradually realized that all these things I was buying weren't making me any happier. My kids were having problems at school. My wife and I were talking about a divorce. Sometimes I would wake up at three o'clock in the morning and just lie there, thinking about what I owed on my credit cards."

"The Traveler made us feel that we weren't trapped," Rebecca said. "He looked at all of us—just a group of ordinary people—and helped us see how to make a better life. He made us realize what we could do on our own."

Martin nodded slowly. "Our friends talked to their friends and, after about a week, we had a dozen families coming to our house every night. Twenty-three days after he arrived, the Traveler said goodbye and went away."

"After he left, four families stopped coming to the meetings," Antonio said. "Without his power, they couldn't break away from their old habits. Then some other people went on the Internet and found out about Travelers and how dangerous it was to oppose the Vast Machine. Another month went by and we were down to five families. That was the core of people who wanted to change their lives."

"We didn't want to live in a sterile world, but we didn't want to give up three hundred years of technology," Martin explained. "What was best for our group was a mixture of high tech and low tech. It's sort of a 'Third Way.' So we pooled our money, bought this land, and came out here. The first year was incredibly difficult. It was hard to set up the wind turbines so that we'd have our own independent power source. But Antonio was great. He figured it all out and got the generators working."

"By that time we were down to four families," Rebecca said. "Martin talked us into building the community center first. Using satellite phones, we were able to go online. Now we give technical support for the customers of three different companies. That's the main source of the community income."

"All the adults at New Harmony have to work six hours a day, five days a week," Martin explained. "You can work at the community center, help at the school or in the greenhouses. We produce about a third of our food—our eggs and vegetables—and buy the rest. There's no crime in our community. We don't have mortgages or credit card debts. And we have the ultimate luxury: a great deal of free time."

"So what do you do with that time?" Maya asked.

Joan put down her glass. "I go hiking with my daughter. She knows all the trails around here. Some of the teenagers are teaching me how to hang glide."

"I make furniture," Antonio said. "It's like a work of art, only you can sit on it. I made this table for Martin."

"I'm learning how to play the cello," Rebecca said. "My teacher is in Barcelona. Using a computer cam, he can watch and listen to me play."

"I spend my time communicating with other people on the Internet," Martin said. "Several of these new friends have come to live at New Harmony. We're now up to twenty-one families."

"New Harmony helps spread information about the Vast Machine," Rebecca said. "A couple of years ago, the White House proposed something called the Protective Link ID card. It was voted down in Congress, but we've heard that it's currently being used by the employees of large corporations. In a few years, the government will reintroduce the idea and make it mandatory."

"But you haven't really broken away from modern life," Maya said. "You have computers and electricity."

"And modern medicine," Joan said. "I consult with other physicians on the Internet and we have basic group insurance in case of severe illness. I don't know if it's exercise, diet, or lack of stress, but people rarely get sick around here."

"We didn't want to run away from the world and pretend to be medieval farmers," Martin said. "Our objective was to gain control of our lives and prove that this Third Way of ours can work. There are other groups like New Harmony— the same mix of high tech and low tech—and we're all connected by the Internet. A new community just started in Canada about two months ago."

Gabriel hadn't spoken for a while, but he kept staring at Martin. "Tell me something," he said. "What was the name of this Traveler?"

"Matthew."

"And what was his last name?"

"He never gave us one," Martin said.

"Do you have a photograph of him?"

"I think we have one in the storage chest." Rebecca stood up. "Should I . . ."

"No need for that," Antonio said. "I've got one."

He reached into his back pocket and pulled out a leather memo book that was stuffed with lists, old receipts, and building plans. Placing the book on the table, he thumbed through the pages, then pulled out a small photograph.

"My wife took this four days before the Traveler left. He ate dinner at my house that night."

Holding one edge of the photograph like it was a precious relic, Antonio handed it across the table. Gabriel took the photograph and stared at it for a long time.

"And when was this taken?"

"About eight years ago."

Gabriel looked up at them. His face showed pain, hope, joy. "This is my father. He was supposed to be dead, destroyed in a fire, but here he is—sitting next to you."

Gabriel sat beneath the night sky and examined the frayed snapshot of his father. More than anything, he wanted Michael to be there with him. The brothers had stood beside the charred remains of the farmhouse in South Dakota. They had driven around the country together, whispering at night when their mother was asleep. Was Father still alive? Was he looking for them?

The Corrigans had searched for their father constantly, expecting to see him sitting at a bus stop or gazing out the window of a café. Sometimes, when they entered a new town, the brothers would glance at each other, feeling tense and excited. Maybe their father was living here. Maybe he was close—very close—just drive two blocks west and turn left. It was only when they reached Los Angeles that Michael announced that the speculation was over. Father was dead or gone forever. Let's forget about the past and move on.

While the stars glimmered overhead, Gabriel questioned the four members of New Harmony. Antonio and the others were sympathetic, but they couldn't give him much information. They didn't know how to find the Traveler. He hadn't contacted them or left an address.

"Did he ever mention that he had a family? A wife? Two sons?"

Rebecca placed her hand on Gabriel's shoulder. "No. He never said anything."

"What did he tell you when he said goodbye?"

"He embraced each of us and then he stood in the doorway." Martin's voice was strained, filled with emotion. "He said that powerful men would try to make us frightened and filled with hate. They would try to control our lives and distract us . . ."

". . . with glittering illusions," Joan said.

"Yes. With glittering illusions. But we should never forget that the Light was in our hearts."

The photograph—and Gabriel's reaction to it—did solve one problem. Antonio no longer believed that he and Maya were Tabula spies. As they finished the wine, Antonio explained that the community was protecting a Pathfinder and this person lived in an isolated location about thirty miles north. If they still wanted to go, he would take them there tomorrow morning.

* * *

MAYA WAS SILENT walking back to the Blue House. When they reached the front door, she stepped in front of Gabriel and entered the house first. There was a feeling of aggressiveness about this act—as if each new location was a place where they might be attacked. The Harlequin didn't switch on the lights. She seemed to have memorized the position of each piece of furniture. She quickly inspected the house and then they faced each other in the living room.

"It's okay, Maya. We're safe here."

The Harlequin shook her head as if he had said something very foolish. Safety was a false word for her. Another illusion.

"I've never met your father and I don't know where he is," Maya said. "But I just wanted to say that—maybe he did this to protect you. Your house was destroyed. Your family went underground. According to our spy, the Tabula thought you were dead. You would have been safe if Michael hadn't gone back on the Grid."

"That might have been the reason. But I still . . ."

"You want to see him."

Gabriel nodded.

"Maybe you'll find him one day. If you have the power to become a Traveler, you might meet him in another realm."

*   *   *

GABRIEL CLIMBED THE ladder to the loft bed. He tried to sleep, but it was impossible. As a cold wind came down the canyon and rattled the window frame, Gabriel sat on the bed and tried to become a Traveler. None of this was real. His body wasn't real. And he could leave it. Just. Like. That.

For an hour or so, he argued with himself. Assuming that I have the power, then all I have to do is accept that fact. A plus B equals C. When logic didn't work, he closed his eyes and was swept away by his own emotions. He could find his father and talk to him if he could break away from this cage of flesh. Within his mind, Gabriel tried to walk from darkness into light, but when he opened his eyes he was still sitting on the bed. Feeling angry and frustrated, he pounded his fist on the mattress.

Eventually, he fell asleep and woke up at dawn with the rough wool blanket wrapped around his body. When the shadows disappeared from the corners of the loft, Gabriel pulled on his clothes and climbed down the ladder. No one was in the bathroom and the bedroom was also empty. He went down the hallway to the kitchen and peered through a crack in the door. Maya sat with her sword case on her lap and her left hand flat on the table, staring at a patch of sunlight on the red tile floor. The sword and the intense expression on her face made him feel as if the Harlequin was cut off from any real human contact. He doubted if there could be a more solitary life: always hunted, always prepared to fight and die.

Maya turned slightly when Gabriel entered the kitchen. "Did they leave us anything for breakfast?" he asked.

"There's tea and instant coffee in the cupboard. Milk, butter, and a loaf of bread in the refrigerator."

"That's enough for me." Gabriel filled a kettle and placed it on a burner of the electric stove. "Why didn't you make something?"

"I'm not hungry."

"Do you know anything about this Pathfinder?" Gabriel asked. "Is he young or old? What's his nationality? They didn't give us any information last night."

"The Pathfinder is their secret. Hiding him is their act of resistance against the Vast Machine. Antonio was right about one thing: this community could get in a lot of trouble if the Tabula knew we were here."

"And what happens when we meet the Pathfinder? Are you going to hang around and watch me fall on my face?"

"I've got other things to do. Don't forget, the Tabula are continuing to look for you. I've got to make them believe that you're somewhere else."

"And how do you plan to do that?"

"You said your brother gave you money and a credit card when you were separated at the clothing factory."

"Sometimes I use his card," Gabriel said. "I don't have any of my own."

"Think I could borrow it?"

"What about the Tabula? Aren't they going to trace the card number?"

"I'm expecting that," Maya said. "I'll use the card and your motorcycle."

Gabriel didn't want to lose the motorcycle, but he knew that Maya was right. The Tabula knew the bike's license plate number and a dozen other ways to track him down. Everything from his old life had to be discarded.

"Okay." He gave her Michael's credit card and the motorcycle key. Maya looked as if she wanted to tell him something important, but she stood up without a word and walked to the doorway. "Eat your breakfast," she said. "Antonio is going to be here in a few minutes."

"This might be a waste of time. I might not be a Traveler."

"I've accepted that possibility."

"So don't risk your life and do something crazy."

Maya looked at him and smiled. Gabriel felt like they were connected to each other at that moment. Not friends, exactly, but soldiers in the same army. And then, for the first time in their relationship, he heard the Harlequin laugh.

"It's all crazy, Gabriel. But you find your own sanity."

*　*　*

ANTONIO CARDENAS SHOWED up ten minutes later and said he would drive them to where the Pathfinder was living. Gabriel took along the jade sword and the knapsack filled with his extra clothes. In the back of Antonio's pickup truck were three canvas bags of canned food, bread, and fresh vegetables from the greenhouses.

"When the Pathfinder first arrived, I spent a month at the site setting up a windmill to power a water pump and electric lights," Antonio said. "Now I just show up every two weeks with food supplies."

"So what's he like?" Gabriel asked. "You haven't really told us."

Antonio waved at some children as the truck moved slowly down the road. "The Pathfinder is a very strong person. Tell the truth and you'll be all right."

They reached the two-lane highway that led back to San Lucas, but turned off a few miles later onto an abandoned asphalt road that cut a straight line through the desert. NO TRESPASSING signs were everywhere, some hanging from steel posts, others left faceup on the cracked ground.

"This used to be a missile base," Antonio explained. "It was active for about thirty years. Fenced off. Top secret. Then the Defense Department took out the missiles and sold the land to the county sanitation district. When the county didn't want it anymore, our group bought all four hundred acres."

"This looks like a wasteland," Maya said.

"As you'll see, it has certain advantages for the Pathfinder."

Bear grass and cactus reached out and scratched the sides of the truck. The road was covered with sand for a hundred yards or so, then it reappeared. As the road slowly gained elevation they began passing piles of red rocks and groves of Joshua trees. Each stubby desert tree raised its spike-leafed branches upward like the arms of a prophet praying to heaven. It was very hot and the sun appeared to grow larger in the sky.

After twenty minutes of cautious driving, they reached a barbed-wire fence and a shattered gate. "We have to walk from here," Antonio said, and everyone got out of the truck. Carrying the food bags, they slipped through a hole in the gate and headed down the road.

Gabriel could see one of Antonio's windmills in the distance. The heat rising from the dirt made the tower waver and bend. Before he could react, a snake slithered across the road. It was about three feet long with a rounded head, a black body with cream-colored bands. Maya stopped and touched her sword case.

"It's not poisonous," Gabriel said. "I think it's a garter snake or gopher snake. They're usually pretty shy."

"It's a king snake," Antonio told them. "And they're not shy around here."

They kept walking and saw another king snake moving through the dirt, then a third one sunning itself on the road. All the snakes had black bodies, but the pattern and color of their bands seemed to vary. White. Cream. Pale yellow.

More snakes appeared on the road and Gabriel stopped counting. Dozens of reptiles coiled and slithered and looked around with their little black eyes. Maya appeared nervous—almost frightened.

"You don't like snakes?"

She lowered her arms and tried to relax. "You don't see many in England."

As they got closer to the windmill, Gabriel saw that it had been built next to a rectangular concrete area about the size of a football field. It looked like an enormous machine-gun bunker abandoned by the army. Directly south of the concrete area was a small aluminum trailer that reflected the desert light. A parachute had been set up as a sunscreen over a wooden picnic table and plastic boxes filled with tools and supplies.

The Pathfinder was kneeling near the base of the windmill, welding a reinforcement strut. He wore blue jeans, a long-sleeved checkered shirt, and thick leather gloves. A welder's helmet covered his face and he appeared to be concentrating on the flame as he fused two pieces of metal.

A four-foot-long king snake slithered by, almost grazing the tip of Gabriel's boots. He could see that the sand on both sides of the road was marked with thousands of faint S curves, a sign of reptile movements across the dry land.

Thirty feet from the tower, Antonio shouted and waved his arms. The Pathfinder heard him, stood up, and raised the welder's helmet. At first Gabriel assumed that the Pathfinder was an old man with white hair. As they got closer he realized that they were about to meet a woman who was more than seventy years old. She had a broad forehead and a straight nose. It was a face of great strength without an ounce of sentimentality.

"Good morning, Antonio. You brought some friends this time."

"Dr. Briggs, this is Gabriel Corrigan. He's the son of a Traveler and wants to know if—"

"Yes. Of course. Welcome." The doctor had a brisk New England accent. She pulled off one of the welder's gloves and shook Gabriel's hand. "I'm Sophia Briggs." Her fingers were strong and her blue-green eyes were intense, critical. Gabriel felt like he was being evaluated and then she turned away from him. "And you are . . ."

"Maya. Gabriel's friend."

Dr. Briggs noticed the black metal case hanging from Maya's shoulder and understood what it contained. "How interesting. I thought all you Harlequins were dead, slaughtered after various self-destructive gestures. Perhaps you're too young for this business."

"And maybe you're too old."

"There's some spirit. A little resistance. I like that." Sophia returned to her trailer and tossed the welder's gear into a plastic milk crate lying on the ground. Startled by the noise, two large king snakes came out of the shadow beneath the trailer and slithered over to the windmill.

"Welcome to the land of *Lampropeltis getula*, the common king snake. Of course, there's nothing common about them. They're brave, clever, perfectly lovely reptiles— another one of God's gifts to a fallen world. What you're seeing is subspecies *splendida*, the Arizona desert king snake. They eat copperheads and rattlesnakes as well as frogs, birds, and rats. They just love to kill rats. Especially large, nasty ones."

"Dr. Briggs studies snakes," Antonio said.

"I'm a biologist specializing in reptiles. I taught for twenty-eight years at the University of New Hampshire until they forced me out. You should have seen President

Mitchell, a silly little man who can barely walk upstairs without huffing and puffing, telling me that I was too frail for the classroom. What nonsense. A few weeks after the retirement dinner, I started getting messages from my Internet friends that the Tabula had discovered I was a Pathfinder."

Antonio dropped his canvas food bag on the table. "But she wouldn't leave."

"And why should I? I'm no coward. I own three firearms and know how to use them. Then Antonio and Martin found out about this site and lured me here. You two are clever schoolboys."

"We knew you couldn't resist," Antonio said.

"You're right about that. Fifty years ago the government wasted millions of dollars building this ridiculous missile site." Sophia moved past the trailer and pointed at the site. Gabriel saw three enormous concrete disks set in rusty steel frames. "Right over there are the silo lids. They could be opened and shut from the inside. That was where they stored the missiles."

She turned on her heel and pointed to a mound of dirt about half a mile away. "After the missiles were pulled out, the county turned that area over there into a dump. Beneath nine inches of dirt and a plastic tarp is twenty years of rotting garbage that sustains an enormous population of rats. The rats eat the garbage and multiply. The king snakes eat the rats, then live and breed in the silo. I study *splendida* and it's been quite successful, so far."

"So what are we going to do?" Gabriel asked.

"Have lunch, of course. Better eat this bread before it goes stale."

Sophia gave them all jobs and they prepared a meal with the perishable food. Maya was in charge of slicing a loaf of bread and she seemed annoyed with the dull knife. Lunch was simple, but delicious. Fresh tomatoes mixed with oil and vinegar. A very rich goat cheese cut into chunks. Rye bread. Strawberries. For dessert, Sophia took out a bar of Belgian chocolate and gave everyone exactly two squares.

Snakes were everywhere. If they got in the way, Sophia picked them up firmly and carried them over to a moist patch of ground near the shed. Maya sat yoga style at the table as if one of the reptiles might slither up her leg. During the meal, Gabriel learned a few more facts about Sophia Briggs. No children. Never married. She had consented to hip surgery a few years ago but—other than that—she tried to stay away from doctors.

In her forties, Sophia began to make annual trips up to the Narcisse Snake Dens in Manitoba to study the fifty thousand red-sided garter snakes that emerged from limestone caves during their annual breeding cycle. She became close friends with a Catholic priest living in the area and, after many years, he revealed that he was a Pathfinder.

"Father Morrissey was an amazing man," she said. "Like most priests, he presided over thousands of christenings, weddings, and funerals, but he had actually learned something from the experience. He was a perceptive person. Very wise. Sometimes I felt he could read my mind."

"So why did he pick you?" Gabriel asked.

Sophia smeared the soft goat cheese on a piece of bread. "My people skills aren't the best in the world. In fact, I don't like people all that much. They're vain and foolish. But I've trained myself to be observant. I can focus on one thing and get rid of the extraneous details. Maybe Father Morrissey could have found someone better, but he got lymphatic cancer and died seventeen weeks after the diagnosis. I took a semester off and sat by the hospital bed while he gave me his knowledge."

When everyone had finished eating, Sophia stood up and looked at Maya. "I think it's time for you to go, young lady. I've got a sat phone in the trailer and it works most of the time. I'll call Martin when we're done."

Antonio picked up the empty canvas bags and headed back down the road. Maya and Gabriel stood close to each other, but neither one of them spoke. He wondered what he could say to her. Take care of yourself. Have a safe journey. See you soon. None of the commonplace farewells seemed to apply to a Harlequin.

"Goodbye," she said.

"Goodbye."

Maya went a few feet, then stopped and looked back at him. "Keep the jade sword with you," she said. "Don't forget. It's a talisman."

And then she was gone, her body becoming smaller and smaller as she disappeared down the road.

"She likes you."

Gabriel turned around and realized that Sophia had been watching them. "We respect each other . . ."

"If a woman told me that, I would consider her to be extraordinarily dim-witted, but you're just a typical man." Sophia returned to the table and began to pick up the dirty dishes. "Maya likes you, Gabriel. But that's absolutely forbidden for a Harlequin. They have great power. In exchange for this gift they're probably the loneliest people in the world. She can't allow emotions of any sort to cloud her judgment."

As they stored the food and washed the dishes in a plastic tub, Sophia questioned Gabriel about his family. Her scientific training was evident in the systematic way she went about getting information. "How do you know that?" she kept asking. "What makes you think that's true?"

The sun drifted toward the western horizon. As the rocky ground began to cool, the wind grew stronger. It made the parachute above them snap and billow like a sail. Sophia looked amused when Gabriel described his failed attempts to become a Traveler. "Some Travelers can learn how to cross over on their own," she said. "But not in our frantic world."

"Why not?"

"Our senses are overwhelmed by all the noise and bright lights around us. In the past, a potential Traveler would crawl into a cave or find sanctuary in a church. You have to be in a quiet environment, like our missile silo." Sophia finished covering the food boxes and faced him. "I want you to promise that you'll remain in the silo for at least eight days."

"That seems like a long time," Gabriel said. "I thought you'd know fairly soon if I had the power to cross over."

"This is your discovery, young man, not mine. Accept the rules or go back to Los Angeles."

"Okay. Eight days. No problem." Gabriel walked over to the table to get his knapsack and the jade sword. "I want to do this, Dr. Briggs. It's important to me. Maybe I can contact my father and my brother—"

"I wouldn't think about that. It's not very helpful." Sophia brushed a king snake away from a storage bin and picked up a propane lantern. "You know why I like snakes? God created them to be clean, beautiful—and unadorned. Studying snakes, I've been inspired to get rid of all the clutter and foolishness in my life."

Gabriel looked around him at the missile site and the desert landscape. He felt like he was about to leave everything and go on a long journey. "I'll do whatever is necessary."

"Good. Let's go underground."

47

A thick black power cable ran from the windmill's electric generator to the missile silo. Sophia Briggs followed the cable across the concrete pad to a ramp that led down to a sheltered area with a steel floor.

"When they stored the missiles here, the main entrance was through a freight elevator. But the government took the elevator away when they sold the site to the county. The snakes get in a dozen different ways, but we have to use the emergency staircase."

Sophia set her propane lantern on the ground and lit the wick with a wooden match. When the lantern was burning with a white-hot flame, she pulled up a hatch cover with two hands, exposing a steel staircase that led into darkness. Gabriel knew that the king snakes weren't dangerous to humans, but it made him uneasy to see a large specimen gliding down the steps.

"Where's he going?"

"One of many places. There are between three and four thousand *splendida* in the silo. It's their breeding area." Sophia went down two steps and stopped. "Do the snakes bother you?"

"No. But it does seem a little unusual."

"Every new experience is unusual. The rest of life is just sleep and committee meetings. Now come along and shut the door behind you."

Gabriel hesitated a few seconds, and then shut the hatch. He was standing on the first step of a metal staircase that spiraled around the outside of an elevator shaft protected by a chain-link cage. Two king snakes were on the stairs in front of him and several more were inside the cage, moving up and down the old conduit pipes as if they were branches of a snake highway. The reptiles slithered past each other as their little tongues darted in and out, tasting the air.

He followed Sophia down the staircase. "Have you ever guided a person who thought he was a Traveler?"

"I've had two students in the last thirty years: a young woman and an older man. Neither one of them could cross over, but maybe that was my fault." Sophia glanced over her shoulder. "You can't *teach* people to be Travelers. It's more of an art than a science. All a Pathfinder can do is try to pick the right technique so that people can discover their own power."

"And how do you do that?"

"Father Morrissey helped me memorize *The 99 Paths*. It's a handwritten book of ninety-nine techniques and exercises developed over the years by visionaries from different religions. If you weren't prepared for the book, you might think it was all magic and moonbeams—a lot of nonsense thought up by Christian saints, Jews who studied the Kabbalah, Buddhist monks, and so on. But *The 99 Paths* isn't mystical at all. It's a practical list of ideas with the same goal: to break the Light free of your body."

They reached the bottom of the elevator shaft and stopped in front of a massive safety door still hanging on one hinge. Sophia connected two parts of the electrical cable and a lightbulb went on near a discarded power generator.

They pushed open the door, walked down a short corridor, and entered a tunnel that was wide enough for a pickup truck. Rusted girders lined the walls like the ribs of an enormous animal. The floor was constructed with flat steel plates. Ventilation ducts and water pipes hung above them. The old fluorescent fixtures had been disconnected, and the only light came from six ordinary bulbs attached to the power cable.

"This is the main tunnel," Sophia said. "From end to end, it's about a mile long. The whole area is like a giant lizard buried underground. We're standing in the middle of the lizard's body. Walk north to the head and you'll reach missile silo one. The lizard's front legs lead to silos two and three, and the two rear legs lead to the control center and the living quarters. Walk south to the end of the tail and you'll find the radio antenna that was stored underground."

"Where are all the snakes?"

"Beneath the floor or in the crawl space above you." Sophia guided him down the tunnel. "It's very dangerous to explore this place if you don't know where you're going. All the floors are hollow, set on steel springs that could take the shock of an explosion. There are levels built on levels and, in some places, you can fall a long way."

They turned into a side corridor and entered a large round room. The outer walls were made of concrete blocks, painted white, and four half walls divided the room into sleeping areas. One of the areas had a folding cot with a sleeping bag, pillow, and foam-rubber mattress. A second propane lantern, a covered bucket, and three water bottles were placed a few feet from the cot.

"This used to be the staff dormitory. I stayed underground for a few weeks when I was doing my first population count of *splendida*."

"And I'm supposed to live here?"

"Yes. For eight days."

Gabriel looked around at the bare room. It reminded

him of a prison. No complaints, he thought. Just do what she says. He dropped his knapsack on the floor and sat on the cot.

"All right. Let's get going."

Sophia moved restlessly around the room, picking up pieces of broken concrete and flicking them into a corner. "I'll run through the basics first. All living things carry around a special kind of energy called the Light. You can call it a 'soul' if you want. I don't worry too much about theology. When people die, their Light returns to the energy that surrounds us. But Travelers are different. Their Light can go away and then return to their living body."

"Maya said that the Light travels to different realms."

"Yes. People call them 'realms' or 'parallel worlds.' Once again, you can use any term that makes sense to you. The scripture of every major religion has described different aspects of these realms. They're the source of all mystical visions. Many saints and prophets have written about the realms, but the Buddhist monks living in Tibet made the first attempt to understand them. Before the Chinese invaded, Tibet was a theocracy for more than a thousand years. The peasants supported monks and nuns who could examine the accounts of Travelers and organize the data into a system. The six realms aren't a Buddhist or a Tibetan concept. The Tibetans are simply the first people who described the whole thing."

"So how do I get there?"

"The Light breaks out of your body. You have to be moving slightly for the process to happen. The first time it's surprising—even painful. Then your Light has to cross four barriers to reach each of the different realms. The barriers are composed of water, fire, earth, and air. There is no particular order to cross them. Once your Light finds the passageway through, you'll always find it again."

"And then you enter the six realms," Gabriel said. "So what are they like?"

"We're living in the Fourth Realm, Gabriel. That's human reality. So what is our world like? Beautiful. Horrible. Painful. Exhilarating." Sophia picked up a shard of concrete and tossed it across the room. "Any reality with king snakes and mint chocolate-chip ice cream has its good side."

"But the other places?"

"Each person can find traces of the realms within their own heart. The realms are dominated by a particular quality. In the Sixth Realm of the gods, the sin is pride. In the Fifth Realm of the half gods, the sin is jealousy. You need to understand that we're not talking about God, the power that created the universe. According to the Tibetans, the gods and half gods are like human beings from another reality."

"And we're living in the Fourth Realm . . ."

"Where the sin is desire." Sophia turned and watched a king snake moving slowly down a conduit pipe. "The animals of the Third Realm are ignorant of all others. The Second Realm is inhabited by the hungry ghosts who can never be satisfied. The First Realm is a city of hate and anger, ruled by people without compassion. There are other names for this place: Sheol, Hades, Hell."

Gabriel stood up like a prisoner ready for a firing squad. "You're the Pathfinder. So tell me what I'm supposed to do."

Sophia Briggs looked amused. "Are you tired, Gabriel?"

"It's been a long day."

"Then you should go to sleep."

Taking a felt-tip marker out of her pocket, Sophia walked over to the wall. "You need to break down the distinction between this world and your dreams. I'm going to show you the eighty-first path. It was discovered by the Kabbalist Jews who lived in the northern Galilee town of Safed."

Using the marker, she wrote four Hebrew letters on the wall. "This is the tetragrammaton—the four-letter name of God. Try to keep the letters in your mind when you start to go to sleep. Don't think about yourself or me—or *splendida*. Three times during your sleep, you should ask yourself, 'Am

I awake or am I dreaming?' Don't open your eyes, but stay within the dream world and observe what happens."

"And that's all?"

She smiled and began to walk out of the room. "It's a start."

Gabriel pulled off his boots, lay down on the cot, and stared at the four Hebrew letters. He couldn't read or pronounce them, but the shapes themselves began to float through his mind. One letter looked like a shelter from the storm. A cane. Another shelter. And then a small curving line that looked like a snake.

He fell into a deep sleep, and then he was awake or half awake—he wasn't sure. He was looking down at the tetragrammaton drawn with red-colored sand on a gray slate floor. As he watched, a gust of wind blew God's name away.

* * *

GABRIEL WOKE UP covered with sweat. Something had happened to the lightbulb in the dormitory and the room was dark. A faint light came from the corridor that led to the main tunnel.

"Hello!" he shouted. "Sophia?"

"I'm coming."

Gabriel heard footsteps enter the dormitory room. Even in the darkness, Sophia seemed to know where she was going. "This happens all the time. Moisture seeps through the concrete and it gets into the electrical connections." Sophia tapped her finger on the lightbulb and the filament lit up. "There we go."

She walked over to the cot and picked up the kerosene lantern. "This is your lantern. If the lights go out or you want to go exploring, take it along with you." She studied his face. "So how did you sleep?"

"It was okay."

"Were you aware of your dream?"

"Almost. Then I couldn't stay in it anymore."

"All this takes time. Come with me. And bring that sword with you."

Gabriel followed Sophia out into the main tunnel. He didn't know how long he'd been sleeping. Was it morning or still night? He noticed that the lightbulbs kept changing. Eighty feet above them, wind was rattling the leaves of the Joshua trees and pushing the blades of the windmill. Sometimes the wind blew strongly and the lights burned brightly. When the wind faded, the only power came from batteries, and the bulb filaments glowed dark orange like embers from a dying fire.

"I want you to work on the seventeenth path. You brought along that sword, so it seems like a good idea. This path was invented by people in Japan or China: some kind of sword culture. It teaches you how to focus your thoughts by not thinking."

They stopped at the end of the tunnel and Sophia pointed to a patch of water on the rusty steel plates. "Here we go . . ."

"What am I supposed to do?"

"Look up, Gabriel. Straight up."

He raised his head and saw a drop of water forming on one of the arched girders above them. Three seconds later the drop fell off the girder and splattered on the steel in front of him.

"Draw your sword and cut the drop in half before it hits the ground."

For a second he thought that Sophia was teasing him with an impossible task, but she wasn't smiling. Gabriel drew the jade sword. Its polished blade gleamed in the shadows. Holding the weapon with two hands, he got into a kendo stance and waited to attack. The water drop above him grew larger, trembled, then fell. He swung the sword and missed completely.

"Don't anticipate," she said. "Just be ready."

The Pathfinder left him alone beneath the girder. A new water drop was forming. It was going to fall in two seconds. One second. Now. The drop fell and he swung the sword with hope and desire.

42

After the confrontation at Michael's apartment building, Hollis went back to his martial arts school on Florence Avenue and taught a final day of classes. He told his two best students—Marco Martinez and Tommy Wu—that he was turning the school over to them. Marco would teach the advanced students and Tommy would teach the lower ranks. They would split the costs evenly for the first year, and then decide if they wanted to continue the partnership.

"Some men might come here looking for me. They could be real police officers or maybe they're using fake identification. Tell them I decided to go back to Brazil and rejoin the fighting circuit."

"You need money?" Marco asked him. "I got three hundred dollars back at my apartment."

"No. That's okay. I'm expecting a payment from some people in Europe."

Tommy and Marco glanced at each other. They probably assumed that he was dealing drugs.

Hollis stopped at a grocery store on the way home and wandered up and down the aisles tossing food into a shopping basket. He was starting to realize that everything he once thought was a big decision—leaving the church, traveling to Brazil—had only prepared him for the moment when Vicki Fraser and Maya walked into his school. He could have turned them down, but that wouldn't have felt right. He had been preparing for this battle all his life.

Driving down the street to his house, Hollis kept looking for strangers who didn't fit into the neighborhood. He felt vulnerable when he opened the driveway gate and parked his car in the garage. Something moved through the shadows as he opened the back door and entered the kitchen. He jumped back, then laughed when he saw Garvey, his cat.

By now the Tabula realized that a black man had fought three of their mercs in an elevator. Hollis figured it wouldn't take long for their computers to come up with his name. Shepherd had used Vicki to meet Maya at the airport. The Vast Machine probably had the names of everyone in the local Jonesie church. Hollis had broken with the church several years ago, but the congregation knew that he taught martial arts.

Although the Tabula wanted to kill him, he wasn't going to run away. There were practical reasons for this—he needed to receive his $5,000 payment from the Harlequins, and remaining in Los Angeles also matched his fighting style. Hollis was a counterpuncher. Whenever he fought in a tournament, he always let his opponent attack at the beginning of each round. Taking a punch made him feel strong and justified. He wanted the bad guys to make the first move so he could destroy them.

Hollis loaded his assault rifle and sat in the shadows of his living room. He kept the TV and radio turned off and ate breakfast cereal for dinner. Occasionally Garvey would wander in with his tail in the air and give him a skeptical look. When it got dark, Hollis climbed onto the roof of his house with a foam-rubber pad and a sleeping bag. Concealed by the air-conditioning unit, he lay on his back and gazed at the sky. Maya said the Tabula used thermal imaging devices to look through walls. Hollis could defend himself in the daytime, but he didn't want the Tabula to know where he was sleeping. He kept the air conditioner on and hoped that the heat of the electric motor would obscure the warmth that came from his body.

The next day, the postman brought a package from Germany: two books about Oriental rugs. There was nothing between the pages, but when he cut open the covers with a razor, he found $5,000 in hundred-dollar bills. The person who paid the money included a small business card for a German recording studio. On the back of the card, someone had written a Web site address and a friendly message. *Lonely? New friends are waiting for you.* Hollis smiled to himself while he counted the money. New friends are waiting for you. Harlequins. The real thing. Well, he might need backup if he had another encounter with the Tabula.

Hollis jumped over the wall and talked to his backyard neighbor, a former gang leader named Deshawn Fox who sold custom tire rims. He gave Deshawn $1,800 to buy a used pickup truck with a camper shell.

Three days later, the truck was stored in Deshawn's driveway with extra clothes, canned food, and ammunition. While Hollis was searching for camping supplies, Garvey got into the attic crawl space. Hollis tried to tempt the cat down with a rubber mouse and a dish of canned tuna, but Garvey stayed hidden in the rafters.

A power company truck appeared and three men wearing hard hats pretended to fix the electric line on the corner. A new postman also made an appearance: an older white man with a military haircut who rang the doorbell for several minutes before he went away. Hollis went up to the roof right after sunset with his rifle and a few bottles of water. The streetlights and pollution made it difficult to see any stars, but he lay on his back and watched the jet planes circle the approach pattern to Los Angeles airport. He tried not to think about Vicki Fraser, but her face floated through his mind. Most of those Jonesie girls stayed virgins until they were married. Hollis wondered if she was that way or if she had secret boyfriends.

He woke up around two o'clock in the morning when the driveway gate made a faint rattling sound. Several people vaulted over the locked gate and landed on the concrete. A few seconds passed and then the Tabula mercs kicked in the back door and entered the house. "Not here!" voices shouted. "Not here!" A plate shattered and a cooking pot hit the floor.

Ten or fifteen minutes passed. He heard the back door squeak shut, then two cars started their engines and drove away. It was quiet again. Hollis slung the assault rifle over his shoulder and lowered himself down from the roof. When his feet touched the ground, he clicked off the rifle's safety.

Standing in a flower bed, he listened to the muffled bass thump from a passing car stereo. Hollis was just about to jump over the wall to Deshawn's house when he remembered the cat. Maybe the Tabula mercs had scared Garvey out of the attic when they were searching the place.

He opened the back door and slipped into the kitchen. Only a small amount of light came in through the windows, but he could see that the Tabula had trashed the place. The closet door was open and everything in the kitchen cabinets had been dumped onto the floor. Hollis stepped on shards of a smashed plate and the crunching sound startled him. Be cool, he told himself. The bad guys are gone.

The kitchen was in the back of the house. A short hallway led to the bathroom, a bedroom, and the workout room where he kept his exercise equipment. At the end of the hallway, another door led to the L-shaped living room. The long part of the L was where Hollis listened to music and watched television. He had turned the small side area into a place he called "the memory room," where he kept framed photographs of his family, old karate trophies, and a scrapbook about his professional fights in Brazil.

Hollis pushed open the door to the hallway and smelled a foul odor. It reminded him of an unclean cage at an animal shelter. "Garvey?" he whispered, suddenly remembering the cat. "Where the hell are you?" Cautiously, he moved down the hallway and discovered something smeared on the floor. Blood. Shreds of fur. Those Tabula bastards had found Garvey and ripped the animal apart.

The smell got stronger as he reached the door at the end of the hallway. He stood there for a minute, still thinking about Garvey. And then he heard a high-pitched laughing sound coming from the living room. Was it some kind of animal? He wondered. Had the Tabula left a watchdog in his house?

He raised the rifle, jerked open the door, and entered the living room. Light from the street was diffused by the bed-sheets he used for curtains, but Hollis could see that a large animal sat on its haunches in the far corner near the couch. As he stepped closer, he was surprised to see that it wasn't a dog but a hyena. It had broad shoulders, stubby ears, and a large powerful jaw. When it saw Hollis, it bared its teeth and grinned.

A second hyena, one with spotted fur, stepped from the shadows of the memory room. The two animals glanced at each other and the leader—the one by the couch—made a throaty growl. Trying to keep his distance, Hollis moved toward the locked front door. He heard a barking sound behind him—like a nervous laugh—and spun around to see another hyena come out of the hallway. This third animal had stayed hidden until Hollis had entered the living room.

The three hyenas began to move into a triangle with him at the center. He smelled their foul odor, heard claws click on the wooden floor. Hollis found it difficult to breathe. A feeling of intense fear surged through his body. The leader made a quick laughing sound and bared his teeth again.

"Go to hell," Hollis said, and fired the rifle.

He shot the leader first, turned slightly and fired a burst at the spotted hyena near the memory room. The third animal leaped through the air as Hollis threw himself sideways. He felt a sharp pain on his upper left arm as he hit the floor. Hollis rolled to his side and watched the third hyena spinning around to attack. He squeezed the trigger and hit the animal at a low angle. Bullets cut into the hyena's chest and it was knocked back against the wall.

When Hollis stood up, he touched his arm and felt blood. The hyena must have slashed him with its claws as it jumped forward. Now the animal lay on its side, making a deep wheezing sound while blood bubbled from a chest wound. Hollis looked at his attacker, but didn't get close. The hyena stared back at him with hatred in its eyes.

The coffee table was lying on its side. He went around it and examined the leader. Bullet holes were in the animal's chest and front legs. Its lips were pulled back and it seemed to be grinning.

Hollis stepped into a pool of blood, smearing it across the floor. Bullets had cut through the spotted hyena's neck and almost severed its head. Hollis leaned down and saw that the animal's yellow-and-black hair covered a thick skin that was almost like cowhide. Sharp claws. Strong muzzle and teeth. It was a perfect killing machine—quite unlike the smaller, cautious hyenas he had seen on nature shows. This creature was a distortion, something bred to hunt without fear, compelled to attack and kill. Maya had warned him that the Tabula scientists had learned how to subvert the laws of genetics. What was the word she used? Splicers.

Something changed in the room. He turned away from the dead splicer and realized that he could no longer hear the wheezing sound coming from the third hyena. Hollis raised the assault rifle, then saw a shadow moving on his left side. He spun around just as the leader scrambled to its feet and leaped toward him.

Hollis fired wildly. A bullet hit the leader and knocked it backward. He kept squeezing the trigger until the thirty-round clip was empty. Reversing the rifle, Hollis ran and began beating the animal with a hysterical fury, crushing the splicer's skull and jaws. The wooden stock cracked, then broke away from the rifle frame. He stood in the shadows, clutching the useless weapon.

A scratching sound. Claws on the floor. Six feet away, the third hyena was getting to its feet. Although its chest was still wet with blood, it was preparing to attack. Hollis threw the rifle at the splicer and ran for the hallway. He shut the door behind him, but the hyena ran at full speed and smashed it open.

Hollis reached the bathroom, shut the door, and braced his body against the thin plywood, holding the knob with his hand. He thought about climbing out the window, then realized that the door wouldn't hold for more than a few seconds.

The splicer hit the door hard. It popped open a few inches, but Hollis pushed backward with his feet and managed to slam it shut. Find a weapon, he thought. Anything. The Tabula had scattered the towels and toiletries across the bathroom floor. Still braced against the door, he knelt down and searched desperately through the clutter. The splicer hit the door a second time, forcing it open. Hollis saw the creature's teeth and heard its frantic laughter as he pushed the door shut with all his strength.

A can of hair spray lay on the floor. A butane cigarette lighter was over by the sink. He grabbed them both, stumbled backward toward the window, and the door slammed open. For one heartbeat he stared at the animal's eyes and saw the intensity of its desire to kill. It was like touching a live electric cable and feeling a snap of malevolent power surge through his body.

Hollis held the button down, spraying the hyena's eyes, then clicked the lighter. The cloud of hair spray caught fire and a stream of orange flame hit the splicer. The hyena screamed with a gurgling yowl that sounded like a human in pain. Burning, it staggered down the hallway toward the kitchen. Hollis ran into the exercise room, picked up a steel barbell rod, and followed the splicer into the kitchen. The house was filled with the sharp odor of scorched flesh and fur.

Hollis stood near the doorway and raised his weapon. He was ready to attack, but the splicer kept screaming and burning and moving forward until it collapsed beneath the table and died.

Gabriel didn't know how long he had been living underground. Four or five days, perhaps. Maybe more. He felt detached from the outside world and daily cycle of sunlight and darkness.

The wall he had created between being awake and dreaming was beginning to disappear. Back in Los Angeles, Gabriel's dreams were confusing or meaningless. Now they seemed like a different kind of reality. If he went to sleep concentrating on the tetragrammaton, he could remain conscious in his dreams and walk around them like a visitor. The dream world was intense—almost overwhelming—so most of the time he looked down at his feet, glancing up occasionally to see the new environment that surrounded him.

Within a dream, Gabriel walked on an empty beach where each grain of sand was a tiny star. He stopped and gazed out at a blue-green ocean with silent waves falling on the shore. Once he found himself in an empty city with bearded Assyrian statues built into high brick walls. At the center of the city was a park with rows of birch trees, a fountain, and a bed of blue irises. Every flower, leaf, and stalk of grass was perfect and distinct: an ideal creation.

Waking from one of these experiences, he would find crackers, cans of tuna, and pieces of fruit left in a plastic box next to his cot. The food appeared almost magically and he never figured out how Sophia Briggs was able to enter the dormitory room without making any noise. Gabriel ate until he was full, then he left the dormitory room and entered the main tunnel. If Sophia wasn't around, he would take the kerosene lantern and go exploring.

The king snakes usually stayed away from the lightbulbs in the main tunnel, but he could always find them in side rooms. Sometimes they were intertwined in an undulating mass of heads and tails and slithering bodies. Often they lay passively on the floor as if still digesting a large rat. The snakes never hissed at Gabriel or made a threatening move, but he found it unsettling to look at their eyes, as clean and precise as little black jewels.

The snakes didn't hurt him, but the silo itself was dangerous. Gabriel inspected the abandoned control room, electric generator, and radio antenna. The generator was covered with mold that clung to the steel like a fuzzy green carpet. In the control room, the gauges and panels had been smashed and looted. Electric cables hung from the ceiling like roots in a cave.

Gabriel remembered seeing a small opening in one of the concrete lids that covered a launch silo. Perhaps it was possible to crawl out of this hole and reach the sunlight, but the missile area was the most dangerous part of the underground complex. Once Gabriel tried to explore a launch silo. He became lost in shadowy passageways and almost fell through a gap in the floor.

Near the empty fuel tanks for the electric generator, he found a forty-two-year-old copy of a Phoenix newspaper, the *Arizona Republic*. The paper was yellowed and brittle at the edges, but still legible. Gabriel spent hours on the folding cot, reading news articles, want ads, and wedding announcements. He pretended that he was a visitor from another realm and the newspaper was his only source of information about the human race.

The civilization that appeared in the pages of the *Arizona Republic* appeared to be violent and cruel. But there were positive things as well. Gabriel enjoyed reading an article about a Phoenix couple that had been married for fifty years. Tom Zimmerman was an electrician who liked model trains. His wife, Elizabeth, was a former schoolteacher who was active in the Methodist church. Lying on the cot, he studied the couple's faded anniversary photograph. They smiled at the camera and their fingers were intertwined. Gabriel had been involved with various women in Los Angeles, but those experiences felt very far away. The photograph of the Zimmermans was proof that love could survive the fury of the world.

The old newspaper and thoughts of Maya were the only diversions. Usually, he walked into the main tunnel and met Sophia Briggs. A year ago she had counted all the snakes in the missile silo and now she was taking another census to find out if the population had grown. Carrying a can of non-toxic spray paint, she would find a snake and mark the specimen to show that it had been counted. Gabriel got used to seeing king snakes with neon-orange stripes on the tip of their tails.

* * *

HE WALKED DOWN a long passageway in a dream, then opened his eyes and found himself lying on the folding cot. After drinking some water and eating a handful of wheat crackers, he left the dormitory room and found Sophia in the abandoned control room. The biologist turned and gave him a sharp, appraising look. Gabriel always felt like a new student in one of her college classes.

"How did you sleep?" she asked.

"All right."

"Did you find the food I left you?"

"Yes."

Sophia saw a king snake moving in the shadows. Moving quickly, she sprayed a band on its tail, then counted the specimen with her hand clicker. "And what's going on with that lovely water drop? Have you split it with your sword?"

"Not yet."

"Well, maybe this time, Gabriel. Give it a try."

And then he was back at the wet patch of floor, staring up at the ceiling and cursing all of the ninety-nine paths. The water drop was too small, and too fast. The sword blade was too narrow. This was truly an impossible task.

In the beginning, he had tried to concentrate on the event itself, staring at the drop as it formed, flexing his muscles, and gripping the sword like a baseball player waiting for a fastball. Unfortunately, there was nothing regular about what happened. Sometimes the drop wouldn't fall for twenty minutes. Sometimes two drops would fall within ten seconds. Gabriel swung the sword and missed. He muttered a curse, and tried again. Anger filled his heart so intensely that he thought of fleeing the silo and walking back to San Lucas. He wasn't the lost prince of his mother's stories, just a foolish young man ordered around by a half-crazy old woman.

Gabriel felt as if today would bring only more failure. But standing alone with the sword for several hours, he gradually forgot about himself and his problems. Although the weapon was still in his hands, he didn't feel like he was holding it in a conscious way. The sword was simply an extension of his mind.

The water drop fell, but this time it seemed to fall in slow motion. When he swung the sword, he was one step back from his own experience, watching the blade touch the water drop and cut it in two. Time stopped at that moment and he saw everything clearly—the sword, his hands, and the two halves of the water drop drifting off into opposite directions.

Then time began moving again and the sensation disappeared. Only a few seconds had gone by, but it felt like a glimpse of eternity. Gabriel turned and ran down the tunnel. "Sophia!" he shouted. "Sophia!" His voice echoed off the concrete walls.

She was still in the control room, writing in her leather notebook. "Is there a problem?"

Gabriel stammered as if his tongue didn't work anymore. "I—I cut the drop with the jade sword."

"Good. Very good." She closed the notebook. "You're making progress."

"There was something else, but it's hard to explain. It felt like time slowed down while it happened."

"You saw this?"

Gabriel looked down at the floor. "I know it sounds crazy."

"No one can stop time," Sophia said. "But people can focus their senses far beyond the normal boundaries. It may feel like the world is slowing down, but it's all going on inside your brain. Your perceptions have been accelerated. Occasionally, great athletes are able to do this. A ball is thrown or kicked through the air and they can see it precisely. Sometimes musicians can hear every instrument in a symphony orchestra at the same moment. It can even happen to ordinary people who meditate or pray."

"Does it happen to Travelers?"

"Travelers are different from the rest of us because they can learn how to control this kind of intensified perception. It gives them the power to see the world with an immense clarity." Sophia studied Gabriel's face as if his eyes could give her an answer. "Can you do that, Gabriel? Can you push a switch in your mind and make the world seem to slow down and stop for a while?"

"No. The whole thing just happened."

She nodded. "Then we have to keep working." Sophia picked up her kerosene lantern and began to walk out of the room. "Let's try the seventeenth path to help your sense of balance and movement. When a Traveler's body is moving slightly, it helps the Light break free."

A few minutes later they were standing on a ledge that was built halfway up the sixty-foot silo that had once contained the facility's radio antenna. A steel girder about three inches wide crossed the length of the silo. Sophia raised her lantern and showed him that it was a thirty-foot drop to a pile of abandoned machinery.

"There's a penny on the girder, about halfway across. Go pick it up."

"If I fall, I'm going to break my legs."

Sophia didn't seem to be worried. "Yes, you could break your legs. But I think it's more likely that you'd break both ankles. Of course, if you land on your head, you'll probably die." She lowered the lantern and nodded. "Get going."

Gabriel took a deep breath and stepped sideways on the girder so that his weight was on the arches of his feet. Cautiously, he began to shuffle away from the ledge.

"That's not right," Sophia said. "Step with your toes pointed forward."

"This is safer."

"No, it isn't. Your arms should be extended at a ninety-degree angle to the girder. Focus on your breathing, not on your fear."

Gabriel turned his head to speak to Sophia and lost his balance. He swayed back and forth for a moment then crouched down and grabbed the girder with both hands. Once again, he started to fall until he threw his legs outward and straddled the girder. It took him two minutes to return to the ledge.

"That was pathetic, Gabriel. Try again."

"No."

"If you want to be a Traveler—"

"I don't want to get killed! Stop asking me to do things that you can't do yourself."

Sophia set her lantern down on the ledge. Stepping onto the girder like a tightrope walker, she moved quickly to the middle of the girder, bent down, and picked up the penny. The old woman jumped a few feet into the air, turned around completely, and landed on one foot. Quickly, she returned to the ledge and flicked the penny in Gabriel's direction.

"Get some rest, Gabriel. You've been awake much longer than you think." She picked up her lantern and headed back to the main tunnel. "When I come back down, we'll try the twenty-seventh path. That one is quite old, thought up in the twelfth century by a German nun named Hildegard of Bingen."

Furious, Gabriel tossed the penny away and followed her. "How long have I been underground?"

"Don't worry about that."

"I'm not worried. I just want to know. How long have I been here and how many more days do I have left?"

"Go to sleep. And don't forget to dream."

*   *   *

GABRIEL THOUGHT ABOUT leaving, then decided against it. If he left early, he would have to explain his decision to Maya. If he stayed for a few more days and failed, no one would care what happened to him.

Sleep. Another dream. When Gabriel raised his eyes, he was standing in the courtyard of a large brick building. It appeared to be some kind of monastery or school, but no one was there. Pieces of paper were scattered across the floor and the wind blew them up into the air.

Gabriel turned, stepped through an open doorway, and entered a long corridor with smashed windows on the right side. There were no dead bodies or bloodstains, but he knew immediately that people had been fighting here. Wind pushed through the empty window frames. A sheet of lined notebook paper skittered across the floor. He went to the end of the corridor, turned the corner, and saw a woman with black hair sitting on the floor holding a man in her lap. As he came closer, he saw that it was his own body. His eyes were closed and he didn't appear to be breathing.

The woman looked up and brushed her long hair away from her face. It was Maya. Her clothes were covered with blood and her broken sword lay on the floor beside her leg. She held his body tightly, rocking back and forth. But the most terrifying thing was that the Harlequin was crying.

* * *

GABRIEL WOKE UP in a darkness so absolute that he found it difficult to know if he was dead or alive. "Hello!" he shouted and the sound of his voice echoed off the concrete walls of the room. Something must have happened to the electric cord or the power generator. All the lightbulbs had gone out and he was a captive of the darkness. Trying not to panic, he reached beneath the folding cot and found his lantern and a box of wooden matches. The match flame startled him with its sudden brightness. He lit the wick and the room was filled with light.

As he adjusted the lantern's glass chimney, he heard a harsh buzzing sound. Gabriel turned slightly to the left just as a rattlesnake rose up two feet away from his leg. Somehow the viper had entered the silo and had been drawn to Gabriel's warm body. The snake's tail vibrated quickly and he moved his head back, ready to strike.

Without warning, an enormous king snake came out of the shadows like a straight black line and bit the rattlesnake just behind its head. The two snakes fell together onto the concrete floor as the king snake wrapped its body around its prey.

Gabriel grabbed the lantern and stumbled from the room. The lights were out down the length of the main tunnel and it took him five minutes to find the emergency staircase that led back to the surface. His boots made a hollow thumping sound as he climbed up the stairs to the hatch cover. He reached the landing, pushed hard, and realized that he was locked in.

"Sophia!" he shouted. "Sophia!" But no one answered. Gabriel returned to the main tunnel and stood beside the line of dead lightbulbs. He had failed at all his attempts to become a Traveler. It seemed pointless to continue. If Sophia was going to keep the hatch locked, then he would have to enter the launch silos and find another way out.

Gabriel hurried north down the main tunnel and entered the maze of passageways. The silos were designed to deflect the explosion of flame when the missiles took off and he kept encountering ventilation shafts that went nowhere. Finally he stopped moving and stared at the lantern in his hand. Every few seconds the flame trembled as if touched by a slight breeze. He moved slowly in that direction until he felt cool air flowing down the tunnel. Slipping between a heavy steel door and a bent door frame, he found himself on a platform jutting out of the wall of the center launch silo.

The silo was a massive vertical cave with concrete walls. Years ago, the government had removed the weapons aimed at the Soviet Union, but he could see the shadowy outline of a missile platform about three hundred feet below him. A stairway spiraled around the silo from the base to the opening. And yes, there it was—a shaft of sunlight pushing through a gap in the silo cover.

Something splattered on his cheek. Groundwater was oozing through cracks in the concrete wall. Holding the lantern, Gabriel began climbing the staircase to the light. The stairs trembled each time he took a step. Fifty years of water had rusted the steel bolts that held the structure to the wall.

Slow down, he told himself. Got to be careful. But the stairs began to shiver like a living creature. Suddenly a bolt was ripped out of the wall and fell through the air to the shadows below. Gabriel stopped and listened to the bolt ricochet off the platform. And then, sounding like bullets from a machine gun, a line of bolts snapped out of the concrete, and the stairs began to peel away from the wall.

He let go of the lantern and held on to the railing with both hands as the upper part of the staircase fell toward him. The weight of the collapsing structure pulled out more bolts and then he was falling outward, only to slam back into the concrete, about twenty feet below the entrance ledge. Only one of the support brackets still held the railing.

Gabriel hung from the railing for a moment, overcome by fear. The silo yawned below him like a portal into endless darkness. Slowly, he began to climb up the railing, and then he heard a roaring sound in his ears. Something was wrong with the right side of his body. It felt paralyzed. As he tried to hold on, he saw a shadow arm composed of small points of light emerge from his body while his right arm fell motionless to his side. He was holding on with one hand, but all he could do was stare at the light.

"Hold on!" Sophia shouted. "I'm right above you!"

The sound of the Pathfinder's voice made the shadow arm disappear. Gabriel couldn't see where Sophia was standing, but a length of knotted nylon rope fell down and slapped against the concrete wall. He was just able to reach out and grab the rope as the support bracket ripped away from the concrete. The railing fell past him, smashing onto the launchpad.

Gabriel pulled himself up to the ledge, and then lay there for a while, gasping for breath. Sophia stood over him, holding her lantern.

"You all right?"

"No."

"I was up on the surface when the generator shorted out. I got it going again and came down immediately."

"You—you locked me in."

"That's right. There was only one more day to go."

He stood up and headed back down the passageway. Sophia followed him.

"I saw what happened, Gabriel."

"Yeah. I almost got killed."

"I'm not talking about that. Your right arm went limp for a few seconds. I couldn't see it, but I know that the Light came out of your body."

"I'm not sure if it's day or night, if I'm dreaming or awake."

"You're a Traveler like your father. Don't you realize that?"

"Forget it. I don't like any of this. I just want to have a normal life."

Without another word, Sophia took a quick step toward Gabriel. She reached out, grabbed the back of his belt, and jerked hard. Gabriel felt as if something was ripping, tearing inside him. And then he felt the Light break out of its cage and float upward while his body collapsed facedown onto the floor. He was terrified, desperately wanting to return to what was familiar.

Gabriel looked at his hands and saw that they had been transformed into hundreds of points of light, each precise and glimmering like a star. As Sophia knelt beside the discarded body, the Traveler floated upward, passing through the concrete ceiling.

The stars seemed to move closer together as he became a concentrated point of energy. He was an entire ocean contained within a drop of water, a mountain squeezed into a grain of sand. And then the particle that contained his energy, his true consciousness, entered into a sort of channel or passageway that propelled him forward.

This moment could have lasted a thousand years or for only a single heartbeat; he had lost consciousness of time. All he knew was that he was moving very quickly, racing through darkness, following the curved edge of a contained space. And then the movement ended and a transformation occurred. A single breath, more fundamental and pervasive than lungs and oxygen, filled his being.

Go now. Find the way.

Gabriel opened his eyes and found himself falling through blue sky. He looked down and from side to side but saw nothing. There was no ground below him. No landing place or final destination. This was the barrier of air. He realized that he had always known of its existence. Attached to a parachute, he had tried to re-create this feeling in his own world.

But now he was free of the jump plane and the inevitable descent back to earth. Gabriel closed his eyes for a while, then opened them again. He arched his back and spread his arms, controlling his movement through the air. Look for the passageway. That's what Sophia had told him. There was a passageway that led across all four barriers and into the other realms. Leaning to the right, he began to spiral downward like a hawk looking for prey.

Time passed and then, in the distance, he saw a thin black line, like a shadow floating in space. Gabriel extended his arms, pulled out of the tight circle, and fell quickly to the left on a sharp diagonal. The shadow grew into an oval shape and he glided into its dark center.

*   *   *

ONCE AGAIN, HE felt a compression of light, a movement forward and the life-giving breath. Opening his eyes, he found himself standing in the middle of a desert, the red dirt cracked open as if it were gasping for air. Gabriel turned on one heel, surveying this new environment. The sky above him was a sapphire blue. Although the sun had disappeared, light glowed on every part of the horizon. No rocks or plants. No valleys or mountains. He was captive in the earth barrier, the only thing vertical in a flatland world.

Gabriel began walking. When he stopped and looked around, his perspective hadn't changed. Kneeling down, he touched the red dirt with his fingers. He needed a second point on the landscape, some other feature that would confirm his own existence. He kicked and clawed at the earth until he scraped together a pile of dirt about ten inches high.

Like a small child who had thrown down a cup and thereby changed the world, he circled the pile several times just to make sure it was still there. Once again, he started walking and counted his steps. Fifty. Eighty. One hundred. But when he looked over his shoulder, the pile had disappeared.

Gabriel felt a surge of panic push through his heart. He sat down, closed his eyes and rested, then stood up again and resumed walking. As he looked for the passageway, he began to feel hopeless and lost. For a while, he kicked at the earth with the toe of his boot. Chips of dirt rose up into the air, fell down, and were instantly absorbed by this new reality.

He looked over his shoulder and saw a patch of darkness behind him. It was his own shadow, following him around on this aimless journey, but the image had an unusual depth and sharpness, as if someone had cut into the ground. Was this the way out? Had it always been there? Closing his eyes, he fell backward and was pulled down the passageway.

*   *   *

BREATHE, HE TOLD himself. Breathe again. And he was kneeling in a dirt street that ran through the middle of a town. Gabriel stood up cautiously, expecting the ground to collapse and drop him into air, water, or the bare desert world. He stomped his feet on the street like a man having a tantrum, but this new reality sustained itself and refused to vanish.

The town reminded him of a frontier outpost in an old-fashioned Western, the sort of place where you'd find cowboys, sheriffs, and dance-hall girls. The buildings were two and three stories high, built with flat boards and shingles. Wooden sidewalks ran on both sides of the street, as if the builders wanted to keep mud from splattering into the doorways. But there was no mud or rain or any water at all. The few trees on the street looked dead; their leaves were dry and brittle-brown.

Gabriel drew the jade sword and held it tightly as he stepped onto the wooden sidewalk. He tried a doorknob—unlocked—and stepped into a one-room barbershop with three chairs. Mirrors hung from the walls and Gabriel stared at his own face and the sword in his hand. He looked frightened, like a man who expected to be attacked at any moment. Leave this place. Hurry. And then he was back on the sidewalk with the clear sky and the lifeless trees.

All the doors were unlocked and he began to search each building. His shoes made a hollow sound on the wooden sidewalk. He discovered a fabric store filled with bolts of cloth. An apartment was upstairs. It had a sink with a hand pump and a cast-iron stove. Plates and cups had been set for three people, but the shelves and icebox were empty. In another building, he found a cooper's shop with wooden barrels in different states of completion.

The town had only two streets and they intersected at a city square with park benches and a stone obelisk. There was no writing on this memorial, only a series of geometric symbols that included a circle, a triangle, and a pentagram.

Gabriel kept following the street until the town disappeared and he reached a barrier of dead trees and thornbushes. He spent some time looking for a path, then gave up and returned to the square.

"Hello!" he shouted. "Is anyone here?" But nobody answered him. Now the sword made him feel like a coward and he slid it back into the scabbard.

A building near the square had a rounded cupola roof, and the front door was made of a dark, heavy wood with iron hinges. Gabriel passed through the doorway and found himself in a church with pews and stained-glass windows that displayed complex geometric patterns. A wooden altar was at the front of the room.

The missing inhabitants of the town had decorated the altar with roses that were dead and faded, showing only a faint suggestion of their former color. A black candle burned at the center of this dry offering. The bright flame flickered back and forth. Other than himself, it was the only thing that was alive and moving in the entire town.

He stepped toward the altar and breathed deeply, like a sigh. The black candle fell out of its brass holder and the flame touched the dry petals and leaves. A rose was set on fire and an orange flame ran down the stem to another flower. Gabriel began searching the room for a bottle of water or a bucket of sand, anything that would extinguish the flame. Nothing. When he turned back, the altar itself was on fire. Flames curved around the posts and touched the edges of the scrollwork.

Gabriel ran outside and stood in the middle of the street. His mouth was open, but he stayed silent. Where could he hide? Was there any place of refuge? Trying to control his fear, he ran down the street that led past the barbershop and fabric store. When he reached the edge of the town, he stopped and looked out at the forest. All the trees were on fire and smoke rose up into the sky like a massive gray wall.

A particle of ash touched his cheek and he brushed it away. Gabriel knew there was no way out, but he ran back to the church building. Smoke leaked out of the crack around the heavy door. The stained-glass windows glowed from within. As he watched, a crack appeared in the center window and grew larger, like a jagged wound on someone's skin. Air expanded inside the building and the window exploded, showering the street with broken glass. Flames reached out of the window frame and black smoke touched the side of the white cupola.

He sprinted down the street to the other side of town and watched a burning pine tree explode into flames. Turn back, he thought. Run away. But all the buildings were burning now. The intense heat caused a wind that made bits of ash swirl around like leaves in an autumn storm.

Somewhere in this destruction was a way out, the dark passageway that would guide him back to the human world. But the fire destroyed all shadows and the rising smoke turned day into night. Too hot, he thought. Can't breathe. Returning to the square, he kneeled beside the stone obelisk. The park benches and the dry weeds were burning. Everything was touched by the flames. Gabriel covered his head with his arms and curled up in a tight ball. The fire surrounded him and pushed through his skin.

* * *

AND THEN IT passed. When Gabriel opened his eyes, he saw that he was surrounded by the charred ruins of the town and the forest. Large pieces of wood were still burning and wisps of smoke rose toward a slate-gray sky.

Gabriel left the square and walked slowly down the street. The church, the cooper's shop, and the fabric store with the upstairs apartment had been destroyed. A moment later, he reached the edge of the town and the remains of the forest. Some of the trees had fallen to the ground, but a few of them were still standing like black stick figures with twisted arms.

He retraced his footsteps through the ash-covered streets and saw that a wooden awning post was still standing in the middle of the destruction. Gabriel touched the post, sliding his hand down its smooth surface. Was this possible? How did it survive? He lingered by the post, trying to understand its meaning, and saw a white plaster wall standing about twenty feet away from him. The wall hadn't existed a few minutes ago—or perhaps he was too dazed to notice it. He kept walking and found a barbershop chair in the middle of the ashes. This object was completely real. He could touch it, feel the green leather and the wooden armrests.

He realized that the town was going to reappear in exactly the same form. It would become whole, only to burn again—the process repeating itself forever. This was the damnation of the fire barrier. If he couldn't find the passageway, he was trapped within this endless cycle of rebirth and destruction.

Instead of searching for a shadow, he returned to the square and leaned against the obelisk. As he watched, a front door appeared, and then part of a wooden walkway. The town began to form and reassert itself, growing like a living creature. The smoke vanished and the sky was blue again. Everything was changed but the same, as ashes melted in the sunlight like flakes of dirty snow.

Finally the process was complete. A town with empty rooms and dead trees surrounded him. Only then did a degree of clarity return to his mind. Forget the convolutions of philosophy. There were only two states of being: equilibrium and motion. The Tabula worshipped the ideal of political and social control, the illusion that everything should remain the same. But this was the cold emptiness of space not the energy of the Light.

Gabriel left his refuge and began to look for a shadow. Like a detective searching for a clue, he entered each building and opened the closets and the empty cupboards. He peered beneath beds and tried to look at each object from a different angle. Perhaps he could see the passageway if he stood in the correct position.

When he returned to the street, the air seemed a little warmer. The town was new and complete, but gaining power for the next explosion of flame. Gabriel began to get angry about the inevitability of the cycle. Why couldn't he stop what was going to happen? He began whistling a Christmas carol, enjoying the feeble noise in the silence. Returning to the church, he yanked open the door and marched toward the wooden altar.

The candle had reappeared as if nothing had ever happened and burned bright in its brass holder. Gabriel licked his thumb and forefinger, then reached out to snuff the flame. The moment he touched the candle, the flame broke off from the wick and began to flutter around his head like a bright yellow butterfly. It came to rest on a rose stem and this dry tinder started to burn. Gabriel tried to crush the fire with the palm of his hand, but sparks escaped and settled on the rest of the altar.

Instead of running from the fire, he sat down in a center pew and watched the destruction spread through the room. Could he die in this place? If his body was destroyed would he reappear again, like the altar and the barbershop chair? He began to feel an intense heat, but tried to deny the new reality. Perhaps all this was a dream, another construction of his mind.

Smoke had risen to the ceiling and now it began to drift downward, pulled toward the half-open door. As Gabriel stood up and began to leave the church, the altar turned into a column of flame. Smoke entered his lungs. He started coughing, then glanced to the left and saw a shadow appear in one of the stained-glass windows. The shadow was black and deep; it floated back and forth like a wavering particle of night. Gabriel grabbed a pew and dragged it over to the wall. He stood on the pew and pulled himself onto the narrow ledge at the bottom of the window frame.

Drawing the sword, he slashed at the shadow and his right hand disappeared into the blackness. *Jump*, he thought. *Save yourself*. He began to fall into the dark passageway, pulled forward into space. It was only in the final moment that he looked back and saw Michael standing in the church doorway.

With Gabriel's motorcycle hidden in the back of the van, Maya drove north to Las Vegas. She saw dozens of road signs advertising casinos, and then a cluster of bright towers popped up on the horizon. After cruising past several motels outside the city, she checked into the Frontier Lodge—ten individual rooms designed to look like log cabins. The shower stall had green stains bleeding from the faucet handles and the mattress was saggy, but she placed her sword beside her and slept for twelve hours.

Maya knew the casinos would have surveillance cameras, and some of the cameras might be connected to Tabula computers. When she woke up, she took out a syringe and injected facer drugs into her lips and the skin below her eyes. The drugs made her look overweight and dissipated, like a woman who had a drinking problem.

She drove to a mall and bought cheap, flashy clothes—Capri pants, a pink T-shirt, and sandals—then visited a shop where an older woman wearing a cowgirl costume was selling makeup and synthetic wigs. Maya pointed to a blond wig sitting on a Styrofoam head behind the counter.

"That's the Champagne Blonde model, honey. You wanna wrap it up or wear it?"

"I'll put it on right now."

The clerk nodded her approval. "Men just love that blond hair. It drives 'em crazy."

Now she was ready. She drove down the main boulevard, turned right at the half-sized Eiffel Tower, and left the van in the parking lot of the Paris Las Vegas Hotel. The hotel was an amusement-park version of the City of Lights. It had a small version of the Arc de Triomphe and painted façades that resembled the Louvre and the Paris Opera House. The ground-floor casino was an enormous room with a domed ceiling that glowed with a dark blue color like an endless Paris twilight. Tourists wandered down cobblestone streets to blackjack tables and rows of slot machines.

Maya walked along the strip to another hotel and saw gondoliers rowing tourists down a canal that went nowhere. Although each hotel had a different theme, they were all basically the same. None of the gambling rooms had clocks or windows. You were there and nowhere at the same time. When Maya first entered a casino, her acute sense of balance helped her realize something most tourists would never understand. The ground floor was slightly tilted so that gravity would pull visitors in an imperceptible manner from the hotel section to the slot machines and blackjack tables.

For most people Las Vegas was a happy destination, where you could drink too much and gamble and watch strange women take off their clothes. But this city of pleasure was a three-dimensional illusion. Surveillance cameras watched constantly, computers monitored the gambling, and a legion of security guards with American flags sewn on the sleeves of their uniforms made sure nothing truly unusual would ever occur. This was the goal of the Tabula: the appearance of freedom with the reality of control.

In such an ordered environment, it would be difficult to trick the authorities. Maya had spent her life avoiding the Vast Machine, but now she had to trigger all their sensors and escape without being captured. She was sure the Tabula computer programs were searching the Vast Machine for a variety of data—including the use of Michael's credit card. If the card was reported as stolen, then she might have to deal with security guards who knew nothing about the Tabula. Harlequins avoided injuring citizens or drones, but sometimes it was necessary for survival.

After checking out the rest of the hotels on the strip, she decided that the New York–New York Hotel gave her the most options for escape. Maya spent the afternoon at a shop run by the Salvation Army where she acquired two used suitcases and men's clothes. She bought a toiletry kit and filled it with a can of shaving cream, a half-used tube of toothpaste, and a toothbrush, which she rubbed on the concrete outside her cabin. The final detail was the most important: road maps with pencil marks indicating a coast-to-coast trip with New York City as the final destination.

Gabriel had left his helmet, gloves, and motorcycle jacket in the van. Back at the tourist cabin, Maya pulled on the riding gear. It felt as if Gabriel's skin, his presence, surrounded her. Maya had owned a motor scooter when she lived in London, but the Italian-made motorcycle was a large and powerful machine. It was difficult to steer the bike, and whenever she shifted gears she heard a grinding sound.

That evening she left the motorcycle in the New York–New York Hotel parking lot and used a pay phone to reserve a suite. Twenty minutes later she entered the hotel's massive atrium and approached the front desk carrying her suitcases.

"My husband made the reservation," she explained to the desk clerk. "He's flying in later tonight."

The clerk was a muscular young man with a blond haze of close-cropped hair. He looked as if he should be running a summer sports camp in Switzerland. "Hope you two have a fun weekend," he said, and then asked for some form of identification.

Maya handed over her fake passport and Michael Corrigan's credit card. Numbers flowed from the desk computer to a master computer and then onward to a mainframe somewhere in the world. Maya watched the clerk's face intently, looking for a slight tension if the words *stolen card* appeared on the monitor screen. She was ready to lie, to run, to kill if necessary—but the clerk smiled and gave her a plastic card key. When Maya entered the elevator she was required to slide the card into a slot and punch the correct floor number. Now the hotel computer knew exactly where she was: in the elevator going up to the fourteenth floor.

The two-room suite had a huge television. The furniture and bathroom fixtures were larger than anything to be found in a British hotel. Americans were fairly big people, Maya thought. But it was more than that—this was a conscious desire to feel overwhelmed by grand furnishings.

Maya heard screaming and then a deep grumbling sound. When she pushed open the curtains, she saw that a roller coaster was on the roof of a building about five hundred feet away from the window. Ignoring the distraction, she ran water in the tub and sink, used a bar of soap, and dampened a few towels. In the suite's living room, she placed the road maps and a pencil on a side table. A paper bag with greasy wrappers from a fast-food restaurant was left beside the television. With each piece of trash and clothing, she was constructing a little story that would be read and interpreted by a Tabula mercenary. It was about ten minutes since the credit card number had entered the Vast Machine. Returning to the bedroom, she opened the suitcases and placed some of the clothes in a drawer. Maya pulled out the small German automatic that she had found at Resurrection Auto Parts and slipped it beneath a folded shirt.

The gun was the ultimate proof that she had been at the hotel. The Tabula would never believe that a Harlequin would deliberately give up a weapon. If the police discovered the gun, it would be registered in their database and the Tabula computers that were searching the Internet would detect it immediately.

Maya was rumpling up the sheets and blankets when she heard a faint click in the outer room. Someone had pushed a key card into the door lock and now he was opening the door.

Her right hand touched the sword case. She had the Harlequin desire to attack—always attack—and destroy the threat to her safety. But that wouldn't accomplish the true goal, to confuse the Tabula with false information. Maya glanced around the room and saw a sliding glass door that led to a balcony. She drew the stiletto and approached the curtains; it took her a few seconds to cut two strips of fabric.

The floor creaked in the outer room as the intruder walked softly across the carpet. Whoever was outside the bedroom door paused for a few seconds and Maya wondered if he was gathering the courage to attack.

Carrying the strips of curtain, she pushed open the sliding door and stepped onto the balcony. Warm desert air surrounded her. The stars hadn't appeared yet, but green-and-red neon lights flashed in the street below. No time to make a rope. She tied both strips to the railing, then went over the side.

The curtains were made of thin cotton and unable to support her weight. As Maya lowered herself, one strip ripped apart and broke away. She dangled in the air, holding on to the other strip, then continued her descent to the next floor. A voice from above. Maybe he saw her.

There was no time to think or feel or be afraid. The Harlequin grabbed the iron railing and pulled herself onto a balcony. Once again, she drew the stiletto and saw that she had cut the palm of her hand. Damned by the flesh. Saved by the blood. She pulled open a sliding glass door and ran through an empty room.

46

One of the reasons Michael enjoyed living at the research center was the way that the staff seemed to anticipate his needs. When he returned from the barriers the first time, he had felt fragile and dazed, not quite sure about the reality of his own body. After a few medical tests, Dr. Richardson and Lawrence Takawa brought him up to the first-floor gallery to meet General Nash. Michael asked for orange juice and they had returned five minutes later with a six-ounce cardboard carton, probably taken from a janitor's lunch box.

Now he was back from his second experience crossing the barriers and everything was prepared for his comfort. On a side table in the gallery was a glass carafe of chilled orange juice. Next to that was a silver tray displaying fresh-baked chocolate-chip cookies as if a team of apron-wearing moms had been making preparations for his homecoming.

Kennard Nash sat opposite him in a black leather chair and sipped a glass of wine. When they first started their conversations, Michael was surprised that the general never took notes. Now he realized that the surveillance cameras were always working. Michael enjoyed the fact that everything he said and did was so important that it had to be recorded and analyzed. The entire research facility was dependent upon his power.

Nash leaned forward and spoke softly. "And then the fire started?"

"Yeah. The trees began burning. That was when I found a path that led to a town in the middle of nowhere. All the buildings were burning, too."

"Was anyone there?" Nash asked. "Or were you alone?"

"At first I thought the town was empty. Then I walked into this little church and saw my brother, Gabriel. We didn't talk to each other. He was going through a passageway that probably led back to this world."

Nash pulled a cell phone out of his suit-coat pocket, punched a button, and spoke to Lawrence Takawa. "Copy the last five seconds of our conversation and send it to Mr. Boone. He needs this data as soon as possible."

The general snapped the phone shut and picked up his glass of wine. "Your brother is still a prisoner of a terrorist group called the Harlequins. Obviously, they've trained him to cross over."

"Gabriel was carrying our father's Japanese sword. How is that possible?"

"Our research indicates that certain objects called talismans can be carried by a Traveler."

"I don't care what they're called. Find one and get it for me. I want a weapon when I cross over."

General Nash nodded quickly as if to say, *Whatever you want, Mr. Corrigan. No problem. We'll arrange it.* Michael leaned back in his chair. He felt confident enough to make his next demand.

"That is—if I decide to visit the different realms."

"Of course you will," Nash told him.

"Don't threaten me, General. I'm not serving in your army. If you want to kill me, go right ahead. You'd be losing the most important element of this project."

"If you want money, Michael—"

"Of course I want money. But that's trivial. What I really want is full information. The first time we met you told me that I was going to help you achieve a technological breakthrough. You said we were going to change history together. Okay, now I'm a Traveler. So why do I have wires in my brain? What's the point of all this effort?"

Nash walked over to the side table and got a chocolate-chip cookie. "Come with me, Michael. I need to show you something."

The men left the gallery and strolled down a hallway to the elevator. "All this started several years ago when I was in the White House and developed the Freedom from Fear program. Everyone in America was going to wear a Protective Link device. It would have ended crime and terrorism."

"But it didn't work," Michael said.

"At the time, our technology wasn't that sophisticated. We didn't have a computing system capable of handling that much data."

As they left the building, two security men followed them across the quadrangle at the center of the research compound. The air was cold and damp and a dense cloud concealed the night sky. Michael was surprised to see that they were headed for the computer center. Only special technicians were allowed inside.

"When I assumed leadership of the Brethren, I began to push for the development of a quantum computer. I knew it would be powerful enough to solve complex problems and handle enormous amounts of information. With a bank of quantum computers, we could literally track and monitor the daily activities of everyone in the world. A few people might object, but most of us would gladly give up a little privacy in exchange for security. Just think of the advantages. No more deviant behavior. No more unpleasant surprises—"

"No more Travelers," Michael said.

General Nash laughed. "Yes. I'll admit it. Getting rid of people like the Travelers was part of the plan. But that's all changed. Now you're on our team."

The security men remained outside when Michael and Nash entered the empty lobby of the computer center. "An ordinary computer runs on a binary system. No matter what the size or power, it has only two states of consciousness: 0 or 1. Ordinary computers may work very fast or in tandem with each other, but they're still restricted to these two possibilities.

"A quantum computer is based on quantum mechanics. It seems logical that an atom can spin up or down: 0 or 1. Once again, it's a binary system. But quantum mechanics tells us that an atom can be up or down or in both states at the same time. Because of this, different calculations could go on simultaneously and at great speed. Since a quantum computer uses quantum switches instead of conventional ones, it has an immense power."

They entered a windowless cubicle and a steel door closed behind them. Nash pressed the palm of his hand against a glass panel. A second door glided open with a soft whooshing sound and they entered a dimly lit room.

At the center of the room was a sealed glass tank, about five feet high and four feet wide, set on a heavy steel pedestal. Thick cables snaked across the floor from the pedestal to a bank of binary computers against the wall. Three technicians wearing white coats hovered around the glass tank like acolytes at an altar, but when General Nash glared at them, they immediately left the area.

The tank was filled with a thick green liquid that moved and churned slowly. Little explosions, like tiny bolts of lightning, kept flashing in different parts of the liquid. Michael could hear a humming sound and there was a burned odor in the air, as if someone had set fire to a handful of dead leaves.

"This is our quantum computer," Nash said. "It's a set of electrons floating in super-cooled liquid helium. The energy passing through the helium forces the electrons to interact and perform logical operations."

"Looks like a big fish tank."

"Yes. Only the fish are subatomic particles. Quantum theory has shown us that, for a very short period of time, particles of matter go off into different dimensions and then return."

"Just like a Traveler."

"And that's what happened, Michael. During our first experiments with the quantum computer we began to get messages from another realm. At first we didn't know what was going on. We thought it was an error in the software program. Then one of our scientists realized that we had received binary versions of standard mathematical equations. When we sent off similar messages, we began to receive diagrams that showed us how to create a more powerful computer."

"And that's how you built this machine?"

"Actually, this is our third version. It's been a continual process of evolution. Whenever we improved our computer, we could receive more advanced information. It was like building a series of powerful radios. With each new receiver you could hear more words, obtain more information. And we've learned about things other than computers. Our new friends have taught us how to manipulate chromosomes and create different hybrid species."

"What do they want?" Michael asked.

"This other civilization knows all about the Travelers and I think they're a little bit jealous." Nash looked amused. "They're trapped in their own realm, but they'd like to visit our world."

"Is that possible?"

"The quantum computer has been tracking you as you've crossed the barriers. That's why we placed the wires in your brain. You're the scout who's going to provide a road map for our new friends. If you cross over to another realm, they've promised to send us the design for an even more powerful machine."

Michael stepped closer to the quantum computer and watched the little flashes of lightning. Nash thought that he understood power in all its forms, but Michael suddenly realized the limits of the general's vision. The Brethren were so obsessed with controlling humanity that they weren't looking very far down the road. I'm the gatekeeper, Michael thought. I'm the person who controls what happens. If this other civilization really wants to enter our world, then I'll decide how that might occur.

He took a deep breath, and then stepped back from the quantum computer. "Very impressive, General. We're going to achieve some great things together."

47

Maya took a wrong turn in the desert and got lost looking for the abandoned missile base. It was late in the day by the time she found the barbed-wire fence and the broken gate.

She felt comfortable wearing dark custom-tailored clothing, but that would have drawn attention in this environment. While she was in Las Vegas, she had gone to a Salvation Army store and bought drawstring pants, skirts, and tops—nothing too tight around the shoulders and legs. That afternoon, Maya was wearing a cotton pullover and a pleated skirt—like something a British schoolgirl would wear. On her feet were steel-toed mechanic's shoes, very effective when used with a roundhouse kick.

She got out of the van, slung the sword carrying case over her shoulder, and then glanced at herself in the rearview mirror. That was a mistake. Her tangled black hair looked like a bird's nest. It doesn't matter, Maya thought. I'm just here to protect him. She marched over to the gate, hesitated, and then felt compelled to return to the van. Maya was furious—almost shouting with rage—as she brushed her hair. Fool, she thought. Bloody fool. You're a Harlequin. He doesn't care about you. When she was done, she threw the brush into the van with an angry flick of the wrist.

The desert air was getting cooler and dozens of king snakes were out, slithering across the asphalt road. Because no one was watching her, she drew the sword and kept it ready in case one of the reptiles got too close. This acknowledgment of her own fear was even more frustrating than the incident with the hairbrush. They're not dangerous, she told herself. Don't be a coward.

All these angry thoughts disappeared as she approached the little trailer parked beside the windmill. Gabriel was sitting at the picnic table beneath the parachute sunscreen. When he saw her, he stood up and waved. Maya studied his face. Did he look different? Had he changed? Gabriel smiled as if he'd just come back from a long journey. He looked glad to see her again.

"It's been nine days," he said. "I started to worry about you when you didn't show up last night."

"Martin Greenwald sent me a message through the Internet. He hadn't heard from Sophia, so he thought everything was all right."

The trailer door popped open. Sophia Briggs came out with a plastic pitcher and some cups. "And everything is all right at this particular moment. Good afternoon, Maya. Welcome back." Sophia placed the pitcher on the table and looked at Gabriel. "Did you tell her?"

"No."

"He crossed the four barriers," she told Maya. "You're defending a Traveler."

At first Maya felt vindicated. All the sacrifice had been worthwhile to defend a Traveler. But then much darker possibilities pushed through her mind. Her father was right: the Tabula had become too powerful. Eventually they would find Gabriel and then he would be killed. Everything she had done—finding this person, bringing him to the Pathfinder—had only pulled him closer to destruction.

"That's wonderful," Maya said. "This morning I was in contact with my friend in Paris. Our spy told him that Michael has also crossed over."

Sophia nodded. "We knew the news before you did. Gabriel saw him just before he left the fire barrier."

* * *

AS THE SUN went down, the three of them sat beneath the parachute and drank powdered lemonade. Sophia offered to make dinner, but Maya rejected the idea. Gabriel had stayed here too long and it was time to leave. Sophia picked up a stray king snake coiling beneath the table and carried it over to the silo. When she returned, she looked tired and a little sad.

"Goodbye, Gabriel. Come back here if you can."

"I'll try."

"In ancient Rome, when a great general came back from a successful war, they would parade him in triumph through the streets of the city. First would come the armor of the men he had killed and the standards he had taken, and then the captive soldiers and their families. Next came the general's army and his officers and, finally, the great man himself in a golden chariot. One servant would guide the horses while another stood behind the victor and whispered in his ear: 'You are mortal. You are a mortal man.'"

"Is that a warning, Sophia?"

"A journey into the realms doesn't always teach compassion. A Cold Traveler is a person who has taken the wrong path. They use their power to bring more suffering into the world."

* * *

MAYA AND GABRIEL returned to the van, then followed the two-lane road that cut across the desert. Lights from the city of Phoenix glowed on the western horizon, but the sky above them was clear and they could see a three-quarter moon and the bright haze of the Milky Way.

As Maya drove, she explained her plan. Right now they needed money, a safe place to hide, and multiple forms of false identification. Linden was sending American dollars to contacts in Los Angeles. Hollis and Vicki were still there and it would be good to have allies.

"Don't call them allies," Gabriel said. "They're friends."

Maya wanted to tell Gabriel that they couldn't have friends—not really. He was her principal obligation. She could risk her life for only one person. Gabriel's main responsibility was to avoid the Tabula and survive.

"They're *friends*," he repeated. "You understand that. Don't you?"

She decided to change the subject. "So what was it like?" Maya asked. "How did it feel to cross the barriers?"

Gabriel described the endless sky, the desert, and the vast ocean. Finally he told her about seeing his brother in the burning church.

"And did you speak to him?"

"I tried to, but I was already in the passageway. By the time I got back, Michael had disappeared."

"Our spy with the Tabula says that your brother has been very cooperative."

"You don't know if that's true. He's just trying to survive."

"It's more than survival. He's helping them."

"And now you're worried that he'll become a Cold Traveler?"

"It might happen. A Cold Traveler is someone who's been corrupted by power. They can cause a great deal of destruction in this world."

They drove in silence for another ten miles. Maya kept glancing in the rearview mirror, but no one was following them.

"Do the Harlequins protect Cold Travelers?"

"Of course not."

"Do you kill these people?"

The Traveler's voice sounded different and Maya turned to look at him. Gabriel was staring at her with a sharp intensity in his eyes.

"Do you kill these people?" he repeated.

"Sometimes. If we can."

"You'd kill my brother?"

"If that was necessary."

"And what about me? Would you kill me?"

"All this is just speculation, Gabriel. We don't need to talk about it."

"Don't lie to me. I can see your answer."

Maya gripped the steering wheel, not daring to look at him. One hundred yards ahead of them, a black shape darted across the road and disappeared into the weeds.

"I have this power, but I can't control it," Gabriel whispered. "I can speed up my perceptions for a moment and see everything clearly."

"You can see whatever you want, but I'm not going to lie to you. If you became a Cold Traveler, I'd kill you. It would have to be that way."

The cautious solidarity between them, their pleasure at seeing each other, had disappeared. In silence, they traveled down the empty road.

Lawrence Takawa placed his right hand on the kitchen table and stared at the little bump that showed where the Protective Link device had been inserted beneath his skin. He picked up a razor blade with his left hand and contemplated its sharp edge. Do it, he told himself. Your father wasn't afraid. Holding his breath, he made a short, deep cut. Blood oozed out of the wound and dripped onto the table.

* * *

NATHAN BOONE HAD studied the surveillance photos taken at the front desk of the New York–New York Hotel in Las Vegas. It was clear that Maya was the blond young woman who checked into the room using Michael Corrigan's credit card. A mercenary had been sent to the hotel immediately, but the Harlequin escaped. Twenty-four hours later, one of Boone's security teams found Gabriel's motorcycle in the hotel parking lot. Was Gabriel traveling with her? Or was all this just a decoy operation?

Boone decided to fly to Nevada and question everyone

who had encountered the Harlequin. He was driving to the Westchester County Airport when he got a phone call from Simon Leutner, the head administrator of the Brethren's underground computer center in London.

"Good morning, sir. Leutner here."

"What's going on? Did you find Maya?"

"No, sir. This concerns another issue. A week ago, you asked us to run a security check on all Evergreen Foundation employees. Along with the standard phone and credit card examination, we tried to see if anyone had used their access code to enter our system."

"That would be a logical target."

"The computer does an access code sweep every twenty-four hours. We just learned that a level-three employee named Lawrence Takawa entered an unauthorized data sector."

"I work with Mr. Takawa. Are you sure this wasn't a mistake?"

"Not at all. He was using General Nash's access code, but the information went directly to Takawa's personal computer. I guess he didn't realize we had added a destination-specific capability last week."

"And what was Mr. Takawa's objective?"

"He was looking for any special shipments from Japan to our administrative center in New York."

"Where is the employee at this moment? Did you check his Protective Link location?"

"He's still inside his residence in Westchester County. The time log says he reported a viral illness and will not be working today."

"Let me know if he leaves his house."

Boone called the pilot waiting at the airport and postponed his flight. If Lawrence Takawa was aiding the Harlequins, then the Brethren's security had been severely compromised. A traitor was like a tumor hidden within the body. They would need a surgeon—someone like Boone—who wasn't afraid to cut out the malignant tissue.

* * *

THE EVERGREEN FOUNDATION owned an entire office building at Fifty-fourth Street and Madison Avenue in Manhattan. Two-thirds of the building was used by the foundation's public employees who supervised research grant applications and managed the endowment. These employees—nicknamed the Lambs—were completely unaware of the Brethren and their activities.

The Brethren used the top eight floors of the building, which were accessed by a separate elevator bank. On the building directory, this was listed as the headquarters of a nonprofit organization called Nations Stand Together, which supposedly helped Third World countries upgrade their antiterrorist defenses. Two years ago at a Brethren meeting in London, Lawrence Takawa met the young woman from Switzerland who answered the phone calls and e-mails sent to Nations Stand Together. She was an expert at deflecting all inquiries in a courteous and bland manner. Apparently the United Nations ambassador from Togo was convinced that Nations Stand Together wanted to give his country a large grant to buy airport X-ray machines.

Lawrence knew that the building had one vulnerability: the security guards on the ground floor were Lambs who were ignorant of the Brethren's larger agenda. After parking his car in a lot on Forty-eighth Street, he walked up Madison to the building and entered the lobby. Although it was cold outside, he had left his overcoat and suit coat in his car. No briefcase—just a takeout cup of coffee and a manila folder. That was part of the plan.

Lawrence showed his ID card to the older guard at the desk and smiled. "I'm going to the Nations Stand Together office on the twenty-third floor."

"Stand on the yellow square, Mr. Takawa."

Lawrence stood facing an iris scanner, a large gray box mounted on the security desk. The guard pressed a button and a lens photographed Lawrence's eyes, then compared the imperfections in his irises to the data in the security file. A green light flashed. The older guard nodded to a young Latino man standing by the desk. "Enrique, please process Mr. Takawa to twenty-three."

The young guard escorted Lawrence to the elevator bank, swiped a card at the security sensor, and then Lawrence was alone. As the elevator glided upward, he opened the manila envelope and pulled out a clipboard holding some official-looking papers.

If he had been wearing an overcoat or carrying a briefcase, the other people in the hallway might have stopped to ask where he was going. But a neatly dressed and confident-looking young man with a clipboard had to be a fellow employee. Perhaps he was a new hire in computer services who had just come back from his coffee break. Thieves didn't carry cups of fresh latte.

Lawrence quickly found the mail room and swiped his ID card to get inside. Boxes were stacked against the walls, and surface mail had already been placed in different mail slots. The mail-room employee was probably pushing a cart down the hallway and would return in a few minutes. Lawrence had to find the package and get out of the building as quickly as possible.

When Kennard Nash mentioned the idea of obtaining a talisman sword, Lawrence nodded obediently and promised to come up with a solution. He called the general a few days later and kept his information as vague as possible. The data system said a Harlequin named Sparrow was killed during a confrontation at the Osaka Hotel. There was a chance that the Japanese Brethren had acquired the dead man's sword.

Kennard Nash said he would contact his friends in Tokyo. Most of them were powerful businessmen who felt that Travelers undermined the stability of Japanese society. Four days later, Lawrence used Nash's access code to enter the general's message file. *We have received your request.*

Glad to be helpful. The item requested has been sent to the administrative center in New York.

Stepping around a half wall, Lawrence saw a plastic shipping box in the corner. Japanese characters were on the shipping sticker along with a customs declaration that described the contents as *samurai film props for movie premiere*. No need to tell the government that they were shipping a thirteenth-century sword, a national treasure created by one of the Jittetsu.

There was a box cutter on the shipping counter and Lawrence used it to slash through the sealing tape and customs stamps. He opened the lid and was disappointed to find a set of fiberglass armor made for a samurai movie. Breastplate. Helmet. Gauntlets. And then, near the bottom of the case, a sword wrapped in brown paper.

Lawrence picked up the weapon and knew it was too heavy to be made of fiberglass. Quickly, he ripped off the paper that covered the sword's handle and saw that the fittings were burnished gold. His father's sword. A talisman.

* * *

BOONE WAS ALWAYS suspicious when a troublesome employee decided not to come into work. Five minutes after his conversation with the staff in London, he sent a member of his security team to Lawrence Takawa's residence. A surveillance van was already parked across the street from the town house when Boone arrived. He got into the back of the van and found a technician named Dorfman munching on corn chips while he stared at the screen of a thermal imaging device.

"Takawa is still in the house, sir. He called the research center this morning and said he had the flu."

Boone knelt on the floor of the van and examined the image. Faint lines showed walls and pipes. A bright patch of warmth was in the bedroom.

"That's the bedroom," Dorfman said. "And there's our sick employee. The Protective Link is still active."

As they watched, the body jumped off the bed and appeared to crawl to the open doorway. It hesitated for a few seconds, then returned to the mattress. During the entire sequence the body was never more than two or three feet off the floor.

Boone kicked open the back of the van and stepped out onto the street. "I think it's time to meet with Mr. Takawa—or whatever is lying on his bed."

*   *   *

IT TOOK THEM forty-five seconds to break down the front door and ten seconds to enter Lawrence's bedroom. Puppy biscuits were scattered across the bedspread where a mongrel dog sat chewing on a beef bone. The animal whimpered slightly when Boone came closer. "Good dog," he murmured. "Good dog." A plastic sandwich bag was taped to the dog's collar. Boone pulled the bag open and found a Protective Link device covered with blood.

*   *   *

AS LAWRENCE HEADED south on Second Avenue, a raindrop splattered on the windshield of his car. Dark gray clouds covered the sky, and an American flag on a steel pole fluttered wildly. Bad storm coming. He would have to drive carefully. The back of Lawrence's right hand was covered with a bandage, but the wound still hurt. Trying to ignore the pain, he glanced over his shoulder at the backseat. A day earlier he had purchased a set of golf clubs and a golf bag with an outer traveling case. The sword and scabbard were nestled between the irons and the putter.

Driving his car to the airport was a calculated risk. Lawrence had considered buying a used car that didn't have a Global Positioning System, but the purchase might be detected by the Tabula security system. The last thing he wanted was a computer inquiry asking him: *Why did you purchase another car, Mr. Takawa? What's wrong with your vehicle leased by the Evergreen Foundation?*

The best disguise was to act as ordinary as possible. He would drive to Kennedy airport, board a plane to Mexico, and reach the vacation town of Acapulco by eight o'clock that evening. At this point, he would disappear from the Vast Machine. Instead of going to a hotel, he would hire one of the Mexican drivers who waited at the airport and head south toward Guatemala. He would use additional drivers for hundred-mile segments, check into small pensions, and find a new driver a few hours later. As he made the transition into the Central American countryside, he could avoid the facial scanners and the Carnivore programs accessed by the Brethren.

Twelve thousand dollars in cash was sewn into the lining of his raincoat. Lawrence had no idea how long this money would last. Perhaps he would have to bribe the authorities or buy a house in a rural village. The cash was his only resource. Any use of a check or a credit card would immediately be detected by the Tabula.

More raindrops fell, two or three at a time. Lawrence waited at a stoplight and saw that people with umbrellas were walking quickly, trying to find shelter before the storm began. He turned left and headed east toward the Queens Midtown Tunnel. *It's time to start a new life*, he told himself. *Throw the old life away*. He lowered the window and began to toss his credit cards into the street. If some stranger found them and used them, it would cause even more confusion.

*   *   *

A HELICOPTER WAS waiting for Boone when he reached the foundation research center. He got out of his car, walked quickly across the grass, and got inside. As the helicopter slowly rose up into the air, Boone plugged his headset into the communication jack and heard Simon Leutner's voice.

"Takawa was at the administrative center in Manhattan twenty minutes ago. He entered the mail room using his ID card and left the building six minutes later."

"Can we find out what he did there?"

"Not immediately, sir. But they're starting an inventory assessment of the mail and packages that might have been in the room."

"Start a full information scan looking for Takawa. Have one of your teams focus on his charge card and bank account activity."

"We've already started that. He emptied his savings account yesterday."

"Organize another team to enter the airline data systems and check for a flight reservation."

"Yes, sir."

"Direct the major effort toward tracking his car. At this point, we have one advantage. Takawa is driving somewhere, but I don't think he knows we're searching for him."

Boone peered out the side window of the helicopter. He saw the two-line asphalt roads of Westchester County and, in the distance, the New York State Thruway. Cars and other vehicles were headed for different destinations. A school bus. A FedEx delivery truck. A green sports car cutting in and out of traffic.

In the past, people had spent extra money to order global positioning technology for their cars, but this was gradually becoming standard equipment. The GPS provided driving directions and helped the police find stolen cars. They gave monitoring services the ability to unlock doors or flash head lights if a car was lost in a parking lot, but they also turned each car into a large moving object that could easily be monitored by the Vast Machine.

Most citizens didn't realize that their cars also contained a black-box system that provided information about what was going on in the vehicle a few seconds before a collision. Tire manufacturers had implanted microchips into the tire wall that could be read by remote sensors. The sensors linked the tire to the vehicle identification number and the name of the owner.

As the helicopter continued to rise, the Brethren computers in London were forcing their way into code-protected data systems. Like digital ghosts, they glided through walls and appeared in storage rooms. The external world still looked the same, but the ghosts could see the hidden towers and walls of the Virtual Panopticon.

* * *

WHEN LAWRENCE DROVE out of the Queens Midtown Tunnel, the rain was falling hard. Raindrops exploded on the pavement and rattled on the roof of the car. Traffic halted completely, then inched forward like a tired army. He exited onto Grand Central Parkway with a line of other cars. In the distance, he could see sheets of rain pushed sideways by the wind.

There was one last responsibility before he disappeared into the jungle. Lawrence kept his eyes on the brake lights of the car in front of him and dialed the emergency phone number that Linden had given him when they met in Paris. No one answered. Instead he heard a recorded voice telling him about weekend vacations in Spain: Leave a message and we'll get back to you.

"This is your American friend," Lawrence said, then gave the date and time. "I'm going on a very long journey and I won't be coming back. You should assume that my company knows that I've been working for our competitor. This means that they will assess all of my prior contacts and every request made to the data system. I'll be off the Grid, but you can assume that the older brother will remain at our research facility. The experiment is going well . . ."

That's enough, he thought. Don't say anything more. But it was difficult to end the call. "Good luck. It was a privilege to meet you. I hope you and your friends survive."

Lawrence touched the switch in the armrest and lowered the electric window. Raindrops blew into the car, striking his face and hands. He dropped the cell phone onto the road and continued driving.

* * *

PUSHED BY THE storm, the helicopter headed south. Rain hit the pilot's Plexiglas windshield with a cracking sound, like little pieces of mud. Boone kept dialing different phone numbers and occasionally lost the signal. The chopper fell through a hole in the sky, dropped down a hundred meters, then regained stability.

"The target has just used his cell phone," Leutner said. "We've established location. He's in Queens. Entrance to the Van Wyck Expressway. The Global Positioning System in his car confirms the same location."

"He's going to Kennedy airport," Boone said. "I'll be there in twenty minutes. Some of our friends will meet me there."

"What do you want to do?"

"Do you have access to his car's location-tracking device?"

"That's easy." Leutner sounded very proud of himself. "I can do that in about five minutes."

* * *

LAWRENCE TOOK THE ticket from the machine and entered the airport's long-term parking lot. He would have to abandon the car. Once the Brethren found out about his disloyalty, he could never return to America.

The rain continued to fall and a few people huddled together in the parking lot kiosks waiting for the shuttle bus to take them to the airline terminal. Lawrence found an empty parking space and slipped in between the faded white lines. He checked his watch; it was two and a half hours before his plane left for Mexico. Plenty of time to check his luggage and the golf clubs, go through security, and drink a cup of coffee in the waiting lounge.

As Lawrence touched the door handle, he saw the lock buttons glide downward as if pushed by invisible hands. A loud click. Silence. Someone sitting at a distant computer terminal had just locked all four doors of his car.

*　*　*

BOONE'S HELICOPTER SETTLED on a landing zone near the private flight terminal attached to Kennedy airport. The main propeller continued to turn slowly as Boone dashed through the rain to the Ford sedan waiting at the edge of the runway. He yanked open the back door and jumped into the car. Detectives Mitchell and Krause sat in the front seat drinking beer and eating sandwiches. "Bring on the ark," Mitchell said. "The flood is on its way—"

"Let's go. The GPS locator says that Takawa's car is in either parking lot one or two near the terminal."

Krause glanced at his partner, then rolled his eyes. "Maybe the car is there, Boone. But he's probably gone."

"I don't think so. We just locked him inside."

Detective Mitchell started the engine and drove toward the guarded exit. "There are thousands of cars in those lots. It's going to take us hours to find him."

Boone slipped on a headset and dialed a number on his cell phone. "I'm taking care of that, too."

* * *

LAWRENCE TRIED PULLING up the lock button and forcing the door handle. Nothing. He felt as if he were sealed in a coffin. The Tabula knew everything. Perhaps they had been tracking him for hours. He rubbed his face with his hands. Calm down, he told himself. Try to be a Harlequin. They still haven't caught you.

Suddenly the car horn began honking while the head-lights flashed on and off. The pulsing noise seemed to jab at his body like the point of a knife. Lawrence panicked and pounded on the side window with his fists, but the safety glass didn't break.

Lawrence twisted around, crawled into the backseat, and snapped open the traveler carrier for the golf bag. He reached into the bag, pulled out an iron, and hit the front passenger window again and again. Cracks appeared like an intricate crystal and then the steel club head smashed through the center of the glass.

* * *

THE TWO DETECTIVES drew their guns as they approached the car, but Boone had already seen the smashed window and nylon carry-on bag lying in a puddle.

"Nothing," Krause said, peering into the car.

"We should cruise the parking lot," Mitchell said. "He could be running away from us right now."

Boone returned to the car, still talking to the team in London. "He's out of his vehicle. Switch off the theft alarm and initiate facial scanning from all airport surveillance cameras. Pay particular attention to the arrival zone outside the terminal. If Takawa grabs a taxi, I want the license number."

* * *

THE SUBWAY JERKED forward, steel wheels screeching as it rolled out of the Howard Beach station. With wet hair and a damp raincoat, Lawrence sat in one end of the car. The sword was on his lap, the scabbard and gold handle still covered with brown wrapping paper.

Lawrence knew that the two surveillance cameras at the airport had photographed him stepping onto the shuttle bus that carried visitors to the subway connection. There were more surveillance cameras at the station entrance, token booth, and platform. The Tabula would feed these camera images into their own computers and search for him using facial recognition technology. By now, they probably knew he was on the A train, heading to Manhattan.

That knowledge was useless if he stayed on the train and kept moving. The New York subway system was huge; many stations had multiple levels and different exit corridors. Lawrence amused himself with the idea of living on the subway for the rest of his life. Nathan Boone and the other mercenaries would stand helplessly on the platforms of local stations while he roared past them on an express train.

Can't do it, he thought. Eventually they would track him down and be waiting. He had to find a way out of the city that couldn't be monitored by the Vast Machine. The sword and its scabbard felt dangerous in his hands; the weight, the heaviness made him feel brave. If he was trying to hide within the Third World, then he needed to find similar places in America. Taxicabs were regulated in Manhattan, but unregistered gypsy cabs were easily found in the boroughs. A gypsy cab traveling on surface streets would be very difficult to trace. If the driver could take him across the river to Newark, perhaps he could slip onto a bus going south.

At the East New York subway station, Lawrence got out and hurried upstairs to catch the Z train going to lower Manhattan. Rainwater dripped down from a ceiling grate and there was a damp, moldy feeling in the air. He stood alone on the platform until the headlights of the train appeared in the tunnel. Keep moving. Always keep moving. It was the only way to escape.

* * *

NATHAN BOONE SAT in the grounded helicopter with Mitchell and Krause. Rain kept falling on the concrete landing zone. Both detectives looked annoyed when Boone told them not to smoke. He ignored them, closed his eyes, and listened to the voices coming from his headset.

The Brethren's Internet team had accessed the surveillance cameras of twelve different government and commercial organizations. As people hurried down New York sidewalks and subway corridors, as they paused on street corners and stepped onto buses, the nodal points of their faces were being reduced to an equation of numbers. Almost instantly, these equations were matched against the particular algorithm that personified Lawrence Takawa.

Boone enjoyed this vision of constant information flowing like dark, cold water through cables and computer networks. It's just numbers, he thought. That's all we really are—numbers. He opened his eyes when Simon Leutner began talking.

"Okay. We just accessed the security system for Citibank. There's an ATM on Canal Street with a surveillance camera. The target just went past the camera, heading toward the Manhattan Bridge." It sounded like Leutner was smiling. "Guess he didn't notice the ATM camera. They've become part of the landscape."

A pause.

"Okay. Now the target is on the pedestrian walkway of the bridge. We've already accessed the Port Authority security system. The cameras are up on the light towers, out of direct sight. We can track him all the way across."

"Where's he going?" Boone asked.

"Brooklyn. The target is moving quickly, carrying some kind of pole or stick in his right hand."

A pause.

"Reaching the end of the bridge."

A pause.

"The target is walking toward Flatbush Avenue. No. Wait. He's waving to the driver of a livery cab with a luggage rack welded to the top of the vehicle."

Boone reached up and clicked the intercom switch to the helicopter pilot. "We've got him," he said. "I'll tell you where to go."

* * *

THE DRIVER OF the gypsy cab was an older Haitian man who wore a plastic raincoat and a Yankees baseball cap. The roof of the car kept leaking and the backseat was damp. Lawrence felt the wet coldness touch his legs.

"Where you want to go?"

"Newark, New Jersey. Take the Verrazano. I'll pay the toll."

The old man looked skeptical about the idea. "Too many miles and no fare back. Nobody in Newark want to go to Fort Greene."

"What's it cost one way?"

"Forty-five dollar."

"I'll pay you a hundred dollars. Let's go."

Pleased with the deal, the old man shifted into drive and the battered Chevrolet chugged down the street. The driver began mumbling a song in Creole while his fingers tapped out a rhythm on the steering wheel.

"*Ti chéri. Ti chéri . . .*"

A roaring sound came down on them and Lawrence watched as an intense wind flung raindrops against the cars. The old man slammed on the brakes, amazed at the vision in front of him: a helicopter slowly landing at the intersection of Flatbush and Tillary Street.

Lawrence grabbed the sword and kicked the door open.

* * *

BOONE SPRINTED THROUGH the rain. When he glanced over his shoulder, he could see that the two detectives were already gasping for air and flailing their arms. Takawa was about two hundred yards ahead of them, running down Myrtle Avenue and turning onto St. Edwards. Boone passed a cash-checking store with barred windows, a dentist's office, and a small boutique with a lurid pink-and-purple sign.

The towers of the Fort Greene housing project dominated the skyline like a broken wall. When the people on the sidewalk saw three white men chasing a young Asian man, they instinctively pulled back into the doorways or hurried across the streets. Drug bust, they thought. Cops. Don't get involved.

Boone reached St. Edwards and looked down the block. Raindrops hit the sidewalk and the parked cars. Water flowed down the gutter and pooled at the intersection. Someone moving. No. Just an old woman with an umbrella. Takawa had disappeared.

Instead of waiting for the detectives, Boone kept running. He went past two rundown apartment houses, then looked down an alley and saw Takawa slip through a hole in the wall. Stepping around plastic bags of garbage and a discarded mattress, Boone reached the hole and discovered a sheet of galvanized steel that once sealed off a doorway. Someone, probably the local drug addicts, had bent the sheet back, and now Takawa was inside.

Mitchell and Krause reached the mouth of the alleyway. "Cover the exits!" Boone shouted. "I'll go in and find him!"

Cautiously he pushed through the metal sheet and entered a long room with a concrete floor and a high ceiling. Trash everywhere. Broken chairs. Many years ago, the building had been used as a garage. There was a tool bench along one wall and a repair bay in the floor where the mechanics once stood to work on cars. The rectangular bay was filled with oily water, and in the dim light it looked as if it could lead to a distant cavern. Boone stopped near a concrete staircase and listened. He heard water dripping on the floor and then a scraping noise coming from upstairs.

"Lawrence! This is Nathan Boone! I know you're up there!"

* * *

LAWRENCE STOOD ALONE on the second floor. His raincoat was sodden with water, heavy with the thousands of dollars concealed in the lining. Quickly he pulled the coat off and threw it away. Rainwater splattered on his shoulders, but that was nothing. He felt as if an immense burden had been taken from his body.

"Come downstairs!" Boone shouted. "If you come down immediately, you won't get hurt!"

Lawrence stripped the wrapping paper off the scabbard of his father's sword, drew the weapon, and examined the shimmery cloud on the blade. The gold sword. A Jittetsu sword. Forged in fire and offered to the gods. A drop of water trickled down his face. Gone. All gone. Discarded. He had thrown everything away. His job and position. His future. The only two things he truly possessed were this sword and his own bravery.

Lawrence laid the scabbard on the wet floor, then walked to the staircase carrying the bare sword. "You stay there!" he shouted. "I'm coming!"

He climbed down the littered staircase. With each step, he lost more of his heaviness, the illusions that had burdened his heart. Finally he understood the loneliness revealed in his father's photograph. To become a Harlequin was both a liberation and an acknowledgment of one's death.

He reached the ground floor. Boone was standing in the middle of the trash-filled room with an automatic pistol in his hand. "Drop your weapon!" Boone shouted. "Throw it on the ground!"

After a lifetime of masks, the final mask was removed. Holding the gold sword, Sparrow's son ran toward the enemy. He felt free, released from doubt and hesitation, as Boone raised his gun slowly and fired at Lawrence's heart.

Vicki was a prisoner inside her mother's home. She was being watched by the Tabula as well as by her church congregation. The power company truck had left the street, but other surveillance teams appeared. Two men working for a television cable company began replacing the relay boxes at the top of the phone poles. At night, there was no attempt at camouflage. A black man and a white man sat in an SUV parked across the street. Once, a police car stopped beside the SUV, and the two patrolmen spoke to the Tabula. As Vicki peered through the curtains, the mercenaries flashed ID cards and ended up shaking hands with the officers.

Her mother asked for protection from the church. At night, one or two people would sleep in the living room. In the morning, the night-shift team would leave and two church members would arrive to spend the day in the house. Jonesies didn't believe in violence, but they saw themselves as defenders of the faith armed with the word of the Prophet. If the house was attacked, they would sing hymns and lie down in front of cars.

Vicki spent a week watching television, but eventually

she turned off the set. Most of the shows seemed childish or deceitful once you realized what was really going on beneath the surface. She got some barbells from a church deacon and lifted weights in the garage every afternoon until her muscles felt sore. At night, she stayed up late and searched through the Internet for the secret Web sites created in Poland, South Korea, and Spain that mentioned the Travelers and the Vast Machine. Most of them seemed to agree that all the Travelers had vanished, destroyed by the Tabula and their mercenaries.

As a little girl, Vicki had always looked forward to the Sunday service at church; she'd wake up early, anoint her hair with perfume, and put on her special white dress. Now every day of the week felt the same. She was still lying in bed late Sunday morning when Josetta entered the room.

"Got to get ready, Vicki. They're sending a car to pick us up."

"I don't want to go."

"There's no reason to be frightened. The congregation will protect you."

"I'm not scared of the Tabula. I'm worried about my friends."

Josetta's lips tightened and Vicki knew what her mother was thinking: *They're not your friends.* She stood beside the bed until Vicki got up and pulled on a dress.

"Isaac Jones once told his brother—"

"Don't quote the Prophet to me, Mother. He said a lot of things and they don't always agree. When you look for the basic ideas, it's clear that Isaac Jones believed in freedom and compassion and hope. We can't just repeat his words and think we're right. People need to change their lives."

An hour later, she was sitting in church beside her mother. Everything was the same—the familiar hymns, the rickety pews, and the faces that surrounded her—but she didn't feel like part of the ceremony. The whole congregation knew that Victory From Sin Fraser had gotten involved with Hollis Wilson and an evil Harlequin named Maya. They stared at Vicki and expressed their fears during the public confessional.

The confessional was something unique to the Jonesie church, a peculiar mixture of a Baptist revival and a Quaker meeting. That morning it developed in a typical manner. First, Reverend J. T. Morganfield gave a sermon about manna in the desert, not only the food provided to the Israelites but also the riches available to any believer. As a three-piece band began to play with a driving gospel beat, the congregation sang "Call Your Faith Forward," an old-time Jonesie hymn. People stood up during the singing and at the end of each chorus expressed their concerns.

Almost everyone mentioned Vicki Fraser. They were worried about her; they were afraid; but they knew God would protect her. Vicki looked straight ahead and tried not to look embarrassed. The way they talked, it was basically her fault for believing in Debt Not Paid. Another chorus. A confession. A chorus. A confession. She felt like standing up and running from the church, but she knew everyone would follow.

As the singing got louder, the deacon's door near the altar opened and Hollis Wilson walked out. Everyone stopped singing, but that didn't appear to bother him. Standing at the front of the church, he reached inside his jacket and pulled out a leather-bound copy of *The Collected Letters of Isaac T. Jones*.

"I have a confession to make," Hollis said. "I have a testimony for all of you. In the fourth letter, written from Meridian, Mississippi, the Prophet says that there is no such thing as a truly fallen man or woman. Anyone, even the most miserable sinner, can make the decision to return to God and the circle of the faithful."

Hollis glanced at Reverend Morganfield and the pastor responded, almost automatically, "Amen to that, Brother."

The entire church of believers took a breath and seemed to relax. Yes, a dangerous man was standing by the altar, but they were familiar with the style of his confession. Hollis looked at Vicki for the first time and nodded very slightly as if to acknowledge the connection between them.

"I have strayed for many years," Hollis said. "I have lived a wayward life of disobedience and sin. I apologize to anyone I have hurt or offended, but I do not request forgiveness. In his ninth letter, Isaac Jones tells us that only God can grant forgiveness—which he gives equally to every man and woman, to every race and nation under the sun." Hollis flipped open the green book and read a passage. "We, who are equal in the Eyes of God, should be equal in the Eyes of Mankind."

"Amen," said an old lady.

"I also do not beg forgiveness for joining with a Harlequin to stand against the Tabula. I did this, at first, for money—like a hired killer. But now the blindfold has been ripped from my eyes, and I have seen the power of the Tabula and their plan to control and manipulate the people of New Babylon.

"For many years, this church has been divided by the issue of Debt Not Paid. I believe, very strongly, that this argument has lost its meaning. Zachary Goldman, the Lion of the Temple, died with the Prophet. That's a fact, and no one disputes it. But what's more important is the evil being done *right now*, the willingness of the Tabula to betray mankind. As the Prophet said: 'The Righteous must fight the Dragon both in darkness and in light.' "

Vicki glanced around the church. Hollis had won over some of them, but definitely not Reverend Morganfield. The elderly believers were nodding and praying and whispering, "Amen."

"We must support the Harlequins and their allies, not only with our prayers but with our sons and daughters. That's why I've come here today. Our army needs the help of Victory From Sin Fraser. I'm asking her to join us and share our hardships."

Hollis raised his right hand and gestured as if to say: Come with me. Vicki knew this was the biggest choice she had ever made in her life. When she looked at her mother, she saw that Josetta was crying.

"I want your blessing," Vicki whispered.

"Don't go. They'll kill you."

"This is my life, Mother. It's my choice. You know I can't stay here."

Still crying, Josetta embraced her daughter. Vicki could feel her mother's arms holding her tightly, and then finally letting go. Everyone watched as Vicki left the pew and joined Hollis near the altar.

"Goodbye," she said to the congregation. Her own voice surprised her. It sounded strong and confident. "In the next few weeks, I might ask some of you for help and support. Go home and pray. Decide if you want to stand with us."

Hollis grabbed her hand and they headed quickly for the door. A pickup truck with a camper shell was parked in the side alleyway. As they got in, Hollis pulled an automatic out of his waistband and placed it on the seat between them. "Two Tabula mercs are out front, across the street," he said. "Let's hope they don't have a second group watching us." Slowly he drove down the alley to a dirt access road that ran between the two rows of buildings. Hollis kept turning until they reached a paved street several blocks away from the church.

"Are you all right?" Vicki glanced at Hollis and he smiled.

"I had a little fight with three splicers, but I'll tell you about that later. For the last few days, I've been driving around the city, going to public libraries and using their computers. I've been in contact with this Harlequin in France named Linden. He's Maya's friend, the guy who sent me the money."

"Who else is in this 'army' you were talking about?"

"At this point, it's just you, me, Maya, and Gabriel. She's

brought him back to Los Angeles. But listen to this . . ."
Hollis thumped his fist on the steering wheel. "Gabriel
crossed the barriers. He's a Traveler. The real thing."

Vicki looked at the traffic as they turned onto the freeway. Thousands of people sat alone, each held within their
little box on wheels. The citizens gazed at the bumpers in
front of them, listened to noise from their radios, and
assumed that this time and place was the only true reality.
In Vicki's mind, everything had changed. A Traveler had broken the restraints that held them to this world. The freeway,
the cars and drivers, was not a final answer, only one possible alternative.

"Thank you for coming to the church, Hollis. That was a
dangerous thing to do."

"I knew you'd be there and I remembered the alleyway.
Besides, I needed the permission of the congregation. I
could tell that most of them supported me."

"What kind of permission are you talking about?"

Hollis leaned back in the seat and laughed. "We're hiding out at Arcadia."

Arcadia was a church camp in the hills northwest of Los
Angeles. A white woman named Rosemary Kuhn, who liked
to sing hymns at the Jonesie church, had given forty acres of
Malibu ranch land to the congregation. Both Vicki and
Hollis had visited Arcadia when they were children, taking
hikes, swimming in the pool, and singing songs around the
Saturday night campfire. A few years ago, the camp's water
well had failed and the zoning board had condemned the
site for different violations. The Jonesie church was trying to
sell the property while Rosemary Kuhn's children were
suing to get it back.

Hollis took Route 1 along the coast, and then followed
the two-lane highway that ran through Topanga Canyon.
When they turned left at the Topanga post office, the road
got narrow and very steep. Coastal oak and dense chaparral
were on both sides of the road. Finally they passed beneath

a wooden archway with the word CADIA painted on a vandalized sign and reached the top of the ridge. A long dirt driveway, eroded by flooding, led them to a gravel parking lot.

The buildings at the camp hadn't changed in the last twenty years. The camp had men's and women's dormitories, an empty pool with a pool house, a water tank, and a large community center that was used for meals and church services. The long white buildings had red tile roofs in the Spanish style. Flower beds and a vegetable garden, once carefully tended by the Jonesies, were now overgrown with weeds. All the windows had been smashed and empty beer cans covered the ground. At the top of the ridge you could see the mountains on one side and the Pacific Ocean on the other.

Vicki thought they were alone until Maya and Gabriel came out of the community center and walked down to the parking lot to meet them. Maya looked the same: strong and aggressive. Vicki stared at Gabriel, searching for a change in his appearance. His smile hadn't changed, but his eyes looked at her with a new intensity. She felt a little nervous until Gabriel said hello and hugged her.

"We were worried about you, Vicki. Glad you're here."

Hollis had gone to an army surplus store and purchased folding cots and sleeping bags for the two dormitories. A camp stove, water bottles, and canned food were in the kitchen of the community center. They used an old broom to sweep away some of the dust, then sat down at one of the long tables. Maya switched on her computer and showed them personal information about Americans their age who had died in car accidents. During the next few weeks, they would obtain the birth certificates of the dead people, then driver's licenses, then passports for different identities. Eventually, they would cross the border into Mexico and look for a safe place to hide.

"I don't want to end up in a Mexican jail," Hollis said. "If we're leaving the country, we'll need money."

Maya explained that Linden had sent thousands of dollars to America hidden inside an antique Buddha. The package was being held by an art dealer in West Hollywood. It was dangerous to ship money and pick up packages if the Tabula were searching for you. Hollis volunteered to guard the back of the building when she entered the front door.

"I can't leave Gabriel alone."

"I'll be okay," Gabriel told her. "Nobody knows about this place. Even if the Tabula found out, they'd still have to drive up that winding road. We'd see the car ten minutes before they got here."

The Harlequin changed her mind twice during lunch, and then finally decided that it was important to get the money. Vicki and Gabriel stood in the parking lot and watched Hollis's truck head back down the hill.

"What do you think about Maya?" Gabriel asked.

"She's very brave."

"Maya's father put her through some pretty harsh training to turn her into a Harlequin. I don't think she trusts anyone."

"The Prophet once wrote a letter to his twelve-year-old niece, Evangeline. He said that our parents give us armor to wear and we decide to put on more armor as we get older. When we become adults, the different pieces of armor don't match and they don't protect us completely."

"Maya is very well protected."

"Yes. But she's the same underneath. We're all the same."

Vicki took the broom and swept the floor of the community center. Occasionally she glanced out the window and saw that Gabriel was pacing around the dirt parking lot. The Traveler looked restless and unhappy. He was thinking about something, trying to figure out a problem. Vicki finished sweeping and was wiping down the tables with a wet rag when Gabriel appeared in the doorway.

"I've decided to cross over."

"Why do it now?"

"I need to find my brother, Michael. I just missed him in the fire barrier, but maybe he's in one of the realms."

"Do you think he's helping the Tabula?"

"That's what worries me, Vicki. They could be forcing him to do this."

She followed Gabriel into the men's dormitory and watched him sit on one of the folding cots with his legs flat in front of him. "Should I go away?" she asked.

"No. It's all right. My body stays here. No flames or angels."

Holding the jade sword with both hands, Gabriel took long, deep breaths. Suddenly he allowed the upper part of his body to fall backward. The quick movement seemed to change everything. He breathed one last time and then Vicki saw the transformation. His body shivered and went completely limp. Now he reminded her of a picture she had seen of a stone knight lying on a tomb.

Was Gabriel above her? Floating through space? She looked around for a sign and saw nothing but the water-stained concrete walls and dirty ceiling. Watch over him, she prayed. Dear God, protect this Traveler.

5°

Gabriel had crossed over, his Light passing through the four barriers. Opening his eyes, he found himself standing at the top of a staircase in an old house. He was alone. The house was quiet. A faint gray light bled through a narrow window.

An old-fashioned parlor table was on the landing behind him. A vase with a silk rose was on the table, and Gabriel touched the stiff, smooth petals. The rose and the vase and the room that surrounded him were as false as the objects in his own world. Only the Light was permanent and real. His body and his clothes were ghost images that had followed him to this place. Gabriel pulled the jade sword a few inches out of the scabbard and its steel blade gleamed with a silver energy.

He pushed back the lace curtains and peered out the window. It was early in the evening, just after sunset. He was in a city with sidewalks and shade trees. A line of row houses was on the other side of the street and the area reminded him of the brownstone neighborhoods in New York City or Baltimore. Lights were on in a few of the apartments, and the window shades had a soft yellow color, like pieces of old parchment.

Gabriel rearranged the sword so that the strap was over one shoulder, the scabbard touching his back. As quietly as possible, he climbed down the staircase to the third floor. He pushed open one of the doors, expecting to be attacked, and discovered an empty bedroom. All the furniture was heavy and dark: a large dresser with brass fittings and a bed with a carved wooden frame. The room had an old-fashioned look that reminded him of movies set in the 1920s. He couldn't find a clock radio or a television set, nothing new and bright and gleaming. On the second floor, he heard the sound of a piano coming from below. The music was slow and sad: a simple melody repeated with slight variations.

Gabriel tried not to make the stairs creak as he climbed down the last flight. On the ground floor an open doorway led into a dining room with a long table and six high-backed chairs. Wax fruit was in a bowl on the sideboard. Crossing the hallway, he passed through a study with leather club chairs and one solitary reading lamp, then entered the rear parlor.

A woman sat with her back to the doorway, playing an upright piano. She had gray hair and wore a long black skirt and a lavender blouse with puffy sleeves. When Gabriel stepped toward the woman, the floor creaked and she glanced over her shoulder. Her face startled him. It was emaciated and pale, as if she'd been locked up in the house and left to starve. Only her eyes were alive; bright and intense, they stared at him. She was surprised but not frightened that a stranger had appeared in the room.

"Who are you?" the woman asked. "I've never seen you before."

"My name is Gabriel. Could you tell me the name of this place?"

Her black skirt made a rustling sound as she approached him. "You look different, Gabriel. You must be new."

"Yes. I guess that's right." He stepped back from the woman, but she followed him. "I'm sorry to be in your house."

"Oh, you mustn't be sorry at all." Before he could stop her, the woman grabbed his right hand. A look of wonder appeared on her face. "Your skin is warm. How is that possible?" Gabriel tried to pull away, but the woman held him with a strength that didn't seem to match her frail body. Trembling slightly, she leaned down and kissed the back of his hand. Gabriel felt cold lips touch his skin, and then a sharp pain. He yanked his hand back and saw that it was bleeding.

A small drop of blood—his blood—was on the corner of the woman's mouth. She touched the blood with her forefinger, studied the bright red color, and then placed the finger in her mouth. Ecstatic, possessed by pleasure, she shivered and closed her eyes. Gabriel hurried out of the room and down the hallway to the front door. He fumbled with the latch and then was outside on the sidewalk.

Before he could find someplace to hide, a black automobile cruised slowly down the street. The car resembled a four-door sedan from the 1920s, but there was a vagueness about the design. It looked like the idea of a car, a gesture, instead of a real piece of machinery built in a factory. The driver was an old man with a pinched, shriveled appearance. He stared at Gabriel as he passed.

No other cars appeared as Gabriel wandered the dark streets. He came to a city square surrounding a little park with benches, an outdoor bandstand, and a few shade trees. Shops with window displays were on the street level of the three-story buildings. Lights glowed through the windows of upstairs rooms. About a dozen people drifted around the square. They wore the same formal, old-fashioned clothing as the woman who played the piano: dark suits, long skirts, hats, and overcoats that concealed thin bodies.

Gabriel felt conspicuous wearing his blue jeans and sweatshirt. He tried to remain in the shadows of the buildings. The shop windows had the kind of thick glass and steel frames that protected displays of jewelry. Each store had one window and each window had one object, illuminated with lights. He passed a skinny, bald man with a twitching face. The man was staring at an antique gold watch in the window. He looked dazed, almost hypnotized, by the object. Two doors down was an antique store with a white marble statue of a naked boy in the window. A woman with dark red lipstick stood very close to the window and gazed at the statue. As Gabriel passed, she leaned forward and kissed the plate glass.

A grocery store was at the end of the block. It wasn't a modern establishment with wide aisles and glass-door freezer cases, but everything looked clean and well organized. Customers carrying red wire shopping baskets walked between shelves of merchandise. A young woman wearing a white smock stood behind a cash register.

The clerk stared at Gabriel when he entered the store, and he went down an aisle to avoid her curiosity. The shelves held boxes and jars without any words printed on them. Instead, the different containers had colorful drawings of the products hidden inside. Cartoon children and their parents smiled cheerfully as they consumed breakfast cereal and tomato soup.

Gabriel picked up a box of crackers; it weighed almost nothing. He picked up another box, ripped open the top, and discovered that it was empty inside. Checking other boxes and jars, he went over to the next aisle and found a little man kneeling on the floor as he restocked the shelves. His starched white shopkeeper's apron and red bow tie made him look neat and organized. The man worked with great precision, making sure that the display side of each box was facing out.

"What's wrong?" Gabriel asked. "Everything is empty."

The little man stood up and looked intently at Gabriel. "You must be new here."

"How can you sell empty boxes?"

"Because they want what's inside them. We all do."

The man was drawn to the warmth of Gabriel's body. Eagerly, he stepped forward, but Gabriel pushed him away.

Trying not to panic, he left the store and returned to the square. His heart was beating quickly and a cold wave of fear rushed through his body. Sophia Briggs had told him about this place. He was in the Second Realm of the hungry ghosts. They were lost spirits, fragments of Light that were constantly searching for something to fill their painful emptiness. He would stay here forever unless he could find the passageway out.

He hurried down the street and was surprised to find a butcher shop. Lamb chops, pork roasts, and sides of beef were lying on metal trays inside the brightly lit store. A heavyset butcher with blond hair stood behind the case with his assistant, a young man in his twenties. A boy wearing a man's apron was carefully sweeping the white tile floor. The food was real. The two men and the boy looked healthy. Gabriel's hand touched the brass doorknob. He hesitated, then went inside.

"You must be a new arrival," the butcher said with a cheerful smile. "I know just about everyone around here and I've never seen you before."

"Is there something to eat?" Gabriel asked. "What about these hams?"

He pointed to three smoked hams hanging from hooks over the display counter. The butcher looked amused and the assistant sneered. Without asking permission, Gabriel reached up and touched one of the hams. It felt wrong. Something was wrong. He pulled it off the hook, dropped it on the floor, and watched the ceramic object shatter into pieces. Everything in the store was false: imaginary food displayed like the real thing.

He heard a sharp click and spun around. The boy had locked the door latch. Turning again, Gabriel saw the butcher and his assistant come from behind the display case. The assistant pulled an eight-inch knife from the leather holder that hung from his belt. The owner held a large cleaver. Gabriel drew his sword and stepped back so he was near the wall. The boy set aside the broom and pulled out a thin, curved knife—the sort of thing that was used to cut fillets off a bone.

Smiling, the assistant raised his arm and threw his weapon. Gabriel jerked to the left as the blade buried itself in the wood paneling. Now the butcher came forward, swinging and twirling the heavy cleaver. Gabriel faked a cut to the head, then came down low and slashed the butcher's arm. The ghost grinned and displayed the wound: cut skin, muscle, and bone, but no blood at all.

Gabriel attacked; the cleaver came up and blocked his sword. Two blades rubbed against each other, the steel screeching like a caught bird. Gabriel jumped to one side, got behind the butcher, and swung low, cutting off the ghost's left leg below the knee. The butcher fell forward and hit the tile floor. He lay on his stomach, groaning and reaching out his arms as if he were trying to swim on dry land.

The assistant grabbed a knife off the chopping board and Gabriel got ready to defend himself. Instead, the assistant knelt beside the butcher and stabbed him in the back. He cut deeply, pulling the blade down through the muscle to the hips. The boy ran over and joined this attack, cutting off pieces of dry flesh and stuffing them in his mouth.

Gabriel unlocked the door and ran outside. He crossed the street to the little park at the center of the square and realized that people were coming out of the buildings. He recognized the woman who had been playing the piano and the little clerk with the bow tie. The ghosts knew that he was in their city. They were searching for him, hoping that he could fill their emptiness.

Gabriel stood alone beside the bandstand. Should he run away from them? Was there a way to escape? He heard a car engine, spun around, and saw headlights coming down one of the side streets. As the car got closer, he saw that it was an old-fashioned taxicab with a glowing yellow light on the roof. Someone began honking the taxi's horn over and over again, then the vehicle pulled up to the curb. The driver rolled down the side window and grinned; it was Michael.

"Jump in!" he shouted.

Gabriel scrambled into the car and his brother circled the square, honking the horn and steering around the ghosts. He turned down a side street and went a little faster. "I was up on the roof of this building and then I looked down and saw you in the square."

"How'd you get the cab?"

"I ran down to the street and this cabdriver showed up. He was a skinny old guy who kept asking if I was 'new'— whatever that means. So I yanked him out of the cab, punched him in the face, and drove away." Michael laughed loudly. "I don't know where we are, but I doubt if I'll be arrested for car theft."

"We're in the Second Realm of the hungry ghosts."

"That sounds right. I stepped into a diner and there were four people sitting in the booths. No food anywhere. Just empty plates."

Michael jerked the steering wheel hard and turned the cab into an alleyway. "Hurry up," he said. "We've got to get into this building before anyone sees us."

The brothers got out of the cab. Michael was holding a sword with a gold triangle embedded in the handle.

"Where'd you get that?" Gabriel asked.

"Friends."

"It's a talisman."

"I know. It's good to have a weapon in a place like this."

The Corrigan brothers left the alleyway and hurried down the sidewalk to a four-story building with a granite façade. The large entrance door was made of dark metal and it was divided into squares with bas-relief sculptures of wheat, apples, and other kinds of food. Michael pulled the door open and the brothers slipped inside. They were in a long windowless hallway with a black-and-white checkerboard floor and lamps hanging from brass chains. Michael jogged down the hallway and stopped at a door marked LIBRARY. "Here we are. Safest place in town."

Gabriel followed his brother into a two-story room with a stained-glass window at one end. All the walls were lined with oak shelves crammed with books. There were ladders on wall tracks running the length of the room and a catwalk fifteen feet up that gave access to another set of shelves. Heavy wooden chairs and reading tables covered with a green leather surface were in the middle of the room. Lamps made of dark green glass illuminated the tables. The library made Gabriel think of history and tradition. Any book of wisdom could be found in this place.

Michael strolled around as if he were the librarian. "Nice, huh?"

"And no one will come here?"

"Of course not. Why would they do that?"

"To read a book."

"No chance of that." Michael picked up a thick book with a black leather binding and tossed it to his brother. "See for yourself."

Gabriel opened the book and found nothing but blank pages. He dropped it on a table and pulled another book from the shelves. Blank pages. Michael laughed.

"I looked in the Bible and the dictionary. Everything's blank. The people who live here can't eat, drink, or read. I bet they can't have sex or go to sleep. If this is a dream, then it's definitely a nightmare."

"It's not a dream. We're both here."

"That's right. We're Travelers." Michael nodded and touched his brother's arm. "I was worried about you, Gabe. I'm glad you're all right."

"Father's alive."

"How do you know that?"

"I went to a place called New Harmony in southern Arizona. Eight years ago, Father met some people and inspired them to start a community living free of the Grid. He could be in our world—this world—anywhere."

Michael paced back and forth between the reading tables. He picked up a book as if it could give him an answer, then tossed it away. "All right," he said. "Dad's alive. That's an interesting fact, but it's not relevant. We've got to focus on our current problem."

"And what's that?"

"At this moment, my body is lying on a table at a research center near New York City. Where are you, Gabe?"

"I'm at a deserted church camp in the Malibu hills."

"Are you surrounded by guards?"

"Of course not."

"When I return to the normal world, I'll tell them where you are—"

"Are you crazy?" Gabriel stepped closer to his brother. "You were captured by the Tabula. They're the same people who attacked our house and burned it down."

"I know all about it, Gabe. A man named Kennard Nash explained everything. But that was in the past. Now they *need* a Traveler. They're in contact with an advanced civilization."

"What difference does that make? They want to destroy any kind of personal freedom."

"That's the plan for the ordinary people, but not for us. There's no right or wrong about this. It's going to happen. You can't stop it. The Brethren are already putting the system into place."

"Our parents didn't see the world that way."

"And what the hell did that get us? We didn't have any money. We didn't have any friends. We couldn't even use our real names and we spent our entire lives running. You can't avoid the Grid. So why not join the people in control?"

"The Tabula have brainwashed you."

"No, Gabe. It's the other way around. I'm the only one in the family who ever saw things clearly."

"Not this time."

Michael placed his hand on the handle of the gold sword. The two Travelers looked in each other's eyes. "I protected you when we were growing up," Michael said. "Guess I have to do it again." He turned on his heels and hurried from the room.

Gabriel stood between the tables. "Come back here!" he shouted. "Michael!" He waited for a few seconds, and then ran out into the hallway. Empty. No one there. The door squeaked faintly as it closed behind him.

51

Michael sat on the surgical table in the middle of the Tomb. Dr. Richardson and the anesthesiologist stood back and stared at him while Miss Yang removed the sensors from his body. When the nurse was done, she took a fleece-lined sweatshirt from the tray and held it on the open palms of her hands. Michael took the shirt and slowly pulled it on. He felt exhausted and very cold.

"Maybe you should tell us what happened." Dr. Richardson sounded worried.

"Where's General Nash?"

"We called him immediately," Dr. Lau said. "He was over in the administration center."

Michael picked up the sheathed sword lying on the table beside him. Like a guardian spirit it had traveled with him through the barriers. The gleaming sword blade and the gold handle were exactly the same in the Second Realm.

The door opened and a thin shaft of light appeared on the dark floor. Michael returned the sword to the table as Kennard Nash hurried across the room.

"Is everything okay, Michael? They said you wanted to see me."

"Get rid of these people."

Nash nodded his head. Richardson, Lau, and Miss Yang retreated through the lab door underneath the northern gallery. The computer technicians were still peering down from the gallery windows.

"That's all!" Nash said loudly. "And please switch off the microphones! Thank you very much!"

The technicians reacted like schoolboys caught peeking into the teacher's room. Immediately, they moved away from the windows and returned to the glowing light of their monitors.

"So where did you go, Michael? A new realm?"

"I'll describe that later. There's a more important issue. I met my brother."

General Nash stepped closer to the table. "That's wonderful! Were you able to speak to each other?"

Michael swiveled so that he was sitting on the edge of the table. When he and Gabriel were traveling around the country together, Michael had spent hours staring out the windshield at the passing scenery. Sometimes he would concentrate on one particular object beside the road and hold that vision in his mind for several seconds until it disappeared. Now that same sensation had returned to him with an increased power. Images lingered in his mind and he could analyze the smallest details.

"When we were growing up, Gabriel never looked ahead or made any plans. I was the one who always figured out what to do."

"Of course, Michael. I understand." Nash's voice was soft and soothing. "You're the older brother."

"Gabe gets a lot of crazy ideas. I need to be objective. Make the right choice."

"I'm sure the Harlequins have told your brother all their foolish legends. He doesn't see the big picture. Not like you."

It felt as if time had slowed down. Without effort, Michael could see the split-second changes in the expression on Nash's face. Normally, everything happened quickly during a conversation. One person was talking and the other was waiting to respond. There was noise, movement, confusion, and all these factors helped people conceal their true emotions. Now everything was clear.

He remembered how his father had acted with strangers, watching them carefully while they spoke. That's how you did it, Michael thought. You didn't read their minds—just their faces.

"Are you all right?" Nash asked.

"After we talked, I left my brother and found the passageway back. Gabriel is still in the Second Realm, but his body is lying in a church camp in the Malibu hills."

"That's wonderful news. I'll send a team there right away."

"That doesn't mean you have to hurt him. Just get him under control."

Nash glanced down as if he was getting ready to conceal the truth. His head shifted slightly and he showed his teeth with a terse smile. Michael blinked and then the world was normal again. Time continued to move forward, each new moment falling into the future like a line of dominoes.

"Don't worry. We'll do everything we can to protect your brother. Thank you, Michael. You did the right thing."

General Nash turned and hurried through the shadows to the exit. The heels of his dress shoes made a sharp noise on the polished concrete floor. Click-click. Click-click. The sound echoed off the walls of the Tomb.

Michael picked up the gold sword and held the scabbard tightly.

52

It was close to five o'clock in the afternoon, but Hollis and Maya still hadn't returned. Vicki felt like a Harlequin, protecting the Traveler who lay on the cot in front of her. Every few minutes, she touched Gabriel's neck with her fingers. His skin was warm, but there was no sign of a pulse.

Vicki sat a few feet away from him and read some fashion magazines she found in the closet. The magazines were about clothes and makeup and finding men and losing men and being knowledgeable about sex. It embarrassed Vicki to read some of the articles, so she skimmed through them quickly. She wondered if she would feel uncomfortable wearing tight clothes that displayed her body. Hollis would find her more attractive, but then she might become one of the girls who received a duplicate toothbrush and a ride home the next morning. Reverend Morganfield was always talking about shameless modern women and the harlot by the side of the road. "Shameless," she whispered. "Shameless." The word could sound like a feather or a slithery snake.

Vicki tossed the magazines into a trash can, went outside, and looked down the hill. When she returned to the dormitory,

Gabriel's skin was pale and felt cold. Perhaps the Traveler had entered a dangerous realm. He could have been killed by demons or the hungry ghosts. Fear came to her like a soft voice growing louder and more powerful. Gabriel was losing strength. Dying. And she couldn't save him.

She unbuttoned Gabriel's shirt, leaned over his body, and pressed her ear against his chest. Vicki listened for a heartbeat. Suddenly, there was a thumping noise, but Vicki realized it came from outside the building.

Abandoning the body, she ran out the door and saw a helicopter descend to the flat area of land beside the empty swimming pool. Men jumped out wearing helmets with bulletproof face shields and body armor that made them look like robots.

Vicki ran back into the dormitory. She put her arms around Gabriel's chest and pulled him, but he was too heavy for her to carry. The cot fell on its side and she had to lower the body onto the floor. She was still holding the Traveler when a tall man wearing body armor ran into the room.

"Let go of him!" he shouted and pointed his assault rifle. Vicki didn't move.

"Step back and put your hands on your head!"

The man's finger began to squeeze the trigger and Vicki waited for the bullet. She would die beside the Traveler, just like the Lion of the Temple had died for Isaac Jones. After all these years, debt paid.

A moment later, Shepherd strolled into the room. He looked as stylish as ever, with his spiky blond hair and tailored suit. "That's enough," he said. "No need for that."

The tall man lowered the rifle. Shepherd nodded his approval, and then approached Vicki as if he was late for a party. "Hello, Vicki. We've been looking for you." He leaned over the Traveler's body, took the sword away, and pressed his fingers against Gabriel's carotid artery. "Looks like Mr. Corrigan has gone off to another realm. That's all right. Sooner or later, he has to come home."

"You used to be a Harlequin," Vicki said. "It's a sin to work for the Tabula."

"Sin is such an old-fashioned word. Of course, you Jonesie girls have always been old-fashioned."

"You're scum," Vicki said. "Do you understand that word?"

Shepherd gave her a benevolent smile. "Think of all this as a particularly complex game. I've picked the winning side."

53

Maya and Hollis were about four miles from the entrance to Arcadia when they saw the Tabula helicopter. It rose into the sky and circled over the church camp like a raptor looking for prey.

Hollis turned his pickup truck off the road and parked in the Jimsonweeds growing near a retaining wall. They peered through the branches of an oak tree and watched the helicopter head over the ridge.

"So what do we do now?" Hollis asked.

Maya wanted to punch the window, kick, and shout: anything to release her anger. But she forced her emotions into a little room inside her brain, and then locked the door. When she was a child, Thorn would make her stand in the corner, then pretend to attack her with a sword, knife, or fist. If she flinched or panicked, her father was disappointed. If she stayed calm, he praised his daughter's strength.

"The Tabula won't kill Gabriel right away. They'll interrogate him first and find out what he knows. While that's going on they'll leave a team at the church camp to ambush whoever returns."

Hollis peered out the window. "You mean somebody's waiting there to kill us?"

"That's right." Maya slipped on her sunglasses so Hollis couldn't see her eyes. "But that's not going to happen . . ."

* * *

THE SUN WENT down around six o'clock, and Maya began to climb the hill to Arcadia. The chaparral was a tangled mess of dry vegetation; it had the sweet, sharp odor of wild anise. The Harlequin found it difficult to move in a straight line. It felt as if the branches and vines were grabbing at her legs and trying to pull the sword case from her shoulder. Halfway up the hill, she was blocked by a thicket of manzanita and scrub oak that forced her to search for an easier path.

Finally she reached the chain-link fence that surrounded the church camp. She grabbed the top bar and pulled herself over. The two dormitories, the swimming pool area, the water tank, and the community center could be seen clearly in the moonlight. The Tabula mercs had to be there, hiding in the shadows. They probably assumed that the only entry point was the driveway that led up the hill. A conventional leader would position his men in a triangle around the parking lot.

She drew her sword and remembered the lesson on soft walking she had learned from her father. You moved as if you were crossing a lake covered with thin ice: extend your foot, judge the ground, and finally step forward with your weight.

Maya reached an area of darkness near the water tank and saw someone crouched beside the pool house. He was a short, broad-shouldered man holding an assault rifle. As she approached him from behind, she heard him whispering into the microphone of a radio headset.

"You got any more water? I'm out." He paused for a few

seconds, then sounded annoyed. "I understand that, Frankie. But I didn't bring two bottles like you did."

She took a step to the left, ran forward, and swung the sword at the back of his neck. The man fell forward like a slaughtered steer. The only sound was the clatter of his weapon falling onto the concrete. Maya leaned over the body and pulled the radio headset off the dead man's ears. She heard other voices whispering to each other.

"Here they are," said a voice with a South African accent. "See the headlights? They're coming up the hill . . ."

Hollis drove his truck up the driveway, stopped in the parking lot, and switched off the engine. There was just enough moonlight to see his silhouette inside the truck cab.

"Now what?" an American voice asked.

"Do you see a woman?"

"No."

"Kill the man if he gets out of the truck. If he stays there, wait for the Harlequin. Boone told me to shoot the woman on sight."

"I only see the man," the American said. "How about you, Richard?"

The dead man wasn't answering questions. Maya left his weapon on the ground and hurried toward the community center.

"Richard? Can you hear me?"

No answer.

Hollis remained in the pickup, distracting them from the real danger. Maya found the next Tabula at the second point of the triangle. Kneeling by the community center, he pointed a sniper rifle at the truck. Maya's footsteps were silent on the hard-packed ground, but he must have sensed her approach. The Tabula turned slightly and her sword blade hit the side of his throat. Blood sprayed from a cut artery as the man collapsed.

"I think he's getting out of the truck," the South African said. "Richard? Frankie? Are you there?"

She made the quick, certain choice of a Harlequin in combat and sprinted toward the women's dormitory. And yes, the third man was standing near the corner of the building. The Tabula was so frightened that he was talking loudly. "Can you hear me? Shoot the man in the truck!"

Emerging from the shadows, she slashed at his right arm. The South African dropped his rifle and she attacked again, cutting the hamstring tendons behind his left knee. He fell forward, screaming with pain.

Almost over. She stood beside the man and gestured with her sword. "Where are the two prisoners? Where did you take them?"

The mercenary tried to get away, but she swung the sword again and cut the hamstrings on his other leg. Now he was flat on his belly, crawling like an animal, his fingers digging into the soft dirt.

"Where are they?"

"They took them to Van Nuys Airport. Loaded them on . . ." He groaned and his body jerked forward. "Private jet."

"What's the destination?"

"Westchester County, near New York City. The Evergreen Foundation Research Center." The man rolled onto his back and raised his hands. "Swear to God, I'm telling you the truth. It's the Evergreen . . ."

Her blade flashed through the shadows.

57

The beams from the truck's headlights skittered across the road as Hollis drove down the hill from the church camp.

Maya leaned against the door with the Harlequin sword on her lap. She had been either fighting or running ever since she had arrived in America, and now she had failed completely. At this moment, Gabriel and Vicki were being transported to the East Coast in a private jet. And the Tabula had control of both Travelers.

"We need to attack the Evergreen Foundation Research Center," she said. "There are only two of us, but I don't see any other option. Drive to the airport and we'll catch a plane to New York."

"That's not a good idea," Hollis said. "I don't have a fake ID and it's going to be difficult to transport our weapons. You're the one who told me all about the Vast Machine. The Tabula have probably entered every police data system in the United States and placed our photographs in a 'fugitive' category."

"Could we go on a train?"

"America doesn't have a high-speed rail system like Europe or Japan. Traveling that way could take four or five days."

Maya spoke loudly, showing her anger. "So what are we supposed to do, Hollis? We have to respond immediately."

"We'll drive cross-country. I've done it before. It takes about seventy-two hours."

"That's too much time."

"Let's say a magic carpet took us straight to the research center. We'd still have to figure out the best way to get inside." He smiled at Maya, trying to look optimistic. "All you need to get across America is caffeine, gasoline, and some good music. While we're on the road, you've got three days to come up with a plan."

Maya stared unblinking out the windshield, then nodded slightly. It bothered her that emotions might be influencing her choices. Hollis was right; he was thinking like a Harlequin.

Cardboard shoe boxes filled with music CDs were on the seat between them. The truck had a pair of large speakers and two CD players stacked on top of each other. As they turned onto the freeway, Hollis loaded a CD and punched the play button. Maya was expecting house music with a thumping beat, but suddenly she heard the Gypsy guitarist Django Reinhardt playing "Sweet Georgia Brown."

Hollis found hidden connections between jazz, rap, classical, and world music. As they cruised down the freeway, he kept his left hand on the steering wheel while his right hand flicked through the CDs in the shoe boxes. He began a continuous soundtrack for their journey, merging one song into another so that a Charlie Parker saxophone solo flowed into Russian monks chanting which led to Maria Callas singing an aria from *Madame Butterfly*.

The Western deserts and mountains seemed to glide past them like a beautiful dream of openness and freedom. Reality was not part of the American landscape; it was only found in the massive tractor-trailer trucks that raced down the highway carrying gasoline, plywood, and a hundred frightened pigs sticking their snouts through the gaps of a cargo container.

While Hollis did most of the driving, Maya sat in the passenger seat and used her satellite phone and laptop computer to access the Internet. She found Linden in a chat room and explained in soft language where she was going. The French Harlequin had contacts with the new tribes forming in America, Europe, and Asia—mostly young people opposed to the Vast Machine. One of these groups met on a renegade Web site called the Stuttgart Social Club. Although none of these hackers actually lived in Stuttgart, the club shielded their identities and gave them instant communication. Linden told them that there was an urgent need to find out everything about the Evergreen Foundation Research Center in Purchase, New York.

At first the Stuttgart Social Club sent Maya downloaded newspaper articles about the Evergreen Foundation. Several hours later, club members began to break into corporate and government data systems. A Spanish hacker named Hercules entered the computer of the architectural firm that had designed the research center and electronic blueprints started to appear on Maya's computer screen.

"It's a big compound in a suburban environment," Maya said, scrolling through the information. "There are four large buildings constructed around a central quadrangle. A windowless building is at the center."

"What's the security situation?" Hollis asked.

"It's like a modern castle. There's a ten-foot wall. Surveillance cameras."

"We have one advantage. I bet the Tabula are so proud and confident that they won't expect an attack. Is there a way to get in without tripping all the alarms?"

"The building that was designed for genetic research has four levels beneath the ground floor. There are water pipes, electric cables, and air-conditioning ducts that follow some underground tunnels. One of the maintenance points for the ventilation system is about two meters outside the wall."

"Sounds promising."

"We're going to need tools to break in."

Hollis slipped in a new CD and the door speakers blasted out dance music by a group called Funkadelic. "No problem!" he shouted and the music pushed them forward across the immense landscape.

55

It was almost midnight when Gabriel's body was brought into the research center. A security guard knocked on the door of Dr. Richardson's room in the administration center and told him to get dressed. The neurologist slipped a stethoscope into his coat pocket, then was escorted outside to the central quadrangle. It was a cold autumn evening, but the sky was clear. The Tomb was lit from the inside and it seemed to float like a massive cube in the darkness.

Dr. Richardson and his guard met a private ambulance and a black passenger van at the entrance gate and walked behind the convoy like mourners following a funeral cortege. When the vehicles reached the genetic research building, two foundation employees got out of the van along with an African American woman. The younger employee said his name was Dennis Prichett. He was in charge of the transfer and was determined not to make any mistakes. The older man had spiky hair and a slack, dissipated face. Prichett kept calling him "Shepherd"—as if that was his only name. A black metal tube dangled from Shepherd's left shoulder and he carried a Japanese sword in a scabbard.

The young black woman kept staring at Dr. Richardson, but he avoided her eyes. Richardson sensed that she was some kind of prisoner, but he didn't have the power to save her. If she whispered, "Please, help me," then he would have to acknowledge his own captivity—and cowardice.

Prichett opened the back of the ambulance. Dr. Richardson saw that Gabriel Corrigan was strapped to a gurney with the thick canvas restraints used on violent patients in hospital emergency rooms. Gabriel was unconscious. When the gurney was pulled out of the ambulance, his head lolled back and forth.

The young woman tried to approach Gabriel, but Shepherd grabbed her arm and held her tightly. "Forget about that," he said. "We need to get him inside."

They wheeled the gurney over to the genetic research building and stopped. No one's Protective Link was authorized to enter the building. Prichett had to call security on his cell phone while the group stood outside in the cold air. Finally a technician sitting at a computer in London authorized the entry for their various ID cards. Prichett pushed the gurney through the doors and the group followed him.

Ever since Richardson had accidentally read the laboratory report about hybrid animals, he had been curious about the top-secret genetic research building. There was nothing imposing about the ground-floor laboratories. Fluorescent ceiling lights. Refrigerators and lab tables. An electron microscope. The building smelled like a dog kennel, but Richardson couldn't see any lab animals—and certainly nothing that could be called a "splicer." Shepherd led the young woman down the hallway while Gabriel was wheeled into an empty room.

Prichett stood beside Gabriel's body. "We think Mr. Corrigan has crossed over to another realm. General Nash wants to know if his body is injured or not."

"All I have is a stethoscope."

"Do whatever you can, but hurry up. Nash is going to be here in a few minutes."

Richardson pushed the tips of his fingers against Gabriel's neck and searched for a pulse. Nothing. He took a pencil out of his jacket, jabbed the sole of the young man's foot, and got a muscular reaction. While Prichett watched, the neurologist unbuttoned Gabriel's shirt and pressed his stethoscope against the Traveler's chest. Ten seconds. Twenty seconds. Then, finally, a single heartbeat.

Voices came from outside in the corridor. Richardson stepped away from the body as Shepherd led Michael and General Nash into the room.

"So?" Nash asked. "Is he all right?"

"He's alive. I don't know if there's been any neurological damage."

Michael went over to the gurney and touched his brother's face. "Gabe's still in the Second Realm, looking for a way out. I had already found the passageway, but I didn't tell him."

"That was a wise decision," Nash said.

"Where's my brother's talisman? The Japanese sword?"

Shepherd looked as if he'd been accused of stealing something. He handed the sword over and Michael placed it on his brother's chest.

"You can't keep him restrained forever," Richardson said. "He'll develop skin ulcers like patients with spinal cord injuries. His muscles will start to deteriorate."

General Nash seemed annoyed that anyone had raised an objection. "I wouldn't worry about that, Doctor. He's going to stay under control until we change his mind."

*   *   *

THE NEXT MORNING, Richardson tried to stay out of sight in the neurological laboratory located in the library basement. He had been given access to an online chess game running on the research center's computer and the activity fascinated him. His black chess pieces and the computer's white pieces were little animated figures with faces, arms, and legs. When they weren't moving across the board, the bishops would read their breviaries while the knights steadied their horses. The bored pawns were constantly yawning, scratching themselves, and falling asleep.

After Richardson got used to the chessmen being alive, he moved up to something called the second interactive level. At this level, the chessmen insulted each other or gave suggestions to Richardson. If he moved a piece the wrong way, the chessman would argue about strategy, then grudgingly move to the next square. On the third interactive level, Richardson didn't have to do anything but watch. The pieces moved on their own and the superior pieces killed the weaker ones, battering them with maces or stabbing them with swords.

"Working hard, Doctor?"

Richardson looked behind him and saw Nathan Boone standing in the doorway. "Just playing a little computer chess."

"Good." Boone walked over to the lab table. "We all need to challenge ourselves continually. Keeps the mind alert."

Boone sat down on the other side of the table. Anyone glancing into the room would have thought that two colleagues were discussing a scientific issue.

"So how are you, Doctor? We haven't talked for a while."

Dr. Richardson glanced at the computer screen. The chessmen were talking to each other, waiting to attack. Richardson wondered if the chessmen believed that they were real. Perhaps they prayed and dreamed and enjoyed their little victories, not realizing that he was in control.

"I—I would like to go home."

"We understand that." Boone offered a sympathetic smile. "Eventually you can return to your classroom, but right now you're an important member of our team. I was told that you were here last night when they brought in Gabriel Corrigan."

"I just examined him briefly. That's all. He's still alive."

"That's right. He's here, he's alive, and now we have to

deal with him. That presents a rather unique problem—how do you keep a Traveler locked in a room? According to Michael, if you keep a Traveler completely strapped down, he can't break out of his body. But it might lead to physical problems."

"Exactly. I said that to General Nash."

Boone leaned forward and tapped a button on the laptop computer. The chess game with all its characters disappeared. "For the last five years, the Evergreen Foundation has sponsored research into the neurological processing of pain. As I'm sure you know, pain is a rather complex phenomenon."

"Pain is handled by multiple brain regions and it travels on parallel nerve pathways," Richardson said. "That way, if one part of the brain is disabled we can still react to an injury."

"That's correct, Doctor. But our researchers have discovered that wires can be implanted in five different brain regions, the most important areas being the cerebellum and the thalamus. Take a look at this." Boone took a DVD out of his pocket and inserted it into Richardson's computer. "This was filmed about a year ago in North Korea."

A brownish-yellow rhesus monkey appeared on the computer screen. It was sitting in a cage and had wires coming out of its skull. The wires were fastened to a radio transmission device strapped to the animal's body. "See that? Nobody is cutting this specimen or burning his skin. All you have to do is press a button and . . ."

The monkey screamed and collapsed with a look of intense pain on its face. It lay on the floor of the cage, twitching and whimpering softly.

"See what happens? There's no physical trauma, but the nervous system is overwhelmed by a massive neurological sensation."

Richardson could barely speak. "Why are you showing me this?"

"Isn't it obvious, Doctor? We want you to insert wires in Gabriel's brain. When he returns from his traveling, he'll be released from his restraints. He'll be treated well and we'll try to change his rebellious opinions about certain issues. But the moment he tries to leave us, someone will press a button and—"

"I can't do this," Richardson said. "It's torture."

"That's an incorrect word. We're just providing an immediate consequence for certain negative choices."

"I'm a physician. I was trained to heal people. This—this is wrong."

"You really have to work on your vocabulary, Doctor. The procedure isn't wrong. It's *necessary*."

Nathan Boone stood up and returned to the doorway. "Study the information on the DVD. In a few days we'll send you some more data." He smiled one last time, then disappeared down the hallway.

Dr. Richardson felt like a man who had just learned that cancer had been found inside him, the destructive cells spreading throughout his blood and bones. Because of fear and ambition, he had ignored all the symptoms, and now it was too late.

Sitting in the lab, he watched as different monkeys appeared on the computer screen. They should break out of the cage, he thought. They should run away and hide. But an order was given, a button was pushed, and they were forced to obey.

56

$\mathcal{B}$reaking into buildings was considered a minor but important Harlequin skill. When Maya was a teenager, Linden spent three days teaching her about door locks, security cards, and surveillance systems. At the end of this informal tutorial, the French Harlequin helped her break into the University College London. They wandered through the empty hallways and slipped a postcard into the black coat covering Jeremy Bentham's bones.

The electronic blueprint of the research facility showed a ventilation duct that led underground to the basement level of the genetic research building. At various points on the blueprint, the architect had written "PIR" in small letters, indicating a system of passive infrared motion detectors. There was a way to deal with that particular problem, but Maya was worried that another security device might have been added later.

* * *

HOLLIS STOPPED AT a mall west of Philadelphia. They purchased rock-climbing equipment from a sporting goods store and a small canister of liquid nitrogen from a medical equipment warehouse. A home repair store was close to the mall, and they spent an hour strolling up and down the enormous aisles. Maya filled the shopping cart with a hammer and chisel, a flashlight, a crowbar, a small propane blowtorch, and a pair of bolt cutters. She felt as if everyone was watching them, but Hollis joked with the young woman at the cash register and they got out of the store without being stopped.

Late that afternoon, they reached the town of Purchase, New York. It was a wealthy community with large homes, private day schools, and corporate headquarters surrounded by landscaped parks. Maya decided that the area was the perfect location for a secret research center. The facility was close to New York City and the local airports, but the Tabula could easily keep their activities hidden behind a stone wall.

They checked into a motel and Maya slept for a few hours with her sword beside her. When she woke up, she found Hollis shaving in the bathroom. "You ready to go?" she asked.

Hollis pulled on a clean shirt, and then tied back his dreadlocks. "Give me a couple of minutes," he said. "A man should look good before he fights."

Around ten o'clock at night they left the motel, drove past the Old Oaks Country Club, and turned north onto a two-lane road. The research center was easy to find. Sodium security lights were mounted on the wall and a security guard sat in a booth at the entrance. Hollis kept glancing in the side mirror, but no one followed them. A mile later, he took a side road north and parked on the shoulder near a grove of apple trees. The apples had been picked weeks ago and dead leaves covered the ground.

It was very quiet in the truck. Maya realized that she'd gotten used to the music coming from the speakers; it had sustained them during the journey.

"This is going to be difficult," Hollis said. "I'm sure there are a lot of security guards inside the research center."

"You don't have to go."

"I know you're doing this for Gabriel, but we got to save Vicki, too." Hollis looked out the windshield at the night sky. "She's smart and brave, and she stands up for what's right. Any man would be lucky to be part of her life."

"It sounds like you want to be that person."

Hollis laughed. "If I was lucky I wouldn't be sitting in a beat-up truck with a Harlequin. You people have *way* too many enemies."

They got out of the pickup and pushed their way through a dense thicket of pin oaks and blackberry bushes. Maya was carrying her sword and the combat shotgun. Hollis took along a semiautomatic rifle and a canvas bag filled with the tools. When they came out of the trees near the north wall of the research center, they found a ventilation duct coming out of the ground. The opening was covered with a heavy steel grate.

Hollis cut off two padlocks with the bolt cutters and pried up the grate with the crowbar. He shone the flashlight in the duct, but the light beam didn't reach beyond ten feet. Maya felt warm air touch her skin.

"According to the blueprint, the duct goes straight to the basement," she told Hollis. "I can't tell if there's room enough to maneuver, so I'll go headfirst."

"How will I know if you're all right?"

"Let me down at three-foot intervals. If I snap the rope twice it's okay to let out some more line."

Maya pulled on the rock-climbing harness while Hollis attached a carabiner and pulley to the edge of the grate. After everything was secure, the Harlequin went down the ventilation duct with a few tools held beneath her jacket. The steel duct was dark, hot, and just wide enough for one person. She felt as if she was being lowered into a cave.

After forty feet of rope was released, Maya reached a T junction where the duct went off in two different directions. Hanging upside down, she pulled out the hammer and chisel and got ready to cut through the sheet metal. When the chisel blade hit the duct, the sound echoed around her. Sweat dripped down her face as she swung the hammer again and again. Suddenly, the chisel cut through the steel and a thin sliver of light appeared. Maya cut out a hole and pried back the steel. She snapped the line twice and Hollis lowered her into an underground tunnel with a concrete floor and cinder-block walls. The tunnel was lined with water, power, and ventilation pipes. The only illumination came from a series of fluorescent fixtures placed at twenty-foot intervals.

It took ten minutes to double up the climbing rope and lower down a knapsack with the tools. Five minutes after that, Hollis was standing beside her.

"How do we get upstairs?" he asked.

"On the north corner of the building, there's an emergency staircase. We've got to find the staircase without triggering the security system."

They went down the tunnel and stopped at the first open doorway. Maya took out a small mirror and held it at an angle. On the other side of the door frame was a small white plastic box with a curved diffuser lens.

"The blueprints said that they're using PIR motion detectors. It senses the infrared energy given off by objects and trips an alarm if it goes above a certain limit."

"And that's why we got the nitrogen?"

"Right." She reached into the knapsack and pulled out the liquid nitrogen. The container looked like a thermos with a nozzle on one end. Carefully, she reached through the door frame and sprayed the motion detector. When it was covered with white frost, they continued down the tunnel.

The engineers who had built the underground area had painted sector numbers on the walls, but Maya didn't understand their meaning. In certain areas of the tunnel, they could hear a constant mechanical hum that sounded like a steam turbine, but the machinery remained out of sight. After wandering around for ten minutes, they reached another junction in the tunnel. Two passageways led off in different directions with no signs indicating the right path. Reaching into her pocket, Maya took out the random number generator. Odd number means right, she decided, and pressed the button. Number 3531 appeared.

"Go right," she told Hollis.

"Why?"

"No reason at all."

"The tunnel on the left looks bigger. I say we go that way."

They went left and spent ten minutes exploring empty storage rooms. Finally the passageway hit a dead end. When they turned back, they found the Harlequin lute that Maya had scratched on the wall with her knife.

Hollis looked annoyed. "This doesn't mean your little number machine gave us the correct choice. Give me a break, Maya. The number doesn't *mean* anything."

"It means we go right."

They entered the second passageway and disabled another motion detector. Suddenly Hollis stopped and pointed up. A small silver box was mounted on the ceiling. "Is that a motion detector?"

Maya shook her head and put her hand to her lips.

"Just tell me what it is."

She grabbed his arm and they ran down the passageway. Pushing open a steel door, they entered a room the size of a football field that was filled with concrete support pillars.

"What the hell is going on?"

"That was their backup system. A sound detector. It probably feeds into a computer program called Echo. The computer filters out mechanical noises and detects the sound of a human voice."

"So they know we're here?"

Maya opened up the top of her sword case. "The detector could have picked up our voices twenty minutes ago. Come on, we've got to find the staircase."

The basement area had only five sources of light: a single lightbulb in each of the distant corners and a fifth bulb in the middle. They left the corner of the room and walked slowly between the gray pillars to the light at the center. The concrete floor was dusty, and the air was hot and stagnant.

The lightbulbs flickered, and then died. For a few seconds they stood in complete darkness until Hollis switched on their only flashlight. He looked tense and ready to fight.

They heard a squeaking, raspy sound as if a door was being forced open. Silence. Then the door was shut with a hollow boom. The tips of Maya's fingers were tingling. She touched Hollis's arm—don't move—and they both heard a quick barking noise that sounded like laughter.

Hollis pointed the flashlight between two rows of pillars and they saw something pass through the shadows. "Splicers," he said. "They sent them down to kill us."

Maya reached into the knapsack and found the propane blowtorch. Her hands were awkward, fumbling, as she turned the steel knob and lit the nozzle with a cigarette lighter. A blue flame came out of the nozzle with a soft roaring sound. She held it up and took a few steps forward.

Dark shapes passed between the pillars. More quick laughter. The splicers were changing position, running in a circle around them. Maya and Hollis stood with their backs to each other within the small circle of light.

"They don't die easy," Hollis told her. "And if you shoot them in the body, the wound heals right away."

"Go for the head?"

"If you can do it. They'll keep attacking until they're destroyed."

Maya spun around and saw the pack of hyenas about twenty feet away. There were between eight and ten splicers—and they were moving fast. Yellowish fur with black spots. Blunt dark muzzles.

One of the splicers made a high-pitched laughing sound. The pack broke apart, ran between the pillars, and attacked from two sides. Maya placed the blowtorch on the floor in front of her and pumped a round into the combat shotgun. She waited until the pack was ten feet away from her then fired at the lead animal. The pellets hit his chest and he was flung backward, but the others kept coming. Hollis stayed near her, firing his rifle at the other group.

She squeezed the trigger again and again until the firing chamber was empty. Dropping the gun, she drew her sword and pointed it forward like a lance. A splicer leaped through the air and was skewered on the blade. His heavy body fell in front of her. Desperately, she pulled out the sword and began swinging with quick, slashing strokes as two more splicers attacked. They yelped and screamed as the sword cut through their thick skin.

Maya spun around and saw Hollis running away from her, trying to snap a new ammunition clip into his rifle while three splicers chased him. He turned, dropped the flashlight, and swung the rifle at the first attacker, knocking it sideways. Two more splicers jumped on him and he fell backward into the shadows.

Maya picked up the blowtorch with her left hand and gripped her sword with her right. She ran over to Hollis while he tried to fight off the two splicers. She swung downward, cutting off one animal's head and stabbing the other in the belly. Hollis's jacket was ripped open. His arm was covered with blood.

"Get up!" she shouted. "You've got to get up!"

Hollis scrambled to his feet, found a new ammunition clip, and snapped it into the rifle. A wounded splicer was trying to crawl away, but Maya swung her blade down like an executioner. Her arms were trembling as she stood over the dead body. The splicer's mouth was open and she could see its teeth.

"Get ready," Hollis said. "They're coming again." He raised his rifle and began murmuring a Jonesie prayer. "

pray to God with all my heart. May His Light protect me from the Evil that—"

A barking laugh came from behind them, and then they were attacked from three sides. Maya fought with her sword, stabbing and slashing at the teeth and claws that came at her, red tongues and wild eyes that burned with hatred. Hollis took single shots at first, trying to conserve his ammunition, then switched to automatic fire. The splicers attacked again and again until the final animal came toward her. Maya raised her sword, ready to swing, but Hollis stepped forward and shot the splicer in the head.

* * *

THEY STOOD TOGETHER, surrounded by the dead. Maya felt numb inside, overwhelmed by the fury of the attack.

"You okay?" Hollis's voice was harsh and strained.

Maya turned to face him. "I think so. What about you?"

"One of them slashed my shoulder, but I can still move my arm. Come on. We need to get moving."

Maya slipped her sword back into the carrying case. Holding the shotgun with one hand, she led them to the outer edge of the underground area. It took them only a few minutes to find a steel security door, protected by electro-magnetic sensors. A cable led from the door to a circuit box and Hollis popped it open. Wires and switches were every-where, but they were color coded. That made it easier.

"They already know we're in the building," Maya explained. "I don't want them to realize that we've reached the staircase."

"What wire do we cut?"

"Don't cut anything. That just triggers the alarm."

Never avoid a difficult decision, her father once told her. *Only fools think they can guarantee the right choice.* Maya decided that the tamper wires were green and the red wires carried current. She used the blowtorch to melt the plastic covering off each pair of red wires, and then attached them together with small alligator clips.

"Is that going to work?"

"Maybe not."

"Are they going to be waiting for us?"

"Probably."

"Well, that sounds promising." Hollis smiled slightly and that made her feel better. He wasn't like her father or Mother Blessing, but he was beginning to think like a Harlequin. You had to accept your fate, and still be brave.

Nothing happened when they forced open the steel door. They were at the bottom level of a concrete emergency staircase with lightbulbs on each landing. Maya took the first step, and then started moving quickly.

Find the Traveler.

51

Kennard Nash spoke to one of the technicians monitoring the quantum computer. He gave the man a pat on the back like a coach sending a player back into the game, then crossed the room and sat down next to Michael.

"We've received the preliminary message from our friends," Nash explained. "That usually means that the main transmission will occur in five or ten minutes."

The general's bodyguard, Ramón Vega, refilled both wineglasses as Michael nibbled on a cracker. He enjoyed sitting in the shadowy room and watching the sealed glass tank filled with liquid helium. Little explosions kept going off inside the green liquid as the electron switches at the heart of the computer were manipulated within a cage of energy.

The electrons existed within this world, but the quantum property of superposition enabled these subatomic particles to be on and off, up and down, spinning left and spinning right—all at the same time. For an almost imperceptible moment, they were both here and there, crossing over into a parallel dimension. In this other realm, an advanced civilization was waiting with another computer.

The computer captured the electrons, arranged them into a packet of information, and sent them back again.

"Are you waiting for anything in particular?" Michael asked.

"A message from them. Perhaps a reward. Three days ago, we transmitted the data obtained when you entered the Second Realm. That's what they wanted from us—a road map from a Traveler."

Nash pressed a switch and three plasma-screen TVs were lowered from the ceiling. A technician on the other side of the room was staring at a computer monitor and he began typing commands. Seconds later, points of light and patches of darkness appeared on the left-hand TV screen.

"That's what they're sending us. It's a binary code," Nash explained. "Light and non-light is the basic language of the universe."

The computers translated the code and numbers appeared on the right-hand screen. Another delay and Michael saw an arrangement of straight and angled lines on the center screen. It appeared to be the blueprint of a complex machine.

General Nash was acting like a true believer who had just seen the face of God. "This is what we were waiting for," he murmured. "You're looking at the next version of our quantum computer."

"How long will it take to build it?"

"My staff will analyze the data and give me a delivery date. Until then, we've got to keep our new friends happy." Nash smiled confidently. "I'm playing a little game with this other civilization. We want to increase the power of our technology. They want to move freely between the realms. You're the one who shows them how it's done."

Binary code. Numbers. And then a design for a new machine. The data from the advanced civilization flowed across the three screens and Michael was swept away by the images flashing in front of him. He barely noticed when

Ramón Vega approached General Nash and handed him a cell phone.

"I'm busy," Nash said to the caller. "Can't you wait until . . ." Suddenly the general's face changed. Looking tense, he stood up and began to pace around the room. "You did what? Who gave you permission to open the cages? So where's Boone? Have you contacted him? Well, hurry up and do it. Tell him to come to the computer center right away."

"Is there a problem?" Michael asked when Nash switched off the phone.

"Someone has entered the research facility. It might be one of those Harlequin fanatics I mentioned to you. All this is highly unusual. Those people don't have the resources to enter our facilities."

"Is this person in the building?"

The possibility startled General Nash. He glanced at his bodyguard, and then controlled his fear. "Of course not. That's impossible."

58

After wandering through the dark city, Gabriel had finally found the passageway home. Now he felt as if he was at the bottom of a deep pool of water, looking up at the shimmering surface. The air in his lungs pulled him upward—slowly, at first, and then with growing acceleration. He was close to the surface, only a few feet away, when he entered back into his body.

The Traveler opened his eyes and realized that he wasn't lying on a folding cot in a church camp dormitory. Instead he was strapped to a hospital gurney, being pulled down a long hallway with recessed lights. Protected by its scabbard, the jade sword lay on his stomach and chest.

"Where . . ." he whispered. But his body was very cold and it was difficult to speak. Suddenly the gurney stopped moving and two faces looked down at him—Vicki Fraser and an older man wearing a white lab coat.

"Welcome back," the older man said.

Looking worried, Vicki touched Gabriel's arm. "Are you all right? Can you hear me?"

"What happened?"

Vicki and the man wearing the lab coat pushed the gurney

into a room filled with empty animal cages and unfastened the straps. As Gabriel sat up and tried to move his body, Vicki explained that the Tabula had raided Arcadia and flown them to a research facility near New York City. The man wearing the lab coat was a neurologist named Phillip Richardson. He had released Vicki from a locked room and then they had found Gabriel.

"I didn't really plan this. It just happened." Dr. Richardson sounded both scared and exhilarated. "A security guard was watching you, but he was called away. Apparently someone is attacking the research center . . ."

Vicki stared at Gabriel, trying to judge his strength. "If we can reach the underground parking lot, Dr. Richardson thought we could drive away in one of the maintenance vans."

"What happens after that?" Gabriel asked.

"I'm open to any ideas," Richardson said. "I have an old college friend who lives on a farm in Canada, but it might be difficult to get across the border."

Gabriel's legs felt weak when he stood up, but now his mind was clear and focused. "Where's my brother?"

"I don't know."

"We need to find him."

"That's way too dangerous," Richardson said. "In a few minutes the staff is going to realize that you and Vicki have vanished. We can't fight them. It's impossible."

"Dr. Richardson is right, Gabriel. Maybe we can come back later and save your brother. But right now, we have to get out of here."

They had a whispered argument until Gabriel agreed to the plan. By now Dr. Richardson was starting to panic. "They probably know everything," he said. "They could be searching for us right now." He peered through a crack in the door, and then guided them down a long hallway to the elevator.

They reached the parking level a few seconds later. The entire floor was nothing but concrete and support pillars.

Three white vans were parked about twenty feet away from the elevator bank. "The staff usually leaves a key in the ignition," Richardson explained. "If we can get through the front gate, we have a chance."

The doctor approached the first van and attempted to open the door on the driver's side. It was locked, but he kept pulling on the handle as if he couldn't believe that fact. Vicki stood beside him. Her voice was calm and soothing. "Don't worry, Doctor. Let's try the next one."

Vicki, Gabriel, and Richardson heard a squeaking sound as a fire door was pulled open, followed by footsteps on concrete. A moment later, Shepherd came out of the emergency stairwell.

"Now this is quite wonderful." Shepherd strolled past the elevators, stopped, and grinned. "I thought the Tabula might get rid of me, but now they're going to give me a bonus. The renegade Harlequin saves the day."

Gabriel glanced at Vicki, then drew the jade sword. He swung it slowly through the air and remembered what Maya had told him. A few human-made objects were so beautiful—so pure—that they were free of greed and desire.

Shepherd snorted as if he'd just heard a bad joke. "Don't be a fool, Gabriel. Perhaps Maya doesn't think I'm a real Harlequin, but that doesn't change my skill as a fighter. I've been trained to use swords and knives since I was four years old."

Gabriel turned his head slightly. "Look inside the other van," he told Vicki. "See if the keys are in the ignition."

Shepherd reached into his carrying tube. He drew his Harlequin sword and snapped the guard into place. "All right. Have it your way. One good thing is going to come out of this. I've always wanted to kill a Traveler."

Shepherd assumed the fighting position and Gabriel surprised him by attacking immediately. Running forward, he pretended to stab at Shepherd's face. When Shepherd parried the blow, Gabriel spun around and slashed at the heart

Steel clashed against steel two, three, four times, but Shepherd defended himself easily. The two swords locked together. Shepherd took half a step back, made a quick movement with his wrists, and twisted the jade sword out of Gabriel's hands.

The sword clattered onto the concrete floor. In the empty parking structure the noise was loud and distinct. The two men looked at each other and the Traveler saw his opponent clearly. Shepherd's face had assumed the Harlequin mask, but something was wrong with his mouth. It twitched slightly, as if the lips couldn't decide if they were going to smile or frown.

"Go ahead, Gabriel. Try to get it back—"

Someone whistled—a sharp, piercing sound. Shepherd spun around just as a throwing knife flashed through the air and buried itself in his throat. His hand released the sword and he fell to his knees.

Maya and Hollis came through the open doorway. The Harlequin glanced at Gabriel—making sure he was safe—then approached the wounded man. "You betrayed my father," she said. "Do you know what they did to him, Shepherd? Do you know how he died?"

Shepherd's eyes could barely focus, but he nodded slightly as if admitting his guilt could somehow save his life. Maya pushed the palms of her hands together like a nun about to pray. Then she made a quick, jabbing front kick that struck the handle of the knife and drove it deeper into his flesh.

59

Maya turned and pointed her shotgun at the tall man wearing the white lab coat.

"Don't!" Vicki said quickly. "This is Dr. Richardson. He's a scientist. A friend. He's helping us get out of here." Maya made an instant evaluation and decided that Richardson was frightened, but harmless. If he panicked in the tunnels, then she would have to deal with that problem. Gabriel was alive; that was all that mattered.

As Hollis explained how they had entered the research facility, Maya approached Shepherd's body. She stepped into the blood that trickled in bright red lines across the concrete floor, knelt beside the dead man, and retrieved her knife. Shepherd was a traitor, but Maya didn't feel happy about his destruction. She remembered what he had told her in the storage room of Resurrection Auto Parts. *We're the same, Maya. We both grew up with people who worshipped a lost cause.*

When she returned to the group, she saw that Hollis was arguing with Gabriel. Vicki stood between the two men, as if she was trying to negotiate a compromise.

"What's the problem?"

"Talk to Gabriel," Hollis said. "He wants to look for his brother."

The idea of remaining at the research facility seemed to terrify Richardson. "We've got to leave immediately. I'm sure the guards are looking for us."

Maya touched Gabriel's arm and guided him away from the others. "They're right about this. It's dangerous to stay here. Maybe we can return some other time."

"You know that's not going to happen," Gabriel said. "And even if we did come back, Michael won't be here. They'll move him to another place with even more guards. This is my only chance."

"I can't allow you to do this."

"You don't control me, Maya. This is my own decision."

Maya felt as if she and Gabriel were tied to each other like two mountain climbers on a rock wall. If one person slipped or if a ledge crumbled, both of them would fall. None of her father's lessons had prepared her for this situation. Come up with a plan, she told herself. Risk your life. Not his.

"All right. I've got another idea." She kept her voice as calm as possible. "You go with Hollis and he'll get you out of the building. I promise to stay here and look for your brother."

"Even if you found him, he wouldn't trust you. Michael has always been suspicious of everyone. But he'll listen to me. I know he will."

Gabriel looked into her eyes and for one breath—one heartbeat—she felt a connection between them. Desperately, Maya tried to figure out the right decision, but that was impossible. This time there was no right decision, only fate.

She hurried over to Dr. Richardson and grabbed the ID card clipped to his lab coat. "Will this open any doors around here?"

"About half of them."

"Where's Michael? Do you know where they're holding him?"

"He usually stays in a guarded suite of rooms in the administration center. Right now we're on the northern edge of the research center. Administration is on the other side of the quadrangle, directly south."

"And how do we get there?"

"Use the tunnels and stay out of the upper passageways."

Maya pulled some shells out of her pocket and began to reload the combat shotgun. "Return to the basement level," she told Hollis. "Get these two out through the ventilation duct while I go back with Gabriel."

"Don't do this," Hollis said.

"I have no alternative."

"Make him come with us. Drag him out of here if you have to."

"That's what the Tabula would do, Hollis. We don't act that way."

"Look, I understand why Gabriel wants to help his brother. But both of you are going to get killed."

She pumped a round into the shotgun's firing chamber and the snapping noise echoed through the empty parking area. Maya had never heard her father say "thank you." Harlequins weren't supposed to feel grateful to anyone, but she wanted to say something to the person who had fought beside her.

"Good luck, Hollis."

"You're the one who needs the luck. Take a quick look around and get the hell out of here."

* * *

A FEW MINUTES later Maya and Gabriel were walking down the concrete tunnel that passed underneath the quadrangle. The air was hot and stuffy. She could hear water running through the black pipes attached to the walls.

Gabriel kept glancing at her. He looked uncomfortable, almost guilty. "I'm sorry we have to do this. I know you wanted to leave with Hollis."

"This was my choice, Gabriel. I didn't protect your brother when I was in Los Angeles. Now I have another chance." She avoided his eyes and tried to sound reassuring. "We're making an emotional decision. Not a logical one. Perhaps they won't anticipate this."

They reached the administration center on the other side of the quadrangle and Dr. Richardson's ID card allowed them to go up a staircase to the lobby. Maya used the card to open the elevator and they went to the fourth floor. Both of them walked down a carpeted hallway, looking inside empty offices and conference rooms.

Maya felt odd holding a shotgun while she stared at a coffee machine and filing cabinets, a screensaver on a computer that showed angels drifting across a blue sky. She remembered her job back at the design firm in London. She had spent hours sitting in a white cubicle with a postcard of a tropical island taped to the wall. Every day at four o'clock a plump Bengali lady came around pushing a tea cart. Now that life seemed as distant as another realm.

She grabbed a wastebasket from one of the offices and they got back into the elevator. When they reached the third floor, she left the basket wedged between the elevator doors. Slowly, they began to walk down the hallway. Maya made Gabriel stay six feet behind her as she opened each new door.

The lighting panels set in the ceiling left a particular kind of shadow on the floor. At the end of the hallway, one of the shadows looked slightly darker. It could be anything, Maya thought. Maybe a dead lightbulb. As she took a step closer, the shadow began to move.

Maya turned to Gabriel and tapped a finger to her mouth. Be quiet. She pointed to a private office and motioned for him to hide behind the desk. When she returned to the corner, she looked down the hallway. Someone had left a janitor's cart near one of the offices, but the janitor had disappeared.

She reached the end of the hallway, moved a few inches around the corner, and then jerked back when three men fired their handguns at her. Bullets cracked through the walls and made a splintery hole in an office door.

Holding the shotgun, Maya ran back down the hallway and fired at the sprinkler head in the middle of the ceiling. The fixture was split open and a fire alarm began ringing. One of the Tabula peered around the corner and fired wildly in her direction. The wall beside her seemed to explode and chunks of plaster were scattered across the carpet. When Maya fired back, the man retreated around the corner.

Water sprayed from the shattered sprinkler head as she stood in the hallway. When most people were in a dangerous situation, their vision became restricted, as if they were peering down a tunnel. *Look around you*, Maya told herself and glanced up at the ceiling. She raised her shotgun and fired twice at an overhead lighting panel above the janitor's cart. The plastic grate disintegrated and a hole appeared in the plaster.

Maya slid the shotgun beneath her belt and climbed onto the janitor's cart. She reached through the hole and grabbed the water pipe. With one quick kick, she shoved the cart down the hall and pulled herself up into the hollow ceiling. All she could hear was the fire alarm and the water squirting out of the sprinkler head. Maya removed the shotgun from her belt. She wrapped her legs around the pipe and hung upside down like a spider.

"Get ready," a voice said. "Now!" The Tabula stepped into the hallway and fired their guns. The alarm stopped ringing a few seconds later and suddenly it was very quiet.

"Where'd she go?" a voice asked.

"Don't know."

"Be careful," the third voice said. "She could be in one of the rooms."

Maya peered down through the hole in the ceiling and watched one, two, three Tabula mercs pass beneath her, carrying their handguns.

"Prichett here," said the third voice. It sounded like he was talking into a radio or a cell phone. "We saw her on the third floor, but she got away. Yes, sir. We're checking each—"

Holding on to the water pipe with her legs, Maya swung through the jagged hole. Now she was upside down, her black hair dangling above the floor. She saw the backs of the three Tabula and fired at the first man.

The recoil from the shotgun snapped her backward and she somersaulted through the air, landing on her feet in the middle of the hallway. Water sprayed from the sprinkler head, but she ignored it and shot the second man as he was turning. The third man was still holding his cell phone as shotgun pellets punched through his chest. He hit the wall and slid to the floor.

The sprinkler stopped spraying water and she stood alone looking down at the three bodies. It was too dangerous to remain in this building. They had to get back to the tunnels. Once again, she saw the shadows change on the wall and then an unarmed man appeared at the end of the hallway. Even without the family resemblance, Maya knew that it was the second Traveler. She lowered her shotgun.

"Hello, Maya. I'm Michael Corrigan. Everyone around here is scared of you, but I'm not frightened. I know you're here to protect me."

An office door opened behind her and Gabriel stepped into the hallway. The brothers faced each other and she was standing between them.

"Come with us, Michael." Gabriel forced a smile. "You'll be safe. No one will order you around."

"I have a few questions for our Harlequin. It's a strange situation, isn't it? If I left with you two, it would be like sharing a girlfriend."

"It's not that way," Gabriel said. "Maya just wants to help us."

"But what if she has to make a choice?" Michael took a step forward. "Who are you going to save, Maya? Gabriel or me?"

"Both of you."

"It's a dangerous world. Maybe that's not possible."

Maya glanced at Gabriel, but he gave no indication of what she should say. "I'll protect whoever makes this world a better place."

"Then I'm the one." Michael took another step forward. "Most people don't know what they want. I mean, they want a big new house or a shiny new car. But they're too frightened to decide the direction of their lives. So we're going to do it for them."

"The Tabula told you that," Gabriel said. "But it's not true."

Michael shook his head. "You're acting just like our father did—making a small life, hiding under a rock. I hated all that talk about the Grid when we were growing up. We've both been given this power, but *you* don't want to use it."

"The power doesn't come from us, Michael. Not really."

"We grew up like crazy people. No electricity. No telephone. Remember that first day at school? Remember how people pointed at our car when we drove into town? We don't have to live that way, Gabe. We can be in charge of everything."

"People need to be in charge of their own lives."

"Why haven't you figured it out, Gabe? It's not difficult. You do what's best for yourself and to hell with the rest of the world."

"That's not going to make you happy."

Michael stared at Gabriel and shook his head. "You talk like you have all the answers, but one fact is clear." Michael raised the palms of his hands as if he was blessing his brother. "There can be only one Traveler . . ."

A man with short gray hair and steel eyeglasses stepped

around the corner of the hallway and raised an automatic pistol. Gabriel looked as if he had lost his family forever. Betrayed.

Maya shoved Gabriel down the next hallway as Boone fired. The bullet hit Maya's right leg, slamming her against the wall, and she fell facedown on the floor. It felt as if all the air had been squeezed out of her body.

Gabriel appeared and scooped her up in his arms. He ran a few feet and lunged into the elevator while Maya tried to pull away from him. *Save yourself*, she wanted to say, but her mouth couldn't form the words. Gabriel kicked the wastebasket out of the doors and punched at the buttons. Gunshots. People shouting. The doors closed and they were moving to the ground floor.

* * *

MAYA BLACKED OUT and when she opened her eyes they were in the tunnel. Gabriel was on one knee, still holding her tightly. She heard someone talking and realized that Hollis was there. He was stacking up bottles of chemicals that he had taken from the genetic research building.

"I can still remember the little red warning signs in my high-school lab. All this stuff is dangerous if it gets near a flame." Hollis turned the nozzle on a green canister. "Pure oxygen." He picked up a glass bottle and poured a clear liquid onto the floor. "And this is liquid ether."

"Anything else?"

"That's all we need. Let's get far away from here."

Gabriel carried Maya to the fire door at the end of the tunnel. Hollis lit the propane blowtorch, adjusted the hissing blue flame, and then tossed it behind him. They entered a second tunnel. A few seconds later, there was a loud popping noise and the expanding air pressure slammed the fire door open.

When Maya opened her eyes again, they were climbing down the emergency staircase. There was a much louder explosion, as if a massive bomb had just hit the building. The power went out and they huddled in the darkness until Hollis switched on the flashlight. Maya tried to stay conscious, but she glided in and out of a dream. She remembered Gabriel's voice and a rope lashed around her shoulders as she was pulled up through the ventilation duct. Then she was lying on her back in the wet grass, staring at the stars. She could hear more explosions and the wail of a police siren, but none of that mattered. Maya knew that she was bleeding to death; it felt as if all the life within her body was being absorbed by the cold ground.

"Can you hear me?" Gabriel said. "Maya?"

She wanted to speak to him—say one last thing—but someone had stolen her voice. A black liquid gathered around the edge of her vision and then it began to spread and darken like a drop of ink in a glass of clear water.

60

Around six o'clock in the morning, Nathan Boone glanced up at the sky over the research facility and saw a hazy patch of sunlight. His skin and clothing were covered with soot. The fire in the tunnels was supposedly under control, but black smoke with a harsh chemical odor continued to pour out of the vents. It looked as if the earth was burning.

Fire trucks and police cars were scattered around the quadrangle. At night, their flashing red lights had seemed bright and demanding. In the early morning, the lights blinked feebly. Canvas fire hoses snaked from the pumper trucks to the vents. Some of the hoses were still spraying water below while firefighters with blackened faces drank coffee from cardboard cups.

Boone had made a general assessment two hours ago. The explosion in the tunnels and the resulting power failure had caused damage in every building. Apparently the quantum computer had shut down and part of the mechanism had been destroyed. A young computer technician estimated that it would take nine months to a year for everything to get running again. The basements were flooded. All laboratories and offices were blackened with smoke. A computerized refrigerator in the genetic research laboratory had stopped working and several splicer experiments were ruined.

Boone didn't care about the destruction. As far as he was concerned, every building in the compound could have collapsed into rubble. The real disaster was that a Harlequin and a known Traveler had been allowed to escape.

His ability to start an immediate search had been undermined by a minimum-wage security guard sitting in the gatehouse at the entrance to the facility. When the explosions started, the young man had panicked and called the police and fire department. The Brethren had influence throughout the world, but Boone couldn't control a team of local firefighters determined to do their job. While the firefighters set up a command post and sprayed water into the tunnels, he helped General Nash and Michael Corrigan leave the quadrangle in a guarded convoy. Boone spent the rest of the night making sure that no one found Shepherd's body or the three dead men in the administration center.

"Mr. Boone? Excuse me, Mr. Boone . . ."

He glanced over his shoulder as a fire captain named Vernon McGee approached him. The stocky little captain had been in the quadrangle since midnight, but he still appeared to be full of energy—almost cheerful. Boone decided that suburban firefighters were bored with checking hydrants and retrieving cats from trees.

"I think we're ready to start the inspection now."

"What are you talking about?"

"The fire is knocked down, but it will take a few hours until we can go into the maintenance tunnels. Right now need to enter each building and check for structural damage.

"That's impossible. As I told you last night, the staff here is involved with top-secret research for the government. Jus about every room requires a security clearance."

Captain McGee rocked back slightly on the heels of hi boots. "I don't give a damn about that. I'm fire captain an this is my district. I have the right to enter any of these buildings for reasons of public safety. Feel free to give me an escort if you want."

Boone tried to conceal his anger as McGee swaggered back to his men. Perhaps the firefighters could do an inspection. It was possible. The bodies had already been wrapped in plastic and dumped in a van. Later that day, they would be shipped down to Brooklyn, where a cooperative mortician would cremate them and throw the ashes into the sea.

Boone decided to check out the administration center before McGee started nosing around. Two security men were supposed to be in the third-floor hallway, ripping up the blood-stained carpet. Although the surveillance cameras were dead, Boone always assumed that someone was watching him. He marched confidently across the quadrangle as if everything was under control. His cell phone rang and, when he answered it, he heard Kennard Nash's booming voice.

"What's the situation?"

"The fire department is going to make a safety inspection."

Nash swore loudly. "Who should I call? The governor's office? Could the governor stop this?"

"There's no reason to stop anything. We've cleaned up the significant problems."

"They're going to find out that someone started the fire."

"That's exactly want I want them to do. Right now, I have a team at Lawrence Takawa's apartment. They'll place a half-made explosive device on his kitchen table and write a revenge letter on his personal computer. When the arson investigators show up, I'll tell them about our angry employee—"

"And they'll start looking for a man who has already disappeared." Nash laughed softly. "Good work, Mr. Boone. I'll talk to you this evening."

General Nash ended the phone call without saying goodbye and Boone stood alone near the entrance to the administration center. If he reviewed his actions during the last few weeks, he had to acknowledge some mistakes. He had underestimated Maya's effectiveness and ignored his own suspicions about Lawrence Takawa. He had given in to anger on several occasions, and that had influenced his choices.

As the fire died down, the smoke changed color from black to dirty gray. It looked like car exhaust—just ordinary pollution—as it came out of the vents, drifted up into the air, and disappeared. Maybe the Brethren had suffered a temporary setback, but victory was inevitable. Politicians could talk about freedom, their words thrown into the air like confetti. It meant nothing; the traditional idea of freedom was fading away. For the first time that morning, Boone pressed the button on his wristwatch and was pleased to see that his pulse rate was normal. He stood up straight, squared his shoulders, and entered the building.

61

Once again, Maya was held captive by the dream. Standing alone in the dark tunnel, she attacked the three football thugs and escaped down the staircase. Men were fighting on the platform, trying to smash the train windows, as Thorn grabbed her with his right hand and pulled her into the car.

She had thought about that incident so many times that it had become a permanent section of her brain. *Wake up*, she told herself. *Enough*. But this time she lingered in the memory. The train lurched forward and she pressed her face against her father's wool overcoat. Her eyes were closed as she bit her lip and tasted blood in her mouth.

Maya's anger was strong and loud, but another voice was whispering to her in the darkness. And then she knew that a secret was about to be revealed. Thorn had always been strong and brave and sure of himself. He had betrayed her that afternoon in North London, but something else had happened.

The Underground train lurched forward, leaving the station, and she looked up at her father and saw that he was crying. At the time, it seemed impossible that Thorn could ever show weakness. But now she knew it was true. A single tear on a Harlequin's cheek was a rare and precious thing. Forgive me. Was that what he was thinking? Forgive me for what I have done to you.

*   *   *

SHE OPENED HER eyes and saw that Vicki was looking down at her. For a few seconds Maya lingered in a shadow land between her dream and the waking world; she could still see Thorn's face while her hand touched the edge of a blanket. Breathe out. And her father disappeared.

"Can you hear me?" Vicki asked.

"Yes. I'm awake."

"How do you feel?"

Maya reached beneath the bedsheet and felt the bandage that covered her injured leg. If she moved her body quickly, there was a sharp pain, like being jabbed with the point of a knife. If she remained stationary, it felt like someone had burned her skin with a branding iron. Thorn had taught her that you couldn't ignore pain; you tried to reduce it to a specific point that was isolated from the rest of your body.

She looked around the room and remembered being placed in the bed. They were in a beach house on the coast of Cape Cod, the curving Massachusetts peninsula that jutted into the Atlantic Ocean. Vicki, Gabriel, and Hollis had driven her there after spending several hours at a private clinic run by a doctor in Boston. The doctor was a member of Vicki's church who used the house as a summer retreat.

"Do you want another pill?"

"No pills. Where's Gabriel?"

"He's walking on the beach. Don't worry. Hollis is guarding him."

"How long have I been asleep?"

"About eight or nine hours."

"Find Gabriel and Hollis," Maya said. "Pack everything up. We have to keep moving."

"That's not necessary. We're safe here—at least for a few days. Nobody knows we're at the house except Dr. Lewis and he believes in Debt Not Paid. He'd never betray a Harlequin."

"The Tabula are looking for us."

"No one's walking on the beach because it's too cold. The house next door is empty for the winter. Most of the stores in the village are closed and we haven't seen any surveillance cameras."

Vicki looked strong and sure of herself, and Maya found herself remembering the timid church girl she approached in the Los Angeles airport just a few weeks ago. Everything had changed, moved forward, because of the Traveler.

"I need to see Gabriel."

"He'll be back in a few minutes."

"Help me up, Vicki. I don't want to be in bed."

Maya used her elbows to push her body up. The pain came again, but she was able to control the expression on her face. Standing on her good leg, she threw one arm around Vicki's shoulder and the two women moved slowly out of the bedroom and down a hallway.

With each halting step, Vicki gave Maya more information. After they had fled the Evergreen Foundation Research Center, Dr. Richardson had kept her from dying as Hollis drove to Boston. At this moment, Richardson was traveling to Canada to stay with an old college friend who owned a dairy farm in Newfoundland. Hollis had parked his truck in a poor neighborhood and left the keys in the ignition. Now they were using a delivery van owned by another member of Vicki's church.

The beach house had a thick Berber carpet; the wood and leather furniture was clean and simple. A sliding glass door led to a deck and Maya got Vicki to take her outside. When Maya lay down on a chaise longue she realized how much effort it had taken to walk thirty feet. Sweat covered her face and her body began to shiver.

Vicki went back into the house and returned with a blanket. She wrapped it tightly around Maya's lower body and the Harlequin began to feel comfortable. The house was built next to sand dunes dotted with wild rose and beach grass and dark green heather. There was enough wind to push the dry blades of grass back and forth and Maya could smell the ocean. A solitary tern circled above the women as if searching for a resting place.

Wooden steps led from the deck to the beach. The tide was out and Gabriel stood about five hundred feet away from her at the edge of the sea. Hollis sat on the sand, halfway between the house and the Traveler. He had something on his lap, wrapped in a bright beach towel, and Maya assumed it was her shotgun. There was no need for a Harlequin at this peaceful, isolated house. Vicki and Hollis had arranged everything without her. She was supposed to protect Gabriel, but he was the one who had risked his life to carry her out of the tunnels.

The overcast sky and the gray-green water merged into each other; it was difficult to see the horizon. Each wave collapsed with a hushing sound, the water flowing across the packed sand and then returning to the sea. Gabriel wore jeans and a dark sweatshirt; it seemed that if he took just one more step he would be absorbed by the grayness and vanish from this world.

The Traveler turned away from the water and looked back at the house. "He sees us," Vicki said.

Maya felt like a child wrapped up in the blanket, but she sat quietly as the men left the beach and climbed up the steps to the deck. Gabriel stood near the railing while Hollis grinned and approached her. "Maya! How you feeling? We didn't think you'd wake up for a few days."

"I'm all right. We need to contact Linden."

"I already did that from a cybercafé in Boston. He'll send money to three different locations in New England."

"Is that all he said?"

"According to Linden, Sparrow's son has disappeared. I guess the Tabula found out that he was—"

Vicki interrupted. "Let's make some coffee, Hollis."

"I don't want any."

"Other people might." There was a slight change in Vicki's voice that reminded Maya of the soft pressure from someone's hand. Hollis appeared to get the message.

"Right. Of course. Fresh coffee." Hollis glanced back at Gabriel, and then followed Vicki into the house.

Now they were alone, but Gabriel still didn't speak. A flock of seabirds appeared in the distance, the black specks circling into a tight funnel that slowly began to descend to the earth.

"Dr. Lewis said you'll be able to walk in a month or so. You're lucky that the bullet didn't shatter the bone."

"We can't stay here that long," Maya said.

"Vicki has a lot of contacts through her church and Hollis knows people from the martial arts world. I think we'll have plenty of places to hide until we get false ID cards and passports."

"Then we should leave the United States."

"I'm not sure about that. People want to believe there's a tropical island or a cave in the mountains where you can hide, but that's not true anymore. Like it or not, we're all connected to one another."

"The Tabula will be searching for you."

"Yes. And my brother will be helping them." Gabriel sat beside her, looking tired and sad. "When we were growing up, I felt like Michael and I were fighting the whole world together. I would have done anything for my brother. I trusted him completely."

Maya remembered the dream of the Underground—her father's sadness—and allowed herself to feel pity for another human being. She offered her hand and Gabriel held it tightly. His warm skin touched her coldness; she felt transformed. It wasn't happiness. No, happiness was a childish, temporary illusion. The pain within her melted away and she felt like the two of them had created a center, a constancy, a whole.

"I don't know if my father is still alive, and Michael has turned against me," Gabriel said. "But I feel connected to you, Maya. You're important to me."

He looked at her with an intense energy in his eyes, then let go of her hand and stood up quickly. Their closeness was painful; it felt as if they had crossed a line.

Alone and unprotected, Gabriel walked back down the steps to the sand. Maya remained on the deck, trying to control her feelings. If she wanted to protect this Traveler, then she couldn't allow herself to care for him. Any emotion would only make her hesitant and vulnerable. If she allowed that weakness, she might lose him forever.

Help me, she thought. It was the first time she had ever prayed. *Please help me. Show me what I need to do.*

A cold wind touched her black hair and she felt a quickness in her body, a gathering strength. So many people drifted through their lives, acting out roles for others and not recognizing their true destinies. All the doubts and hesitations she felt in London had vanished. Maya knew who she was: a Harlequin. Yes, it would be difficult, but she would stay with Gabriel.

She sat up slightly and looked toward the ocean. The flock of seabirds was resting on the beach and, as the Traveler approached them, they rose up to heaven, keening and calling to each other.

The End

Book One of The Fourth Realm

About the Author

JOHN TWELVE HAWKS lives off the Grid. This is his first novel.